LIVECELL

LIVECELL

A Novel by

Eric Green

Printed in the United States of America

Copyright © 2011 by Eric Green

Library of Congress Control Number: 2012954257

ISBN 9871937644178 (paperback)
ISBN 9781937644048 (eBook)

Interior design by North Wind Design & Production

Interior art credit: Eric Green

Cadent Publishing
9 Gleason Street
Thomaston, ME 04861
www.cadentpublishing.com

Distributed by University Press of New England
1 Court Street
Lebanon, New Hampshire 03766
www.upne.com

For Amanda

AUTHOR'S NOTE

The first draft of *LiveCell* was begun in 2001 and finished about a year later. I continued to work on the novel intermittently over the next ten years, but the world I initially envisioned was locked into the early part of the new century, and I decided to leave it that way. I felt that keeping the earlier time period lends the book an interesting mix of retro and new. Hopefully readers will find the blend intriguing as well.

ACKNOWLEDGMENTS

Over the ten years I worked on *LiveCell*, the book made some friends. These mean a great deal to a writer because it's not always easy to maintain faith in a project over extended periods of time. Therefore I wish to thank the following people: Ben Taylor, Ben Duffy who never flagged for an instant, Margo and Jay Davis, Sterling Watson who early on showed me three major mistakes I was making with my prose, Susan Kelly, Rick Russo, Carl Hays, Pete Llanso who mailed me the largest hunk of coal anyone has ever received for Christmas, Nina Young, Richard Silliboy who told me about Micmac culture, Kathy McCarty Thornberry, Jake MacKenzie who is vaguely related to Mary, Elisabeth Green to whom I so wish I could hand the paperback, Barbara Verbrick, Helen H. Clark whose enthusiasm generated quite a following for the novel in an assisted living residence in upstate NY, Buck Sawyer, Marsea Ryan, Tris Coburn, Jon Eaton, Kathrin Seitz, Lionel Tardif, and my wife Amanda who transformed my writing, tenderly, patiently, and edited the book so many times she probably knows the thing better than I do. Without her efforts there wouldn't be a *LiveCell*.

That a life will be spent gaining inches,

When this distance is read in miles.

—Kelly Harris

PROLOGUE

Occasionally something that changes our world is discovered quietly, without reporters or cameras, without showing up on the Internet or in a newspaper, without being witnessed. The invention is even missed by the usual corporate radar and remains hidden for some time because the inventor isn't willing to share it. The inventor wants complete control.

Jay Chevalier glanced around the room though no one else was working this late. His lone companions were the mechanical churn of one bioreactor, an intermittently flickering fluorescent tube, and a cat with a missing ear, a feral stray that normally would never have been allowed into the lab. Outside was only the humid chaos of the city, Wilmington, Delaware, a place that had remained alien for Jay during the eight years he'd been employed at DuPont. When the bioreactor coasted to a halt, he meticulously transferred the inert gray cell structure to the holding vessel and set the timer for the final incubation interval. There was nothing to do now but wait.

He settled on a metal chair. "Inside," he said to the cat, his voice hollow in the cavernous room, the animal arching its back in response. "I'm always inside. Working." He reached down to stroke the neglected fur, praying that the fundamentals of his life might soon change.

His eyes focused uncertainly on the impenetrable blackness beyond the glass-brick windows, the future, but his mind slid into the past and the purity of the wilderness. Hadn't he always sought the refuge of the wilderness when his life became desperate or untenable? Even with the precise warmth of the controlled laboratory air, for an instant he shivered as if from cold. Ten years ago he'd left New York City. Ten years ago his life had reached a nadir of emptiness and despair. And what had he done? Though he hadn't realized it at the time, this instinct to return to Maine was what had been so crucial to everything that followed.

Like a wing-damaged carrier pigeon, he had homed north, not knowing where else to go. With a bitter wind coming off the Hudson River, he stood in the breakdown lane next to the highway, the collar of his jacket turned up, one sore hand stuffed into a pocket, the other with thumb out, a duffel bag at his feet. Dried bodies of dead leaves leapt in a spiral when trucks roared past. He felt about like those leaves; he had been close to so few people in his life, and he'd lost yet another.

A week before, his boxing trainer Pete had grabbed his arm and slumped to the gym floor. Jay had sat in the hospital waiting room for nine hours, but his friend never regained consciousness. At the age of twenty-six, Jay had begun to understand that we rarely get second chances; he'd never gotten the opportunity to tell Pete how he felt about him, or even to thank him for his kindness. After the funeral, he'd returned to the gym for one last workout and unloaded his frustration into the rough weave of the heavy bag.

Jay had earned a living for two years in New York as a sparring partner and by working in the gym, but with Pete gone that was over. Pete's brother, in a moment of sentiment at the funeral, had asked Jay to stay, but he couldn't—they'd never gotten along that well anyway. So he'd left the city and hitchhiked home to northern Maine.

The driver of a massive logging truck dropped him off between distant towns before turning farther north into the great tracts of forest owned by the paper mills, the grumble of diesel stacks gradually absorbed by the stillness of the woods. It had been so many years since he'd heard real quiet. Mount Katahdin was above the deep reach of pine, its remembered shape like a forgotten lullaby, its bald crown already beginning to luminesce with snow. He drew the icy air into his lungs as if it were an antidote for despair. Finally toward late afternoon a Canadian motorist stopped and took him the last stretch.

Using up the little money he'd saved from New York, he ate in the same diner every day, the narrow restaurant with its hand-painted *Cafe* and rough wooden booths so different from the rampant electricity, massive steel and mirrored glass of the city. One of the waitresses was friendly—lank black hair, bad skin, middle-aged, always cheerful. He felt awkward around someone so content, and at first he couldn't talk to her, but one afternoon when the diner was empty, she brought over a mug of coffee.

"Okay if I sit down?" she said.

He nodded.

"You're not from around here, are you?"

"I was born here."

"Madawaska?" She examined his face. "What's your name?"

"Jay Chevalier."

She shook her head. "I don't know any Chevaliers, and I know just about everyone around here."

"I grew up in the boys' home."

"That explains it," she said.

On his arrival into town he'd located the building first thing, pathetic in the early dusk, all the windows smashed, his childhood home so obviously abandoned. He'd sat on the curb until dark, his mind stumbling through the past, a slide show run amok.

"I was sent there as a kid when my mom died."

"And your dad?"

"He wasn't from around here. I never knew him."

"So why'd you come back then?"

He thought a moment. "I think I came to see my mother's grave."

That had taken him some time to locate. She was buried in a section of Saint David's Cemetery across the road from the Catholic church. Of course it made sense that her legal name was on the cross, but it took him a couple hours of roaming between the headstones to remember that. The weather had caught a last caress of warmth, the sky incongruously blue compared to the somberness of his mood. When he finally found her grave, he kneeled on the thick mat of damp leaves and scrubbed his fingers over the small iron cross, loosening the rusty scale until some of the black metal showed through, her name and 1934–1966. He cleared the leaves from around the grave as well, but when he stood, the isolated patch of grass looked so lonely and separate that he brushed them all back.

"What was her name?" the waitress said.

"What?"

"Your mother's name, her family's name."

"Oh . . . Madeline Katliin."

"She was Micmac?"

He nodded and her eyes lit.

It turned out the waitress was Micmac as well. She offered him a place to sleep, but he refused though he'd been stretching out on burlap sacks in a deserted potato barn. He had this fear that if he gave in to any human kindness, he might shatter. Two days later she told him his grandfather might still be alive.

"There's a cabin in the woods," she said, "just under the border by the Beaulieu. Be real careful approaching is what I heard."

Within the hour Jay walked north out of Madawaska toward the cabin. The sky had a dull sheen like raw metal, and he could already imagine the coming snow. As he made his way through dense secondgrowth woods, he realized how much better he felt in the wilderness even though he had some trouble staying on the vague dirt path.

The cabin was chained to a white pine to keep it from toppling, wood smoke a drifting smudge from a stovepipe chimney. An old man in a wool shirt and knitted cap was outside splitting firewood in the cleared yard. He was strong; Jay could see that by the way he swung the maul in a hard clean arc. As Jay approached, his heart started to pound. The man looked up from his work, and Jay searched the face under the dirty orange tuque for resemblance.

"What do you want?" the man said.

"I'm Jay Chevalier."

"So?"

"I'm Madeline's kid."

The old man didn't say a word, just leaned the maul against the pile of split birch and went into his cabin. Jay waited ten minutes, maybe longer, stood there as it began to snow, the woods fading to a chalky monochrome, disappointment choking him. He was about to walk off when a head stuck out of the cabin door and said, "Are you coming in or not?"

There was a wood stove with chinks in the iron drum revealing hot ember, a dry sink with a galvanized pail of river water next to it, a yellow enameled breakfast table and two rusted chrome chairs with most of the rubber feet missing, a half-loft with a steep ladder and a mattress. A Pyrex pot steamed on the table. The old man poured the hot liquid into two thick mugs, gestured for Jay to take a seat, picked up a mug and blew across it to cool the tea, a bitter concoction of dried Labrador leaves and spruce shavings as it turned out.

Then he said, "Are you angry with me?"

The question surprised Jay. "Why would I be angry?"

"You should not be, but you might be. If you did not understand." He examined Jay for what seemed like a couple minutes. "I did not take you in after Madeline died. I knew they could take better care of you, those state people. I liked to drink then and was not willing to raise a young kid. I never let them know I existed. I'm glad you are not angry with me."

And so Jay moved in with his grandfather. They extended the loft with scrap lumber so there would be an extra place to sleep. He slept on blankets, telling his grandfather he was too young to need a mattress. It was luxury after the potato barn. From the first day, they seemed to get along as if they'd always lived together, Jay willing to fit himself to his grandfather's routine.

One day his grandfather said, "I named you. When you were being born I was waiting outside in the yard, letting the women be. A large blue jay flew on a birch limb, looked at me for a long time, said nothing. They usually come in pairs, but this one was alone. Just so you know."

His grandfather had not stopped drinking. Not in the least. He made his own liquor using a wood-fired pot still, and though hesitant at first, he began to teach Jay his secrets. The moonshine itself was straight forward, mostly a potato mash with some corn thrown in. What made it remarkable was the inclusion of *Amanita muscaria* mushrooms.

"Most people will tell you they are poisonous," he said, holding Jay for a moment with his deadpan stare. "They are, but I know a few things."

The mushrooms grew in a certain part of the woods among the birches near the river. Jay and his grandfather harvested them as the veil ruptured and the gills began to open. They carefully cleaned the cap of nubs, trimmed the root, and hung the mushrooms upside down from the cabin's rafters with bits of string. Once dried, the fungus was simmered in river water for hours, creating a rust-colored tea, his grandfather very attentive as he stirred the pot. To this cold tea they added measured amounts of raw moonshine, along with an essence boiled from black birch buds and fresh shoots of red spruce; herbs—dock, saxifrage, bettony, and wild sage; and roots of young borage and elecampane. The mixture sat for several months in white-oak barrels and once ready was strained into clean quart beer bottles and stoppered with whittled-down wine corks. It was an ancient recipe and one that his grandfather adhered to like an alchemist. He was precise about this one aspect of his life and nothing else.

They made enough extra liquor to sell to a few customers so they could buy shells for the .30-30, his grandfather's Bull Durham or Bugler, and the few things they couldn't shoot, trap, forage or grow—salt, flour, sugar, and yeast. They drank almost every evening. Did nothing but hunt, fish the Lower Beaulieu, garden some, distill, chop wood, and drink. It was quite a change for Jay who had never drunk anything stronger than a little wine. After all the years he'd spent studying and working indoors, or training as a boxer, he was finally back in the wilderness, and as he continued to live with his grandfather, something began to gather inside him.

There was an old sweat lodge down near the river. It hadn't been used in many years, and Jay asked his grandfather about it, wanted to rebuild it. His grandfather resisted. "Why mess with the past? Let it rest where it died. Most Micmacs are Catholic now anyway. They made sure of that. Never understood why Madeline gave in. I guess after she got sick, she weakened. It is difficult to be strong when you are sick." But after a few weeks of Jay's prodding, they dug a new fire pit, cleared and deepened the earthen hollow inside the lodge, cut young alder and black ash and repaired the canvas canopy, spread cedar boughs inside. They started to take sweats.

They heated rocks in the pit. Jay shoveled the glowing stone into the hole in the center of the lodge. Both of them inside, the door flap pulled closed, they poured water on the rocks and added sweetgrass. His grandfather told him, "What matters in the sweat is the heat of the rocks. Let the rock bring the smell of the earth into your lungs. Let the steam bring you out through your pores. Know you are nothing. Then you can start to become something. You can bring questions into the sweat. Many times they are answered."

Jay had a question.

One night he took a long sweat alone. When he finally crawled from the heat, he stretched out against the cold ground, steam pouring off him as if his skin were smoldering. He could feel the entire enormous mass of the earth against his naked back, the curve of the planet as it moved through space. He stared up at the sky, at the infinite heavens, got that incredible understanding of distance, where everything is so close and so far away in the same instant. A meteor cut an acid-green pathway across the sky, the woods springing alive in a flare of radiance. And then there was a voice inside his mind. At first he did his utmost to ignore it, to shut it out with the boundaries of logic, but soon he knew it was real, and though it didn't speak in clear words, he sensed exactly what it was saying.

The next morning he packed his duffel bag. He explained his decision to his grandfather and thanked him. The old man listened, barely nodding his head, his face expressionless. Jay waited. He gave it a few minutes, then simply shook the callused hand one last time and walked off down the dirt path after two years in the woods.

The timer signaled the end of the final incubation interval, and Jay's thoughts returned to the laboratory, the cat having long since asked to rejoin the outside world. As dawn began to blue the glass-brick windows, he noticed something he'd never seen before or ever expected to see. The structure in the holding vessel seemed to be pulsing, not from movement but with shifting color. A prismatic rainbow beauty not unlike the wet skin of a trout just pulled from the Beaulieu. He almost turned, half-expecting to see his grandfather standing behind him. Instead he reached down and touched the cell aggregate with his fingertips.

What happened next changed his life and many lives forever, like a fresh channel of rushing water broken free from a river that can never be held back again.

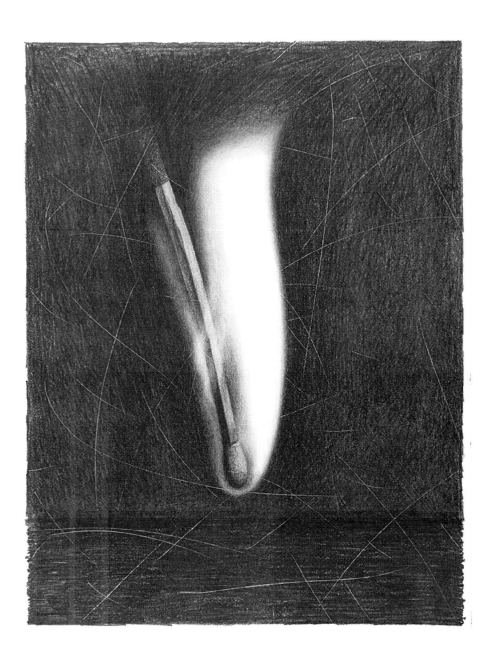

TWO YEARS LATER

ONE

Mary hated her new car. As she waited in a crawling line of traffic over the Bay Bridge, her mind veered into the same annoying quicksand that had mired it for a week—anemic engine, buzzing speakers, and worse, a wheel vibration so evil the car needed an exorcism. Even the horn had laryngitis. What was she doing in this twenty-year-old Fiesta? The car had become a symbol, and she couldn't seem to stop obsessing about it or transferring her other frustrated emotions to the pathetic thing.

Part of her resentment came from the loss of her Porsche convertible. Unable to manage the payments, she'd been forced to hand over the keys at the dealership, the same salesman who'd always beamed kilowatts suddenly treating her with bored condescension. Forget him, she told herself, but she wanted to be back in the silver Porsche, rocketing up the steep streets around San Francisco, through morning fog, that gentle moisture misting her face from over the windshield, then sunlight warming her skin. Instead she hobbled along in the lime-green Fiesta, feeling robbed.

Two weeks ago she'd asked her boss what he planned to do with the company, and though everyone in management had been strung along for months, he'd refused to tell her anything. This morning, in less than an hour, he was finally going to reveal their future, and she was worried. At a stop sign onto Market Street, she waited again, tapping her fingernails impatiently, the van in front of her eventually pulling forward. But then, inexplicably, it stopped and its backup lights flared. She pounded her horn to alert the driver, got only the feeble bleat, and the van rammed her car with a sickening crunch, her forehead almost hitting the steering wheel. At least the Fiesta didn't have an airbag.

For a moment she couldn't seem to move, her heart pounding, the whole miserable month cloaking her like a rotting cape. "Great," she muttered. "What next?" She got out her cell phone, pressed 9-1-1 and gave the dispatcher the location of the accident through a jumble of poor reception. Then she rang her office.

"Clicksave, marketing your internet future, may I help you?"

"Deirdre, it's Mary MacKensie." She attempted to control her voice. "Something unexpected's come up, and I'm going to be late. If anyone asks, tell them I'll be there by nine for the meeting." She wasn't about to explain. The other execs had already made enough stupid jokes about the Fiesta. "That thing's not a lemon, it's a lime." Well, they'd be delighted; now it was juiced.

The van's door opened, and the driver stepped out and walked toward her. He placed his hands on top of her car and leaned in—eyes unfocused, his skin like wet saltines, spinnaker-sized sweat suit bulging in unpleasant places. "What the fuck's wrong with you, tailing me like that?"

His breath pushed her back like a filthy hand. For the moment she was too startled to be scared. "Bitch, you hear me?"

Suddenly he slammed his massive fist down on the Fiesta's roof. Mary jumped and edged farther away, wondering if she should roll up the window and lock the door or try to get out the other side. She was maneuvering toward the passenger door when she heard a voice behind her.

"Wasn't enough to smash up the car, you gotta pound in the roof?"

Mary turned. Just behind her, a small guy in a cowboy hat was leaning against a muddy pickup. Not a dude, she decided, this one looked like the real thing, like a worker, though these days with bankers and brokers wearing five-hundred-dollar tattered ranch outfits, who knew. Whatever he was, she was relieved he was there. He spit a stream of chew onto the street and walked up to her, ignoring the big guy.

"You okay?" he said.

She nodded.

"That was quite a bump. Your neck all right?"

"Whaddaya think *you're* doing?" It was the big guy again.

The cowboy looked up at him. "Haven't you caused enough trouble?" His voice was easy, melodious, but there was something hard underneath. "What the hell is it with you anyway?" He spit next to his boot. "Vet can't get your medication right?"

"This ain't none of your business, dickwad."

The cowboy continued to stand calmly—if anything, he seemed amused—as the other guy glared and tightened his fists. Then a police car arrived, siren strangling into silence, and the big guy headed back to his van. The cop said something to him, and soon the ball hitch complained with a metallic groan as it released the Fiesta's radiator, the car bleeding its paint color, antifreeze still spreading, a rivulet nosing into the gutter.

Mary curbed the Fiesta, and the cowboy moved his truck. Although hesitant to admit it, she was mildly intrigued by him. He had an unpretentious confidence though he seemed younger than her by at least a few years, probably mid-twenties. She was reminded of farm kids back home, something she realized she missed after being in the city for so long.

The cop arrived to collect her license and registration. The cowboy stepped forward.

"Sir, name is Hank McKeen from Likely. That's up near Alturas." He extended his hand. "Modoc County," he added as if it would make a difference.

The cop glanced at the hand. "What do you want?"

"Saw the whole thing. Saw the smash, him pound her roof. All of it." His grin spread.

"If I need to, I'll talk to you in a minute." He walked off to his cruiser.

Mary opened the door and went to examine the front of the Fiesta. It wasn't terminal, despite the sprung radiator, but it wasn't drivable. She glanced at her watch—she had to get to the office.

"You know about cars?"

There he was again. "Some," she said. "My mother taught me."

"Name's Hank, Hank McKeen." He started to lift his hand, hesitated. "Well, actually . . . it's Garland McKeen, but I'm known as Hank. 'Cause of Hank Williams, the singer. Senior, not the son. Big favorite of mine. You need to get somewhere? Got the truck right there." He pointed to his pickup.

She continued to study him. "Okay," she said. "I really need a ride to work." She was willing to take the gamble that he was safe even if he wasn't clean because at this point she couldn't take a chance at finding a cab. She circled the puddle to the cruiser. The cop told her that from the antifreeze trail he could tell what had happened, asked if she wanted to file a charge of criminal mischief over the damaged roof. She shook her head; the meeting was the only thing that mattered right now. The officer handed her the accident report and wished her a better day. She took it as a positive sign.

Hank McKeen maneuvered his pickup along Market Street and couldn't think of a thing to say. Nobody had ever done this to him before; he always had something to say. While she'd talked with the cop, he'd frantically tidied up his truck. He'd found the cleanest towel and spread it over the dirty vinyl of the bench seat, wiping the seat back with another rag. Everything else: assorted tools and rope, stained styrofoam coffee cups, a Rainier pounder with the bag twisted around the neck, and his spit can, he tossed into the bed. He dug his chew out with his finger and rinsed his mouth with some water left in his canteen. He even wet back his hair in the rearview mirror before remounting his hat. Maybe Pa had a point after all—the right woman could civilize you.

She broke the silence: "Garland, what are you doing in San Francisco?"

"Cousin's in the hospital. Cancer. Came down to see her."

"Is she going to be okay?"

"Nope."

"I'm sorry," she said.

He glanced over at her for a second; his eyes returned to the road. Goddang, there was a mad herd of traffic in this city. He didn't want to depress her about his cousin. He also didn't tell her how much she reminded him of Patsy—way she used to look when she was living at the ranch. Same smooth whitish skin with the round face, same mouth just like you'd draw one, and those stern sun-bleached eyes seeing everything, but with the glitter of wildness.

He'd been with Patsy all night in that stuffy room, trying not to reflect in his face what he saw on the bed. Every time he truly focused on her it hurt him, but there was nothing he could do. Something in him wanted to bundle her up and get her out of there, take her up to the ranch, make her a warm spot on the porch glider with blankets where she could look out over the fields and feel the late-summer breeze. But he knew it wouldn't do a lick of good. Patsy had asked to hear some stories during their vigil, begging him to stay with her, and he tried desperately to recall some of their best times together from when they were teenagers and later on before she left. He got her laughing a few times, at least a little. As the hospital room slowly sharpened with daylight, she'd been able to fall asleep. He got out of his chair and kissed her forehead. Then he took the stairs down two at a time—unable to wait for the elevators—and located his truck. He'd been so upset he'd needed to drive around, and that's when he'd pulled up behind the Fiesta.

Reaching up now and feeling his chin, he wished again that he'd shaved. He kept his left hand positioned on the steering wheel so she wouldn't notice the missing joints of his index finger, and for the first time in his life he worried about the appearance of his hands. Their size and strength were good for ranching, but he wasn't so sure how a woman like Mary would feel about them.

"Buy ya breakfast?" he said after contemplating the appropriateness of the question.

"No thank you, Garland. I just need to get to the office. You'll want to turn left here."

"Okay." A pause. "What's in the box?"

"A pool cue."

"What for?"

"To shoot pool with?"

Ouch. Was he only going to say dumb things? First all that stuff about Hank Williams, now this. She'd also called him Garland, again. This wasn't going so good. "I mean—you the player?"

She told him she was. He was about to ask more when she said, "Anywhere up here on the right is fine." As they drew up to the office building he panicked. What should he say to her? Can I see you again? Ask for her phone number? Yet when he ground to a stop in front of the big glass doors, all he managed was a grin. She thanked him, hopped down from his truck, and with a walk that broke his heart, pool cue on one side, briefcase on the other, she entered the building and was gone.

Hank sat and stared at the closed doors for maybe two or three minutes as if he half-expected her to return. Finding a pencil stub with some difficulty, and frustrating himself further by having to sharpen it with his Buck knife, he wrote down the address of the Harcourt Building. Behind him someone started honking. He almost shot the cabby the finger, but instead looked back and waved. Then he eased the Chevy forward, back toward the hospital and his sick cousin.

TWO

Mary greeted Manuel at the front desk—that ever-present whiff of cologne or hair oil—and walked across the polished marble to the elevators. Once again she tried to ignore the huge tangle of modern sculpture in the lobby. It wasn't easy. She stood waiting for an elevator but changed her mind and returned to Manuel. Handing him the cue case, she asked if he would look after it until that evening. No one at the office knew about her other life, and she wanted to avoid explanations. Manuel confirmed her hunch.

"Oh my, a musical instrument?"

"Kind of. Let's hope it plays sweetly tonight."

"Sweetness is good, dear."

As she approached the elevators a second time, a bell dinged, doors whispered open, and she entered without breaking stride. Maybe she was back on track? Pressing the button for the fifth floor, she glanced at her watch. Eleven minutes until Wendell's declaration.

She figured Wendell Alden III had never experienced a bad moment. Until recently. He'd come to San Francisco from Connecticut and started Clicksave.com a little over six years ago. The company provided internet marketing, and with the strong financial backing he'd brought with him from the East, Clicksave had grown rapidly. As he liked to tell everyone, he'd outperformed his peers since prep school. His education and business decisions were guided by his father, an investment banker, and everything had gone exactly according to the family's plan. She had to admit, he possessed the height, the build, and the self-assurance of the archetype. If he lacked anything, maybe it was heart. But what use had Boy Wonder, as she privately called him, with such a thing? This wasn't the *Wizard of Oz*. About a year ago, an Alden family friend at Goldman Sachs had overseen the release of Clicksave's initial public stock offering, and the IPO had performed miraculously. The Aldens were heavily invested, and everything had run perfectly.

Until now.

Mary had a theory about what destroyed Clicksave.com. When the IPO was launched, the stock price doubled the first day, then leveled, fluctuating but generally climbing. After months of this pattern, it surged unexpectedly. While everyone at the office celebrated, she researched online and found some revealing traces. She suspected their main competitor, Buynow.com, of purchasing large blocks of stock using surrogate investors to veil the transactions, then salting internet chat rooms with false prophesy about Clicksave's potential earnings. She told Wendell and a few coworkers, but they dismissed her fears, said she worried too much, but if she hadn't been obligated by her lockup agreement, she would have sold all her stock. While everyone else in the office was still grinning, Buynow yanked the stopper, selling all their Clicksave holdings. The same henchmen peppered the Internet with predictions of doom. Clicksave's stock plummeted.

With his family holding sixty percent of the company, Wendell stepped in and bought back shares, but the other stockholders panicked. Wendell insisted publicly, "Clicksave is a sound company. It's growing daily. The stock will rebound." It didn't. In the past weeks, a rumor that Buynow would be investigated by the Securities and Exchange Commission circulated around the office, and her theory suddenly had credibility.

On the fifth floor of the Harcourt Building, a narrow room next to the elaborate grid of work cubicles was designated as a lounge. A few molting sofas, a pink wicker rocker, two kinds of coffee makers, a small fridge, a standing lamp with a dented shade, sea-green walls with some Edward Hopper prints—Mary considered the room a subtle, or not so subtle, dig at Wendell, who had sent an office memo requiring that the door always be kept closed. The rest of the floor, and those above and below it, reflected Wendell's taste: off-white walls, chromed chairs, pickled hardwood floors, brushed metal desks, recessed fluorescent ceiling lighting, and *the* paintings. She stepped into the lounge and closed the door.

"Why are you so late?" It was Duncan; otherwise the lounge was empty. Duncan hated to sit in the boardroom waiting for meetings to start. "You want some coffee?"

She nodded. His espresso with foamed milk balanced out some of his other traits. Duncan had trouble meeting her eyes and blushed if she caught him staring at her breasts, made comments behind her back about Vermont dairy farms not just producing great milk. Obsessed with the fact that she'd grown up on a farm, he repeatedly questioned her about it, as if being a farm girl might mean something unusual sexually. "Do cows do it the same as horses?" "Cows don't *do* it, Duncan." She knew he didn't have a social life, but she wanted him to stop hoping for one with her. Then one night she dreamed she was milking him, squatting naked on a three-legged stool, liquid ringing the metal pail beneath her hands until she awoke horrified. After that—blessedly—he'd stayed out of her subconscious.

Duncan was the only one who'd taken her Buynow subterfuge theory seriously, but when Wendell had asked his opinion, he hadn't spoken up. He was far too shrewd for that, realizing no one ever wanted the truth of failure when they could have the illusion of success. He'd never be shot for being the messenger. Yet if Clicksave was restructured, he might be let go. With his quirky personality, unsavory humor, and sloppy appearance, he probably wouldn't impress new owners.

"So, any brilliant insights?" said Duncan. "What's your old dowsing rod say?"

"I think you should consider a new career . . . dairy farming. You could milk cows every day." She regretted the comment immediately, and it triggered his self-conscious giggle, belly shaking uncontrollably. She noticed he'd trimmed his goatee and was wearing a new suit. Though the fabric was expensive, it still looked grabbed off the rack, reminding her of a kid dressed by a grandparent, and she felt a ripple of tenderness and pity. Did he buy the suit to impress new owners? Where had he gotten the money? Actually, he probably saved every dime he'd ever made; after all, he still lived with his mother in Santa Rosa. Mary wished again that she'd saved. No one in upper management had been paid in months, and she'd maxed out her cards. Wendell had begged them to "fight along with him" as he deferred their checks, promising he would make it right in the end. Today they should be paid their back wages, hopefully with a nice bonus. She could finally pay off some of her debt. Otherwise she'd simply have to win the pool tournament tonight.

When Mary and Duncan walked into the boardroom, the other senior executives were already inside, most seated. She greeted a few and nodded to the others. Chet Simmons had his electronic notebook lined up exactly with the table edge, his glass of water exactly in front of that. Cliff Thompson looked like a cadaver, probably hung over, and who could blame him considering the stress they'd been living under. Nancy, the only other female, was as usual stationed next to Wendell's chair. She certainly didn't have on jeans. For the third time that morning, Mary questioned her decision to wear jeans to the office. She wanted them for the pool tournament—she played best in them, a superstition—but they'd bug the hell out of Wendell. Something had made her wear them anyway. To hell with Wendell's dress code.

The boardroom continued the bleached Clicksave look; it certainly had the worst paintings. To avoid them, she took a seat facing the picture windows, preferring the middle floors of other buildings and the pinch of bay in the distance. The conference table, a massive slab of oiled cherry beginning to crack at one of its glue joints, floated on spindly legs in the center of the room. She rather liked it—at least it was raw wood. By now, everyone had taken one of the chrome and black leatherette chairs. Duncan, who read Wendell's habits like a weathervane, always took his seat moments before he appeared, a door between Wendell's office and the boardroom reserved for this.

First thing she noticed about Wendell was that his hair, as on every Monday, sported the same expensive haircut, and though it looked great, it annoyed her. She couldn't remember the last time she'd had her hair done. He greeted everyone solemnly, allowing Nancy his secret little glance even today, and opened the meeting.

After the usual formalities, he clasped his hands together and said, "This is not a pleasant day for me. You have all worked very, very, hard. All of you. And I thank you for that. Clicksave is a viable concept. I know that. You know that. It's a great company, and what has happened, should not have happened. But it did. And if there had been any other way out of this, I would have taken it, believe me. I am not happy with the way things have turned out. Know that. We all deserved better." He scanned their faces. "I have sold my family's sixty percent of the company."

He took a long sip of water.

"My suspicion is that Buynow is the purchaser, though the on-paper name is LiveCell. My lawyers have been unable to ascertain the identity of this *Live-Cell* or what they do. LiveCell doesn't seem to exist. Therefore, it must be Buynow using another name. We certainly know how dirty they can be."

Something is not right, she thought. Something false in his face.

Wendell reached up and touched the knot of his tie. "All financial responsibility will be absorbed by the new owners."

A grumble ricocheted around the table. Feeling as if she'd been run over, not merely backed into, she realized he wasn't going to pay their back salaries or leave them with any kind of severance. Her devalued stock was to be the sole legacy of four years of constant work. Duncan looked wilted. Chet Simmons, exhumed. Cliff Thompson and Randy Dyer had been with Wendell from the beginning; they looked outraged. Jack Wingham and Wendell golfed together at The Presidio every weekend. Jack looked ready to kill. Even Nancy's cover-girl serenity was majorly disturbed. No one was on the inside. Everyone had gotten screwed.

But before anyone could confront Wendell, the boardroom door opened, and a stranger walked in. The pursuing receptionist, Deirdre, a big surfer girl, said, "Sir! You can't like, *go* in there. *Sir!* . . . I'm so sorry, Mr. Alden, he just won't listen."

Wendell seemed relieved to have their attention diverted, and Mary wondered if the disturbance was a set up.

In a faded blue T-shirt, jeans, worn loafers, his skin pallid and pocked along the temples, the stranger contrasted with the tanned and suited group around the table. Though of ordinary height, his body was proportioned like a gymnast's, his arms and shoulders the kind that would normally have a few tattoos. Mary's impression was that he'd just gotten out of jail and might be dangerous. She couldn't stop staring at him, though something self-protective in her wanted to turn away. As if he sensed this, his eyes found hers. And she—Mary of the cool gray gaze—looked down.

Wendell was by now in front of the stranger. Cliff Thompson and Jack Wingham were on their feet.

"What're you doing in my boardroom?" said Wendell.

The stranger's voice was calm and straightforward, without emotion. "Are you sure it's your boardroom?"

Wendell hesitated but only for an instant. "I want you out of here immediately."

The stranger didn't move.

Mary glanced at the others. Cliff said, "Who is that guy?" Duncan, still seated, shrugged.

"Did you hear me? I want you out of here," said Wendell again.

"Mr. Alden, it's you who're leaving."

"Should I, like, go get security?" said Deirdre halfheartedly.

The stranger answered though she'd been talking to Wendell. "There's no need. Mr. Alden will go quietly."

"Who the hell are you?" said Wendell, his face slack.

"Jay Chevalier." He pronounced it Cheval-*yer*, something guttural yet sensual in his tone. Likely a New England voice, thought Mary, though she couldn't quite place it.

"And that's supposed to mean something to me?"

"It's not your company any more."

"How the hell do you know that?"

"Because I own half."

"*You?*"

The interest in Jay Chevalier magnified. Even the lanky Deirdre straightened her posture. Some of the executives moved toward the new owner, wanting to be introduced. Others got up from the table.

"You're going to believe him?" said Wendell, his face contorted. "Look at him."

"Mr. Chevalier, I'm Cliff, Cliff Thompson, head of investor relations. This is . . ." and he started to introduce the others who clustered around Jay.

Mary remained seated. She was still reeling from her financial ruin. At least now there was some hope, but there was something about Jay Chevalier that bothered her. She realized she was attracted to him and resented it. He'd looked at her as if he could see right into her, as if he knew her secrets. She didn't want to introduce herself.

Wendell pushed into the group. "What are you people doing? Cliff, come on . . . You don't know who this guy is. He could be some nut."

Jay Chevalier faced him again. "Mr. Alden, I purchased your half of Clicksave. Now, please, if you would," and he gestured toward the door. "I'm sorry, but there's nothing more for you to do here." He grasped him by the arm the way an orderly would assist someone confused or hurt, and he guided him firmly out the boardroom door. From there, Wendell Alden seemed to exit their lives.

Mary figured it wasn't completely his fault. After all, she'd worked four years for him, and knew he was spoiled, but not a total bastard. She had a strange intuition that there was more to the failure of Clicksave than anyone realized, even Wendell. Why hadn't the father stepped in and helped? With his power and money he probably could have, yet he'd let his son and the company fail. She'd met the man once and he'd truly frightened her. Unlike Wendell, he was of common stature and ordinary handsomeness, scrupulously polite, generally bland in manner, almost bored. But under that unassuming manner, she had sensed evil. At the time she'd dispelled the reaction, but now she wondered. Wendell had even told her once: failure wasn't tolerated in his family. Maybe the father had wanted to prove something to someone, perhaps Wendell's mother? It made her almost feel sorry for Wendell, even if she never wanted to see him again.

When Jay Chevalier returned, everyone in the room quieted. He sat down in Wendell's chair and fanned out his hands, his palms against the tabletop. Then he closed his eyes. Mary questioned what he was doing. This was her new boss? With his eyes closed, just sitting there, his fingers splayed in that odd arrangement as if he were trying to read some divine message through the wood. She could finally study his face: the uneven brow, slightly crooked nose, jaw like a fist. Graceful hands with long fingers. She imagined those hands touching her, caressing her, and was startled by the intensity of the thought. She glanced at Nancy to see if she was affected, but she only seemed moody and unsure; maybe the new boss hadn't appropriately acknowledged her charms yet. Mary wondered if the stunning blue of his eyes was from colored contacts. It was an eye color she'd never seen before, bordering on violet, but she doubted he'd wear tinted lenses.

Finally, Duncan, "Mr. Chevalier? May I ask you a few questions, sir?"
Jay shook his head.

Duncan was sweating. Mary could almost hear his mind grinding, trying to work this all out. He was also probably lamenting his new suit as a wasted investment. Her jeans had been the right choice after all.

The silence started ticking again.

This time, Nancy, "Mr. Chevalier,"—in her sweetest voice—"maybe you'd like a hot coffee, or a mineral water, or something . . . I could get it for you." He glanced abruptly at her, frowned slightly, and shook his head. She continued to watch him, as if expecting more of a reaction, but he ignored her. Soon a chair sighed, high heels snapped on hardwood, and the door closed. She must've had second thoughts and went to find Wendell, decided Mary. After all, he was still very rich.

Jay's eyes closed again, and the silent waiting folded in like a fog of claustrophobia. Everyone was looking at each other, raising eyebrows, mouthing comments. Then—

"Your lives are about to change. More than you ever thought possible. That is if you stay with me."

He opened his eyes and they were slightly wet. She hadn't considered that. He must have a tender side, or at least an emotional one.

He continued, "If you stay with me, you will also make a great deal of money. But after a while that won't matter to you. Other things will become more important. What you must ask yourselves right now is: Do I want to stay? Does it feel right? Rely on your intuition. If you stay, I will hope for a high level of commitment from each of you. I want you to decide in the next ten minutes."

Some of the execs started to complain. He raised his hand. "I will pay your back salaries, stay or not. I also offer anyone who wants to leave a fifty-thousand-dollar settlement for doing so. However, your stock in the company will transfer to me with the acceptance of this offer. Please discuss it among yourselves." He glanced pointedly at Mary and walked out of the room.

As everyone else started to discuss the situation, she wondered why he'd looked at her like that again, as if he knew her or knew something intimate about her. She had never experienced a look like his before. There was something magnetically compelling about him, and she couldn't decide if it was just sexual attractiveness or something more. It scared her.

Then her mind flickered to her car problem. She decided to dump the Fiesta and get a rental for the time being. Should she still enter the pool tournament?

Duncan cut into her thoughts: "Mary . . . What are you going to do?"

The group stopped talking.

"Stay. Why wouldn't I?"

This triggered more discussion. Who was he? Was he crazy? Did it matter? What did he plan for the company? Should they grab the fifty thousand and run? Their stock options weren't worth anything now anyway. Did you see him handle Wendell?

"One good thing," said Cliff Thompson, "at least we won't have to worry about a dress code." This raised a few grins.

"Hey, Duncan," said Mary. "Intuitive move with the new suit by the way. Armani?" Everyone started laughing. That was when Jay Chevalier returned.

And he smiled; it softened his face, gave it an odd innocence. He walks into a room of strangers laughing, and he smiles, she thought. Not a nervous smile, not a questioning smile, doesn't look down at himself to see if he's untucked or unzipped, just seems pleased they're laughing. This time he carried a briefcase. One of those old-fashioned leather briefcases with the double handles and the accordion effect on the ends, the corners tipped in brass, the flanks worn to a polish like the skin of a fallen chestnut. He sat back down, set the briefcase beside him, looked up and made the circuit of their faces. "Well . . . what are your decisions?"

Duncan spoke first. "Mr. Chevalier, you haven't explained what you expect out of us, or told us if our salaries will remain the same, or defined our job descriptions. Everyone, I'm sure, is very relieved that you've rescued the company and are willing to pay us to date, but this entire morning has been a bit confusing."

"Linden—"

"Duncan."

"Sorry. Duncan. I want you to make your decision intuitively. Without facts. Now, if you would."

Duncan looked away, at Mary, Cliff, back at Jay. He was sweating heavily, and his hesitation bugged her. Why didn't he take off his suit jacket if he was so warm? His boss was in a T-shirt.

"Duncan?" said Jay again.

"You mean make my decision right now?"

Jay nodded.

"For how long? Do we have to sign a contract?"

Jay waited.

"Okay. *Okay*. I'll stay."

"Thank you." Turning to Myron Banks, next in line, "Well?"

"I'll take the money. I'd need to know more to make an informed decision."

"Then please leave."

"Right *now*?"

"Anyone who is leaving should go now."

"When will we be paid?" said Myron.

"I'll need three weeks to a month. Again, anyone not staying, please leave."

Everyone churned with unanswered questions, and they hesitated, but eventually four of the executives stood. The four, including Myron Banks and Jack Wingham, waited by their chairs. Someone asked a question. No response from Jay. Eventually there was nothing for them to do but walk out.

Jay said, "You know very little about me, yet you have stayed. Your motives in staying are important to me. Everything about you is important to me. But allow me to tell you a little about myself.

"I am not a businessman and I have never run a company before. I'm an inventor." He reached down and unclasped his briefcase. From it he drew a dull gray object approximately the size of an enlarged deck of playing cards and placed it in front of him. The surface began to shimmer, reminding Mary of an early season brook trout lifted from a stream. Then it went dull again. She looked up, wondering if a fluorescent tube was flickering.

Jay picked up the object and whacked it on the edge of the table. A startled cry escaped from Chet Simmons who'd barely moved since he'd aligned his electronic notebook. Now his eyes jumped between Jay and the object. An obvious dent was in the gray surface. As it oscillated between dull and glowing, she had the peculiar notion that it was upset from being whacked. The dent gradually filled in and the object recovered its former round-edged shape.

"Is it some kind of new packing foam?" said Cliff Thompson, sounding unimpressed.

"Patience," said Jay.

Reaching into the briefcase again, he extracted a small black box fitted with two thin polished-metal prongs. He attached this to the gray object by pressing the prongs imprecisely into one end, the gray material yielding and aligning itself slowly. From the pulsing glow against his hands, she realized that the iridescence was inherent.

"Cliff? Do you have an answering machine?" said Jay. Cliff nodded. "Your phone number please?" He gave the ten digits. Jay whispered *okay* to the object and handed it to Cliff. "Place it against your ear." He did, looking foolishly around at the group, clowning a little. Mary worried for the first time that Jay might actually be a nut.

Cliff leapt to his feet and dropped the object as if it had shocked his hand.

"Jesus Christ, how in the hell did you do that?"

"Do what?"

"*How* did you do that trick?"

"It's not a trick."

"What happened?" said Duncan.

Cliff glared at the object as if it were possessed.

"Come on, Cliff—*tell*," said Duncan again.

"I heard my outgoing message through that *thing*."

"Maybe there's a tape inside?"

"No. You don't understand, you don't understand at all." He shook his head back and forth, looking ill. "I heard it inside my head. Like a thought. Like thoughts. Like there was a speaker, or voice, inside my brain somewhere. Damn it, *what* is going on here?"

"It's a new telephone," said Jay.

"A *telephone*?"

"Yes. I've created a new kind of telephone. Allow me to show you."

He reached over and took the object.

"Mary, what's your cell phone number?" She gave it to him. Had she told him her name? She didn't think so. His attention was on her now, the length of table between them. "Please turn on your cell phone," he said. She took it out of her briefcase and did. He whispered *okay* to the gray object in his hand and her phone started to ring. She answered it, feeling silly. He started talking to her through the gently pulsing object, explaining about his invention, his voice through her cell phone even more sensual than in person. Those incredible eyes on her eyes. His look pouring into her. She clutched her phone, feeling very self-conscious. Her heartbeat and breathing quickened. She began to sense a warmth between her thighs. She wished her legs weren't crossed, yet she was incapable of moving them, wished that her jeans weren't pressing her just there. He kept staring at her, talking about something. She couldn't understand his words, couldn't turn away. It was almost like being hypnotized but wasn't. It was something else. She had never felt anything like this, this level of pure attraction. And then she felt something more, the confusion and fear that she might orgasm.

Mary rose blindly from her chair almost knocking it over and half-ran from the boardroom. She didn't know what else to do.

THREE

The day finally over, the lounge empty, Mary was settled on one of the tattered sofas when she opened her briefcase and glanced at the new phone. Toward the end of the afternoon, Jay had given one to each of the remaining executives. Hers rested against the red lining, dull gray now, inert. It seemed to luminesce only when touched. She ignored it for the moment and picked up a folded letter. Though she'd read it four times since she received it last week, she read it again:

Cage Dairy Farm, Monkton, Vermont
*August 7, 200_*

Dear Mary,

Your letter upset me deeply because I hate to hear you're not happy and that you're lonely. Not that we can be fulfilled all the time, but having someone to share things with helps. Life doesn't work out that great for most people, and it's wicked hard to accept this. We have all these dreams when we're young, and few of them ever make it. Of course some of us barely even have the dreams. As you requested, I've kept everything in your letter confidential from your parents.

When I moved into the old trailer, before you were born, Patty had just died and I was desperately alone. Boy do I know about loneliness! What you don't know is that the reason your father brought me back to Vermont with him is he was worried I wouldn't make it. He was right. When I told you I had been a pool hustler in New York, I told you that because I didn't want to be a bad example. The truth is that I was a junkie. I shot pool to make money for dope. Patty helped me get straight—not that anyone can ever really do that—and we went to Wisconsin together after she got sick. Now you realize why your mother never liked me so much, and worried about our friendship. I don't blame her. She can't understand someone who would throw his life away like that. Of course, she's never done junk. (Just kidding.) I know I should have told you sooner, I just couldn't. I pray that you will be able to accept this part of my past.

You say you don't have a life except work, and I know how you long ago decided to save yourself for that one perfect guy. You wanted to share yourself with only one man, one love, forever. It's a noble idea but a rougher reality. But then I wonder, if you gave up your dreams, if you would be pleased with that. I remember you learning pool and how if you missed a shot, you would keep practicing the same shot over and over until you had it cold. Your determination never to be weak in the same way twice always impressed me. If only life were as fair as a level pool table. If only gravity and time were what decided winners—

She stopped reading for a moment and skipped to the end.

The dogs are fine, but I'm sure Pilgrim misses you terribly. Will you visit soon? We all miss you. I want to see that massé in action.

My love to you,

Kelly

P. S. I had a visit a few months ago from someone I knew in New York. A secretive fellow, but brilliant.

She read the postscript twice, refolded the letter, placed it back in her briefcase. Then she thought of Jay—his face, his voice, his hands.

After running to the bathroom and sitting in a stall until she calmed down, she'd patted her face with cold water, touched up her mascara.

She'd never been so affected by anyone in her life, and it made her uncertain and nervous. She didn't like the feeling. On reentering the boardroom, she'd apologized to Jay for leaving, explaining she'd not felt well. With a concerned look, he said it was a trying day for everyone. Glancing around at the table of faces, she figured no one had noticed. Then they had all gotten down to work.

Some of the executives questioned Jay about the new phone: How did it work? What comprised its unusual structure? Who had previously manufactured it? He said, "I don't think the phones' secrets are decipherable." He remained deadpan, not giving the group anything further. She decided he wasn't very forthcoming, but why should he be? Then he said, "All I can tell you is I discovered the cell aggregate while working in the forgotten laboratory for DuPont. Now, there is more pressing business to address first.

"We're to become manufacturer, marketer, and retailer of the phone. We need an ad campaign and press releases, phone-marketing and public-relations strategies, packaging and shipping. The pronged black boxes need to be farmed out. They send radio waves, carry the battery and charging system, allowing our phones compatibility with all conventional systems. Our phone must be licensed and agreements must be established for the use of existing telecommunication pathways. Your job descriptions and salaries must be settled, and a new board of directors chosen. One of my stipulations for purchase was that I could appoint a new board. With my sixty-percent ownership, the stock holders' approval should be a formality."

He may not have had any experience in running a company, but he seemed to know exactly what he wanted and how to achieve it. He asked her to design a new web site, which he wanted compelling and informative in a completely fresh way. My God, she thought, he only wants the future.

Mary looked at her watch: if she was going to this tournament she'd better get moving. For a moment she considered skipping it, but her fifty-dollar greens fee was mailed in, and she was too wound up to be stuck at home. Nine-ball might provide a good distraction. Besides, she hated to ask Jay for an advance and reveal her finances. The thousand-dollar first prize, if she won, would be heaven-sent.

Finally she reached for the new phone. So much was riding on it that she'd been nervous to examine it before now. As she picked it up, the surface started to pulse with that eerie phosphorescence. The texture surprised her—something like skin, though cool to the touch, more firm and almost but not molding itself to her hand, so sensual and appealing that she wanted to keep holding it. She told it the numbers of Manuel's desk phone, feeling slightly foolish. Said okay. Within a moment, Manuel's voice spoke inside her mind, just as Cliff had described it, saying he still had her instrument case, and for some reason she knew he'd looked at her cue. She asked him to call her a cab, giggling with excitement. And Jay had been so modest about it: "I've never owned a company, I'm only an inventor." My God, they were going to make a fortune, an absolute fortune. Nokia, Motorola, and Samsung, look out. Gathering her things, she headed for the elevator. From the cab she'd reserve a rental at the airport for later on. Right now she was headed directly to Jake's poolroom. She needed a sandwich and a cold beer.

When she collected her cue from Manuel, he said with a conspiratorial wink, "Have a lovely *concert*, dear."

Outside, the sun gilded the tops of the tallest buildings, the sky a vibrating cerulean, the air with that faint brininess of the sea. She walked toward the cab, noticing a police cruiser across the street. Oh Christ, it couldn't be. She recognized the truck—the worst-looking one in San Francisco. She was tempted to hop quickly into the cab, but with a sigh she asked the cabby to please wait and headed across the street.

"Garland, what's going on?"

His smile spread as he sat calmly on the bench seat.

"Do you know this man?" said the officer standing by Garland. The other cop was still in the cruiser, talking on the radio.

"Yes," she said, reluctantly. "What's he done?"

"He refuses to move, and he's about to get a citation. Or we may haul him in."

"Officer, could I speak to you for a minute? In private, please." She used her eyes. A curt nod. They walked to the tailgate. He scowled down at her. She introduced herself. "And you are?"

"Sergeant Boronski."

"Thanks, Sergeant, for talking with me. Garland's cousin is—"

"Who's Garland?"

She pointed.

"He said his name is Hank."

"Hank's his nickname. He's from Likely—"

"Believe me, we know. Likely, near Alturas. Moduck County. He told us about six damn times."

She smiled, hoping to lighten him up, wondering why she was doing this. "Garland's cousin is dying of cancer. He's been with her in the hospital for days. He might not be himself."

"That's no excuse for ignoring a police officer."

"No. No, of course not. But I'm sure I can get him to move."

"Believe me—*we* can get him to move."

They were interrupted by a blast from the cabby's horn, the driver signaling impatiently. The cop frowned and went back to the front of the pickup. She followed.

"Hank, are you going to move now?" he said.

"Yep. Sure will."

"You might get away with this kind of behavior up there in Likely, but not here, Hank. Okay?" Garland nodded. "You behave yourself while you're in San Francisco."

"Yes, sir, sure will."

Now the sergeant turned to her. "Good luck," he said, smiling.

She suddenly realized the cop had been toying with her, had been amused by Garland all along, had probably heard about that morning and expected her to get into his truck. Oh, what the hell, after all this, Garland could at least provide another ride. She waved off the taxi, the cabby muttering and shaking his head, tires squawking.

When she circled around the hood, Garland leapt across the bench seat to open the door for her. She settled onto the tan vinyl, quite a bit cleaner than that morning. Garland was sporting a new shirt, his boots shined, and a shave.

"Garland—"

"Wish you'd call me Hank."

"I like Garland."

"You do?"

She nodded.

"Well, all right then." The grin. Getting the truck rolling. Waving to the cops. Was he always this cheerful?

"What are you doing here, anyway?" she said.

"Waiting."

"*Waiting?*"

"Thought ya might need a lift."

"How long have you been waiting?"

"Since three."

"Three? That's two and a half hours."

"Didn't wanna miss ya. Thought I mighta though. Guy inside your building kept getting up and peering out at me. He musta called the cops."

"That was probably Manuel."

"The guy with the big hair, looks like a fag."

Mary turned to stare at him, decided to let it go. "*Garland*, you shouldn't be waiting for people you don't know."

"Can't help it."

His cheeks went red through the tan. *Oh, great.* She told him to turn right on 16th Street and head over to Dolores.

"How's your cousin?"

"Maybe just some better. She et something." A silence. "You going that pool tourney?"

"Jake's Billiards, on Van Ness. If you wouldn't mind dropping me off?"

"Anything. Just ask." A pause, and he blurted out, "I know a lot about ranching. If you wanna know something."

"So you know a lot about ranching?" she said.

"Yes, ma'am. Been ranching since I had memory. Pa too. Mean, Pa ranched from when he was a kid. My family's always ranched, came over from Wyoming." He swallowed nervously. "We run three hundred head of Black Angus."

"The Cage farm milks thirty head of Jersey and Holstein."

He slowed the truck for a red light, stopped, people walking in front of the hood.

"*You?* That your last name?"

"I grew up on a dairy farm. Monkton, Vermont. That's near Lake Champlain. Addison County."

The loud hoot made her jump, along with a few pedestrians. "Goddang! Just knew it. I just knew it." He pounded the steering wheel, the horn going off.

"*Garland*, for Christsakes, calm down."

"Sorry. Can't help it."

They drove together through the soft evening light, Garland asking questions, telling a couple of stories, angling his hat back, his confidence seeming to grow each time he made her laugh. Mary knew she shouldn't encourage him but got swept along. He told her about playing shortstop as a teenager and how a stray bull had wandered into the game. The bull was about to charge the first baseman when Garland beaned it with a hard throw right between the eyes, and the animal had bellowed angrily but loped away. He told her about how happy his cousin had been at the ranch.

They pulled up outside the pool hall. Thanking him for the ride, she jumped down, slammed the rusty door, and he drove off. She was finally rid of him, yet for the first time wasn't so sure she wanted to be.

She climbed the dark stairwell over the Chinese dry cleaner, the chemical smell assaulting her until she reached the entrance, then the familiar rhythm of colliding pool balls, the din of voices, jukebox thump, the nervous energy of everyone practicing for the event. Jake's was an older billiard room, in business long before the pool craze glossed the game and hundreds of thousands of dollars funded new designer pool palaces. Jake's was no-frills. It offered twenty-two level regulation tables with worn cloth, good sandwiches and cold beer, and held the best regional tournaments in the area. Mary favored Jake's as a nod to Kelly Harris who had grown up in such places. In many ways she would have preferred the luxurious trappings of the new rooms, the designer carpet instead of crumbling linoleum, incandescent lighting instead of fluorescent, better air, but she remained loyal to Jake's and Kelly Harris. Besides, she liked the bartender, Sammy, and the owner, Nick Brignolia, even if he was a bit dour.

At the bar, she asked Sammy for a Weinhard's draft and a crabmeat roll and passed him her briefcase to stash. She imagined the wrong person stealing it and finding the phone, but knew it was safe with Sammy. As she stared blankly at the enormous oak beer cooler with all its fogged glass doors, he set down her draft, the frozen base inching fractionally along the Formica. Now that she was finally at rest, she was suddenly exhausted; it had been quite a day.

"Not seen you 'round much," he said.

"Work, too much work."

"How that Porsche runnin'? Nice you take me out that day. I still think on that." He slid her a saltshaker.

"Gone." She shook a few grains into her beer, a habit copied from her dad.

Sammy looked concerned. "Accident?"

"No." She took a long sip. "Repo."

"Damn, girl, this recession gettin' *ugly*—everybody juss losing and losing. I shoulda listen to you. Or stuck with my horses. Odds be a hell of a lot better, and you get something pretty to view while they takin' your money. Crab be right out." Sammy turned, his huge shoulders moving under a vintage mint-green bowling shirt, though she knew he didn't bowl. But he always wore the shirts—he must collect them. Against his skin color the bright green looked great, a tone that would've only made her appear sickly.

She was on her second beer and halfway through her crab roll when someone took the stool beside her. She couldn't believe it.

"Took a bit to find parking. Goddang, lot of people live down here." He signaled Sammy, who sauntered over, looked curiously at the two of them.

"He with you?" he asked her.

"I suppose so," she said. "We met during a car accident." She introduced them.

"Hey there, Sammy,"—Garland standing up, extending his hand—"Hank McKeen from Likely, that's up near Alturas, Mo—"

"Garland," she said, "you don't have to announce to everyone you meet *exactly* where you're from, they already know, believe me."

He looked confused, then his grin spread. He shook hands with Sammy. "Worked with a black guy on our ranch one year, great big fella. Real good worker. Looked like you. Lemay Jefferson. Maybe you know him?"

"*Garland*," she said. "Why don't you have a beer or something?"

Sammy took the whole thing in, seemed barely to keep from cracking up.

Garland ordered the same as Mary. "Glad you're not drinking that micro stuff. Tried one the other day. Just asked for a draft and that's what they give me. I tell you what, I gave it right back to 'em."

Sammy placed a beer in front of Garland. He drained it in one pull, thumped the glass down on the Formica. "This city stuff makes me thirsty. Again, Mary too."

"Not for me." She took out her wallet.

"Mary . . ." he said, "I got it."

"What're you saying?"

"I'm paying. Goes without saying."

"I can't let you do that."

"Just let me. Look, I know I ain't no good at all this kinda stuff, but let me just pay supper. *Please*."

What was she getting herself into? She would have to have a talk with Garland, though now wasn't the moment. What she needed now was some table time.

Armed with a plastic tray of balls, she walked toward table fourteen as the fluorescent light flickered on above it. Endlessly coached by Kelly Harris that a smooth and consistent stroke was the foundation of the game, she always began a practice session with table-length straight shots. Her forearm hung straight down from the elbow, moving like a pendulum, till the whole arm followed through. She was surprised to be in stroke. Maybe days like this were good for her game?

As she practiced, Nick Brignolia walked over. He wore his uniform: shiny black wing tips, pressed black slacks, starched white shirt with the top button closed. It made him look like a stocky Sicilian waiter. He watched her shooting long shots off the rail for a few minutes before speaking.

"You know what I nickname you after that shot in the semi-final last month?" His voice was gruff. "Mary Massé."

"You saw it?"

"Saw it? Course I saw it. What's wrong with you, *saw it?* You know I saw it." He was already getting angry. Nick was always getting pissed off about something.

"I still lost in the final."

"Mary." He paused, peering at her through his thick glasses, the heavy black frames contrasting with his papery skin. "What do I keep telling you? *Safety.* You gotta play safe. You, you shoot at anything, so what happen, you miss. Safety, you get the table back. But you won't listen to Nick."

"I just love making the crazy ones."

"Make them when you not play for money. Money, you gotta play smart. I'm telling you, you got the nerves, the heart. That's what it takes. All in the head." Nick tapped his white hair with his index finger. "And the stroke. But you, you make that massé, but you make Nick mad." And he walked off.

All around her women were practicing, the clicks and taps of varied shots ringing in the big room, the jukebox still thumping. She glanced over at the bar; Garland had Sammy laughing. She sensed that he was taking his cousin's illness very hard, yet outwardly he still managed to be so cheerful, so positive. He seemed to accept things as they were and go on from there. Maybe that was the secret? She sighted down the row of support columns that bisected the room, the same two-tone as the wainscoting and the walls, a dingy green with a cream above, and wondered if Nick's North End room in Boston had been painted in the same combination. She would have to ask him, but you could never tell what would make him mad. Most questions about his past in Boston upset him. Even her cue irritated him. "What you need all that inlay for? That don't make a stick play better. And that fancy box. You waste your money, Mary." And as if he'd heard her thoughts, there he was ringing the bell signaling the start of the tournament.

She drew Karen Valdez as her opponent for the first round and won the coin toss. Mary shattered the rack, holing the three ball and the seven. Break patterns, like most things in nature, are never the same, each with its own quirky perfection. She examined the lie of the seven remaining balls as she rubbed her cue tip with the edge of a chalk cube. As the balls lay, she couldn't quite *see* the one. She considered calling a *push-out* or playing a safety. Instead, checking quickly to see if Nick was watching, she lifted the butt of her cue so that the whole stick was at a forty-five degree angle to the cloth; then she stroked in a downward motion onto the top of the cue ball. It curved in a gentle arc around the six and pocketed the one, Karen Valdez tapping her cue on the linoleum in recognition of the shot. "Another massé for you, Nick," she said under her breath. "Maybe I am Mary Massé." She ran out the remaining balls. As the nine ball fell into the pocket, she heard a hoot. Actually, everyone in the entire poolroom heard a hoot. He stood by the bar, draft in hand, mouthing Sorry, and she had to smile. He gave her a thumbs up and walked over.

"You didn't miss," he said in a whisper. She was waiting for Karen to rack the balls.

"Isn't that the idea?"—though secretly pleased.

"And that curving thing was frigging unbelievable."

"Massé shot. The guy who invented the leather tip, Mingaud, discovered the shot while in prison because there was so little room in his cell. The more you lift the butt of your cue, the more the ball will curve. I love them, but they're inconsistent."

"Something special to see. You mind me watching from here?"

"Are you going to hoot every time I win?"

He blushed again. "Couldn't help it. Never seen them all run out like that."

"It happens a lot around here. It's stringing the runs together that's tough. The best I've run is a four pack, but only once during a tournament."

"Four pack?"

"Four in a row."

"You ran out four games in a row? . . . No misses?"

She nodded and walked over to check the tightness of Karen's rack. A loose rack could lose a match. Another Kelly Harris admonition.

The match with Karen went to Mary, Garland only letting out a chirp when she dropped the last nine ball into the pocket. As she played out the set, Jay kept intruding into her thoughts. Each time she waited for her opponent to rack, he was there again. Only when she was shooting did her thoughts of him recede.

Late now, a settled quiet blanketed the poolroom. A crowd of beaten players and stragglers watched from the shadows, slumped in chairs or leaning on nearby tables, all the other table lights turned off, the one rectangle of chalky green everyone's focus; Sammy was out from behind the bar, the kitchen long closed, the jukebox mute. There was an intimacy to the moment, a closeness that a group of people can encounter when they are all concentrating on the same thing, sharing the same momentary obsession.

Mary was in the finals with Laura Sedgewick, who, as she insisted on telling everyone, had played snooker in England for two years. Tall and blonde and snobbish Laura Sedgewick. Mary had wanted to crush her quickly and collect her money, yet after sixteen games they were both *on the hill*. Mary had missed a few crazy ones and let Laura back in, Nick frowning at her from the duskiness at the edge of the audience. She just wished she wasn't so tired.

As fate would have it, the final game hinged on her decision between a safety shot and a nearly impossible ninety-degree cut down the rail, the bank shot blocked. She didn't want to find Nick's eyes. She did see Garland smiling confidently at her, looking certain she couldn't miss, no matter the difficulty. If she fired the cue ball with full left English into the cushion just behind the two, the cue could kick off the bank at enough of an angle to clip the ball down the rail and into the pocket. About to attempt this shot, she inadvertently caught Nick's expression.

She stood back up. Looking the table over again, she played a perfect safety, delicately touching the two and trapping the cue ball behind the seven. Nick smiled. At least for Nick it was a smile. No one else would have noticed, but she did.

Laura rose from her stool and addressed the table. For her even to touch the two was unlikely, and if she missed, Mary would have ball in hand and a likely win—the one large. Laura, her arrogance finally looking ruffled, stared at the lie of balls. She was stuck. *Snookered.* Her only chance was a three-rail hit, but with all the other balls on the table in the way, the shot had slim odds. She had to try it. Laura stroked smoothly and the cue ball bounded off one rail, then two, whispered by the eight ball, cleared the six by a wish, off the final cushion to contact the two perfectly, running it down the rail and into the pocket. A unified shout from the shadows. The crowd quieted and Laura, back to her cocky blonde self, carefully ran out the remaining balls. Mary congratulated her with a firm handshake.

As she was unscrewing her cue Garland walked up.

"You were great," he said.

"Thanks."

"Never seen no one play like you."

"As my dad says, God loves a trier."

Garland thought a moment. "I like that. *God loves a trier.* That is dang good." Garland nodding his head, looking serious, then brightening. "Hey, you hungry or thirsty or anything?"

"I just need a ride to the airport."

"You flying somewhere?"—sounding concerned.

"I've got a rental waiting."

"You don't need no rental. Drive you anywhere you wanna go."

"Just the airport. *Okay?*" She looked at him, hoping he would read her expression. She was too exhausted for anything else.

When she collected her five hundred for second place from Nick, he wouldn't meet her eyes. He handed her the envelope full of bills. As she turned to leave—

"Mary."

She stopped.

"You play the right shot. You lose the match, but you play the right shot. Over time you win. Believe me. No one beat the odds. You play the right shot. I feel this."

She glanced down at him, studying him for a moment. "Thanks, Nick. Thanks for caring about me."

The old pool player looked up at her, and if he'd ever smiled in the last twenty years, now was that time.

FOUR

Friday morning she awoke before her alarm went off and lay there tired. Last night, that dream again. For months now, about every dozen days, the dream returned. It always ended with his head on her chest, Mary crying as she gently stroked his brow with her fingers. Now she believed *he* might be Jay Chevalier.

Her hand appeared out of the sheets, and she switched off the alarm, turned on the radio. ". . . stupid and contagious," she heard, "here we are now, entertain us," and the band exploded into electric fury. God, Nirvana had such a sense of dynamics—building tension by withholding. Such a simple concept, though like many simple things, they only seem simple after you understand them. But to think of them first, that's the difficult part, she thought, and got out of bed.

She walked into the kitchen naked, still a little sweaty from her night of dreams. Adhering to her workday ritual, she filled and switched on her coffee grinder, that irritating whine. She shut off the machine and lifted it to her nose, the reassuring aroma of French Roast beans. It seemed like the first casual thing she'd done in four days. She poured boiling water over the coffee and watched it drip for a moment, then walked to the window. Outside, as dawn began its slow focus, early-morning mist wreathed the few eucalyptus trees that bordered her un-mown yard. She gazed idly at the fog and shivered, her eyes no longer seeing anything.

Jay Chevalier had more energy than anyone she'd ever been around, and if there'd been a clue on Monday what her week would be like, she would've forgone the pool tournament and headed to bed early. Entering the Harcourt Building on Tuesday morning—punctually and without incident—there was the smell of paint in the elevator. Jay had painters redoing the walls, each floor a different color. A soft rust on four where reception was, a gray-mauve surrounding the computer cubicles on five, and for the executive offices, a muted sage-green similar to the old lounge color, though to her eye a more refined hue. The lounge itself he left alone. The new colors, along with the removal of *the* paintings, transformed the place. It was now LiveCell.

At Tuesday morning's meeting, Jay insisted she head up the entire advertising department, though she argued for hiring an outside professional firm. From head web-designer to advertising manager seemed like too much of a jump. "We'll try it and see how it goes," he said. So she not only had this new web site to design, but ads to formulate: print, newspaper, radio, TV, bus cards; there were people to interview and hire, drawing from inside the firm if she could. She'd never had so much responsibility. On Wednesday, he handed her an envelope and said, "Get the Porsche back if you want." How had he known about her Porsche? But she didn't have time to think about leasing a new car. On Thursday she told him she wasn't sure she could handle the job. "I have faith in you, please have faith in me," was his reply. Not knowing quite what he meant, she went back to work.

Now on Friday morning, waiting in line for the Bay Bridge toll, she listened to the radio again. With her FasTrak renewed, the wait was brief this early—nice to have money again. Her rental car had clear speakers and an emphatic horn. As she scanned through different radio stations, she heard something, and her finger locked it in:

" . . . and in financial news today, the new firm LiveCell, which recently acquired Clicksave.com, says it has a new telephone that it's bringing to the market place. The new phone apparently works on a completely new technology, and allows for hand-held, static-free communication."—she recognized some of the copy, pleased that *new* was repeated four times—"I hear it utilizes paper cups and kite string but might lead to severe ear infections . . . and now stay tuned for your Bay Area forecast." The last line was slipped in by the announcer using a different tone of voice. A damn sarcastic tone.

On reaching the garage, she jerked the rental into her space and went directly to Jay's office, the only room painted a burnt orange. She wasn't sure about the color. His door was open, it was always kept open, and there he sat behind a large thirties-style battered oak desk that he'd had hauled in. Sentimental, he explained it. She knocked on the doorframe.

"Jay?"

He looked up and waved her in.

"Did you hear the news on the radio? From the press release?" she said.

"Duncan called me. He's up early too."

"Jay, I did *not* write that copy. About the cups and string."

"Kind of funny," he said. "Mary, sit down. Don't look so worried."

She chose one of the mismatched chairs. Where had he unearthed all these relics? She had to admit she preferred them to Wendell's chrome and white world, but there must be something in-between. She looked at Jay, able to look him in the eyes now. As the days passed, she'd been too busy working to contemplate other kinds of thoughts. They were still there nonetheless.

"We can only expect this kind of thing," he said. "There will be ridicule; there will be controversy; there will be sabotage. To be expected. We have a new product and it must prove itself."

"Do you think the radio announcer ad-libbed, or did someone write that copy?"

"Does it matter?"

"Doesn't it?"

"Not to me."

She wasn't even sure now why it had bothered her, but on hearing it, she'd had a disquieting premonition.

"Are you okay?" he said.

She didn't answer.

"Do you need to take the day off?"

She shook her head.

"This evening, where would be a good place to get a drink?"

"You drink?" Somehow she didn't think he did.

"Sometimes wine."

"You want a wine bar?"

"Where do you go?"

"Usually Jake's. It's a poolroom. I don't think they have much wine."

"We'll go there then. Okay?"

"Jay, I don't know anything about you. I shouldn't tell you this, but Duncan has spent a few nights online trying to find out about you. He's usually incredible at hacking information, but even he couldn't find much."

"What did he find?"

"You were born in Madawaska, Maine, in nineteen-sixty. You went to Harvard at seventeen, went from undergrad to finish your doctorate in biochemistry in a record seven years. Then you seem to have disappeared."

"And?"

"Is it so wrong to want to know something about your boss?"

"What do you want to know?" His eyes moved to the window. They appeared to focus on the one slice of blue bay between the buildings, or maybe she imagined it since that's where she usually looked. He leaned back in his chair and folded his arms across his T-shirt. He always wears blue, she thought, wondering if maybe he did have some vanity.

"You don't mind my asking?" she said. "I know I should get to work."

"Why did you come in so early?"

"Well, . . . I thought you might be here." *He knows.*

"So let's have our talk."

"You really don't mind?"

"What do you think?"

She searched him for a second. "I don't understand where all the money's coming from. Duncan couldn't find any indication that you're wealthy yourself. You don't act rich, but then it can be hard to tell. Duncan thought you must have financial backing from somewhere. Is that true?"

"I recently sold a patent to Swatch in Switzerland."

"One of the patents for the phone?"

"No. I didn't patent the phone."

"What? Why *not*?" His words brought her out of her chair. *Everything* rested on patents for the phone as far as she could tell.

"The phone's cell makeup is not its only secret."

"It isn't?" She stood there, stunned. "Then what is?"

He didn't answer.

"Whatever it is, it needs to be patented. All its innovations need to be patented. Believe me, otherwise it will be stolen and we'll be out of business. Someone will be making it overseas for half the price in no time. Jay, I can't believe this. We have to hire a patent attorney immediately."

"It's not possible. Please, sit down."

She found her chair again. "I can't help being upset. Patents for new inventions are imperative. You must know that."

He held her with his calm look and she quieted outwardly, but it lessened none of her uneasiness. How could he leave himself so unprotected? It was crazy, insane. There was that fear again.

He continued to study her. "You'll have to trust me."

She nodded and looked away, trying to calm herself. Her entire future, all her financial dreams, rested on LiveCell's success.

"Can you tell me about the Swiss patent?"

"I invented a new way to indicate time."

"And?" she said, using his technique.

For a moment he seemed to listen to the silence of the empty offices. Then, in an almost bored tone, "My watch utilizes colored light to indicate time. Three colored fiber-optic dots move in the same orbit at the perimeter of the watch face. Blue for the hour, red for the minutes, yellow for the seconds. It runs off of a single LED and has the advantage of being visible in all conditions, even under water. People with poor eyesight will be able to use the watch. It also keeps the center of the watch face free for other uses, such as digital readouts, or three-dimensional designs. As a clock, in a steeple for instance, time can be read from much farther away. It's also visually appealing—at least I think so—because as the dots of light pass each other the color blends for an instant. Kids could learn about mixing color from the watch. When all three primaries meet you see white light for that split second."

So simple when you understood, but to think of it first—

Every time she started to worry about him, he amazed her again. But the phones still needed patents; she didn't care what he thought.

"Other questions?" he said.

He always sensed when she was frustrated with him and gave her just enough. She nodded, and he continued.

"I was born to a single mom in northern Maine. She told me my father was French and Finnish. He was a *voyageur*, a trapper, one of the last of the breed. From the other side of the Saint Lawrence River, the north side. Though they didn't marry, she still took his name. My mom died when I was still fairly young, and I never knew him. I became a ward of the state, and as Duncan found out, got myself an education. Then I searched for meaning for a few years, changed course again and started working as a neurobiologist for DuPont in Delaware."

"The lost laboratory?"

"You remembered. What a place. A big thirties building with those ochre-colored bricks. You know the kind?" She nodded. "The entrance was curved glass-brick shaped like a bell, rather appealing. I think the lab was basically a tax write-off for DuPont. They also used the publicity. We all worked exclusively for environmental causes, and in my case they'd employed a Micmac, probably filling some quota. All the neurobiologists and biochemists worked pretty much separately—they barely spoke to me—and all DuPont required was a progress report every six months. They were generous with equipment, and I liked the feeling of being forgotten, liked the old building though I didn't care for Wilmington."

He glanced away as if deciding something.

"I was originally convinced that the right combination of cells could feed on varied air impurities—or what the human body considers impurities—similar to how plants feed on carbon dioxide. Over the years it led me to experiment with a diversity of cells, but I always ran up against the same problem. I could support cell life, but the extraction of impurities was so minute as to be meaningless in cleaning the air. So I was forced to accept a new vision. I searched for combinations of cells that would replicate with unusual intensity, yet also be able to stabilize and maintain a specific solidity at a desired proportion. This I achieved."

He stopped talking for a moment, and Mary wondered if that was it.

"Then I made a breakthrough. No one had ever managed to reproduce mature brain cells. I found that certain cultured neuronal cells could be mutagenized to alter their genetic makeup by infecting them with a viral DNA. These mutant neurons once triggered by a variety of differentiation factors had the exceptional capacity to form unusually high numbers of axonal processes with similar electrophysiological properties to the human brain. They acted almost like a silicon chip. The trouble was that they were completely unstable. So I amalgamated these cells with other more stable aggregates, and added the cells that would support the matrix by absorption of impurities. Basically I combined the knowledge of all three kinds of cells I had worked with over the years. At first I thought I was on to a novel kind of computer biochip, vastly superior to silicon in storage capacity and speed. And then I made a discovery that startled me. Terrified me at the time." He pulled on his ear for a moment.

"I realized instantly that I wasn't willing to share the discovery with DuPont, or anyone for that matter. People who had not spoken to me in years sensed it, began nosing around, unnerving after being ignored for so long. I was suddenly not so lost. I quit. Disappeared so I could finish the work. Was fortunate to sell the watch patent, borrowed money from a Swiss bank against future royalties to fund my project. Bought Click-save to market the phone, and here we are."

She sat for quite a while in silence, processing it all. He didn't interrupt her. Though she hadn't understood all his words, she still sensed what he meant, that he'd cloned the phones out of a mixture of cells, including brain cells. "Where did you get these, *cells*?" She hesitated to say *brain*.

"You mean the brain cells?" he said.

She nodded. Sometimes she felt he really could read her thoughts.

"Initially I worked with stem cells." He paused. "I discovered I needed fresh brain cells. I knew a surgeon at a nearby hospital, and I used my own." He watched her carefully. "It was only a limited series of very minute extractions, everything was reproduced from those. It was the extraction from my pineal gland that really changed things."

"You used your own brain cells to make the phones?"—knowing the answer but not wanting to believe it.

He nodded.

She didn't say anything for some moments. She couldn't.

"You okay?" he said.

"What was this discovery that you didn't want to share?" She was apprehensive, but too curious not to ask.

But he said, "Let's get to work now, okay? We have a lot to do," and stopped her with his look. Was he concerned that he'd revealed too much? Not that she thought it was too much. Maybe he's worried that I think it's strange? But it *is* strange!

"You won't tell me?" she said.

"No. Not yet. We have other things to concentrate on first."

She would have to be patient. She moved her mind reluctantly back to the morning's business. "So you don't want me to follow up on that?" He didn't understand her at first. "The radio press release?"

"Leave it, it's meaningless. Nothing at all to be worried about. Someone goofing around. We have much better things to do."

Mary retreated to her office. For the first fifteen minutes or so she couldn't get to work. She still had so many questions: what did he do during those missing years? where did he live now? how did the phone work? what was the discovery he wouldn't share? why no patent? did DuPont know about the invention? would they sue? and why did he buy Clicksave?

She thought about him having his own cells extracted to seed the LiveCell phones, and it bothered her, even made her queasy. But maybe it was like some things on the farm—they were strange until you got used to them. She could only hope. She imagined him working year after year in that forgotten laboratory by himself, carrying his worn leather briefcase past the glass brick every morning, making his discoveries, accepting his defeats, continuing on because he believed in himself, in his vision. He had followed his intuitions and decided to have his own brain cells extracted. She kept coming back to that. Could having certain brain cells removed affect a person, change him? What if you removed the wrong cells? And this was the man she was *so* attracted to? With part of his brain missing?

Her coworkers started to arrive, and her attention was required for advertising LiveCell phones, not worrying about her boss's peculiarities. Duncan, one of the first to arrive, looked annoyed that she was already there; he was probably worried she'd been alone with Jay and found out things he hadn't. And as usual, he was correct. He seemed even more stressed since Jay had taken over the company, if that were possible.

Mary spent the morning writing a radio ad, then devised a unique way to navigate the new web site and met with her programmers, took the usual flotilla of phone calls. A short lunch and an equally busy afternoon. At five-thirty people started to leave for the weekend. At six she wandered down the corridor and looked in on Jay. He glanced up at her. "Are you ready?" she said. His face remained blank. "To go out for a drink? . . . the poolroom?" That got a response.

They took his car to Jake's. It made her Fiesta seem like an indulgence. An avocado-green mid-seventies Cutlass with the driver's side badly scarred. "Came that way," he said. When he opened the mildly blemished passenger door for her, it complained loudly. She slid onto the bench seat, and something hiding in the ripped cover spiked her. She winced, yet managed not to cry out. Jesus, she muttered, *quite* the ride.

"How did you know I had a Porsche?" she said, as he followed her directions to the poolroom.

"I just heard about it." There was something odd in his tone, but she let it go. Being around him you had to let go of a lot of things, but then he was her boss after all.

Driving along the same route with Jay reminded her of the evening in Garland's pickup. She wondered how Garland was, how his cousin was doing, and decided to call or write him to find out. She still carried the slip of paper he'd given her with such seriousness. *Call me for any reasin* was written across the top with the address of the ranch carefully penciled below the phone number.

"We're already getting inquiries about the phone," she said. "That banner ad I placed, and some of the radio releases. We had over ten-thousand unique users today alone. Have you decided where to price it?"

He glanced at her. "Mary, no more work. Tell me about Porsches. Or about something else."

She did, and soon they pulled up near the poolroom and parked.

Sammy set down her draft as they approached the bar.

"Hey girl, twice in one week. Now that *is* nice. Where's the cue?"

"Sammy, this is Jay Chevalier, my new boss."

At the introduction they shook hands, nodding cautiously to each other, looking as if they might be checking the other's grip. Probably both alpha males. She knew men had all these odd rituals to show their masculinity, though she wouldn't have thought Jay was that way.

Sammy turned to her. "Where you working now?"

"Same building, new boss, new name. LiveCell."

"LiveCell? 'Nother dot com?"

"We're going to sell phones. A new kind of telephone."

"H-m." Sammy slowly moved his focus to Jay. "Man, what you want to drink?" He was never in a hurry, and with his size why should he be? He was wearing another one of his bowling shirts, orange with navy blue stripes.

"You have any Chianti?" said Jay.

Sammy started to chuckle in his low almost soundless way. "No one ever ask for wine. Man, I sure don't recommend it. The house red's ugly. Sure ain't no *Chian*-ti. Come in a plastic cup."

Jay decided on a draft and Sammy turned to pull it, set it beside hers. No one else was sitting at the bar. One or two players drifted up for drinks and sandwiches, or to cash out table time, and Sammy took care of them. As Mary sipped her beer, she watched Jay looking around the poolroom. Over half the tables were full of Friday night players, a less serious crowd than on other evenings. A group of Asians ganged around two adjoining tables, laughing and yelling excitedly when someone missed an easy shot or pocketed a good one. She had seen them every Friday night she'd been there. Nick was sequestered in his office, a glow of diffused light visible through the opaque glass of the door, the transom window angled. Nick practically lived at his poolroom, always there; she was pretty sure he didn't have a family.

"So, tell me about this *new* telephone?" said Sammy, when he was free of other customers.

"Jay?" She looked to him.

"You have yours?"

She dug it out of her purse and laid it on the bar top. Was about to explain it when she noticed a slight negation in Jay's expression.

"This? A phone?" Sammy reached for it. The minute he touched it, the surface started to shimmer. "*Hey*. This damn thing's glowing. Feel all funny. What kinda plastic's this?" He looked it all over, the phone pearlescent for only an instant, then abruptly turning dull gray. "This one funny ass telephone. No screen, no buttons, no nothing, juss this funny little box sticking out."—with a perplexed expression now as if he'd eaten something strange.

"It shut itself off," said Jay, "because it doesn't know you."

They both stared at him.

"Each phone gets to know its owner, and when it does, no one can use your phone unless you tell it okay."

"Man, you joking me, right?"

"You dial it by speaking the number to the phone; it does the rest. You can even tell it to keep dialing a busy number."

Sammy incredulous.

"Try it if you like. Call someone." He asked Mary to release her phone. She did and it began to pulse again in Sammy's hand. He didn't drop it; he glared at it as if it were alive.

She turned to Jay. "No one could steal someone else's phone?"

"It wouldn't do them much good."

"So, they can't be stolen *or* damaged?"

"What you talking about, can't be damaged?" said Sammy.

She took her phone from Sammy and whacked it on the bar edge hard enough to make a fair-sized dent. As it healed Sammy started to chuckle.

"Man, what is this crazy shit? Damn! Where'd you get this thing?"

"He invented it," she said, "and LiveCell will manufacture and market it—Jay's company."

"You got to be fucking with me."

"Try it."

Sammy did, hesitating before he told the phone his home number in Oakland, addressing it as if he knew they were playing a practical joke on him and there was no way he was going to fall for it, maintaining full cool. This cool, however, completely deserted him when his wife answered. He tried to explain to Jolene about how he had called her, about the new phone, about her voice sounding as if it were inside his head. She told him to get out of Felix's Lounge right that instant. "And *you* should be at work," she said. "And you sober your ass up before you come home to me and the kids or you got *some*thing else coming."

Mary watched the usually calm and cool Sammy.

"This the most amazing fucking thing I ever seen." He held it out in front of him as if it were a divine object. "Damn." He stood there shaking his head, placed the phone carefully in front of Mary again. He turned and walked over to the tap and drew himself a beer, came back to them. "Jolene thinks I been drinking anyhow." He lifted his glass to Mary. Then to Jay.

"Man, you some kind of motherfucker." He downed his drink in a long swallow, hummed his approval. "Okay, tell me more."

"Hey?" said a new voice, "Can I get a hot dog?"

Sammy turned to the teenager, not saying anything. The kid looked nervously over his shoulder at his friends and then down at his sneakers as if the solution might be there. Then Sammy broke into a grin and went off to fix the kid a hot dog.

"Is there anything that's not incredible about your phone?" she said.

"You don't know all of it yet."

"Well? . . ."

He said nothing.

"How do you expect me to market these things if I don't know everything about them?"

"You're doing fine. You hungry?"

"Why did you want Sammy to know about the phone?"

"You certainly are perceptive, aren't you?"

"And are you always this forthcoming?"

It took him a moment to answer. "I've lived alone most of my life. Worked alone. Maybe it makes me too careful, a bit withdrawn with people."

"I shouldn't have said that. It was rude."

"Let's eat something. And another beer. I think I like beer. Then we'll have a game of pool."

"You shoot?"

"No, but I want to watch you."

"I'm not any good," she said, and he smiled slightly. Maybe he does have a sense of humor even if he always acts serious? He was so hard to read.

Sammy took their dinner order and poured three more drafts, refilling his own glass though Nick didn't like him to drink on the job. Soon he brought out two cheeseburgers crowded by chips and nudged by a few pickle spears. He waited while they ate, sipping his beer this time, looking as if he was trying to be patient, but soon—

"Man, you gotta tell me more about this telephone."

Jay wiped his mouth with a paper napkin. "I think a lot of people don't realize one thing about the phones. They're alive."

Sammy dropped his glass of beer and Mary choked on a potato chip. Four eyes stared at him: *Alive?*

"All the cells are maintained in a sleep-like state when not in use. Some of the aggregate feeds on air impurities to sustain the neurons and the substrate. That's how they heal, they're genetically coded to have memory of their shape, same as they remember their owners. When you use the phone, or while it heals, it phosphoresces at its core as kinetic energy floods it, similar to a firefly."

He examined Mary. "You going to be okay?" She was still choking a little. She nodded, though she wondered. "I thought you realized that this morning," he said to her.

Sammy broke in, "This thing is *living*? That the wildest shit I ever heard! Man, oh, man . . ." He chuckled, slapping his thighs. "Everybody going to want this here phone. *Everybody*. Be like having a pet, much as owning a phone. How long they last? How much they gonna cost?"

"As far as how long they will last, that I don't know. But feeding off air impurities they should last many years—we have a lot of impurities. As far as cost, how much would you pay for one?"

"Are you joking me? I'd pay next to anything for one a these things. Man, that is just the coolest kind of shit."

"Give me a figure. What would you *like* to pay?"

"What I like to pay." Sammy thought a minute. "Hundred and a half, two bills, anyway. And that would be cheap. I never heard a telephone that clear. And the way you talk to the thing and the way those things heal up. Damn, man, that *is* some very outrageous shit." Sammy shook his head back and forth again, still chuckling. "Mary, I tell you girl, you bring some crazy people in here. Monday that cowboy, now this cat. I tell you . . . can I invest in this?"

"LVC," said Jay.

"That the ticker symbol? I'm down with that. Monday, I'm buying."

She had stopped coughing, her dinner left unfinished. Why hadn't she realized they were living? But why would she?

Sammy went to get a bar rag to clean up the spilled beer.

She looked at Jay. "You really are something. I mean it all makes sense now, if you can call it that. Do you realize your brain is living in all those phones?"

"Does it bother you?"

"I don't know. Growing up I got used to some strange things. I suppose I'll get used to this. Sammy seems to have no problem with it being alive. I wonder if anyone else at LiveCell has any idea."

Sammy straightened up, the cracked beer glass in his hand. He started questioning Jay about the stock again. Moved over and dropped the glass in the trash as he talked.

"Sammy, no stock is foolproof," she said, annoyed *that* was what he was concentrating on.

"I got a hunch with this one, girl. Big hunch. Jay is the man."

"Where do you work out?" said Jay. He always gets uncomfortable with praise, she noticed.

"Cyclone Gym. Over in Oakland on Ninety-eighth and Edes. Southeast of the Coliseum. You looking for a place?"

Jay nodded.

"This mainly a boxing gym. But we got all the free weights you want. You box?"

He nodded again.

"Man, I thought so. You got the nose and scar tissue. You also shake hands like a boxer. Tough guys always wanna break your fucking hand, show you how damn tough they are. Boxer always shakes soft 'cause his hands sore lot of the time."

"So you boxed?" she asked Jay.

"Yeah. Those missing years I did a lot of stuff."

"Is there anything you don't do?"

"I be at the gym tomorrow," Sammy broke in. "You wanna come? I show you round. Best you go with me, first time."

They arranged to meet in front of the gym at ten o'clock. Sammy explained that the Cyclone looked like an abandoned storefront from the street, there was a small sign. "Anybody try an bother you, you juss mention my name, Samuel Holmes." Then some customers pulled him away.

"He really likes you," she said.

"I like him."

"I shouldn't have said that about your not being forthcoming."

"There's truth in it."

"People seem so drawn to you. I bet you could get along with anyone."

"Not anyone." His eyes shifted. She wanted to but didn't ask. He broke the silence. "That was a good hamburger."

"Except the cheese. I've asked Nick to buy a Vermont cheddar, or even a jack, but he always gets that same rubbery provolone."

"I guess you would know about cheese."

"What do you mean?"

"Didn't you grow up on a dairy farm?"

How did he know that? Maybe Duncan told him, or maybe Jay had been asking about her. "How do you know these things about me?" she said.

"Let's play pool."

He is a very closed person, she thought again. But then, she knew she was as well. But in a way he wasn't closed—it was confusing. She wanted to find a way to get to him, yet had no idea how. He was so straightforward about everything, so honest, so directed. She wondered if he ever joked around or just acted silly.

She went to retrieve a tray of balls from Sammy, but didn't ask for her usual table because there were too many noisy players on the adjacent tables; he must have kept it open for her. Slightly guilty, she asked for a different table. She wanted quiet, and certainly wasn't concerned about the cloth's action tonight. Sammy reached for the switch, and they both watched the fluorescent flicker on in the far corner, the cloth turning a vivid green. The sight always stirred her.

"Sammy?" she said, and he leaned across the counter to her, his shoulders pulling the bowling shirt taut. "There is something about him, isn't there?"

"Girl, I never met the likes."

Jay and Mary played a few games of eight-ball. She considered shooting one-handed, hoping to make their games more competitive, yet hesitated to show off in front of him. She attempted more questions about the phone, but he refused, so she tried to relax and just shoot pool. He played pretty poorly, and she considered giving him a few pointers but rejected the idea. She eased back her game and watched his arm muscles move as he stretched for certain shots. Then, as she sank her third eight ball in as many games, he said something that stopped her.

"Your stroke is like Kelly's."

She straightened.

"I know I should have told you sooner. I was worried you might leave the company if you knew. I was so relieved when you decided to stay that first day, and I didn't want you to change your mind."

She didn't respond.

"I'm sorry," he said. "I wanted to tell you sooner, but it's so important to me that you stay. I couldn't risk it."

It took her a moment more before she spoke. "Why?"

"Why what?"

"Why is it so important?"

"I need someone I can trust."

"And Kelly told you that."

"Yes. I went to see him. Actually, at first I thought he might be the one to help me, then he told me about you, and I knew. Difficult fellow to find. We'd been out of touch for many years. Though Kelly had been an addict, even drugs couldn't destroy what he has inside him."

"Can we sit down?"

They moved over to the wood bleacher seats against the wall. Neither of them said anything, the noisy room filling up more now as it neared nine o'clock. She broke their silence.

"I'm very confused by all this. Kelly wrote me and said he'd had a visitor. It was you."

"I asked him not to say anything, but in his affection for you he probably wanted to."

"Where did you meet?"

"New York. Twenty years ago."

"Jay? What's this all about?"

"I need someone I can trust completely. After I received the patent money from Swatch, I could proceed with the phone, but wasn't sure how to go about it, it was all new to me. I decided to find Kelly. I had a premonition that he might be able to help. When I found him, he told me about you, and then I knew. I checked into Clicksave and it looked okay."

"I still don't understand?"

"I bought Clicksave to get you."

She leaned back against the darkened seat.

This was all getting stranger and stranger.

FIVE

Cage Dairy Farm, Monkton, Vermont

*November 2, 200_*

Dear Mary,

It was great to talk. When Jay gave me the phone, he said you'd call one day, and there you were. The way they don't ring but you hear the call is something.

I felt that you should meet Jay, and I'm glad it's worked out. You asked, so here's what I remember. In the city, he was in two worlds. He had the physical with the boxing and the fitness, but when he wasn't in the gym, he was in the Bowery. With all the druggies and drunks. He'd help out the sick, but wouldn't lay out for smack or booze. Some days he'd arrive with these stuffed grocery bags and make everyone sandwiches. It was funny because we only ate the sandwiches to please him. All we wanted was junk! What the hell did we want bologna for? He couldn't seem to understand that (or maybe he did). I guess he just wanted to do something good for others. His street name was Boxer, but actually, as a boxer he sucked. No killer instinct. If he had an opponent in trouble, he'd back off. Drove his trainer crazy. I went to a cou-

ple of his fights, and he could've won both. He'd go with me when I hustled pool. Once, he knocked down two guys who'd attacked me in this hellhole, but he never liked to hurt people. Actually, he was embarrassed when he knocked the two guys down, and you should've seen them! I don't know what obsessed him to be a boxer.

It means a lot to me that you've accepted my past. I was worried about it. Your father said tell her. Your mother was against. I'm just glad it's out in the open.

It's great to know you and Jay are going well. And again, I don't need any money. I'd just use it for junk. (Kidding!) Your mom, though, was delighted by your gift, and your dad walks around floating on air, talking you up to everybody. Everyone is buying a phone. People around here say, "You got your Live one yet?" Old Vermonters jabbering on those crazy glowing phones. It's a strange world. You must be making the fortune you always wanted.

My love to you,

Kelly

Mary thought about the letter again as her newly leased Porsche carved through another corner; the pewter sky echoed in the macadam, the monochrome of the weather the antithesis of her emotions. The windshield wipers removed a slowly gathering mist every four or five seconds with one quick sweep. A new Porsche has a smell like no other car, she thought, breathing it in. More than just the scent of leather, it had a quality she couldn't quite define. And the roar of the engine behind her, vibration like pleasure.

Before leaving Berkeley that morning, she'd examined the brooding sky to the north and reluctantly left the top up. She'd headed down the narrow driveway, her last days in the apartment. Most of her belongings were boxed and lined up near the front door ready for the movers, and she'd taken one small overnight bag. Two weeks ago she'd rented a house north of San Francisco—modern with lots of open space, light, clean lines, a huge kitchen with noble materials, large redwood deck, garage underneath, and most importantly, a fantastic view of the Pacific.

After about half an hour on the 101, she exited at Cotati in the direction of the coast and was soon pointed north up Route 1. The highway was empty, maybe because it was Saturday morning or maybe just the gloomy November day. At the end of a tree-lined straightaway, the taillights of a logging truck appeared, and she rapidly closed the gap. She shifted down one gear, and with a brisk thrill of acceleration, the rear tires biting into the damp pavement, passed the truck as quickly as the thought. She surprised herself by letting out a little shout. It was a shout describing not only being in a Porsche again but the last few weeks as well.

Then a single headlight grew in her rearview mirror, and she negotiated a few corners faster than she normally would have, wanting to outrun the light. "Get used to the car before driving it hard," the salesman at the dealership had told her. "Break it in carefully. This is much more powerful than your other one. It handles differently." She ignored the advice, the headlight remaining annoyingly in her mirrors even with the increased speed. Entering a long straight section, she stamped the accelerator and the car twitched on the greasy surface as it shot out of the corner. Both her hands tightened on the wheel, the tachometer and speedometer needles blurred, her right hand darted down for the shift. The mist changed to a light rain and she adjusted the wipers. The power of the car scared her, and maybe because it scared her, she repeated this severe acceleration twice more, braking late and violently for the corners. She searched her mirrors and the headlight wasn't there. Though she knew she was acting foolish, she couldn't suppress a grin and looked again to make sure it was truly gone. It was this second scan for the motorcycle that was her mistake.

Her foot dove for the brake pedal, but her car was already at the corner. A yellow highway sign read CAUTION 35; she was traveling nearly three times the speed. Wrenching the steering wheel toward the curve and jamming the brakes, she felt the rear tires break loose, the car slide. *Fuck!* The car snapped around on the wet road, careening backwards. A telephone pole darted toward her like the dark ax of an executioner. Something intuitive made her accelerate. Anything not to hit the pole, anything to get away from it. The car spun one more half-revolution and lurched to a stop a few feet from the pole. Tire smoke shrouded the car, and an eerie silence pulsed.

The motorcycle passed her, the rider slowing. He turned and came back as she restarted her car, pulling it parallel to the shoulder to clear the lane. He got off his bike and walked up, stood a moment beside her window until she lowered it. "You okay?" he said. She nodded. "You're some lucky. If a vehicle had been coming the other way . . ." He waited as a logging truck roared by, the one she'd passed earlier. "I was just entering the straight when I saw your brake lights vanish, headlights appear, and I thought, *Oh, shit*."

She couldn't say anything.

"Well, I'm glad you're okay. And I think the car is fine. You're lucky Porsches don't usually roll."

He was holding some kind of old helmet with canvas earflaps, wore a leather jacket soaked black by the drizzle, had pushed his goggles into his hair, a drop of rain hanging from his nose.

"You just get this?"

"Yeah," she finally managed.

"You should take it a bit easy at first. You were driving too fast for the conditions. Porsches have a hammer effect when they break loose."

"You were hardly going slow yourself."—annoyed by his didactic attitude.

"I know the road. I practice here all the time."

"What are you, a racer?"

"Naw—writer, a novelist. The bike helps clear my head. Allows me to see my characters better." He examined her again.

"I've owned a Porsche before," she said, wondering why she needed to explain herself to him.

Two campers passed, their tires hissing as they rounded the corner. His face turned to watch them, if he was even watching.

"Well, take care," he said.

She was intentionally silent this time.

He walked back to his bike, strapped on his helmet, pulled on gloves, and turned his machine around by lifting and pivoting it, the weight of the motorcycle balanced on its kickstand. She watched him without wanting to. He fired up his Ducati—she read the name on the tank—and without a backward glance slowly accelerated the big twin down the glistening road as if he were making a point, the low growl absorbed by the rainy fog. She pressed the button to raise the window, pressed it much harder than she needed to.

She continued north more slowly. Maybe the bike rider had a point after all. The near-accident disturbed her. Fate was like a jack-in-the-box thrusting up its cackling head just when you were your most content. She'd felt so on track that morning, felt as if her run of luck couldn't be touched, and then she'd almost been split in two by a pole. How could such a perfect moment be shattered? Was this a balance within nature? Must everything always be balanced by its opposite? She wondered if Jay knew.

That morning when she'd dressed, she couldn't decide on her underwear. She'd rejected black silk as too stark, red seemed suggestive, white didn't set off her skin enough. Eventually she'd chosen a powder-blue bra and panties. Over these she wore a plaid skirt and cashmere sweater in a soft gray-green. It did the most for her eyes. She'd inherited her father's eyes, her irises an even paler gray than her dad's, delicately flecked with yellow at the rim of each pupil. Her russet hair, which she biannually contemplated dyeing redder though never did, was pulled back with a bow. Maybe she should've gone with braids? *No*, she didn't want to look like a Catholic schoolgirl. She giggled, checked her face quickly in the rearview mirror. It was too round, she thought, and lacked the high cheekbones and full lips that everyone seemed obsessed with these days. "At least I have nice skin," she muttered. It had an almost luminous purity, one benefit of all her years spent inside studying and working.

As she drove farther north, her thoughts began to overrun her enjoyment of the new car. The emotions of the near-crash allied with the somber weather and turned her mind ever more inward. All the years growing up on the farm tumbled in on her: getting up at dawn, the same chores, the same concerns and worries with every passing season. The University of Vermont had been much the same kind of life, commuting back and forth from Monkton every day, continuing to help out with farm chores, working diligently at her classes, having virtually no time for herself. Her whole life had been about discipline and patience, about trying to progress toward the things she craved. Her parents had always lived modestly, the farm barely sustaining itself, the debt increasing with each unlucky season. There was never money for extras, let alone extravagance. Nevertheless, her family had refused the many offers from developers, and though selling would've garnered significant capital, she understood what the homestead meant, particularly to her mother and her grandparents. Her father, having grown up in a mill town in New Hampshire, had never wanted to be a farmer, yet he consistently made the best of it. The house and barns might not be much, everything old and worn, but the land was exceptional, the Adirondacks visible from the higher fields.

Even as a teenager she'd wanted to get away. It wasn't that she didn't love the place and love her family. Those gentle hills and weathered structures, her unassuming father, strong-willed mother, the reclusive Kelly Harris, and her stoic grandparents—they were the foundation of all she believed was good. It was just that the world beyond the farm had beckoned with such promise, like a child's vision of a carnival's fluorescent whirl from across a dark field. She would move away, earn the things she wanted, get the high-paying job, a modern house against the ocean, and her life would be perfect. She would pay off her student loans and send money home so her parents wouldn't have to worry anymore. She would find the perfect guy, have a family of her own.

But what was it about desires that, once you achieved them, they could tarnish in mere weeks? Or in a matter of seconds. There was something in that motorcycle rider's manner that unsettled her more than she liked to admit. He hadn't been impressed by her at all. To him she was just a self-indulgent rich girl who didn't know the limits of her new toy. It simply wasn't true, quite the opposite, and it made her wonder all the more why his opinion bothered her. Maybe she was just hungry. She decided to look for a restaurant.

There was a roadside diner near the Oregon border, its half-lit neon winking in what was now heavy rain. She almost didn't park the Porsche out front, not wanting anyone to notice her car, an inclination new to her. When she entered the warmth of the diner, five or six patrons at the counter turned. Ignoring them, she picked up a Portland paper from the stack resting near the door and chose a booth. She looked out at her car curbed under the window, the rain beaded evenly across the silver paint. It looked so lovely that her self-assurance began to return.

With the paper open, a coffee in front of her and a BLT on order, she scanned the headlines. On page two she found:

New Phone Merits Confidence

A new cell phone design has been selling in unprecedented numbers, outselling every other phone on the West Coast in only its third month. LiveCell phones also rate an unusually high 97% in Consumer confidence. The phone has become a cult phenomenon in California and has spread to the East Coast as well. LiveCell is at the moment targeting only the US, but many international sales have been confirmed. A mail-order-only product, the phone offers a five-year unconditional guarantee. The two-month predicted waiting time for the phones has generated black-market sales of three times the retail price. LiveCell's stock price has reflected the craze for the new phone, investors scrambling to buy shares. Dr. Jay Chevalier, majority owner and CEO of the new firm LiveCell, has refused all attempts to be interviewed by—

She set the paper aside as her sandwich arrived. The *doctor* tag bugged Jay. She wasn't sure why the media insisted on using it; they must have gotten it from his Harvard records. She had tried to erase its use with repeated requests but without avail. She ate her sandwich. It matched her coffee, warm and tasteless, though she was too hungry to care.

The waitress, a woman about her age, cleared the plate. "That yours?"

"Excuse me?"

"That your car?"

She nodded.

"That thing is *so* awesome. Is it new?"

"Just got it."

"Wow. What is it?"

"A Porsche Carrera."

"God, would I love to have one of those. That is *such* a cool car. You are *so* lucky."

Mary smiled up at her, though it wasn't a smile she felt. The waitress envying her or admiring her only because of something she owned made her slightly queasy for the first time.

"You want more coffee, some dessert?" the waitress asked.

She shook her head. "Just a check please."

After a few more hours north, she glanced down at the written directions on the seat beside her. Darkness tinted thick fog, the gray shifted to a cold blue. The turn had to be around here somewhere, though in this weather she might have missed it. Finally, OLD SIUSLAW ROAD was visible on a canted signpost, the words blistered. The transmission whined in the stillness as she backed up. She headed along a paved road that soon changed to gravel toward what might be the Pacific; the map had indicated that it must be close. She rolled down the window to try to see better, and yes, heard a rolling swell pounding a rocky coast. Fog laced with salt and wet pine chilled her face but still felt wonderful, the heater automatically adjusting to the brisk air, fan humming. After a few more miles the car's fog lights picked out a mailbox with *Raymond Madsen* lettered across it. She pulled into the drive, a soaked matting of pine needles and some exposed roots of scrub pine. Stopping, she examined her hair and mascara in the lighted vanity mirror under the sun visor, took a few deep breaths, smelling the ocean, trying to calm herself.

His house on that November evening was an image painted from a lost Herman Melville manuscript, a painting hung in a dim hallway of a forgotten hotel, varnish darkening, its surface obscured by a smudged patina of endless neglect. Surrounded by porches, graced by multiple dormers, covered in weathered shingles, the structure had never been finished—the uncompleted wing like the skeleton of a failed hundred-year-old dream. Scrub pine grew so close to the walls it seemed as if the trees were cupping the building in a giant verdant hand, silver shimmers of ocean through the outer fingers.

She parked near the one light, a porch light, a yellow nimbus in the ultramarine, and got out, the waves louder, coming from below on the far side of the mansion. As she climbed the rotten porch steps, there was another sound, so peculiar she questioned her hearing. It was a muffled train whistle, the lonesome cry of a locomotive. But how could it be? She hadn't crossed any railroad tracks, and beyond the house was only the Pacific.

There was no bell, just a knocker corroded into silence, so she tapped on the oak door with her knuckles. She waited and then tapped a second time. She pounded with her fist, heard only the dirge of the waves. A gust of cold fog brought a shiver, and her hand moved to the doorknob. She cracked the door open and called. As she stepped into the dark foyer, a train whistle cried out again, louder this time, and a tiny light approached her. Above it roiled a plume of ghostlike smoke. The diamond-ring-sized headlight gradually illuminated its surroundings and she realized the hallway was crossed by miniature railroad tracks. She waited, astounded, as a toy passenger train roared past just in front of her, the engine chuffing realistically, smoking, the many passenger cars filled with two-inch people relaxing in well-lit interiors.

"Jay?" She stepped over the tracks and followed them into a cavernous room, a snapping fire in a fieldstone fireplace brushing light over the dusky interior, over pine-paneled walls. And there he sat, his hands at the controls of a black Bakelite transformer.

On noticing her he hopped up, slowing and stopping two trains in the process, silence expanding after the clatter and chuff. One hand wiped quickly across his eyes, but not so quickly that she didn't notice.

"You made it," he said. "Any trouble finding me?"

"Your directions were perfect."

He walked over to her, extending his hand. They shook awkwardly, and she wondered if he ever hugged anyone.

"Hungry?" he said. "Or can I get you a beverage? I bought some beer for you."

"A beer would be good. I had a sandwich at the border." She looked around. "This is some place."

"It's the first house I've ever owned."

"Kind of matches your Cutlass." She regretted the words immediately. "Are you going to fix it up?"

"Why?"

"Well, I just thought you might . . ."

"Let me get you a beer."

She followed him into the kitchen, watched those arms pull two beers out of a fifties icebox, the ivory enamel discolored by rust. She took in the peeling wallpaper, the worn floor, a double slate sink on cast-iron legs, a wood-burning cook stove accented in chrome, a galvanized bucket collecting a roof leak.

"This place is something. Looks completely original," she said, trying to be positive.

"I don't think much has been done to it since it was built. Glass?"

She nodded and he retrieved a glass from a built-in oak cupboard.

"Do you have running water?" *And hopefully a working bathroom.*

"Of course. I installed a generator and got the pump working again. Plenty of fresh well water."

"When did you buy this place?"

"When I left DuPont, I searched the coast for a remote location. I wanted to get as far away from the East as I could. Something about this place got to me. I loved the fog and the ocean being so close. It wasn't even listed when I found it. When I started negotiating for Clicksave, I realized it was too far from San Francisco and got my room at the Y. This place was very reasonably priced."

No wonder. "Had anyone been living here? I mean before you."

"An elderly lady died here about twenty years ago. It's been empty since then. I guess potential buyers saw it as too much work or too far from anywhere."

"Is that her husband's name on the mailbox?"

"I wrote that on the box." He started pouring the beer. "I bought this house under that name. You are the only person who can connect me to this place. That's one reason I wanted you to visit, so you would know how to find it. It's our secret."

She shivered. The wind had come up from the ocean and was ignoring the walls. After the warmth of her car, it was an abrupt change, and she wished she'd brought her jacket in with her. She looked out through a bank of small-paned windows, trying to see the ocean, but it was too dark now for anything except the rain streaming down, some beading on the inside of the mullions, seeping through cracked glass.

"Come back by the fire." He handed her the beer, and they headed into the parlor. "I wish I had a brandy or something for you."

"It would certainly fit this place. Or some whisky. My dad drinks Scotch. He likes this one from some island over there. Jay—maybe we could just turn up the heat?"

"Fireplaces are the heat. Don't worry, I've laid a fire in your bedroom." *Separate bedrooms?*

A dark shape shifted in the shadows of the hall. "Jay, something is moving over there." She pointed anxiously.

"The cats. They get spooked by the trains." He made a kissing sound and three motley looking cats, one even missing an ear, surrounded him, rubbing against his legs, arching up to brush their half-open mouths on his jeans.

She reached down to pet one, but it shied away from her. She knew animals well enough not to persist. Holding their drinks, they moved near the fire. She set hers on the mantle so she could wring her hands over the flames.

"Are these your childhood trains?" The second she asked she knew it couldn't be true. All these months around him and he still made her nervous. And he was always so calm it was infuriating.

"I always wanted trains as a kid. Any kind of trains. Used to spend hours studying train catalogs, and every Christmas I put in my plea at the orphanage. I guess trains were too expensive. When I finished the first phone, I bought these to celebrate."

"Did you work on the phone here?"

"I set up a simple lab, mostly dismantled now. Just a UV culture hood and basic bioreactor. It was difficult—"

"A bioreactor?"

"It's an apparatus that slowly spins the developing cells so they can form three-dimensional shapes. Running all the stuff off the one generator and maintaining temperature was difficult. And contamination was a problem. While the phones are forming they're delicate, fragile. Once they've matured they're completely stable. Kind of strange, but nature is strange. I had a firm in San Francisco fashion a few black boxes. An electrophysicist I knew from Harvard designed the conversion device that translates brain waves to digital sound waves. But all the real work was done before I left DuPont."

He drained his beer. "The final modification of the cell aggregate was with me when I left. I destroyed all the others. That one was all I needed, but it was indispensible. I drove across the country with it packed in a sterile beer cooler like a harvested organ. Kind of funny. I was so nervous something would happen to it or someone would stop me. I took secondary roads the whole way west, only that yellow tomcat for company."

"In the Cutlass?"

He nodded. "I bought it just before I left Delaware." He reached down for a log and placed it on the fire. He added another. "You should warm up soon in here. Please, Mary, sit down."

She told him she was okay, she was warm. Actually the fire felt wonderful, the storm now increasing outside, the wind rattling the loose windows. She settled into the sofa facing the fireplace. He moved to an easy chair that looked a week away from a dump run, and she glanced for an instant at the empty section of sofa beside her. Here she'd finally found the one person she was completely attracted to and he seemed *completely* unaffected by her in that way. Why had he asked her to come here then? "Can we run the trains?" she said.

He leaned over and slowly rotated the transformer handles, and the trains came to life. The two trains departed and reentered the living room as whistles cried out echoing in the hall and the far room of darkness. Bells sang, smoke curled madly from the stacks, passenger car lights illuminated the floor like great ethereal centipedes.

She took a chance. "Jay, were you crying when I arrived?"

He slowed the trains and they came to a rest, all the tiny lights blinking out. She studied his face in the resonating silence but couldn't read it. Did he ever open up?

"The trains allow me to remember," he said finally.

"I thought you said you'd never had them before?"—almost angry.

"To remember about people, about what they want, about their desires, their needs. When I watch the trains I imagine people riding in them, and I think how they are all going towards or away from something—maybe a lover, their family, a home, their work, even their hopes and dreams." The firelight exaggerated his face as he paused, tough looking but still so gentle. "We seem to believe there must be something more to life than mere sustenance and procreation. We all have an emptiness inside us that yearns to be filled. We find different ways to try to fill this emptiness."

"You get all that from these trains?"

He grinned.

At least she'd made him smile. She knew he was trying to tell her something, but all she could think about was her *emptiness* for him. "What do *you* want?"

"I have everything I want."

She searched him again and worried it might be true. "Then why do you work so hard, why are you making all this money?"

"I work because it's what I believe in. I believe in the process of working. It helps fill the emptiness for me. When I said I don't want anything, I should have said, for myself. There are things I want for humanity."

"But aren't there things you want *just* for yourself?"

He didn't answer her this time, and she felt foolish for asking again. She always felt so unwise when she was with him. The flames twisted around the logs; they appeared to her like creatures with too much desire. What was she supposed to do with her desire? The storm slapped the house and the drip in the kitchen struck the rain-filled bucket like a slow metronome.

Eventually she said, "What did Kelly tell you?"

"You mean why did I purchase a company just to get you to work for me?"

She nodded.

"He told me about your dog."

"My *dog*? Pilgrim?"

"About the dog that disappeared when you were sixteen. Kelly told me how you knew something was wrong right away. Everyone on the farm assured you the dog would return soon—it had run off many times before, especially during deer season—but you insisted on going to look. When you found it, the poor animal had been shot in the leg and was dragging itself home. Kelly told me you led him almost directly to the dog. He said it terrified him that you were so intuitive, that sometimes you could sense things before they happened. He also told me you could be trusted with anything."

"He told you all that?"

"You saved the dog's life."

"She lost the leg but she's still alive though very old."

The fire snapped, a glowing cinder striking the hearth.

"You can do it too," she said. "Can't you?"

"Sometimes."

She wanted to go to him, to touch him, hold him. Instead she did nothing, started feeling uncomfortable, wondering if he knew what she was thinking.

"Are you hungry?" he said finally. "I'm afraid all I have are chicken pot pies and some russet potatoes. We can bake those. Let me get the stove in the kitchen going." He got out of his chair, gathered an armful of kindling and newspaper, went to fire the stove, leaving her on the sofa.

Was this why he'd chosen her? She didn't want to tell him that since coming west five years ago, her ability—she wasn't sure what to call it—was probably gone. She was uncertain about it now. It was hard to tell if it was still an ability or if she just happened to guess correctly sometimes. She had never been able to do it on demand, but occasionally she'd simply known things, as with Pilgrim.

She continued to stare into the flames, wondering what she was going to do about these feelings for him. She wanted to touch him, have him touch her, but he was so remote towards her as if none of that could ever be a possibility. Was it from being an orphan? Or maybe he was gay? Had he been close to anyone in his life? Was he simply not attracted to her? Was this her punishment for turning down other men? She'd had such hopes driving up to see him today.

Since their first talk that one Friday morning he'd been shut tight—as if he'd decided he'd shared enough and that was the end of it. He was all work, work, work, from then on. Maybe if she could just hold him once. But he never touched anyone. He was such a loner. Here he had millions and he still drove that horrible junker, had that room at the YMCA, and now this place. Out of politeness, she hesitated to call it a dump. At least he'd bought the toy trains. Somehow that seemed like a good sign. But why had he wanted her to drive all the way up here if not for sex? It couldn't be only to show her his house and trains. It didn't make sense.

She moved from the sofa and stood close to the fire, absently wringing her hands near the flames again, waiting until her whole body was warm. Then she walked into the kitchen to be with him.

SIX

Deirdre Holly didn't understand why some authors used foreign phrases in their writing. Like we all spoke Latin? or even French? And some writers didn't even offer the English translation. She understood that by doing so they were exhibiting a class thing, showing up the rest of us. She'd learned recently that a lot of things in life are about class snobbery. Deirdre had only come to reading fiction in the last few years. In her twenty-eight years she'd come to many things late. As she put it, "I came to the bad things way early, the good things a little late."

She had left home at fifteen, left Monrovia and the San Fernando Valley and headed up the coast to Santa Cruz. Surfing had changed her life, her awkward body finding balance and confidence as her ability grew, her strong shoulders finally an asset. But surfing hadn't changed her life as much as Jay Chevalier was changing it now. It had only been slightly over six months since she'd followed him into what had then been Wendell Alden's boardroom, yet it seemed like years.

Jay had interviewed everyone in the company during the first month and a half of his takeover. Her interview, about two weeks after the famous Monday, stunned her. First thing he said when she walked into his office was, "Hey Deirdre, how are you? Thanks for not calling security." She realized he wanted her to know he'd remembered. Then he asked her a lot of questions about herself. Wanted to know all about her. *Like everything.* And she felt comfortable around him, which hadn't happened with most men. She had never had a boss treat her this way. A week later, he dropped the bomb.

Jay asked her to be in charge of the LiveCell manufacturing facility. "I've only had two years of community college. I have no background in any of this," she reminded him. His response was, "You are the one I want—it has nothing to do with formal education or previous experience."

She ended her relationship with Cathy, a decision that was long overdue, and moved into her own place. A really nice place too, south of Market. If only she still communicated with her family, something in her wanted to show it off to them, wanted to make them envious. Yet she knew better: like how many blows to the head do you have to take till you wise up? It hadn't really started until her father was injured on the job, but then he'd been home all the time, her mother working, and with nothing to do but drink and smoke pot, that's when the real trouble started. But when she finally rebelled after a year, her mother took his side, believed him not her, almost seemed to blame her, and Deirdre had fled and tried hard never to look back.

LiveCell needed a factory to fabricate the phones, though the phone's cell aggregates were replicated rather than fabricated. This required a unique environment providing sterility and a precise control of temperature and humidity—a *clean room*. The delicate cultures of cloned neurons, which had been seeded from Jay's initial pineal gland extraction, were added to the collagen and proteoglycans used as a supportive matrix. This mixture grew best at $37°$ C in a carbon-dioxide oxygen blend, and a clean room would provide this environment.

So Jay and Deirdre had the interior of an old warehouse renovated during an intense three weeks, the place saturated twenty-four hours a day with builders and contractors. She watched the transformation with a conflict of emotions, eager and nervous to begin her new job. Eventually they were finished: the floors gleaming white tile, the main room full of perfectly aligned stainless-steel lab tables canopied with multiple culture hoods and growth-inducing apparatuses, the lighting as bright as an operating room. She even had an office, a small unrestored room to the right of the double front doors, across the hall from the changing cubicle for the workers' sterile gear. She told Jay that she preferred the rough warehouse flooring and the old plaster walls, sensing that would please him and not wanting him to spend extra money just for her. After everything was completed, the building from the outside matched her office; it offered no clues to the high-tech facility that was now inside.

While the factory was being renovated, and with Jay assisting her, she hired two dozen workers. Sharing the factory-hiring process with him, she better understood the method by which he'd hired her. It was by believing in something he must have sensed—it sure wasn't on her resume. That was how he hired everyone. She had to admit some of the choices simply baffled her. *Like made no sense at all*. He even hired a few Santa Cruz gang members, and they really looked like gang members, too. His print ads in the newspapers attracted all kinds of strange applicants. Too many applicants. Who didn't want to work for LiveCell? The pay and the benefits were unrivaled. And in a barren job market, everyone showed up to interview for the two dozen positions. Deirdre was exhausted and impatient by the end, Jay unaffected. Did anything ever get to him?

So LiveCell began production with this collection of carefully chosen misfits, Deirdre applying herself to her new job with the same big-boned intensity she'd used to master the waves. As the weeks passed she came to respect Jay's hiring decisions, even the few that had really surprised her, but she was learning not to be overly surprised by anything having to do with Jay Chevalier. As the workers adjusted to their jobs, LiveCell gradually increased output to around five-thousand phones a day. The procedure wasn't as complicated as she'd first thought. It was almost like baking bread or something. You just had to be really precise and thorough. It was simply amazing watching the cells replicate and then solidify as they achieved maturity. She never tired of watching the process, knowing she was creating something important.

It took about a week to make a phone. The basic cell aggregate first grew in bioreactors, the quick-replicating cells turning and rotating until they reached the phone's basic dimensions. Jay had developed an improved bioreactor that could form a long cylinder of cell matter, creating dozens of phones with one unit. As this fragile mixture multiplied, feeding on the substrate host, the stainless culture hoods that supplied the perfect air mixture and the UV-irradiation to prevent contamination were lowered. On the fourth day, the hoods were lifted, and the young phones could be disassociated from the host by proteolysis, carefully segmented and cradled in phone-sized plastic vessels where they matured and reached full structural density. Before they finished curing, she oversaw the injection by pipette of viral DNA into the center of each young phone. Over the next two days, the virus spread through the cells and modified the neurons, elongating and intensifying their electrophysiological capacity.

Every evening, after the work crew had gone for the day, Jay would stop by to check the finished phones. She staggered the replicating process so that a new batch of phones would reach maturity at the end of each day. The warehouse would be empty, the day's freshly finished phones ready, laid out in an exact grid on the polished metal tables, thousands of them, missing only their pronged black boxes. She always waited for him, though he told her many times that she worked too much.

"Don't wait for me, there is no need," he'd say.

And she would answer, "I just want to be sure that everything was done right."

It was a point of inflexibility between them. Jay, however, insisted she not watch him do whatever he did in the clean room with the phones. Made her promise. He was adamant about it, asking her to wait in her office. It made her very curious, particularly since he always looked changed somehow after he was finished. Each time he went in there, he turned off all the rows of fluorescent lights, so she began to leave it that way for him. But like what can you *check* in the dark?

This was the routine through the fall and the winter, production increasing with each season, until LiveCell was outputting over ten-thousand phones a day. It was in early spring that she came to appreciate fully Jay's choice in workers.

One morning two men in ill-fitting dark suits and bland ties sauntered arrogantly into her office. She came out from behind her desk and politely asked if she could help them. They flashed IDs and said they were from the FCC, were there to investigate the premises. She ignored their bluster, explaining that no public access was permitted, to *anyone*. Like what would the Federal Communications Commission want with Live-Cell? She knew the licensing and all the permits were in order because the company lawyers had gone over everything carefully. Jay had been very thorough. And even if there was a problem, would this be the way the FCC would address it?

They argued with her, demanded admittance, became increasingly rude as she held ground, she more and more convinced they weren't FCC. "*Miss* Holly, do you realize the ramifications of obstructing a government investigation?" said the burlier of the suits. Like this was a government investigation? She didn't answer. She'd already told them to contact Jay Chevalier, made it repeatedly clear that only a search warrant would get them through the clean-room door. Like why waste more words? But the burly suit suddenly shoved her out of the way, her body banging into the doorframe with a painful thud, and the two men headed down the hallway toward the clean room.

Jimmy Hakken was one of the Santa Cruz gang members whom Deirdre hadn't wanted to hire—she'd heard about his reputation over the years—until Jay insisted. He was changing into his sterile gear when she called out for help. In black chinos and sleeveless T-shirt, six-two, shaved head and fully tattooed arms, he charged out of the cubicle. The suits froze at the sight of him. Hakken stopped a few feet in front of the two men, blocking access to the clean room. He said nothing, his posture erect, his body dead still. His look said everything. It almost projected an eagerness for the suits to make a move, but his expression was too neutral for that, too unreadable. She decided there was something about absolute willingness that was really scary. Three other workers emerged from the clean room and blocked the doorway. She figured it was overkill.

The suits muttered a few more threats, backed up and left. She thanked her crew. "No problem, Dree," said Hakken with a quick nod. The others smiled, everyone going back to work as if nothing had happened. She returned to her office and livecelled Jay.

"So you're okay? Everyone is okay?" he said.

She reassured him.

"Did you get a look at their IDs?"

"They were weird about showing them. Just flipped them like, and wouldn't let me examine them. Made me suspicious right away. Classic suit cop types, you know? Really forceful, in-your-face kind of bullshit."

"You did great."

"You should've seen Jimmy. He like really turned the tide. He comes blazing out and one of the suits like yelps. This little squeak. *Really* funny." Now that the tension had passed, she started to giggle. Her mind flashed to when she'd pursued Jay into Wendell Alden's boardroom trying to stop him. How different it was to work for Jay.

"This won't be the end of it," he said.

"You think they really were FCC?"

"We've been fully cleared with the FCC. And they would have contacted our legal department in writing if there was a problem."

"That's exactly what I thought." She wasn't laughing now, worried again. "It just seemed *too* weird. They were somebody with power. Real cocky, you know?"

"I don't want you or anyone to get hurt."

"You should have seen the crew—they were ready."

"Not the point."

"I'm just saying—they're loyal. *Really* loyal."

"Deirdre, you have great people. I know that."

"I mean, you chose them, but they're really like my crew now. I can't tell you how good that feels." She paused. "They talk about you. You know what they say?"

He was silent.

"Because of Jimmy Hakken they think you're some kind of knight now or something. That's why he calls you *The* Chevalier and doesn't use Jay. Like you're from the Round Table or something. 'He's a knight, Dree—Chevalier suits him,' he says. Like just *Jay* isn't cool enough. And now he thinks he's this *yeo*man or something, that's what he calls himself. He takes it serious, too. I shouldn't have loaned him those books to read, but I told him I was trying to educate myself more, and he was all into the idea. He said he'd read a bit as a kid but then stopped. I think Dumas really fired him up, and now he's got everyone at the factory into it. He's really a natural leader, you know." *God*, these phones were so intimate. Like she could almost feel him, she understood him better, he got inside her somehow. Not that she could hear his thoughts unless he spoke or anything like that. "Jay?"

He answered.

"You know how much all this means to me, like what you've done for me and the rest of the crew, right?" Silence. "You there?"

"Shall we all go eat Mexican tonight? I'll invite everyone."

"You got to stop this."

"Dos Reales?"

"You're too generous, it's ridiculous. You don't need to do this."

"You like Dos Reales, don't you?"

"That's *not* the point."

"Think of that cactus salad."

"Cut it out."

"Those flautas?"

"*Jay!*"

"Mole Poblano?"

"Okay, what time?" She was laughing again. He could talk her into anything, always made her feel better about everything.

"I have to tend to the phones, then I'll meet you. You get everyone started. Tell them it's on me—they've earned it."

"I'll send them ahead and wait for you here."

"You don't need to."

"I know."

That evening when Jay arrived at the warehouse, Deirdre's sixties Dodge wagon was alone on the lot near the front entrance, illuminated by one of the two security lights. Then he noticed a black late-model sedan parked along the darkest side of the building, March twilight almost hiding the car.

He parked the Cutlass next to her wagon and got out, irritated that his door squawked so loudly when he opened it. He left it that way and quickly climbed the steps to the front doors. He rotated the steel knob slowly, pulled on it gently. Locked. It was unlikely it would have been Deirdre; she always kept it open for his arrival.

He leapt down the steps and sprinted to the far side of the building, his passkey in his hand by the time he reached the emergency exit. He unlocked the metal door, jerked it open, and was in the factory. All the banks of fluorescent lights were on. Normally they would have been off. He moved between the laboratory tables, the bioreactor apparatus humming. At the doors leading into the front hall, he cracked one, stood for a few seconds and listened. Muffled sounds were coming from the half-open door to Deirdre's office. As he entered the hall he heard her yell, "Fuck you," obviously terrified. There was a hard slap.

She was trapped awkwardly in her office chair, hands taped behind the chair's back, ankles taped to the rungs, her cheeks marked by red welts, mouth bleeding, eyes bleary with tears.

"Leave her alone," he said.

The two men in front of Deirdre turned to face him, a hulk in a rumpled suit and a smaller one with almost no forehead lazily pointing an automatic in his direction.

"Doctor Chevalier, I presume," said the one with the gun, a bored smile barely changing his expressionless face.

Jay moved straight at the voice and threw a right uppercut into the jawbone so hard it almost lifted the guy off his feet. The body slumped heavily against the desk and pitched loudly to the floor, the gun clattering across the unpainted floorboards.

The large guy stared in disbelief at his downed partner. "What the fuck?" he said, grabbing inside his suit jacket. He fumbled a few seconds, and there was the black glint of a snub-nosed revolver. Jay stepped toward it, trying to get inside the gun's reach before the angle of the barrel found him. Using his left arm to deflect the weapon, he drove a straight right into the guy's lower ribcage. He heard the explosion but didn't feel the bullet or suspect that he'd been shot; the pain would come later. The impact spun him off balance and back a few feet. Deirdre screamed.

The guy swayed, bent over, wheezing painfully, the gun smoking in his hand. There was a second report and a dull thud, the bullet lodging into one of the thick planks inches from Jay's shoe. Jay recovered as his assailant began to straighten. He stepped in and started to throw a left hook when he realized his arm wasn't reacting. A spike of nausea jabbed him in the gut, flashing him back to his days in the ring. The same sensation as when he'd been stunned by a punch, but now covering up wasn't going to save him. The gun rose slowly and inexorably toward his head. Someone cried out. With the gasping face before him, the leaden cruelty of the eyes, he swung a brutal roundhouse right, his fist contacting the soft tissue and arteries at the side of the gunman's neck. The third shot remained unfired.

"Jay, Jay, Jay, . . ." he heard her saying between sobs.

Shocked by the violence of his punch, he looked down at the two splayed men and worried that he might have killed the second one. He'd never throw a blow that fierce in the ring, but there was nothing he could do about it now. Though he figured he didn't need to, he still kicked the two guns into a corner of the room. His left arm was numb, covered in blood. Blood was dripping freely from his hand as he attempted to wriggle his fingers, testing the damage. Nausea hit him again, and for a moment he thought he might go down. Supporting himself by grabbing the desk with his good arm, he could vaguely hear Deirdre saying something. He waited and his head started to clear.

"Jay, you're shot!"

"I think I'm okay. Just some blood."

"You need a doctor."

"We better call an ambulance."

"I can drive you. It would be faster."

He found a serrated plastic knife among her papers, guided himself along the desk's edge to her chair, and with a sawing motion cut through the duct tape. "I mean for these two."

"You're the one who needs a hospital. To hell with those fuckers." She lifted herself clumsily out of the chair, rubbing her wrists.

"All I need is a flauta," he said, and winked at her. "And maybe a beer."

Slowly, the smile appeared.

It was almost eleven o'clock when they finally sat on the tattered bench seat of the Cutlass headed to Dos Reales. She called the restaurant as Jay drove. Her Dodge was left on the lot; it was not a night to be alone. Ricky, the owner, explained that a few of Deirdre's crew were still hanging around drinking beer and he would be glad to stay open for her and Jay. "Food? No problem. I make whatever you guys want." They were both hungry, and she'd never craved a vodka rocks more than at that moment. Like who wouldn't?

"How's the arm?" she said.

"Fine," he said, but she knew it wasn't. She'd cleaned and bound his flesh wound, which was similar to some of the worst surfboard cuts she'd seen, except for the ugly powder burn. She'd sterilized and butterfly sutured the gash in his bicep, using a first-aid kit from the factory. It still needed stitches, more than a few, but at least the bullet hadn't done as much damage as it could have. She'd urged him to let one of the paramedics examine his arm, but you couldn't get him to do something he didn't want to do. Like *way* stubborn.

"How can you say fine?" she said. "It must hurt like crazy. That thing is nasty." As the streetlights washed over his face, he appeared even paler than normal. Like a ghost. A real stubborn one.

"The trouble with complaining," he said, "is once you start you can't stop."

They drove awhile, both locked in their own thoughts.

She broke the silence: "The cops acted a little weird, don't you think? Like they didn't really believe you. Like you couldn't possibly have taken out those two guys with guns. Or maybe the whole thing didn't make sense to them either. But that one detective seemed to like you. Otega? Something like that. The Puerto Rican looking one. The others though . . . This whole thing is really *too* weird." She looked over at him, waiting for him to say something. "I thought we would never get out of there. Took for*ever*. They sure had enough cops and paramedics running around. Like the whole force. I still can't believe you wouldn't let a medic look at your arm. You can be pretty weird, you know? And you sure won't talk to the press. Like not at all."

He still didn't say anything. She didn't care. He probably realized she just needed to talk. It made her feel better. Her face had even stopped stinging so painfully, though the inside of her mouth was still raw and getting itchy. The vodka would help that. She'd told the police that one of them was the same guy who'd visited the factory that morning insisting he was from the FCC. She'd never seen the other, the one who looked like a rat. He'd questioned and beat her. He was the one she hated.

What she didn't know was that Jay had quietly noted the serial number from the .38 before the police arrived. It told him something that the gun still had its number, belonging to the hulk. The one on the automatic had been filed off. She also didn't know that as he drove he kept replaying the event, realizing it had probably been a setup. He still had the mushy collapsing sensation of the guy's neck in his memory and was sickened by the violence. If they were after something in the factory, wouldn't they have entered at night? And why involve Deirdre? It was obvious to him now that they'd been waiting for him, using Deirdre as bait, had half-hidden their car so he could spot it. Were they testing him? Trying to scare him? Kill him? No, there were much easier ways to kill him if—

"Jay?" she said.

He moved his eyes from the street to her. "You okay now?"

To Deirdre he looked drawn and tired. She realized with a pang that he was vulnerable, that he had weakness. She wanted to bring her hand across the seat fabric to touch him.

"Thanks," she said instead.

He smiled at her, and she could tell he was mustering his energy.

"I wish I could fight like you. Then those assholes couldn't have pushed me around. They were all over me with their bullshit questions about you and the phones, and I'm all *yeah right*, like I'm going to tell you fuckheads anything. Maybe I should've locked the door, but I figured you'd be coming any minute, and I never lock the door until we leave. That gun really scared me. I hate guns. Seen too many horrible things happen with guns."

She looked out at the shadowed facades of city buildings, a small late-night grocery, closed shops, a brightly lit gas station as it flashed by in a fluorescent blur. Absently these images flickered across her consciousness as the fight dominated her mind.

"Jesus you can sure throw a punch," she said. "You lifted that one guy right into the air. That was *so* amazing. The rumor is you used to fight in the ring. It's true, isn't it?"

"What I did wasn't good. There was nothing good about it. I should have known better . . . but they hurt one of my family, and I overreacted."

That stopped her. "You feel that way about me?"

He nodded.

She glanced out the window again, not seeing anything this time.

Soon, there was the Dos Reales neon in the distance. He took his good arm off the wheel to reach across and flip on the blinker.

"I could have driven you know," she said. "Your arm must be killing you."

"We're here."

Jimmy Hakken listened without moving as Deirdre described what had happened. Only Hakken and Ramon had waited for them in the big padded booth. In the parking lot, Jay had asked Deirdre not to mention the incident, but she'd convinced him otherwise. She told him it was their workplace, she was their boss, and they had a right to know. Besides, he was bleeding through his bandage, like what was she supposed to tell them? Jay cut himself shaving? And how about the newspapers tomorrow? She continued to be put out that he wouldn't go to the hospital. His wound needed stitches. Tape wasn't going to hold the skin together long enough for it to heal. He was even paler, dabbing at the leaking blood with a paper napkin. But food was on its way, she'd already downed one of her signature vodkas, the second on order. Jay worked at a can of beer.

Jimmy Hakken sat immobile after she'd finished the story. He rarely spoke, and he was difficult if not impossible to read. He was the tall silent type, who just happened to be covered in too many medieval tattoos and have a shaved head with reddish sideburns. The ugliness of his face was almost handsome because of his eyes, the lightest of blue like a Nordic sled dog.

"Chevalier," he finally said. "Anything like this ever happens again, say the word, and my guys are there."

Jay took a sip. "Jimmy, we're not about violence. We make phones so people can communicate better."

"They fucked with you and Dree, man. That burns my ass. All I'm saying is, you need us, we're there. I don't give a fuck who they are."

"Let's hope this is the end of it."

Hakken examined his beer can, shook his head back and forth for what seemed an eternity. "Man, you know it ain't over. Look—understand—it would be a fucking honor to move on this. You gave me a chance. No one else would've. I don't forget. Ever."

"I have your work. You do great work. That's all I need."

Hakken paused again, staring at Jay as if he were trying to memorize everything about him, scowling slightly. "Chevalier, you know I dig you. You know I respect your ass. But *no one* can go it alone." He crushed his beer can, dropped it, slid out of the booth and stood. He held out his hand to Jay with intense seriousness. They shook and released. "Take care of the wing," he said. He nodded to Ramon, blinked quickly with both eyes at Deirdre, and lumbered out of the restaurant.

SEVEN

Her curiosity was simply too much for her. And she was worried about him. That was how she rationalized it.

The day after the shooting, he came by as usual to check on the phones. When he walked into her office at the factory, he was so pale she thought he was about to faint. Again she urged him to see a doctor, said she would drive and go in with him, but he refused. Maybe that was why she broke her word. Her anger and concern made her disregard everything else.

Deirdre watched, spied on him from behind the hallway doors, her foot holding one cracked about an inch. The room looked so dark with the multiple banks of overhead fluorescent lights off, only a vague haze entering through the windows of the hallway doors, the few emergency exit signs glowing red. Thousands of newly matured phones cradled in their plastic vessels lay symmetrically arranged on the polished laboratory tables. She could faintly hear the electric motors in the bioreactors as younger phones replicated, the tissue culture hoods exhaling their air mixture and UV-irradiation onto the cells. Jay, in his usual blue T-shirt, didn't wear the sterility gear of the other workers. He'd explained to her that once the cells reached their final shape and solidified, they were immune to contamination. She still worried about the younger phones under the hoods, but you couldn't argue with him. Like about anything.

There he kneeled, his back half-turned to her, his face in three-quarter profile rimmed by the eerie light. His muscular arms were stretched out in front of him, the one with the bandaged bicep quivering slightly. She couldn't quite tell but thought his eyes were closed and his lips were moving.

He didn't seem to be doing anything else, so what was all the exclusion fuss about? She kept watching anyway, *Like who wouldn't?* But what was he up to, just kneeling there like that in the dark as if he were blessing the phones or something? And why no lights? It didn't make much sense unless he used some kind of instrument that required darkness, some kind of laser or something. He never carried anything in with him though—she'd checked. When you only wore T-shirts and jeans, it was hard to conceal things. Now she realized he wasn't checking anything.

He became completely still after a few minutes, his arms relaxed, his lips quiet, and that was when she first noticed a humming inside her brain, the way a nasty headache starts. The humming increased, an inexplicable nervousness enclosed her, and she felt as if something terrible was about to happen. She considered retreating to her office but couldn't seem to move. The sensation in her brain got worse and she fought against it, blinked rapidly, rubbed her temples; everything only seemed to intensify the pain. Maybe Jay had a good reason for demanding she didn't watch? But all he was doing was kneeling there.

And then he collapsed. Fell over on his side as if he'd passed out. The pain in her head subsided almost at once.

She pushed the door open. "Jay? . . . Jay, are you all right?" Called out again but there was still no response. Something must be very wrong, and she ran to him. Kneeled down beside him and shook him by the shoulder. Nothing. His wounded arm was crushed under his torso and she carefully rolled him on his back, straightening it. Was he breathing? She felt for a pulse. Found none. The panic started choking her. Knowing some CPR from her years of surfing, she leaned over him and placed her mouth on his, forced her breath into him, figuring it was the only thing to do. He can't die, she screamed to herself. Don't let him die. *Please.* She straightened, placed her hands on his chest and pressed down hard three or four times, then switched back again. As she inhaled and exhaled, her mouth on his with each arduous out-breath, an upsetting, confusing thought crossed her mind—that since her father's unwanted kisses, Jay's lips were the first male lips that had touched hers.

And he opened his eyes.

"Deirdre," he said.

There was a long intense moment—Deirdre hovering over him, Jay breathing strangely beneath her, their bodies touching as if they were lovers—and then she started to cry. Silently, but the tears kept coming.

"Deirdre. Please," he said.

He struggled out from under her into a sitting position, his face ashen, the pock marks on one of his temples accentuated by the light of an exit sign, his wound bleeding a little through the bandage, the blood black in the reddish glow. He reached out with his good arm and took her hand in his. After a long silence her tears stopped and he released it. She got to her feet awkwardly and looked down at him. It was only then, noticing something greenish-yellow in the periphery of her vision, that she turned and saw with a sudden gasp that all the phones had begun silently pulsing in their vessels.

It took him over half an hour to quiet her. They drove to a nearby tavern in his Cutlass because he felt she needed a change of scene; she had eyed the luminous pulsing phones with terror. In the darkened clean room, the thousands of phones were like a sea of undulating phosphorescence. For Jay they were always a vision of great beauty, yet he understood she had seen them differently at that moment. With one vodka rocks in her and a second in front of her, color was returning to her freckled skin, her spiked blonde hair a turmoiled crown above tear-marked eyes.

"Are you feeling better?" he said.

"Jay, I'm so, so, sorry I watched. I was just really worried about you. You always look so strange after you come out of there, and you looked totally sick going in today. I know I promised to never watch." Her face begged forgiveness. "What happened to you anyway? Did you like, *die* for a minute?"

"When I'm already tired, sometimes the infusing can be exhausting."

"I took your pulse. There was none. *Jay!* No pulse—none."

"Maybe my heart stopped for an instant. Actually I haven't had a problem in a long time."

She looked into her drink. "You got to be *really* careful."

There was a lull and she wouldn't look at him.

"I'm wondering if your touching me didn't help break the bond," he said, wanting to reassure and console her.

"What bond?"

"Between the phones and me."

She took a sip of her drink. "I had this sick feeling come over me. Not sick maybe, but real *freaky*, uneasy, you know? Like my brain felt weird and then I just knew something terrible was going to happen."

"I worried it wouldn't be good." He didn't tell her that she probably had something to do with his collapse, that somehow her resistance and fear had contributed to his blackout. He was fairly certain it had been her anxiety along with his exhaustion that had complicated the infusion. They usually went smoothly.

"No one else knows?" she said.

He shook his head. "I'm sorry you saw it, that it upset you so much."

"I'm okay now. I'm cool."   Jay studying her—"Really. I'm okay. But you got to admit, this whole thing you're doing is totally strange. I mean—my God . . . What were you really *doing* anyway? I know you said infusing, but what's *that*?"

"Will it be our secret?"

She paused to look at him. Studying *him* now. Her expression saying to him, Like there is anything I wouldn't do for you?

Jay looked around the bar. They sat in a back booth where he'd led them, so she could have some privacy until she calmed down. The tavern was almost empty, everyone home for supper. Though she had been overwrought, she had just as quickly returned to her usual composure. She never stopped impressing him.

"I was programming the phones," he said. "I do it by channeling energy through my brain. My neurons in the phones respond to my brain waves. I'm wondering if what you felt, what you called freaky, might not have been your brain fighting against mine."

"Oh my God. Brain waves?"

"That's how they work. The phone becomes a medium and allows brain waves to be passed."

"Passed?"

"From a LiveCell to a human brain. Though brain waves had never been sent any distance, I discovered they could be, that my cell combination was capable of it once infused by my brain. LiveCell phones have identical cloned structures to each other, something that has never existed before, since no one had figured out how to replicate mature brain cells."

Her face twisted in a confusion of emotions. Awe won out.

"That is simply so amazing. I mean, my God. That is just *so* cool." She hesitated again. "I asked everyone. No one has any idea how they work. I was nervous to ask you."

"Believe me, a lot of people ask."

"Even if you told them, I don't know if they'd believe it. Jay, this is just *so* incredible."

"I'm used to it now, though it was strange at first."

"How do the phones remember what you tell them, or think at them, or whatever?"

"The neuron progenitor cells in the structure have become so elongated that they're sensitive to low-frequency impulses. So this particular aggregate is capable of absorbing and transmitting brain waves over the short distance we hold the phones from our brains."

"I thought maybe the black boxes carried all the electric stuff and the living part was like a special speaker or something."

"No, the cell tissue is what matters. It activates the number sequence in the black box to send the call and then translates the voice into a conventional digital code. The infusing is similar to downloading information into a computer. Imagine condensing human memory and filling a brain with a year's learned information in a couple minutes. That's what I do every evening at the factory. Once the phones are programmed, infused by the energy passing through me, they actually acquire an intelligence. This allows the phone's owner to program it by speaking to it. Just like a brain, the phone remembers, but unlike a brain, it never forgets. Better diet and no booze, I suppose." He winked at her.

He watched her face as it all sank in. "Another secret is that you don't have to speak out loud to the phones. Just think the instructions and the phone will usually respond if your thoughts are clear enough. Of course when you talk to another person through the phone, you must speak out loud for them to hear you, or for their brain to hear you. It's only the phone that can sometimes translate your thoughts without speaking. I figured people wouldn't be ready to accept something that unusual yet, so we pretend you must speak to the phones to get them to work—it's simpler."

"How did you discover all this?"

"By chance, I guess. Following my hunches. I was lucky, though sometimes I felt as if I was almost guided." He paused. "I suppose it's all possible within the randomness of life . . . though I keep wondering about randomness."

"You think everything happens to us for a reason?"

"Probably not. I don't think we're that important. Though overall, within the infinite balance of everything, I'm not so sure if some occurrences aren't calculable probabilities, even the future."

She took another pull on her drink, looking confused.

"In other words, if I pick a number between one and a hundred, and if you were to allow yourself, it is more likely for you to pick that number than any other, only because it *is* the number I thought of, because it exists. The future is the same, because it actually *is* going to happen. The problem is believing that you can do it, and then emptying yourself of everything else." She stared at him, and he liked her more than ever. "Of course, in a way, it will always be a guess. But sometimes it just might be the right one."

"That is *so* fucking cool."

"I wonder."—almost to himself.

"What do you mean?"

"I wonder how the whole thing will turn out, if I'll have enough time. Time can be misleading."

He studied her, hoping she was okay. It had been two rather intense evenings in a row for them. Everything always seems to come at once.

EIGHT

Jay Chevalier was hunched over his battered desk on the sixth floor of the Harcourt Building. He looked worse than usual. Though he was reluctant to admit it, Deirdre had been right about his arm—it wasn't healing correctly. He straightened and picked up his LiveCell phone, sensing he had a call.

"Chevalier, Hakken."

They exchanged minimal greetings. *Very* minimal, it being Jimmy Hakken. "Listen, this new woman, something's not right."

"What do you mean?"

"Dree ain't herself."

"Jimmy, could you clarify that a little more please?"

"Chevalier, I'm telling you man, this new one is working Dree."

"How?"

A long pause. "Look, I said enough."

"Are you referring to Wendy Smith?"

Hakken grunted.

"I'm sure Deirdre can handle it."

"Chevalier . . . Would I rat on Dree if I thought she could?"

"Have you discussed this with Deirdre?"

"Some."

"Why not talk to her again? I'm sure she would listen."

A longer pause. "Chevalier. I never had your advantages."

"What do you mean?"

"Fancy schools, Harvard, all that shit. That's what I heard told."

"So?"

"Look—you know I dig you."

"It's not about how you talk or your background, it's about who you are now."

Hakken was silent again. Then he grunted and ended the call.

Jay sat for a while, his eyes traveling to the rectangle of bay out the window, which on this spring afternoon was horizonless with dense fog. This was about the only nature he got these days, this pathetic view from a window, this minor scrape of weather. He longed for the wilderness, for the northern Maine of his childhood, for the days he'd spent with his grandfather. So many years he'd been inside, and every one of them was a splinter under the skin. His phone signaled him again.

"Jay, Sammy. How you hanging?"

"Fine. You?"

"Fine too, *real* fine. We miss your ass over at the gym. Three Saturdays, still no Jay. Reggie call you the mighty Frenchman now, though you don't look any too French to me."—Sammy chuckling in his throaty almost silent way—"'Where that mighty Frenchman at?' he say. 'Man use to be in twice a week.'"

"I should have called you."

"No sweat. I juss wanna make sure everything cool." He paused. "I read about that bullshit stickup in the paper. That all true?"

"More or less."

"They make it sound like a publicity stunt by LiveCell in *The Chronicle*, but I know you better than that."

"It was an ugly thing. It shouldn't have happened."

"You know who was behind it?"

"Not certain yet."

"You got an idea?"

He was silent.

Sammy continued. "A bunch of us is in now. The stock make a wiggle, they *all* ask me, they *all* wanna know what's goin' down. These people can't afford to lose—you know what I'm sayin'?" He paused. "So we cool?"

"I don't watch it."

"Jay. I make a lot already, and I thank you. Man, my children thank you, my wife, she *really* thank your ass. I only ask for the others that got in late. I mean, all the brothers is in now, whole neighborhoods. They all listen to me. They ask me to ask you."

"I don't pay attention to it."

Sammy didn't answer right away. "All right man, that's cool. You comin' our way this Saturday?"

"Maybe. I'll see how it goes."

"How's Mary?"

"Are you going to be bartending at the poolroom tonight?"

"Man, you know, with all the *long* bread I make I think a quitting, and I talk to Nick. He look at me like I his son saying I's going off to war, so yeah, I be there all week. Every week till who knows."

"We'll be over."

"All right, that excellent news. . . . Jay?"

He answered.

"Man, sorry to ask about that other shit."

"Sammy, I truly don't follow it. All I can tell you is that everyone should put their money in what they believe in, that's what matters."

No sooner had they concluded the call than he had another. It was Jimmy Hakken again. He took it reluctantly.

"Chevalier. You ever read this book *Count of Monte Cristo*?"

"A long time ago."

"Dree gave it to me. It's good."

Another Hakken pause. "You didn't grow up rich?"

"I became a ward of the state at age seven."

Another. "No shit. Later, Chevalier."

Mary walked to Jay's office and peered in the open door. He waved her in, and by the time he put his phone down she'd seated herself.

"Finally talking to the press?"

"Jimmy Hakken."

"Oh, *him*."

"You don't like him?"

"He's a little scary, isn't he?"

"How's that?"

"Well, to put it politely, he's hardly a wizard at communicating. He stares at me and I get shivers."

"I'm thinking of putting him in charge of the old factory when Deirdre moves to the new one."

"Jimmy *Hakken*?"

"Yes."

She glanced away, found the only picture he had on his walls. She'd examined it before and asked him about it. Ryder's *The Toilers of the Sea*, a small boat at the crest of a wave careening toward a full moon. She focused back on Jay. Sometimes she couldn't figure out what he was up to, but this was completely ridiculous. He wanted a former gang leader to run a high-tech factory?

"Did you read the latest?" she said.

"I don't read that stuff."

"Well, the headline was something like, Do They Clone Phones or Death-metal Fans? There was a photo of Hakken and another worker leaving the factory."

"Kind of funny. What's death metal?"

"It evolved out of heavy metal. It's sort of Gothic and dark. Like Black Sabbath on amphetamines."

"Oh," he said, sounding as if he didn't have a clue.

"Why are we getting so much bad publicity? I'm trying my best, but something's not right. As a matter of fact, something is wrong."

"Let's not worry about it."

"How can we not worry about it? For the first time our stock price has dipped. We're selling more phones than ever and our stock price goes down."

"The stock price is not what's important."

"What is then?"

"People are communicating better."

"You don't care about the stock price?"

"No."

She stared at him. And actually saw him this time, realizing he was grumpy today. *Really* grumpy. Maybe he wasn't feeling well. "Are you okay?"

"I'm fine."

"Jay, have you been eating, sleeping, taking care of yourself at all? You look feverish."

"Sammy asked about you. He called this morning. He's worried about the stock price too. He tells me a lot of people in Oakland have invested."

"Isn't that the main reason you showed Sammy the phone?"

He stared at her now.

"Have you ever eaten sushi?" she said.

He shook his head.

"Would you let me take you out tonight?"

"I told Sammy we might stop by. We haven't been at the poolroom for over two months."

"You don't need a greasy burger, you need some raw fish." She giggled. "My grandfather would growl at me if he ever heard me say that." She paused. "How's your arm? *Fine?*" she said before he could answer. He turned his head to glance out the window, and she followed his eyes. Fog drifted up the bay toward the Golden Gate Bridge, the distant shoreline barely visible.

"Do you want me to start talking to the press?" he said, facing her again. "Maybe that will fix our stock price. That seems to be the only thing anyone cares about."

She'd never heard him so sarcastic, but she ignored it. "The problem runs deeper than that. I think we're being sabotaged. I don't know what to do about it. Did you hear from Duncan?"

"Yes."

"And?"

"The gun was government issue registered to an address in Brooklyn."

"How does Duncan hack into that stuff? He's really remarkable at finding out things, isn't he? Does the address lead to anyone?"

"According to the police both men were using fake IDs, so we can't be sure. Besides, the guy who lived there moved out two weeks ago—Michael Pegonis."

"So?"

"He worked security for Alden Stone Associates four years ago."

"*Jesus.* Is that Wendell's father?"

"I doubt it has anything to do with the father. The more I've thought over the whole incident, I think it was Wendell getting even with me, hoping I might get intimidated, or at least beat up. After all, we didn't like each other on first sight, and then I humiliated him, intentionally or not."

He reached with his good arm and rubbed his ear. "Wendell probably knew Pegonis when he worked for his father and hired him. When they came to the factory that morning pretending to be FCC, Deirdre told me one of the men was frightened by Hakken."—*who wouldn't be?* she thought—"Pegonis, or whoever, must have replaced him by that evening with the small guy who slapped Deirdre around. Maybe Pegonis got more than he bargained for with this new man, and things turned messy. I haven't told you, but the father, or Alden Stone Associates, has been trying to buy us, or buy me out. Maybe Wendell thought he might expedite the negotiations for his father if I were scared or hurt, I can't imagine he wanted me shot. That might have been his rationale for sending those men."

"The father's been trying to buy you out? Why don't you tell me these things?"

"I just did."

She almost shook her head in frustration. "So *they*'re the ones dumping the stock. I figured they had been buying it. And why wouldn't they? They're not fools. But what *bastards*. God, I'm so glad I don't work for him anymore. Are you thinking of selling?"

"That's not what this is about."

"I wish you would tell me what it *is* about."

"I have. It's about people communicating."

She sat there quietly though what she actually wanted was to go to him, place her hands on his shoulders, stroke his pale face; he really looked sick. Instead she said, "Jay, we need to hire more people. We need a good PR person who does only that, who knows the business. This press issue is hurting us, and I can't seem to straighten it out."

"Your work is superlative. You've been everything I hoped you'd be."

Did he really think that? "I need to know what you want so I can do my job. You don't run a company like any I've been associated with. It makes it a bit difficult sometimes. I wish you would at least hire a secretary."

"Are you working too hard? Do you want to take some time off?"

"Yeah," she said, and watched him suppress his surprise and distress.

"When? How much time would you like?"

She paused as if considering, letting him suffer, but relented since he felt terrible anyway. "A few hours. Tonight. Please let me take you out for sushi." *Wow*, a little smile.

"Okay," he said, "but allow me to treat you."

"No, *I* would like to pay for once; you're always so generous. And we take my car. You haven't even ridden in it yet."—*and* it doesn't have a bench seat with springs that jab and that's covered in cat hair. "Okay?"

He nodded.

She stayed in her chair, examining him, then stood slowly, adjusted her skirt, and headed toward the door. She wanted to know if he was watching her walk away, hoped he was, yet wasn't willing to turn around and check. God, he still made her nervous.

Jay knew he'd missed a few calls during his discussion with Mary. His phone remembered. For the moment he ignored the two from project managers renovating the new manufacturing facility. With the one from Deirdre he thought *dial* and she immediately answered.

"Deirdre. Jay."

"Hey," she said. "You know that kind of rhymes—Jay-*hey*. I know I called you, but can I call you back? Wendy needs me right now, if that's okay?"

"Of course." The call ended. He received another almost immediately.

"Mr. Chevalier?"

"Yes."

"Detective Artega. From the armed assault on March twenty-eighth."

"Right. I remember."

"I'd think you would. Mr. Chevalier, this is not an official call, but I noticed you're not pressing charges."

"That's right."

"May I ask you why?"

"May I ask your interest?"

"Off the record?"

"Sure."

"A lot of money was thrown at cleaning this thing up. And I mean a *lot*. I wondered if you'd been threatened in some way not to press charges. We can protect you if that's the case."

"Detective, I appreciate your concern. My reasons for not pressing charges have nothing to do with fear."

A silence as Jay wondered about the true intent of the call.

"I'll say good-bye then," said the cop.

"Detective Artega?"

"Yeah?"

"Thanks for calling."

Both listening, saying nothing. Then Artega said, "You make a great phone. Say hey to Sammy. We used to box together as kids, before he got so damn big," and he rung off.

So that was it: Sammy had called Artega.

He rotated out of his oak swivel chair and headed down the hall to Mary's office. Most of the office doors on the sixth floor were left open now though he'd never mentioned or recommended it. He glanced through her doorway—no one—greeted a few coworkers on his way to the elevators. He could've found her with his LiveCell yet rejected the idea, and rejected the elevator as well, passed by and entered the stairwell. Something in him wanted to be with her, just to feel her presence.

On the landing between the two floors, he stopped and gazed out the window. Though all but a sliver of bay was denied him, he could still tell that most of the fog had dissipated. He turned away from the view and threw maybe two dozen quick punches, shadowboxing fiercely for perhaps half a minute until the pain in his left arm and a rising nausea forced him to stop. Frustration flooded him. There was still so much to do. And he was sick, worn-out, impatient, angry. Some part of him wanted to desert all his goals and just disappear. If only he could be back in the wilderness with his grandfather. If only for a week. One week of the sweat lodge, the woods, the elixir! How he missed those days.

He descended the stairs and walked into the lounge, that door kept open now as well.

"I thought I might find you here," he said.

"You want a cup?"

"Okay." He took a seat in the wicker rocker.

"Did you go to my office?"

He nodded, but she missed it.

"Did you notice that new print ad layout on my screen?"

This time she saw him shake his head.

"It has the headline, 'Is your two-year-old using your cell phone as a hammer again? Not a problem if it's a LiveCell.' I'm trying to show that our phones are safe even for babies, along with, of course, their healing properties, and I figured a little humor wouldn't hurt. I suppose the signal boxes could be damaged though if a baby hammered on them. I'll have to think about that. We need a third supplier for those by the way. At over eighteen thousand phones a day now, it makes Chet Simmons too nervous with only the two suppliers. He told me our Mexican supplier's been repeatedly late in shipping us product over the last few months. I know it's overkill, but he'd like to have three."

"He can tell me these things, can't he?"

"Chet's still a little shy around you."

"Shy?"

"Well, scared I guess."

"I'll talk to him."

She brought the coffee, and he reached up to take one of the mugs from her, thanking her. She sat beside him on the leather sofa, took a sip of hers. "It's a little strong."

"It's fine," he said. She was examining him again, always watching everything. So aware.

"Jay? Are you sure you're okay?"

He nodded.

"I don't think you'd ask for help if you needed it. Would you?"

A pause, his nose pointed into the steam. "Wendy Smith. Do you know her?"

"I've met her a few times. Deirdre promoted her to personal assistant. Did you know that?"

"She told me."

"I don't think it was Deirdre's idea. What do you want to know about Wendy Smith?"

"Your intuition."

"The truth, no politics?"

He nodded again.

"She's very ambitious. I don't really trust her though I've no reason not to, and I wonder if her beauty doesn't make people envious and react differently than they might otherwise. She seems cold though, unemotional, controlling. Very directed. She's after something, and I think she's dangerous for LiveCell. I'm not sure about any of this; I'm only giving you my gut reaction. That enough?"

"Yes. Thanks."

"Jay?"

"Yeah?"

"Does Deirdre know how the phones work?"

"A lot of it."

"Does anyone else know?"

"I don't think so."

She hesitated. "Are you ever going to tell me?"

"I've planned to all along. There is a lot to tell you."

A silence had spread between them when she said, "Can we leave early for just once? It's almost five now. The sushi bar will be open by the time we get there. It's best when it's empty and the chefs aren't too busy."

He took a single sip from his coffee, his hands cradling the warm mug. "Sure," he said finally. "Let's go."

As they left the lounge he said he wanted to get something from his office, and they took the elevator up together. When they entered the orange room, he walked over to a standing coat rack and retrieved a jacket she hadn't seen before. *Actually* a sports coat. He shrugged it on over his sweatshirt.

"Where did you get *this*?" she said, feeling the material of the sleeve. "This is a really nice jacket. What is it, silk? Let me see the label."

He showed her.

"I can't believe it. She's a hot designer. What's happened to you? When did you buy it?"

"Deirdre gave it to me."

She was silent, not telling him how handsome he looked in it. Deirdre seemed to be everywhere these days. She just wished she'd thought to give it to him, but he'd always seemed so uninterested in clothes.

"Why did she give it to you?"

"I guess she wanted to thank me."

Even with his new jacket on, he didn't look any healthier in the Porsche. She retracted the cloth top so he could admire the full effect of the car, but he ignored even his seat belt, merely settled into the leather bucket and stared up at the sky as they drove through San Francisco. The day was clear now, a perfect late April afternoon, the sun on buildings and pavement and trees crystalline as fresh lacquer. She told herself not to drive too fast, but he seemed completely oblivious to the speed. He took out his phone.

"Duncan, Jay. . . . Fine, and you? . . . What I need is some information on a Wendy Smith. . . . You did? And? . . ." He listened for a while. "H-n. . . . Thanks. . . . No, it's all right that you did."

He put his phone away.

"Well?" she said.

"Well, what?"

She slowed for a red light, shifting down through two gears, not getting her usual pleasure from the sound of the engine.

"What did Duncan find out?"

"Wendy Smith doesn't exist. There are lots of Wendy Smiths of course; none matches ours. Duncan is sure it's an alias, probably chosen because it's such a common name, but he couldn't uncover a link, as he called it. He doesn't know who she is."

"What are you going to do?"

"Nothing."

"*Nothing?*"

"Nothing."

"How about Deirdre?"

"I trust Deirdre."

"Are you going to warn her about Wendy?"

"No."

"Isn't that a lot to risk? Aren't we both thinking the same thing, that this woman is probably an industrial spy trying to get our secrets through Deirdre? Not that I understand everything about it, but it sure seems that way."

He glanced at her. "It's a lot to risk, that's true. I still trust Deirdre. That's what trust is."

"Without a patent? And Deirdre knowing how the phone works? What's going to keep other companies from stealing the secret? You know how strongly I feel about this."

The light turned green and she eased the car forward.

"Soon you will know why I can't patent the phone."

She could tell he'd ended the conversation, and she accelerated, not caring what he thought of her driving.

As she'd anticipated, the sushi bar was empty except for three chefs in crisp white jackets. They were seated by the equally immaculate Japanese hostess, the chefs greeting Mary by name and nodding to Jay. No sooner had they sat down at the polished wooden bar than a smiling waitress offered them a hot cloth dangling from a pair of bamboo tongs. Mary ordered a couple bottles of Japanese beer and a plate of mixed pickles. She tried to put the Deirdre thing behind her. It wasn't easy.

Jay looked up at the chef who bowed a few inches in response. Jay bowed, and the chef bowed again. Jay was starting to bow a second time when she came to the rescue.

"We'll start with sashimi, please." She turned to Jay. "Iso will give us what he feels is best today."

With a quick practiced motion, the chef slid open a glass door at the back of one of the refrigerated cases and selected three different rectangles of glistening fish, examining each for a second before slapping them down on his cutting board. One piece he tossed back and exchanged for another. He picked up his knife.

The beer and pickles arrived.

"These are pickles?" said Jay. "What unusual colors."

She poured soy sauce into both saucers and separated her chopsticks. "Some people rub their sticks together thinking they're removing splinters. These sticks are high quality, and by trying to build a fire you show you haven't noticed. It would be an insult."

She ate a few pickles and took a long pull on her glass of beer. This was one of her favorite places, he was finally here, and now she was in a lousy mood and worried he wouldn't like it.

Iso reached behind him and selected a large sea-blue plate. On it he mounded three hillocks of finely shredded radish against which he arranged the slices of fish he'd cut. He added some pickled ginger. "*Toro, hamachi, katsuo*," he said as he handed the plate to her. "*Katsuo* for spring time season. Very good." Iso grunted when she thanked him, reaching over quickly to toss a dot of *wasabi* onto the plate. It landed perfectly and she wondered again if he practiced the move. She turned to Jay.

"Add a little *wasabi* to your fish if you want with the tip of your chop stick. Don't mix it in your soy sauce. The Japanese believe any cloudiness in soy sauce is an indication of the impurity of the soul." Was she wasting her time explaining these things to him? She wondered why everyone tried to impress when they came to a sushi bar, herself included.

He stared at the raw fish in front of him for a long minute. Then struggling with his chopsticks, the fish slipping away twice, he dipped the edge into the soy sauce—following her admonition not to soak it—and levered it into his mouth, almost dropping it. He chewed thoughtfully, swallowed. Her concern increased as she waited.

"This is actually delicious. I'm surprised it's even fish. Almost melts on your tongue. What did I just eat?"

"That was a rare belly cut of tuna. Try the next one."

Iso was observing them without watching them.

"How do you know so much about Japanese food?" Jay asked her.

"I eat here a lot and I ask questions. This food gives me energy, and I find eating here relaxing."

He nodded to Iso. "This is delicious," he said across the fish case, Iso bowing. "Mary, thanks for this."

"I've wanted to take you here for a long time," she said, the beer, the food, and his appreciation improving her spirits.

Toward the end of their meal, she on her fourth beer as he finished his first, she ordered another round, asking the waitress to bring a beer for Iso as well. They had eaten a variety of sushi, bisecting the meal with a hot miso soup swimming with seaweed. Jay had liked most of it, particularly the raw shrimp where the heads are deep-fried and served separately. He hadn't been so sure about *ika-natto*—squid and fermented soybeans topped by a fresh quail egg yolk all stirred together into a strange porridge. She said it might be an acquired taste. She hadn't been so keen the first time either but hadn't had the heart to tell Iso what she really thought. She was relieved it grew on her.

As they dined, the restaurant and bar progressively filled so that now there was a clatter and murmur of many people around them, lending something intimate and private to their being together. Iso no longer concentrated his efforts on them; he rapidly assembled platter after platter of sushi for different tables, whisked away by the waitresses. Maybe from the beer, or maybe from being embarrassed that she'd gotten so jealous and worried, she suddenly felt an unusual openness toward him.

"You've never been to my new place," she said. "I look out over the entire Pacific, it's really something. Of course you have a similar view in Oregon. Have you been back up to the Siuslaw place?"

"Only once. I really haven't had time, though it breaks my heart. I love it up there."

"You bring those cats every time?"

He nodded.

"You don't know this, but I almost died the day I went up to see you."—her skin felt flushed, her eyes slightly unfocused—"It really frightened me. I guess I was too happy. Everything was so perfect that day. I was so excited to be visiting you, and I drove too fast. This guy on a motorcycle saw me spin and stopped. He treated me as if I were a careless rich idiot, and it bugged me."

"How come you didn't tell me?"

She shrugged and wet her lips. "Can I tell you something?" He nodded. "I'm always a little nervous around you."

He continued to look at her.

"I shouldn't have told you that." She glanced down for a second, wondering if she was getting drunk. He didn't say anything. "Will you tell me about yourself? You never do that. Most men, all they talk about is themselves until you think you're going to scream, but you . . ."

"What do you want to know?"

"You really don't mind?"

He shook his head, and she wondered again how much he'd shared with Deirdre.

"The boxing," she said. "It doesn't make any sense to me."

He took a sip of his beer. "You want the long or the short version?"

"Long." Though she was sure he sensed what she wanted.

He picked up a last pickle with his hand, a purple one, and examined it before tossing it into his mouth.

"I scored well on tests as a kid and was pushed into more and more schooling. I had this obligation to perform, to live up to the opportunities that were offered me. After all, other people were paying for it and I owed them. I was the orphan Indian kid from northern Maine who made it through Harvard. But when I finished there, I felt like I didn't exist. As if I wasn't anything—just all this learned information. You can only live the way other people expect you to for so long."

She knew how that was. Now he picked up a chopstick and started to toy with it, watching his hand as he played with the stick. She was relieved that he didn't drum with it as some men insisted on doing.

"I hitchhiked from Cambridge to Manhattan, not telling anyone I was leaving. Basically I disappeared, knowing it was the only way out. I got a room at the Y and wandered around for a couple of weeks. I remember looking at all the bricks in all the buildings, so many bricks, and thinking that each one had been placed by a human hand. That seemed incredible. One day I walked into a boxing gym. I watched for a while, and the owner and I got to talking. I knew right then I wanted to box. He tried to talk me out of it. 'You're too old to start boxing,' he said, and he was right. I had no illusions, no desire to become a great fighter. I didn't care about that. I just liked Pete. He'd been in the fight game a lot of years and was a terrific trainer. He wasted his time on me though. Until then I'd never had the opportunity to use my body much, but I found out I was naturally strong. My father must have been a very strong man. He might still be alive. Somewhere."

Maybe his father was the reason he didn't want the publicity? She took another drink. She really liked Japanese beer.

"I didn't mind getting hit. Actually, I liked it. I also loved the hard workouts, craved them. Boxing cleared up my complexion. So that's the story—I wasn't much of a boxer."

"Not what I heard."

"That should never have happened."

Iso at this moment reached over and set a plate in front of them with *yamagobo* and *umekyu*. "Good for finish," he said and returned to cutting fish.

"Tell me about these." He pointed at the new plate.

She looked down at the sushi. "They're good for digestion. The burdock root you eat fat end first and the other is full of pickled plum paste. So that's when you met Kelly?"

"About a year after I started boxing."

"He told me you made sandwiches for all the bums."

"He told you that?"

"Said they all ate the sandwiches only to please you."

He looked at her solemnly, and she worried she shouldn't have revealed that, but then he smiled.

"You want another beer?" she said, knowing she shouldn't have another but not caring. He declined. As their waitress passed she ordered it and some tea for them both.

There were so many things she wanted to share, yet she didn't know how to approach him, how to get close. She was used to men always coming at her, wanting her, and she knew how to respond to that, how to handle them. But with Jay, she felt off balance, careening toward him. Just like that boat toward the moon in the painting he had in his office.

She waited for him to speak, but he said nothing more. Was he going to clam up again? "Do you miss your mother?"

"Yes." He reached for another piece of *maki*. "Do you miss yours? You don't talk about her much."

"Did you meet her when you went to the farm?"

"Briefly."

"She's a strong woman. My grandparents are the same way. Solid Vermont Yankee stock is what she calls it. Mother can be tough to be around but everyone respects her. She never took to Kelly much. She was always strange around him, as if she watched him out of the corner of her eye. Did Kelly tell you about any of it?"

"In the city he used to talk about growing up with your dad in, wasn't it northern New Hampshire?"

She nodded. "Irving."

"At the farm I met your dad. Kelly told about how your father rescued him after Patricia died. They came back east together and Kelly moved into the abandoned trailer on the farm."

"My mom wasn't so keen on it, let me tell you. They used to fight about it. Made me really mad because of how I felt about Kelly. Kelly sure liked my mom though. I've always wondered if he didn't have a crush on her. Maybe that's where the tension came from."

The waitress arrived with the tea and beer.

She filled her glass and took a long sip. "Jay, what are you really up to with the phones?"

"Besides people communicating?"

"I'm starting to believe it has nothing to do with money."

"Is this Jay-tells-all-his-secrets night?"

"So will you tell me?"

He looked around at the other diners, reached for his tea, sipped. "The world has always been manipulated by basically the same type of person. This self-professed *aristocracy* do whatever they want—they lie and deceive, they embezzle and steal, they murder and start wars—and so many lives are destroyed, and the rest of us sadly never seem to know what's going on, and it's this ignorance that keeps this group in power. This elect group, they—"

"You're after *them*?"

He paused. "My hope is that our phones will increase intuitiveness over time. People will become aware through using LiveCell phones, and collectively know how they are being manipulated and what to do about it. It won't happen with everyone, but it should affect enough—"

"I never thought of that," she said almost in a whisper. "They do increase intuitiveness, don't they?" She saw so much of it finally. It made sense and it excited her. She reached for her beer to be doing something with her hands. Being with him was always so complex.

"Did I answer your question?" he said.

It took her a minute. "Jay, wouldn't that make an incredible new ad slogan: Change The World, Use LiveCell Phones."

A grimace. "Maybe we better leave that alone for now."

"It's what you always insisted, people communicating better," she said, the feeling between them overwhelming her. Just ask him, she told herself. If you don't ask him nothing will ever happen.

"Jay," she said softy. "You want to come see my place tonight?"

He said nothing.

She tried again: "Maybe you could explain the phone to me if you came over?" God, she was sounding like a slut. This was ridiculous. *Here he tells me about changing the world, and all I want is him.*

"Actually I still have to stop by the factory," he said. "What time is it?"

In confusion she checked her wrist and told him it was twenty to eight. He never wore a watch. "So, are you coming over?" she said, taking another long swallow of beer, feeling really stupid, blushing again.

"I need to stop by the factory. I'm a bit late as it is."

"What's at the factory?"

"I need to do something."

"You go there every damn night. Why?"

"You want to come with me?" he said quietly.

"Precious *Deir*dre won't mind?" Why did she blurt out these things? The sad smile that came to his face made her doubly regret what she'd said.

"I'll show you. I'll call Deirdre, and if she's still there, I'll ask her to go home. Okay?"

She reached out and touched his shoulder.

NINE

Mary looked out across the endless reach of the Pacific. After a few minutes her glance shifted, focused on the scattered pile of mail on her dining room table. She spotted the corner of a postcard she hadn't noticed earlier. The face of the card was a main-street view of Alturas, California. She turned it over. It had been forwarded from her address in Berkeley.

Dear Mary, it started.

Hows everything going? I'm doing OK. Was sad about Patsy but I'm OK now. Been ranching alot which helps. Lot of work in the Springtime as you know. Hows the pool playing going? I read about you and your company in the paper. Wow you are something! I bought one. If you ever need anything you know where I am. Anything!!!

Sincerely,

Garland McKeen (Hank)

His signature was in an elaborate script. Mary wondered if she still had the slip of paper with his address; she knew she hadn't thrown it out. It seemed so long ago. She'd meant to call him and ask about his cousin.

She would write him a card of condolence. Thinking of Garland reminded her of the tournament, and her hands yearned to hold a cue again. Too much time had passed since she'd last played.

Today she finally had a Saturday all to herself—a day off. And all she could think about was Jay. She imagined preparing dinner for him, something special to usher in the summer season; she'd have it all ready to serve, then take a long bath, put on her new outfit—she had bought so many new clothes, yet he never seemed to notice any of them—and wait for him to arrive. They could share a bottle of champagne. Lately she'd been ordering it by the case. Though she still liked beer, she was amazed at how good really fine champagne tasted. Her house was already tidy as her maid cleaned Fridays. Would he come if she invited him?

While she was rinsing her hair in the bathtub, her phone signaled. The thought that it might be Jay and that she was naked excited her. But when the phone was close enough, she knew it wasn't him.

"Hello?" she said.

"Hey Mary, it's Duncan."

"*Oh*, hi, Duncan."

"Did I get you at a bad time?"

"Actually, could I call you back?"

"Will it be soon? I need to talk to you." A slight pause. "What're you doing, washing dishes?"

"I'll call you back in a little while, okay?"

Drying herself, she wandered over to one of the huge windows over-looking the ocean. Her thoughts ran to Jay again.

On the sushi night, she'd watched him minister to the phones for the first time. They'd pulled into the empty parking lot, Deirdre gone as promised. He unlocked the factory, turned on the hallway lights, but left the clean room in darkness, only the metal edges of the lab tables high-lighted in red from the exit signs. She didn't comment. He turned to her, seeming nervous. "If you feel strange in any way, stop me. Any way at all." She wasn't sure what he meant by strange; she already felt strange, and his unusual nervousness was infectious. She couldn't remember him being even mildly nervous before.

He kneeled in front of the phones with his arms held out. She stood close beside him, no idea what he was doing, a thrill of anticipation mix-ing with the beer and her general excitation. His arms dropped and a still-ness settled over everything, almost as if there was no time. A humming started in her brain; was that what he meant by strange? After a few more minutes the humming moved lower between her legs. Unlike in the boardroom, she wasn't afraid. Quite the opposite. Strange or not, there was no way she was going to stop him! With a sharp thrill, maybe because she was allowing herself a newfound freedom, she knew she wanted it and wondered if he would notice, if she could do it soundlessly. She bit her bottom lip, feeling her orgasm rising, but just as it was about to happen, the phones began to throb with their eerie iridescence.

Afterwards, he'd questioned her. How had she felt? Had watching the infusion bothered her at all? She couldn't tell him the truth, not yet anyway, but wondered if he'd guessed, or if there was something else he was after. What did he mean by saying that humility was the beginning of salvation? Why had he said that? It was so hard to tell with him.

She stopped looking out the window and picked up the fallen towel. As she walked into the bedroom she brought her hand to her nose and smelled herself, rubbing the silky wetness between her fingers and thumb. She dressed slowly and decided to stop thinking about him, to contemplate her options for the day instead. Maybe she should head to the poolroom, say hello to Sammy and Nick, run a few racks, find that part of her life again? But her longing for Jay continued, much as she suppressed it. She made a deal with herself: "If he calls me, I'll ask him to dinner, I'll insist he come." She concentrated, attempting to will him into calling her.

And her LiveCell told her there was a call. She reached for it eagerly.

It was Duncan again.

"I was just about to call you, what's up?"

"Mary, I'm sorry to bug you on your day off," he said with his tense giggle.

"What's on your mind?"

"It's this Wendy Smith thing. I've been making some headway. I think she's a fucking spy. My guess was that she's working for a cell phone manufacturer. But the weird thing is, her phone records show that she's made two calls to New York. Alden Stone Associates. Is that a weird coincidence or what? And you know I don't believe in weird coincidences."

"Have you told Jay?"

"That's just it, Jay doesn't seem to care. I've told him, and he just says things will take their course, for me to leave it alone. I mean, what the hell is that? Doesn't he realize how important this is? He runs this company like a—" He hesitated. "Do you know Wendy Smith is moving in with Deirdre?"

"When did that happen?"

"They just announced it. What a fucking company. What a *lovely* group. I go over there to warn *Miss* Deirdre Holly about Wendy Smith and you know what she does? She tells me to mind my own business. Then that tattooed totem pole Hakken shows up and stands there glaring at me. I mean, why is he working at the factory? He's like the grim reaper in a B movie. A real wacko. Put him in some satanic rock band, but keep him away from me and LiveCell. Hopefully Jay will fire him when they move to the new factory next week."

She didn't tell him that Jimmy Hakken might soon be running the old factory. Instead she said, "Duncan, you should worry about doing your work and let everyone else do theirs."

His voice jumped an octave. "We have a chance to make a fucking fortune here. Don't you realize that? But if we don't play smart, we're *fucked*. You know what else really bothers me?" He didn't wait for her reply. "I can't find *any* patents on the phones. Not a one. Nothing pending. *Nothing*, nada. And I still don't even understand how the fucking things work. I've analyzed the boxes. They're basic electromagnetic senders and receivers, standard to every cell phone, have the same battery and charging system. The inexplicable thing is that they're missing the central processing unit, the brain chip."—*he doesn't realize how close he is*—"And on top of that there's an analog preamp that translates digital code connected to the prongs, but why the signal even translates to the cell structure I can't figure out. Those prongs are highly sensitive, low-frequency electrodes, but beyond them are just cells. I've cut a few phones apart, but there aren't any other electronics or chips inside. And let me tell you, you cut into a LiveCell phone—it dies. Fast. Darkens a little and that's it. You can whack them, nick them, but don't cut them open. I'm there with this razorblade, and right after my first slice the phone starts blinking like crazy, like it's going insane. My second deep slice and it turns dull and hard. Thing wouldn't work at all. Does Deirdre know how the phones work?"

She sensed he was trying to sneak the question in.

"No," she said.

"Are you sure?"

"Yes."

"I don't think you're telling me the truth. I think you and her both know. You must because you and Jay are like—" He stopped again.

There was a long silence.

"Are you going to report this conversation to Jay?" he said. Again he didn't wait for her answer. "I'm only trying to look out for the good of the company. Here we might have a spy getting our secrets from Deirdre and no one listens to me. An industrial spy and no patents. What a *great* combination. I mean, we have the best fucking product since the silicon chip and he runs the company like— Oh, the hell with it. And everyone treats him like a goddamn saint. I know you think he's perfect." Tears crept into his voice. A brilliant guy but what an emotional wreck.

"Duncan."

"*What?*"

"Have you been taking any time off?"

"I'm just a little worried about the future. Our stock price slipped again last week."

"Only a fraction."

"Yeah, but it should be going through the roof."

"Everything is down. Besides we've already both made a lot of money."

"It depends what you call *a lot*."

"You can't tell me you need more."

"Listen, do you rent or own?"

"It isn't any of your business."

"My point. Mary, we could all become *really* rich. Super rich. Have anything we wanted."

Her eyes went out to the horizon. So clear this morning. The blue above blue like the tone of two harmonizing bells.

"And last week he brings the price of the phones down again. It looks bad, as if there's not enough demand, and here we are months behind in filling orders. At a hundred a phone we were giving them away, but now—

"Duncan, I've got to get going."

"You do? Where are you going?"

"Good-*bye*, Duncan."

"Okay. Listen, thanks for talking to me. And Mary?"

"Yeah."

"Talk to Jay. We need to get rid of Wendy Smith. We need to raise the price of the phones. *And* find out where the patents are. He'll listen to you." He terminated the call before she could reply.

Duncan had depressed her, and she longed to talk to Jay more than ever. What she really wanted was for him to call her. She knew she had to stop chasing him.

She reached for her phone, thought a number, waited.

"Hey Kelly."

"*Mary*, what's going on?"

"You have a minute?"

"Sure. Just came in from mending fences. Was about to fix myself something to eat."

"It's Saturday. Why aren't you eating with the family?"

"Tonight I will."

"I got your letter. Thanks."

They were both quiet. She realized again how amazing the phones were. Sometimes you didn't have to say anything.

"Was Jay changed when you saw him again?"

"Fifteen years is bound to change someone."

"How was he different?"

"Well, in New York, he was unsure of himself. Seemed lost. When I saw him in Vermont he was at peace, seemed to know exactly what he wanted."

"He's hard to read."

"Doesn't talk much about himself."

"I *guess!*"

"Mary, are you okay?"

A silence. "I just keep thinking about him too much. And I still don't really understand him. I mean, I understand some things, but there's something I'm not getting. Here he is the CEO of this company and he doesn't want any kind of publicity for himself. I keep wondering if there's some reason, if there's something in his past. I've had to take a lot of the press responsibility, and I get asked about him all the time. I never know what to say. And he's always so calm about everything, like nothing could ever go wrong."

"Is that what's bothering you?"

"Maybe. Maybe it's that he has so much confidence in me. The responsibility can be overwhelming. What if I let him down?"

He didn't reply.

"Jay never really tires," she said. "Even when he was shot he just kept working. He almost had blood poisoning and had to be hospitalized, but he worked the whole time. He's so disciplined it makes me feel I have to perform at his level. Sometimes I can't, and he's eleven years older. He never even gets angry with anyone if he likes them, no matter what they do. He's hired some very strange people, and there are all these problems in the company because of it, but he doesn't intercede. He just has faith that people will do the right thing. If he likes you, he trusts you, and that's the end of it."

"Is it that you *sense* something is going to go wrong?"

They were silent again. Then she said, "I get the feeling he sort of knows everything, like he has this master plan and everything is just as it should be, so what do I know." She paused. "Kelly, why did Jay go find you?"

He didn't answer.

"You have it too, don't you?" she said.

"I did. The drugs dulled most of it."

"That's why you were so upset about me finding Pilgrim, wasn't it? You knew I had it and thought I'd fall apart like you did."

"I had it so bad as a teen, I couldn't stand it. I foresaw my father's death. I knew he was going to die in the mill. I'd seen the red pulp-water. No one believed me, I *begged* him." He paused. "After he died, Addison took me in, and I lived on a cot in the back of the poolroom, cleaned up and racked balls all day. No one except Addison and your father gave a rat's ass about me. I did every downer I could get my hands on. They helped. Smack was even better. That slowed things down. For me it was a huge relief."

"You asked Jay not to say anything. He knew you had the ability when you were together in New York."

"Yeah. He sensed it and I told him. I foresaw his boxing trainer's death. Sucked because of course it didn't make any difference."

"Do you still?"

"Rarely."

"You could have told me."

"I was too scared to reveal it. I wasn't even sure about telling Jay about you."

"It got him off your back."

He was silent.

"Sorry," she said. "I don't mean to be so bitchy, don't know what's wrong with me." A pause. "Since we're being so honest. Did he ever have any lovers, male or female?"

"I don't know."

She waited.

"That's the truth." Another lull. "He's the one, isn't he?"

"Yes." She could sense Kelly's emotion overwhelming him and his need to change the subject.

"What are you going to do today?" he said.

"I think I'll head to the poolroom and practice. I haven't been on a table in months. I need to do something."

"Get out of your head for a while. Pool might work."

"Instead of drugs, you mean." She meant it as a joke but realized it sounded cruel.

"Too bad we couldn't run a few racks together. We had some good afternoons, didn't we?"

"We did . . . You're about the only person I can really talk to." Her throat was tight. She told him she had to go and went to retrieve her cue.

For once the traffic on the Golden Gate Bridge was moving briskly. With the top down and the sounds of a CD sailing just above the noise of the car, she glanced out past the sienna-red fencing to the flashing blue of the water. Her glance was habit instead of the yearning it had once been. " . . . a fire, these dreams that pass me by, this salvation and desire, keeps getting me down . . ." The sensuality of the singer's voice stirred up thoughts of Jay again. At least she was doing something besides waiting. Maybe Nick would shoot a few racks; she'd even play him straight pool if he wanted.

Once on Van Ness, she parked near the familiar sign, the neon *Jake's* script unlit and sad-looking. She battened the top, bleeped the locks, and walked toward the poolroom, her cue case gently nudging her thigh. As she climbed the stairs, nostalgia for the place increased with each step. The door was open but the room empty, the jukebox mute, and there was that almost brittle smell of old wood, chalk and wax. Four sconces were lit behind the bar, the cavernous room so dark and silent, the few window shades muddy green against the sunshine, a slice or two of dusty daylight angling to the floor. She set down her cue case on the bar, sat at one of the aligned stools, and stared at the beer cooler lost in thought. Nick's office door opened and he peered out through his thick glasses.

"Can I help you?" he said as he walked over. "—*Mary!* How nice, you come and see Nick."

She greeted him.

"You wanna cup of coffee or something?"

"Sure. That would be great."

"You wanna espresso? We got a new machine."

"Just regular would be fine."

"Okay. I put on the pot."

As he filled the coffee maker with water, she realized she didn't know anything about him. It was strange how you could feel close to someone without that knowledge, or how you could have a close relationship with someone on just one level. The machine gurgled and the aroma lent a freshness to the stale air.

Nick brought her a steaming cup along with a small plastic container of half-and-half and two packets of sugar. She ignored the sugar.

"You no take sugar?" he said.

She shook her head.

"Espresso I take sugar, no milk," he said.

"You're not going to have one?"

"One in the morning is good. Two is no good."

She took a sip of her coffee.

"How you been? You not practicing no more?" he said.

"I've been too busy, Nick."

"Yes, I know. I read about you and your special telephone in the papers. Sammy, he makes lotsa money."

"Do you invest in the market?"

"What do I need the worry for? Too many people lose lotsa money in that place. I have all I need anyway."

"Nick? Can I ask you something?"

"Sure, you go ahead."

"What do you do when you're not here?"

"I'm at home. I have a small apartment, a very nice neighborhood. I have a garden, some roses, some vegetables. I like opera. I listen to opera and I cook sometimes. I read books. My brother, he send me books in Italian, send me whatever I need. No TV. I don't like TV."

"You have a brother?"

"In Boston. He come over before me. He is different from me. He is a very important businessman, very powerful, many people work for him."

"You ever see him?"

"No."

"Why not?"

He didn't answer. He glanced toward a vibrating sliver of sunlight on one of the pool tables.

"Sorry, Nick. I didn't mean to pry."

"It's okay. Boston make me sad. I don't go back there."

"I'm sorry, Nick. I didn't mean to upset you."

"It's okay."

"You want to shoot some straight?"

It took him a little while to answer. He gave her one of his cryptic smiles. "Sure. Let's play some straight pool. We shoot some straight."

They played a couple of seventy-five point games, Mary running forty-two balls in the second game. Nick still won both games, yet only by a few points, and she wondered if she really wanted to beat him. There was such beauty in his careful, gentle stick-work, in the way he controlled the cue ball using mostly topspin, in his cautious safety play. No wonder he had been New England champion. They didn't talk, except to communicate about the game, and that was seldom. She relished it, this midday stillness of the old room with just the melody of clicking balls, the *k-nock* of successful shots striking wooden bottoms of leather pockets, Nick chalking his unadorned cue and slowly circling the table, examining the lie of balls through his glasses, then calculating his score and sliding the wooden beads into position on the overhead wire with his cue shaft.

On their third game, the poolroom began to fill, and Nick was intermittently pulled away to help customers. They decided to forgo the match.

She practiced for about an hour and kept making deals with herself—if I can run two tables of nine-ball in a row he'll call me, if I can make three massé shots in a row he'll call me—but kept missing, so she boxed her cue and went to the bar for a beer. She'd have to wait until Sammy arrived at four to order a sandwich though she could almost taste the crabmeat roll. She felt a little guilty being inside when outside such a perfect spring day waited. The poolroom languor and sipping drafts in the afternoon reminded her of being naughty as a child. Those times when she knew she was doing something she shouldn't, but the knowledge intensified the pleasure, just as it made her uneasy. Such a seductive decadence.

Twice she was offered nine-ball games, but she didn't feel up to playing for money. Then, half an hour early, Sammy walked in.

"Hey girl. How's things?"

"Okay. You?"

"I'm good, *real* good. Attended a workout with my man Jay. Good to see his ass after so many months. And now you back, makes it all doubly fine."

He sat down beside her. *So* that's where Jay was. She was relieved she hadn't called him. His arm must finally be better.

Sammy continued, "That boy got hisself some kinda punch . . . Hey, that thing yours?"

"What thing?"

"That silver bolt-a-lightning parked on Van Ness?"

She grinned.

"Goddamn girl, you gotta give me a ride."

"Anytime."

"I got me something German now too."

"What'd you get?"

"Mercedes, convertible."

"New?"

"Girl, I got a big family. Two-eighty SL—she used, but she smooth and silver too."

They grinned at each other.

"It's good to see you, Sammy."

"It fine to see you. Always fine to see you. Glad to see you got your cue."

"I shot some straight with Nick."

"How'd you do?"

"He beat me two games."

"You ease up on him?"

"I'm not sure. Just watching him play is kind of mesmerizing."

"He still a beautiful shooter, no doubt about that."

"What's between him and his brother? I asked a question about his brother and he went all sad on me—wouldn't say a thing."

Sammy glanced around him. "He don't talk to me none about that neither, and you know how close we are. I find out about it though. You cool right?"

She waited.

The smile. "This the story I hear." He leaned toward her and lowered his voice. "The poolroom Nick run in Boston, his brother own. Or brother and his *associates*. The brother a real big deal now, *real* big. Took over the whole fucking thing from these associates from what I hear. Anyhow, back then, I'm not so sure Nick know everything his brother involved in. They use the poolroom for certain things, meetings in the back, drug deals, shit like that. Maybe Nick juss turn the blind eye, maybe he not hip, but he probably know—it his brother after all, right?"

Sammy glanced around again. "Then everything go south for a time, and there these shootings. Usual shit, retaliation over territory, like that. No big deal. Except—Nick's wife and son get gunned down. It some stupid fucking mistake. A *mistake*, can you believe that shit? Nick lost it, really fall apart. He in and out of an asylum out there. The end of his pool career as a stick, he all nerves now. Eventually, his brother buy him this joint, and he take care of everything. This place don't take in all that much, and the rent real steep in this neighborhood, so the brother juss send checks. I suppose he feel responsible. That the word I got anyway."

"*Jesus.*"

"Sucks, don't it?"

They were both quiet.

"Like some months ago, I tell Nick I wanna quit, and you shoulda seen his face. He *still* ain't over that, and it musta been twenty years ago."

"I knew he didn't have a family, but I had no idea."

"Yeah, more you learn about other people, more you know we *all* carrying something around."

"Was Jake his son's name?"

Sammy nodded and looked at his watch—a new one. "I got to get working. You want a crab roll, 'nother beer?"

She didn't respond right away, but after a few moments she said, "Sure, why not?"

TEN

Deirdre Holly was relieved that she didn't have to look at the bullet hole in the floor of her old office any longer. The bullet hole in the wall had been patched, but the one in the wood floor, though the police had dug out the slug, remained, reminding her of a poorly healed wound. She'd felt chills every time she walked over the spot. Not the same chills as when Wendy's fingertips brushed along her naked body, but chills nonetheless. She missed Jimmy Hakken though—even if he'd been a bit icy towards her over the last few months. Let him be cold: *Hey*, she wasn't going to explain the situation to him. When she'd first come to Santa Cruz she'd heard rumors about Jimmy Hakken, but moving in different worlds—he was hardly a surfer-type—they hadn't run into each other until he'd applied for the job with LiveCell. Then she'd been so against hiring him, and now he was running the old factory. It showed her how presumption could mess you up. He wasn't a yeoman anymore; he'd become a knight. At least in his mind. In hers he was more of a Visigoth.

Wendy Smith had helped decorate her office in the new factory. Jay told Deirdre, "It's your office, do whatever you want," but Wendy had been uncompromising, insisting on white walls. Maybe because of this, Deirdre chose a muted copper similar to the orange of Jay's office. Wendy hated the color and had refused to help with the painting. That the color irked her, secretly pleased Deirdre. Perhaps to make amends she accepted

Wendy's preference in furniture: modern, blonde satin-finished maple; "simple but elegant" was how Wendy phrased it. Deirdre also agreed to hang framed vintage movie posters on the walls. They were an extravagance, like way too expensive, but she could afford it now. The one of Mary Pickford was Wendy's favorite, Deirdre quietly noting that her own appearance was nothing like the star's. She preferred the poster of Veronica Lake, who at least looked somewhat like Wendy.

With her new lifestyle, Deirdre had decided to see a therapist, choosing a name out of the Yellow Pages. She didn't know how else to go about it. Just as she never spoke about her family to anyone, she wasn't willing to mention this either. During the seventh session, the therapist had asked if she'd considered that her lesbianism might be a defense mechanism fostered by a fear of physical contact with men. She told the therapist, "I was gay before my father ever touched me, if that's what you're driving at." The therapist must have gotten her diploma from Walmart. Deirdre rejected the idea of further therapy, wondering why she'd entertained the notion in the first place. She supposed her impulse for help was some kind of media conditioning: like, get rich, get therapy. Wendy Smith's beautiful body was the kind of therapy she wanted. She'd deal with the pain from her past in her own way.

Deirdre headed for work in her Dodge wagon, no surfboards riding in back for almost a year. LiveCell and Wendy took all her time now. Wendy had stayed home that morning, saying she wasn't feeling well, and since Deirdre was alone and early for work—for once not having had to wait for Wendy to get out of the bathroom—she considered swinging by the old factory and attempting to patch things up with Jimmy Hakken. But just before the turnoff, she vetoed the idea. She'd be seeing him later on at the department heads meeting anyway. Her thoughts wandered back to when Jay had offered Hakken the job, asking him to run the old factory. Hakken had just stared. Then, without a word, he'd walked out of the office, leaving them both standing there. They'd looked at each other, not sure what was going on. When Hakken returned about four or five minutes later, he stood in front of them. "Chevalier, you will never regret this."

Jimmy Hakken metamorphosed her old office into what reminded her of a medieval dungeon. On the walls he hung an authentic hangman's noose with thirteen knots—he proudly pointed this out to her—three sets of crossed swords and some ancient axes with two blades; he even set out a human skull on the desk. She didn't check to see if it was real. He probably prized the bullet hole in the floor. Deirdre had taken many of the original crew with her to the new complex, and Hakken filled the vacancies with some of his old gang, the Druids. She had to admit though, all the gang members he hired worked hard. He ran the factory with intense almost military seriousness. She didn't ask Jay if Hakken knew about infusing the phones. She doubted it. Jimmy Hakken would never break his word by spying as she had—he lived to keep his word. She wondered if Mary MacKensie knew.

With the station wagon's windows rolled down, a July breeze trifling with her hair—she was letting it grow out—she pulled in and parked in the empty lot; no one had a reserved space. Jay had unearthed another solid though dilapidated warehouse to hold the new facility, and again the exterior of the building hid the technologically sophisticated interior. As she unlocked the front doors, Luke, exactly fifteen minutes early as usual, rode up on his Panhead, the straight pipes barking, making a racket. He barely fit on the motorcycle, and it was a *large* bike. Jimmy Hakken had insisted she take one of his people for security, and he'd sent Luke Delamar. Jay okayed it; though as he stipulated with all the gang members, Luke wasn't to carry a gun. She didn't think he needed a gun. When she greeted him, he grunted. Jimmy Hakken was verbose compared to Luke.

She activated the voice lock and opened the inner doors, Luke following like a giant black bear. He began turning on lights and checking the humidity, temperature, and carbon-level of the clean room from the set of gauges in the hallway; soon he'd be preparing coffee. She'd explained to him many times that he didn't *have* to do those things, but he'd only stared at her. The one time she'd intentionally stared back and waited, he'd said, "Okay, so what? So God beat me with his ugly stick," and stomped off. She hadn't meant *that* at all. Since his beard and hair covered most of his face, it was impossible to tell what he actually looked like anyway, besides the large nose that reminded her of a rutabaga. After the staring confrontation he even cleaned up around her office and took out the factory's trash at the end of each day. She couldn't figure him out, so she just attempted to get along with him as best she could.

Walking into her office, she closed the door and settled in behind her desk. She pressed PLAY on her answering machine and began listening to messages—there were forty-seven. Every morning it was like that. Once she identified a person, she usually skipped the message, returning to it later. One message she listened to all the way through. It was from Chet Simmons, left at 10:21 last night. He *would* use her answering machine instead of her LiveCell. In his nervous apologetic voice he explained that he was still having trouble filling the orders for the electromagnetic boxes. Those damn black boxes. First the long wait for FCC approval, now their latest supplier raising the price every month. LiveCell had been forced to give up on the Mexican firm, and the one in Korea was about to—

A knock. "Come in," she said.

It was Luke with a mug of coffee. He set it down carefully on her desk, grunted when she thanked him, and left. She'd given up explaining she could get her own coffee. What she hadn't been able to tell him was that she would *prefer* to get her own coffee. She went back to work.

There was a message from Mary's secretary reminding her of the one-thirty meeting. The majority of calls were from unauthorized retailers insisting their orders be filled. On a few of the messages they sounded irate, and that pleased her. LiveCell was a direct-order-only business. By ordering online, by phone, or by mail, a customer received a phone based on when the order came in. Simple. Until a secondary market mushroomed that resold LiveCell phones. These vendors ordered large quantities of phones, then resold them for double the price. Since LiveCell orders were backlogged for months, many consumers paid the higher price rather than wait. It bothered Deirdre—*Like what greedy pricks these phony retailers were*—but Jay told her not to worry about it for the time being. "As long as people are talking on our phones, that's what matters," he'd said. She still tried to fill small orders before the really large ones even though it was against company policy. The last message on her machine was from Wendy. She didn't return the call.

As workers entered the factory and changed into their sterile gear, she checked the inventory of black boxes. They had only enough for less than a week of production. Something had to be done immediately. Should she call Jay and tell him? But he probably knew about the problem though who could tell with Chet Simmons—he was still so nervous around Jay. She decided to wait until the meeting.

Her day proceeded through its normal pattern: she checked with shipping to see how the new ecological shipping-carton insert was working out; she reviewed a bundle of invoices before sending them to Randy Dyer in financial; she answered a few questions from the lab techs; she forced herself to do Wendy's job and returned ten calls to unauthorized retailers, trying hard to be polite—*Like it's not your company, she reminded herself*. She attempted to reach Chet Simmons. Was he hiding?

Twice she almost called Wendy, and twice put the phone back on her desk. At noon she heard Luke kick-starting his big bike. It finally caught, reached the main road, shifted up through three gears, and the exhaust's bellow receded to silence. She thought of ordering out for a hot sandwich and chips, but she was trying to diet, so she reluctantly retrieved a yogurt from the fridge, added some fresh fruit, and ate outside on the back steps in the sun. As she finished her lunch she heard Luke return, and this prompted her to get ready for the meeting; he was always precisely on time. She went back inside, gathered her briefcase and headed for her wagon, figuring no matter what traffic was like it couldn't take her more than a half-hour to get to the Harcourt Building.

When she entered the elevator there, she was tempted to hit the fourth floor button and walk past her old reception desk, then take the stairs up to the boardroom. "Like what am I today? Miss Nos*talgia*," she said to herself and pressed six.

Jay was the only one in the boardroom, wearing one of his blue T-shirts again. Jay always in blue, Jimmy Hakken always in black, Mary liked silver—she wondered if she shouldn't appoint herself a color but had no clue what to choose.

"Hey, Deirdre," he said. "How are you?"

"I'm really great." When he asked the question she felt as if he really wanted to know. "Am I early?"

"A couple minutes."

The ugly red scar across his bicep made her wince. Though the wound was completely healed, some part of her still felt responsible. "Not much traffic today. You been outside? It's *so* beautiful."

"Not yet."

"You know, you really do work too much."

This slowed their conversation, and during the pause, other department heads arrived.

Mary arrived in the boardroom, her hair pulled back with a diamond clip, her face and neck radiant paleness. She greeted Jay and Deirdre. Duncan walked in next, no longer last as in the Wendell Alden days. He still wore a dark suit, but with an open collar on his dress shirt, no tie. Once a rumpled misfit among impeccably dressed men, now he was the only one in conservative clothes, an indication of how much things had changed. Mary had joked with Deirdre that there was no way Duncan wasn't going to get full use out of those expensive suits once he'd spent the money. Chet Simmons, also in a jacket, a sports coat similar to the one Deirdre had bought Jay, greeted no one and went straight to his seat. He looked a bit strange, and Mary wondered what was up with him. Randy Dyer, who had worn suits all his adult life, was in khakis and a wildly floral sport shirt. He stopped to chat with Mary, Jay, Deirdre, and Cliff Thompson. Eventually, they all took their places around the table. The crack where the glue joint was failing had lengthened by a few inches, and Clicksave's modern chrome chairs had been exchanged for some darkened oak ones. During the year, each person's seat choice had become an unspoken agreement developed over the five bimonthly meetings. It was when everyone was settled that Jimmy Hakken lumbered in. This was his first department heads meeting, required now that he was running the old factory.

He lifted his hand at the wrist to Jay and flicked his fingers horizontally in a kind of cutting motion, walked to the far end of the table, settled into an empty chair. He slumped back, his long legs awkwardly clamped under the rungs, the tattooed arms sticking out of a fringed black leather vest. Duncan turned his head away abruptly after a cursory glance. Mary figured any glimpse of Jimmy Hakken was too much for Duncan. She was amused by how much he detested him.

Jay opened the meeting in his usual way and welcomed Jimmy Hakken to the boardroom. Hakken nodded solemnly.

"It's been about a year since you joined me," said Jay. "I hope you're as satisfied with being here as I'm satisfied with each of you. We still have a lot of work to do, but LiveCell is making progress and that's what matters. As you see from the agenda, today each of you will update the rest of us about your department. Feel free to suggest changes, anything that concerns you, any problems you might have or foresee." Jay asked Randy Dyer, the CFO, to start.

Randy passed out copies of the financial report and went over each item carefully. LiveCell had sold around two million phones and generated over fifty million in net profits its first year. As he spoke, Duncan tapped quietly at his calculator. When he finished his report, Duncan's head came up, and his mouth twitched a little.

"By my estimation there's about three and a half million dollars unaccounted for."

There was a silence. Randy glanced at Jay, and Jay nodded vaguely.

"Some money has been moved to another account," Randy said.

"*Some* money?" said Duncan. "Three and a half million is *some money?*"

"Well . . ." he said, looking embarrassed.

"I asked him to do it," said Jay.

"You can't tell us what this is about?" said Duncan.

"No. Let's proceed—"

"Jay. Wait a minute, I think you owe us an explanation."

A long etched arm pointed at Duncan. "You heard the man. He said no."

Duncan rolled his eyes.

"Duncan," said Jay.

"What?"

"It was a charitable contribution."

"Oh yeah, which one?"

Jay hesitated. "Orphanages." A silence. "Can we move along now? . . . Cliff, are you ready?"

Cliff Thompson, head of investor relations, addressed the drop in the stock price. He explained that compared to the rest of the market, Live-Cell was holding and had only slipped marginally.

"I mean, we've gone from a low of eight cents to a high of twenty-seven and a half dollars a share in one year. The fact that we've eased back to the high nineteens recently is not a cause for alarm; instead we should be celebrating." He paused, then grinned. "I don't mean celebrating that we've eased back but celebrating that our stock is selling for a hundred and fifty times its former value. There, I think I have it right this time.

"What is interesting is that by my most recent calculations, institutional buyers make up only twenty-one percent of our investors, which is remarkably low. It used to be much higher. I think many of our new investors simply bought our phones, believed in them, and decided we were a company they wanted to support. Personally, I find that very gratifying."

"My boys are all in," said Jimmy Hakken, winking at him.

Cliff smiled back hesitantly. Mary figured that Deirdre Holly as a company director had probably been unusual enough for Cliff, but Jimmy Hakken? Cliff hadn't been the same since Jay had handed him the untried LiveCell phone nearly a year ago.

"I read in this article," said Deirdre, "that lots of lower-income people who have never even thought of being in the market or anything are investing in LiveCell. They're using the money they used to spend on lottery tickets."

"Where did you read that?" said Mary. "Was it online?"

"Just one of the small local papers. They had like a whole thing on it. I'll save it for you."

"Please do."

"Chet, you okay?" Jay said, studying him across the table.

He nodded vaguely.

"Would you care to go next?"

"Maybe if I could excuse myself for a second first?" He jerked to his feet and left the boardroom.

"What's with Chet?"

"He left a message for me at ten o'clock last night," said Deirdre. "I think he's like, not got the best ever news to report." She waited. "Don't you know about it?"

"How can I know if I don't know?"

Mary cut in. "I was hoping he'd talked to you, Jay. I guess he didn't."

"What's this all about?" said Jay.

"I'll go get him," said Cliff just as Chet returned. A pasty perspiring Chet. He stood by his chair and faced Jay.

"Mr. Chevalier, I'm sorry. I should have alerted you to this sooner. It was just that I thought I could resolve the problem in time, before today's meeting, but I simply can't. I don't understand how it went so wrong. If you so wish . . . I will tender my resignation as manager of purchasing."

"Chet, please, sit down. Maybe you could tell me what you're so upset about?"

He stood frozen. Then in a rush of words, "I simply can't get anyone to supply us with the sender-receiver any longer. Mr. Chevalier, it is simply inexplicable. First I had trouble with our Mexican supplier, as you know, then with our Korean supplier. As problems mounted with Korea, I started to investigate other firms. I shook hands on the deal with the Chinese only four weeks ago, and I truly believed our problems were behind us. I mean, we had *a deal*. Now they have declined to fill our orders, and I can't even get the principals on the phone. I've never been treated this way. You know what I went through trying to get them made here. The few companies that *could* fabricate them felt they were undermining their relationships with larger clients by supplying us. I did not see the possibility of this occurring in China. I still don't. I thought with the world economy the way it is, they would be delighted to have the work. This refusal we've just received from the last Asian manufacturer has completely floored me. I keep asking myself if it's my fault, if someone else could have done better, but believe me, sir, I tried."—he was near tears, and Mary wished she could think of something to say—"I understand that our phones are useless without the black boxes. Now in retrospect I realize I should have built up a larger inventory, but at the time I didn't want to tie up capital needlessly. I should have told you sooner. I just—"

"Chet, please. Sit down."

"Chevalier." It was Hakken.

Jay looked across at him.

"Fuck them all. My boys can make them. Get me the parts, we can put them together. They can't be that hard."

Jay ignored this and asked Chet, again, to please sit down. Finally, he did.

"LiveCell," said Jay, "is a young company without allies, and we have a product that is encroaching on the market share of some powerful corporations. I believe this is our difficulty with finding a supplier for the black boxes. Chet, please, from now on, come to me with these problems. Do not suffer like this on your own. We are in this together, and in the coming months things may get much more difficult. We need to stick together. We are a team. You are all here because I believe in you."

Mary noticed that Jimmy Hakken nodded at the end of each of Jay's sentences, his concentration such that he probably wasn't aware his head was moving.

"In the past month," said Jay, "I've had another offer for my share of LiveCell. I will not sell this company. Your jobs are secure, and no one will ever be fired when they are doing their best. And that means you, Chet."

Chet Simmons thanked him. He had four kids.

"There is nothing to thank me for. I know I demand a lot from all of you." A pause. "Don't worry about the black boxes."

"But Jay," said Deirdre, "I've only got enough boxes for like, less than one week of production. Then we're out of business."

"Same at my plant," said Jimmy Hakken.

"Duncan?" said Jay. "Have you done any snooping on this? I know how good you are at finding things out."

"You mean have I researched the unwillingness of these Asian manufactures to supply us?"

"Precisely."

"Actually, I have been online some since I knew Chet was experiencing problems."—Chet's head snapped around toward Duncan—"Jay, I believe your supposition is correct. I think in every case the companies have been offered more money not to produce the boxes for us."

Jay thanked him, and oddly enough he looked almost pleased.

He leaned back in his chair, placed his hands behind his neck, searched the ceiling. It reminded Mary of the first day, that endless lull when he seemed to be listening to the table wood. Today it seemed to be the ceiling that held the message.

"Mary," he said suddenly. "Set up a radio interview for me as soon as possible. Choose a program that we can trust, public radio please, and select a competent interviewer with a liberal bent. I am sure you would anyway, but this is important. I don't want to be censored."

She stared at Jay. An interview? Publicity? Even Jimmy Hakken exhibited a modicum of uncertainty.

Duncan broke the silence: "What are you going to say?"

"You'll have to tune in. Mary will tell you when."

"Do you think this interview will affect our stock price?" said Cliff Thompson.

Jay smiled. "Definitely."

"Which way?" said Duncan, the pitch of his voice revealing his emotion.

"Who knows."

"I think we need to know! . . . Jay?" He waited for an answer, his face turning red. "Jay? . . . This is ridiculous. You have to tell us. It's our money too."

"Drop it," said Jimmy Hakken.

Duncan swiveled violently in his chair. "I've had about enough out of you, you—"

Hakken calmly fixed his eyes on Duncan and said quietly, "Don't even go there."

"Duncan." It was Jay. "Let's have your report. I've made reservations for this evening at Dos Reales for everyone, and I don't want to have to carry anyone on a stretcher."

He's getting a sense of humor, she thought. And well timed, too. In a flash of insight, she saw how tense the year must have been for him, how much he'd agonized over the creation of LiveCell, and how as the company blossomed he was finally achieving success. This change in him excited her. Maybe it would lead to other changes in him? She couldn't help hoping.

Duncan shuffled his papers. He flipped open his notepad and started to read his report.

"As director of order operations," he said, "I've installed new software allowing for easier secure online purchasing. These improvements should precipitate a trend toward online buying and will allow us to reduce our staff of order takers by at least half."

Jay cut in. "Don't let anyone go yet."

Duncan, after a muted grumble, continued. "LiveCell must create an electronic customer-service answering system to facilitate a reduction of personnel in that area as well."

"We'll keep things as they are."

"But Jay, you haven't even looked at the figures. Look at the potential savings of my plan."

"When someone calls LiveCell, I want them to hear a human voice immediately."

Duncan swallowed and moved on. "This new secondary retail market is selling every phone they can get their hands on for two-hundred dollars and up. We have to price our phones accordingly. I mean, why not? The demand is certainly there and we can *double* our profits."

"I have to admit," said Deirdre, "This thing is really annoying me too. Can't we sue them or something?"

"I could check with legal," said Duncan, looking surprised that she was agreeing with him, "but I doubt there is any possibility of litigation. We don't have a contractual agreement with our purchasers, so they can do whatever they want with the phones once they own them."

"I just feel people should be able to get our phones at the best possible price. Like why assist these greedy . . . ? People are being cheated. They may not realize they can get our phones for like half the cost directly from us. And these huge orders force everyone else to wait for their phones."

"That hardly seems to be the point," said Duncan with a frown. "If we raise our phone price, we won't care who has them or sells them afterwards because the out-of-company profit margin will evaporate. No one is going to be able to resell a two-hundred-dollar phone for twice the money."

"Why have we reduced the price of our phones anyway?" said Cliff Thompson. "I've been wondering if it isn't one of the reasons our stock price has dipped slightly. It signals weakness to the Street."

Everyone looked to Jay. He rubbed his ear and glanced out the window. "I appreciate all your suggestions, but LiveCell is making a fair profit at our current price. It will stay where it is. As far as the outside retailers, we will limit all purchases to six phones once every year."

"But Jay," said Duncan, "that is absolutely ri—" He stopped.

Jay waited for him to continue, and when he didn't, he nodded to Mary.

Mary could see that Duncan was having difficulty containing himself. As she made her report, quickly updated now that Jay was willing to do an interview, she watched Duncan peripherally. Could his brain grasp Jay's reasoning? It was based on things only she knew, or things she assumed he'd told only to her. She wondered if Jay grasped Duncan's. Duncan's priorities were based purely on mercenary gain. Was that something Jay could comprehend?

As she continued with her report, she suggested that LiveCell reduce its advertising budget since the demand for the phones was so high. Jay agreed. She finished her report with the news that she'd managed to get LiveCell phones into a new movie with Mark Wahlberg. The actor had really taken to the phones. Everyone else was excited, but Jay disappointed her by asking who Mark Wahlberg was. Even when he finally said, "Oh, sure, *him*," she didn't think he had a clue. Where had he been all his life?

After Deirdre and Jimmy Hakken had given their factory reports—Hakken's of course rather terse—Jay looked around the table. "So, is there any other business?"

When he first took over the company, he'd told them if they had a grievance, any kind of issue, they should air it at the end of these meetings. "Get it out in the open so we can get rid of it."

Duncan spoke first: "*Miss* Holly. Perhaps you might inform us about your *assistant*, Wendy Smith?"—a sarcastic smirk. Mary knew that smirk. What was he up to?

"What do you want to know?" Deirdre said hesitantly.

"Maybe you could start by telling us her name?"

"What do you *mean*, tell you her name? You know her name."

"So you think Wendy Smith is her real name?" he said smugly.

"What are you talking about?"

"Just what I said—Is Wendy Smith her given name?"

"Where are you going with this, *Duncan*?" Her anger apparent.

"Will you just answer my question?"

"This is really dumb. I don't have to answer your questions. What are you, a prosecuting attorney?"

Everyone in the room studied her, waiting for her answer. She glanced at Jay as if hoping for support. There was none. Obviously everyone was concerned.

"No." She spit the word at Duncan.

"No, what?" he said.

"*No*, I don't think *Wendy Smith* is her real name."

"You don't?" he said without quite the same confidence. "Well, can you tell us her name then?"

"It's Jennifer Stoddard."

"How the hell did you find that out?"—his voice up an octave again.

"Like everyone has a *mother*."

"What's *that* supposed to mean?"

"Simple. She writes her mother and a piece of paper underneath picked up the imprint. She was careful, but when you live with someone they're bound to make a mistake eventually."

She turned to Jay, ignoring Duncan. "Wendy, or Jennifer, what*ever* you want to call her is working as a spy for someone. She's like, *very* eager to find out how our phones work. Anyway, I knew Wendy was after our secrets, but I'm all, what are you going to do for me? I'm just a dumb surfer chick who runs the factory, and they aren't paying me enough. I figured two could play the game and I doubted she would suspect me. So I've been pretending like I might be willing to sell the phone's secret— not that *I* know it—and she's real close to making me an offer. Like days. Then I'll know who's behind it." She paused, glared at Duncan. "I *so* wanted it to be a surprise."

There was a silence. Then Jay started to laugh. No one had heard him really laugh before and the sound was strange, but then Mary joined him and almost immediately, Deirdre, and soon everyone was laughing, even Jimmy Hakken, if what he was doing could be called laughing. All except Duncan. He just sat there looking bitter.

ELEVEN

Mary wanted to drive Jay to the radio station in her car, but he insisted on going alone in his scarred wreck. "That will certainly make an impression," she said to herself. In fact, she wasn't particularly concerned about how he got there as long as he was still willing to do the interview once he arrived; he wasn't exactly headed for the public radio station he'd requested. She had tried to convince him of a televised interview, sensing how well he would come across on TV and knowing there was no better form of exposure, but he'd insisted on radio, so radio it was. Her choice of station though. That was why she wanted to drive him.

Jay pulled up in front of the *KBAY* building, towing a long plume of blue smoke. Twice he compared the street address to the one on Mary's typed directions, then parked the Cutlass in one of the visitor's slots out front. He rammed shut the groaning door, his eyes bumping along the dented body. Maybe it was time to get something else after all? The car had barely passed the smog test when he'd first registered it in California, and with the impurities this thing was putting out, it could feed a million LiveCell phones for a year. He would talk to Mary about buying another car; that would please her.

In the lobby of the radio station, lurid oversized headshots of radio celebrities smirked from the walls. A large three-dimensional aqua-blue and silver THE BAY hung behind a young woman at the reception desk. She looked like a fashion model. He glanced around in confusion. Everything looked wrong. "I'm here for an interview, I think—Jay Chevalyer."

"*Doctor* Chevalier, oh my God—you're here," she said, her very white teeth surrounded by a violent lipstick.

"Jay is fine."

The smile widening.

"This isn't public radio, is it?" he said.

"Heavens *no*."—as if such an inference was unthinkable. "We're number one in the Bay Area."

"And this is where I'm to be interviewed?"

"Keith Radmond's doing it," she said as if that would explain everything. "You must listen to his show?"—surprise touching her voice by degrees as he remained blank. "*What Gets Heard*? The highest-rated talk show in central Cal?" Jay shook his head. "You really haven't heard of him?" She pouted for an instant, but brightened immediately. "I have two of your phones, you know. I just *love* them. Jay, they are *so* amazing. I saw that ad with the baby and I bought my first one." She paused. "You're not at all like I imagined you." The white smile again. "Let me ring Keith for you, he's really eager to meet you. Just one moment, please." As she spoke into the receiver, she kept smiling at him. "Keith, Doctor *Jay* Chevalier is out front."

In just moments Keith Radmond walked into the room and extended his arm. "Doctor Chevalier, this is *certainly* a pleasure and an honor, sir." His voice had the archetypical ingratiating cadence and confidence. The short, balding radio-show host obviously knew exactly what the interview could mean to him. Everyone seemed to know exactly what was going on except Jay. Radmond's goatee was carefully manicured, and what was left of his hair hung to the shoulders of a new designer shirt. They shook and Jay offered his first name again. "Jay? Great, super. Would you care for a coffee, a latté, or maybe a spring water?" Jay declined. "Okay then. Please, follow me and we'll get set up. We have about—" He glanced quickly at his wrist. "—seven minutes until show time."

When they entered the sound studio, a producer and technician, both positioned behind a large plate-glass window in an adjoining room, waved and smiled. Jay returned a nod of greeting. As soon as he was seated on one of the padded stools, another dazzling young woman fitted him with headphones and adjusted a microphone to a precise angle to his mouth. "So you don't pop your Ps," explained Keith Radmond.

They were each asked to speak a few words, and the tech behind the glass set the sound levels and gave them the thumbs up. Everything seemed ready.

"Keith?" said Jay.

"Yes Jay, what's up? Do you need to use the men's room? I should have asked you sooner. We don't actually have the time for that at the moment."

"I'm fine."

"Great, super." Keith watched the producer as he signaled through the window by forming a cupped C with his hand. "Thirty seconds," said Keith, his eyes returning to Jay.

"I was just wondering if you use a delay?"

"We have one—a six-second digital delay—but we rarely use it. If people swear, no big deal, we mostly just leave it, so there's nothing to worry about. You okay, all set?"

Jay nodded. Over the headphones he could hear the top-of-the-hour jingle. Then, with an emphatic downward hand motion, the producer pointed at Keith through the glass.

"Good afternoon and welcome," Keith said, exaggerating the low officious sing-song voice, "to a very special edition of *What Gets Heard* on *K-B-A-Y*, ninety-eight-point-five FM, where what *you* want to hear gets heard first. I'm your host, Keith *Rad*mond, and today I'm talking with Doctor Jay Chevalier, CEO of LiveCell and the inventor of a new cellular telephone that's taken the West Coast by storm. Jay—up until today you've avoided all press coverage. You've been called The Man of Mystery. What made you decide to talk to *What Gets Heard* today?"

"My advertising head—*Mary MacKensie*—set it up." He said it so Mary would get the message as she listened.

"Jay, I mean, why have you decided to break the long silence, why have you finally decided to be interviewed?"

"There's something I'd like people to know about our phones."

"We'll talk about your amazing phones in just a moment, but I'm sure our listeners are eager to hear all about you first. Today we want to remove the mask of mystery and get to the man underneath. Can you tell us a little bit about your background?"

"Background?" said Jay.

"You know, your childhood, growing up, who was Jay as a boy?"

Jay paused. "I'd prefer to discuss our phones."

"Jay, we will shortly. But right now I think our listeners would be fascinated to learn more about *you*, about the inner person that makes up the Man of Mystery."

Jay said nothing.

"Were you always interested in science?"

"Pretty much."

"Could you tell us about how and when you became interested in telecommunications?"

"Actually, I discovered the phone more or less by accident."

"By accident? That sounds remarkable. Please tell us the story."

"There is not that much to tell. I'd been genetically modifying organic structures in my lab when I realized that one of them had some unusual properties. I was originally working with cells that were intended to absorb air impurities, but that proved to be a bit of a dead end. I began concentrating on alternate problems, combining a variety of cells into my matrix, and eventually arrived at a mixture of cells that had certain unusual capabilities." He glanced over at the technician behind the large window.

"And these capabilities?"

"That became our phone."

"Can you tell us more than that?"

"I'm afraid some things need to remain secret."

Keith Radmond hesitated, but only for an instant.

"You are listening to *K-B-A-Y*, The *Bay*, ninety-eight-point-five. Call us at one eight-hundred the-*K*-Bay. Our guest this afternoon is Doctor *Jay* Chevalier. Jay, as an inventor, did you have any idea as to the magnitude of your invention at first? Did you realize that the phones would be so successful?"

"I thought they would be a good way for people to communicate."

"Can you elaborate on that a little?"

"They allow people to communicate in a new way."

"Tell me a little more about that."

"With the use of our phones some people's intuitive abilities seem to intensify over time, allowing people to communicate more fully. It doesn't happen with everyone." He reached up to readjust the headphones.

"That is simply awesome, Jay, just *super*. I've heard people say that, that they can almost sense what another person is feeling when they're on LiveCell phones. It's great to hear it from the phone's inventor. How do your phones do that, Jay?"

"It's within the nature of the communication."

"Can you elaborate?"

"Our phones are clear, the communication is precise, it allows people to concentrate on what is important."

"Yes, true, but how do the phones do that?"

"It's simply within their nature."

Keith hesitated again, but only fractionally.

"Jay, I was reading an article in the *Chronicle* on how telemarketers are complaining that they have a much higher failure rate with potential customers who are speaking on LiveCell phones. Some telemarketers are now determining what kind of phone they've called and are rejecting LiveCell users. There has even been some talk of a ban on your phones. How do you feel about that?"

"I don't concern myself. We attempt to manufacture the best product for the fairest price. We can't control people's response to our product."

Keith Radmond examined the computer screen in front of him and signaled his producer. "Jay, we're going to take a few calls now."

"Calls? What calls?"

"Many of our listeners are very eager to talk with you. As a matter of fact, our switchboard is receiving a record number of calls at the moment. You are a very popular man, Jay. Our first caller is Jesse from Santa Cruz. Jesse, you're on the air."

"Am I on?" she said.

There was a high-pitched quavering.

"Jesse, turn down your radio, please."

"My radio?"

"Yes, Jesse, the volume on your radio. Please turn it down."

The quavering stopped.

"Am I on the air?"

"Yes, Jesse, you're on the air."

"*Oh.* Hello Keith."

"Hello, Jesse."

"Doctor Chevalier?"

Jay nodded, rubbed his knee through his jeans, forcing himself calm. "He's right here. Go ahead Jesse."

"Doctor Chevalier, I just want to thank you for what you've done for me and my family. My daughter hadn't spoken to me for three years, which felt like forever. We had this bad fight because of this awful, awful boy she was seeing who was just no damn good, and I told her that—"

"Jesse, tell us about the phone, please," cut in Keith Radmond.

"*Oh*. Well, as I was saying, my daughter and I hadn't spoken for three years because of this awful boy, and then I got one of your phones because all the wonderful things people were saying about them. I liked it so much I sent one in the mail to my daughter as a present just praying, hey, you never know, right? And then I called her and I said hello dear, and she said Mom? and then we just listened to each other for a while saying nothing, and then we just started bawling. Both of us! Doctor, you're right in what you say. You feel other people on them phones and you feel what's in their hearts. I'm a believer. You have a wonderful phone and you brought our family back together and may God bless you."

Jay was silent and even more uncomfortable.

"Thank you, Jesse," said Keith. "I'm sure we're all happy you're reunited with your daughter. That *is* a lovely story, isn't it, Jay?"

"Jesse," he said.

"Yes, Doctor Chevalier."

"Jesse, I appreciate your kind words, but you have nothing to thank me for. I did not do anything for your family. You did it yourselves. Our phones allow only for the possibility of better communication, but it's you who must communicate."

"Okay, let's take another caller," said Keith Radmond. "Bob from Hillsborough, go ahead Bob."

"Jay, the name is Bob Reikhart, and I'd like to tell you a little story that might just happen to interest you." He chuckled in a self-satisfied way. "I was fly fishing with my nine-year-old son in Wyoming on the Snake River. We always have our LiveCell phone with us in case Mother needs to call; she worries of course." He chuckled again. "The old-fashioned cell phones just don't have the reception of a LiveCell phone, particularly out there in the wilderness. Somehow, while wading up the stream, my phone must have fallen out of my fishing vest. I had no idea where or when it fell out. Well, to make a long story short, my son Jamie found the phone. But not by looking. He swears to this day that he just knew where the phone was, as though the phone were calling to him. Now is that something or what?"

There was nothing for Jay to do but answer. "The same way our phones allow you to sense when you have a call, your son must have sensed the location of the dropped phone. He might have a psychic predisposition. If you empty yourself of all anxious desire to find something, you can sometimes simply know where it is."

"That's very interesting, Jay," said Keith Radmond. "Sounds a little like Eastern philosophy. Are you a doctor of that as well?"

"No. I've never studied philosophy."

"But you do have a doctorate in biochemistry from Harvard. Can you tell us a little about your time there?"

"I studied a lot."

"Can you tell us a little more?"

"There really isn't all that much more to tell."

Keith Radmond studied his screen and signaled his producer again. "Do you miss the East Coast? I understand you're originally from Maine."

"I think we all have feelings about where we were born. I miss the change of seasons. I remember the stillness sometimes in winter on a clear night. I miss that."

"Jay, we have another caller. Roger from Marin County, you're on the air."

"Doc Jay—I just want to know why your phones can't take messages?"

"They aren't programmed for that. They allow you to sense any unanswered calls, but they don't record messages."

"Ain't that like a big drawback?"

The producer signaled Keith Radmond again, this time with a raised rapidly circling finger.

"Yes, I suppose it is," said Jay, "but there are many devices capable of that. It's simply not what our phones are about."

"Well, I think it sucks and it's—"

"You're listening to *What Gets Heard* on *K-B-A-Y*, ninety-eight-point-five on your FM dial, and I'm Keith *Rad*mond, your host. Call me at one eight-hundred the-*K*-Bay and talk with The Man of Mystery, Doctor Jay Chevalier, CEO of LiveCell. We're going to take a sixty-second commercial break, please stay with us."

Keith pulled off his headphones and smiled at Jay.

"Jay, you're doing great. You seemed a little surprised about the callers. Didn't Mary tell you?"

"Not a word."

"I guess you don't know the format of the show."

"I'm afraid not."

"I would've called and briefed you, but Mary said she thought it would work best this way."

"Oh, definitely."

"Yeah, no doubt." Keith nodded in agreement. "You're doing great, super, really great. The continued mystery thing is super. At first I thought it was a little bumpy, but I'm digging the dynamics of it now. I like that you're going with your first name, feels right, opens up the folk hero bit, and we already have plenty of doctors on the air. The whole interview is working super—you're burning up the phones."

The producer held up the cupped-hand signal.

"At some point," said Jay, "I would like to present something about our phones. It's really why I'm here."

"Let's save it for the end of the half-hour if that's okay. How long will it take?"

"Just a few minutes."

"Okay, I'll leave enough time."

They went back on the air and continued to take callers. There were people raving about the effect the phones had on their lives, there were calls about the stock price, people wanting to know how the phones worked, one call from someone who had lost her LiveCell phone and wanted to know if Jamie, the nine-year-old, could find it for her.

Finally, Keith Radmond said, "Jay, we only have a few minutes left. I understand there's something special you'd like to share with our audience? You are hearing it here, live, on *What Gets Heard*, K-B-A-Y, where what *you* want to hear gets heard first. Jay?"

Jay waited for an instant. He imagined Mary and everyone at Live-Cell listening to him, wondering nervously what he was going to tell the world. He hadn't given much to Keith Radmond. He hadn't intended to until now.

"On every LiveCell phone there is a small black metal box pressed into the end. This box allows our phones to communicate with all conventional telephone systems. As all LiveCell owners know, it requires a battery and must be recharged, same as any other cell phone. The box makes our phones similar to all other telephones, similar to the old technology. LiveCell phones are actually more radically different than that." He paused, feeling annoyed that his heart was racing involuntarily. He so wanted to say this intelligently. He had waited a long time for this moment.

"Our phones can be modified so they become the future. I want to let all LiveCell owners know, that if they wish, they can remove the black boxes simply by pulling the pronged end out of the rest of their phone.

The two holes will heal rapidly. Once you do this, you will be able to communicate with any other LiveCell phone anywhere in the world perfectly, and you will have the same LiveCell quality of communication. However, you will only be able to communicate with LiveCell phones. If you wish to call a conventional phone, simply reattach the black box." He paused again.

"A naked LiveCell allows you a few benefits. First, it will no longer be necessary to charge up your phone as it won't require a battery to work. Second—your calls will be completely safe. Without the black boxes, LiveCell phones cannot be bugged, no one can ever listen in on any of your conversations again. Third—all your calls will be absolutely free no matter the distance you call or the length of time you spend communicating. No more phone bills with a LiveCell . . ."

It was early afternoon when Jay got back to the Harcourt Building. Manuel turned off some salsa music and came out from behind the front desk.

"Jay! Say it is really true."

"What's that, Manuel?"

"I can call my mother and sisters in Mexico City and talk as long as we want and it will be free, no charge at all?"

"If they have a LiveCell phone."

"I'm going to kiss you!"

Jay grimaced and Manuel laughed.

"Okay, no kiss if you insist. But I'm going to send them one tomorrow. I can't believe this, it's just *too* fantastic. You know how much money I'm going to save? People are going to *love* you."

"Not everyone."

Manuel thought a second. "I guess you have a point—not everyone. You're going to piss off Ma Bell and her sisters very very much."

Mary was waiting with the others when Jay reached the sixth floor. Everyone clapped as he got off the elevator, and she was certain he blushed. He really *was* changing. She was so proud of him her throat tightened and at first she couldn't say anything. After everyone was finished congratulating him and he'd answered their questions, she was finally alone with him in his office, the two of them standing near his desk. He seemed riveted by the Ryder image on the wall; then he turned to face her, scowling. With each second, her elation diminished by another degree.

"What is it, Jay? What's wrong?"

"That was hardly a public radio station."

"I guess it wasn't. The Bay is the most—"

"Yes, believe me, I know. *K-B-A-Y*, the *Bay*, where *you* hear what *you* want to hear," he imitated Keith Radmond.

"Jay, the ratings were fantastic. I just got off the phone with them. And I haven't even told you the best news yet. I asked everyone to keep it a surprise."

"Well, I have a surprise for you."

"You do?"

He was still frowning and her stomach clamped.

"You're fired," he said.

Her mouth opened as if she'd been slapped.

"Mary, I'm just teasing you," he said immediately. She hung her head. "Please, don't look so upset. I'm not good at teasing. I didn't realize . . ." She tried to recover. "Mary, please. Don't cry—please. I'm so sorry."

She lifted her face. "You're not mad at me?"

"Of course not."

"I'm not fired?"

"Of course not."

She embraced him. The first time. Fully. His body stiffened, her tears against his neck. She felt him slowly relax as she held him, and gradually his arms came around her, one hand rubbing the small of her back. She breathed in his smell and liked it. After perhaps a few minutes, he took hold of her shoulders and moved her away.

"Shall we go out for sushi tonight?" he said. "I was going to invite everyone out to eat, but maybe you prefer we go alone."

"I would love to." She wiped her eyes. "I'm sorry I got so emotional. I'm not usually like this. I guess my New England ancestry deserted me."

"I shouldn't have teased you."

"Was doing the interview so terrible? It sounded so good. It really did."

"I expected a more sedate atmosphere. All these people called in. It was embarrassing. Why didn't you warn me?"

"Would you have gone?"

He thought a moment. "I suppose not."

"See! You wanted exposure. This was the best exposure I could get you outside of television. I know Keith Radmond seems a little commercial, but you have to admit he did a great job. I knew he would."

"We needed to get used to each other. Though you should have seen his face when I made my announcement."

"The only time I've heard dead air on his show."

"He looked at his producer and signaled a cut-off-his-head sign with a question mark drawn in the air."

"He did that?"

"His producer shook his head, and you heard the rest."

"I'm surprised Keith did that. What a wimp. Or maybe he owns a boatload of AT&T stock. I would have killed him if they'd cut you off. Maybe then you *would* have fired me."

"I would never fire you."

They looked at each other for a moment.

"Can I tell you my news now?" she said.

He nodded.

"Our stock went up four dollars a share and was still rising at the close. Cliff thinks it may go over thirty dollars a share by the end of the week. There was record volume in that half-hour after your announcement." She searched his face. "Aren't you pleased?"

"I'm pleased. Now Manuel can call his mother for free."

"You really are strange, you know that?" She leaned over and kissed him on the cheek. She wanted to tell him something else. It was still so difficult to get close or be intimate.

"Shall we leave early today?" he said. "Go see if Sammy approves of my new career as a radio celebrity? Then we can go for sushi."

"Yes, let's."

They paused, still a little awkward with each other.

Jay broke the silence: "I don't remember seeing Duncan when I came in—"

"Oh. I forgot to tell you. You better go and talk to him."

"Why, what's up?"

"He did something stupid, and he's very angry. *Very.* I've never seen him like this."

"What did he do?"

"Maybe he should tell you."

"Tell me."

"Well . . . he sold all of his LiveCell stock this morning."

TWELVE

Friday morning of the same week that Jay made his radio announcement, Mary left a note for her house cleaner: *Dear Trisha, I have company coming this evening. Please wash the ocean-side windows and check the wine glasses for spots.* She realized it was a silly request as soon as she was in her car. Trisha always did a fine job on the glasses, and Jay probably wouldn't notice the windows anyway. For a moment she considered going back and tearing up the note.

On her way home from work she picked up two bottles of very expensive champagne, and again she wondered if she wasn't being foolish. But what was more seductive than good champagne? At least the ceviche, which she'd prepared the night before, he would enjoy since he liked sushi. She wanted the evening to be special; there was so much to celebrate.

As Cliff Thompson had predicted, LiveCell's stock price accelerated throughout the first week and passed thirty dollars a share like a Porsche around a hay wagon. LiveCell now sold two versions of their phone—with and without the black box, the plain one fifteen dollars less. Though the naked phone could only communicate with other LiveCell phones, almost everyone ordered this version. Who wanted to pay for phone service when it could be had for free? The night after the interview, Mary watched the news, and the story of the free telephone crossed the nation like a cheer. Two days later the media attention disappeared without explanation. This worried her, and she wasn't sure what she could do about it.

But the influx of phone inquiries was staggering, and within less than a week LiveCell was swamped, then deeply submerged with orders. To ease the demand, Jimmy Hakken suggested he run his crew around the clock in eight-hour shifts, and Jay had to agree, stipulating that the extra work load only last a few months until they were caught up. He also explained to Hakken that he required ten minutes alone with each batch of newly matured phones, which occasionally was as often as three times a day. Hakken never raised an eyebrow: he never questioned a Chevalier decree. Deirdre ran two shifts yet produced almost double Hakken's output because of her factory's extra capacity. Jay worked constantly, administrating the company, infusing phones at both factories, fending off reporters. Yet even in his exhaustion, Mary had never seen him so content.

Now as she waited for him to arrive, she kept impatiently walking to the window to check for his car. Finally, at the end of her road there was a drift of blue smoke, and the Cutlass thumped up her driveway. She went down the stone steps to greet him.

"You finally made it," she said.

"Sorry I'm a little late."

"I mean, you finally made it *here*, to visit me." She gestured for him to come in, feeling slightly awkward, excited to be alone with him again.

He followed her into the house, and ignoring the expensive fawn-gray interior she was so proud of, he headed immediately for the floor to ceiling windows. He looked out across the water for a moment as she waited; then he reached into his sports coat pocket.

"I brought you something." He held out a small unwrapped pale-gray box on the flat of his palm.

She lifted it from his hand. "Shall I open it now? Or would you like something to drink first?"

"As you wish."

She studied his expression. "I'll open it." She delicately lifted the lid, her heart pounding more than she would have liked. She unwrapped the blue tissue paper. When she saw the face she knew what it was.

"Your watch."

"Swatch mailed me an early prototype."

The three colors of orbiting light radiated just on the surface of the crystal.

"Jay, it's beautiful."

"I think they're doing an okay job. You said you wanted one."

"It's mine?"

"Of course."

She leaned over and kissed him on the cheek. She placed the watch on her wrist, buckled the muted-silver band, held out her arm to admire it, viewing it from various distances. "It's even more incredible than I thought it would be. You really are something." She continued studying it, thrilled when the color mixed to neutrality for an instant as the dots of light met. "Would you like some champagne? I don't even know if you like it, but I bought two special bottles."

"I'm not sure I've ever had good champagne. You are my guide in these things."

She went to open one, pleased to be his guide in something. She returned with tall flutes, handed him one, the bubbles rising madly. "How about a toast?" she said. "To LiveCell."

They drank. "It's very good," he said. "You keep introducing me to new things."

They walked out through French doors onto the large crescent-shaped redwood deck and settled into two teak Adirondack chairs angled toward the sea. The gilded rim of evening was just beginning to show as a mid-September breeze lifted off the water, blunting the warmth of the sun. Jay still removed his jacket and tossed it over a vacant chair.

"Your arm looks much better."

He glanced at the scar on his bicep and rubbed it slowly.

"Do you ever get cold?" she said.

"What do you mean?"

"You always wear just a T-shirt, no matter how cold it is."

"Where I grew up we didn't have coats, just big wool shirts. I guess people donated more shirts than coats, so we would just keep piling on the shirts the colder it got outside. If it was anything above the mid-fifties we wore T-shirts. I got used to dressing that way."

"Do you ever buy anything for yourself? Except those toy trains."

"How about a car? I was going to ask you what to get."

"You're going to buy a new car?"

"The Cutlass is burning oil. It won't pass the emissions test again without major work, and the body's not that great, so I need something else."

"Let's go tomorrow," she said eagerly. "I'll help you find the perfect car."

"Not new though, and nothing fancy."

"Jay, why *not*? Do you realize how much you're worth? You could buy anything you wanted. We could get you something really nice. A Ferrari maybe. I've always wanted to test-drive a Ferrari. Let's." Her eyes pleaded with him.

"I'd rather have an old car. A fancy new car would make me uncomfortable. Besides, I like bench seats. I bet Ferraris don't have bench seats."

"Do you only like old stuff?"

"I like things people have touched, with their marks on them. They absorb joy and pain and a sense of time, or at least a sense of time passing. And if they haven't been discarded over the years, there must be one good thing about them. Maybe they develop a kind of integrity for me because they've survived."

"You still don't have to drive the worst car in California."

He smiled, and she shivered a little. She excused herself and went inside the house, returning in a button-down cardigan, carrying a silver bucket with the champagne bottle sticking out of it.

"Are you hungry?" she said, filling their glasses.

He shook his head, examining the champagne against the light of the sky, the thin lines of bubbles rising. "I'm surprised I like this wine so much. You know, I think I prefer drinks with carbonation."

"Didn't you drink in college?"

"I just studied."

She took a long sip. She knew what that was like, but she didn't want to interrupt when he might talk about himself.

"Remember when I told you about my grandfather?" he said.

She nodded.

"What I didn't tell you is that he made his own liquor. In the two years I was with him I became quite a drunk."

"*You?*" she said.

He nodded.

"No way."

"*Way*," he said and smiled a little. "We drank every day. It was a wonderful couple years."

She never knew when he was going to surprise her. "Is he still alive?"

"He died a few months after I left him. Sometimes I think he was waiting for me to come to him before he died. He taught me so many things I needed to know." His eyes went out to the horizon. She followed his glance. The gradual shifting tones of sunset had intensified over the darkening water. He took a long sip of wine, examined the horizon again. "I think we might be in for quite a storm."

"I doubt it. It would be very unusual for this time of year." She paused. "Jay—" He turned to face her.

"Will you tell me how the phones really work?"

"You've already sensed that I want you to know." He upended his drink and nodded slowly, set the glass on the arm of the chair. "This wine is wonderful. Nice to drink it outside like this with the air so fresh and clean."

She noticed again how much he enjoyed certain things, how he paid careful attention to everything around him. He would be a good lover, probably a great lover. She filled their glasses, emptying the bottle, thought of getting another but wanted to hear what he was going to tell her. Maybe champagne was the secret to loosening him up. She hoped so. He rubbed his scar again absentmindedly, glanced out at the ocean and began talking.

"The phones can communicate with each other because their final matrix is identical, because they are all cloned from the same cells, all modified by the same viral DNA."—*his*, she couldn't help but remind herself—"Just as two similar human brains can sometimes know what the other is thinking, like identical twins for instance, LiveCells, being exactly the same, have complete synergy."

His eyes came back to her. "This sameness is a rare occurrence in nature, and LiveCells don't have chromosomes that alter genetic makeup over time—they remain identical. This makes them unique, like nothing else in nature. When two LiveCells communicate with the black boxes installed, the boxes send the call and log it for billing, but, as you now know, they aren't required."—*maybe that's why Duncan was so confused*— "I wanted to keep that secret, until LiveCell gained more momentum. When LiveCell calls are being sent over conventional pathways, the black boxes translate the brain waves into digital code to be sent as radio waves. I had hoped to leave the black boxes in longer, but my hand was forced." He took a slow sip. "I knew once the phone was free and the calls untraceable, real trouble would start. Now you understand why I couldn't patent the phone, besides the obvious fact that DuPont would've sued for the intellectual property. If certain people learn how the phone works, LiveCell will be simple to destroy."

He searched her face as he took another sip. She remained quiet, hiding her emotion.

"So two human brains can hear each other talk through the Live-Cells, and depending on the natural intuitiveness of the user, sometimes more. As the human brain forms low-frequency wave-code, as it thinks words, the LiveCell absorbs the code over the short distance we hold the phones from our brains, and instantly the other person's LiveCell knows the coding, and that user's brain absorbs the words through their Live-Cell. At first I was worried that LiveCells wouldn't be able to differentiate specific users, but through my program infusion they can. The unusual part is really in the programming." He paused, as if deciding how to tell her.

"Mary, I believe there's a continuum of energy. Anyone who really wants to can access this energy in varying degrees. It allows one to perform and create beyond conscious ability, to understand things outside of conscious thought, and it allows one to simply know things; it's like the clarity we sometimes get in pure nature. You and Kelly can both access it, I know that. Others can, even if they're not sure that's what they're doing. There is so little that we really understand about the human brain."

She hugged her chest, felt the cold air on her face, her hair unruly in the increasing wind.

"I program the phones by accessing this energy. My brain becomes a conduit from this vast intelligence into the LiveCells. When I'm infusing, the closest phone responds and then the energy spreads rapidly through the other phones. You've seen it, but it happens so quickly it seems as if they all infuse at once.

"I think much of our creativity or wisdom comes from this same source. Those years with my grandfather changed me. Without realizing it at first, my intuitive abilities, or my abilities to access this energy, kept increasing. It guided me in my eight years at the forgotten laboratory."

She still said nothing. Her mind was a confusion of conflicting thoughts and emotions, not to mention champagne. He watched her now expectantly, as if he needed her to say something, to respond to what he'd told her. He reached—she thought almost nervously—and picked up his glass from the teak arm, was about to take a sip when he noticed it was empty.

"Shall we open the second bottle?" she said.

"That's up to you."

"Let's." She reached for the empty bottle. She wanted to stand up and do something. *Anything.* She really needed another drink. She was realizing more and more that LiveCell wasn't just another phone company, and Jay certainly wasn't just another CEO.

"Can I get it for you?" he said.

She shook her head. "I'll be right back." She watched him from the French door, his head leaning against the slats of the Adirondack chair, above him infinite chaos, the minute points of colored light that make up an evening sky.

She retrieved the wine and handed him the bottle. He screwed it down into the ice of the bucket.

"Jay, I think I'm getting overwhelmed by all this. I mean, you definitely told me all along what LiveCell was up to; I guess I just didn't realize the magnitude. This is all much more involved and complicated. It's giving me a very odd feeling."

He reached down for the fresh bottle. His hands made quick work of the neck-foil, and after a moment's study he unwound the wire stay to the cork. He looked at her. "I've never opened a bottle of champagne."

All she had to do was imagine opening it, and there was a delicate *pfft.* She'd chosen the brand simply because out of all the expensive bottles in the wine shop, the silver of the neck-foil was her lucky color.

He poured. "I have a toast." He lifted his. "To you. We could never have accomplished what we've done, without you." He leaned toward her, stretched out his arm, and they touched glasses.

She wasn't sure if she believed him—he still acted as if he didn't need anyone. But maybe he did need her?

He'd been correct about the storm. The summit of color at the horizon was past, the advancing clouds a dark blind slowly and methodically pulled shut. They listened to the call of a last mockingbird as it found a roost for the night, the only voice besides the wind and the waves, the rumble of breakers brought to them more and more fiercely as the storm approached.

"I have a favor to ask you," he said. "More than just a favor."

She waited, conscious of her own breathing. *She knew there was something else!*

"It's crucial to what I'm trying to do."

"Tell me."

"I want you to learn how to infuse the phones."

"*Me?*"

"Yes."

"Jay, that's crazy. How could *I* learn to infuse the phones? You think I can simply connect to this continuum thing?"

"Mary, I shouldn't tell you this. And I don't want you to worry, but I've had a death threat. It's most likely a prank, but it made me realize that as things now stand, if they kill me, LiveCell will end. I need someone to carry on if I'm not here."

It was then that the storm reached them from out of the blackness—first a wave of sweet ozone, then large raindrops striking the deck with careless fury. She just sat there, feeling even more scared. Neither moved. Eventually Jay drained his glass and stood, gathered his jacket and the bucket.

"Shall we?" he said.

Once they were inside sitting at the dining room table, with only a low table lamp on, the storm lashing the west-facing windows, he filled their glasses again.

"This is so odd, this storm. It never rains this time of year." She tried to see out through the streaming glass. Just saying something simple made her feel better.

"You're wet."

"I don't mind." She took off her sweater, draping it over the back of a chair. She combed her hair behind her ears with her hands. The rain had soaked the front of her blouse and her bra straps were visible under the dark-pink linen. She could feel the wet material against her breasts, against her nipples. She heard the heat in the house come on.

"Do you have any idea who the death threat is from?"

"Does it matter? When they figure out what I'm up to, that their imperium might be in jeopardy because people's consciousness is changing—you know they're going to have to stop me."

She nodded. The anxiety she'd been feeling on and off for months was clear now. A violent gust drove a sheet of rain against the window and she started.

"Maybe I shouldn't have told you all this," he said. "I thought if you understood, it would help you find what you need to infuse the phones."

"You really think I could infuse the phones?"

"You once asked me why I wanted you to work for me. I always had the gut feeling, ever since Kelly told me about you, that you were the one who could do it."

"You're a very unusual person with abilities others don't have. I'm just ordinary."

"You know that's not true."

"Jay, I'm not sure I understand all this. I don't know what to say."

"You don't have to say anything. Let's not worry about it now. Let's drink our wine."

She sensed that he was embarrassed, that he felt he'd revealed too much, been too vulnerable for a moment. He was beginning to withdraw again. She got out of her chair, walked behind him, put her hands on his shoulders, his muscles reacting to her touch. She wanted to slide her fingers over his damp chest. Did he want her to? All these months and she still didn't know. If only he would give her an indication, any kind of a sign about how he felt. She waited. Then her hands took on a will of their own, the champagne guiding her, her emotion guiding her, and she began to massage his arms, the lean dense muscle under her touch. It made her feel calmer immediately. He turned his body toward her, rose out of the chair.

"Mary!" But as he started to say more, she brought her hand to his lips. Her mouth followed her hand, and with her heels lifting off the floor a little, she kissed him, his mouth at first unyielding, then beginning to open, her tongue now tracing the inside of his lips in a slow circular pattern, the wet tip against his teeth. She felt him shudder, a spasm that ran through his entire body; felt him harden against her center as she clutched him tighter, her hands working across his back. She was getting very excited, and feeling more daring, slid her hand lower to his front, rubbing him through his jeans.

And he pulled away.

Even in the dim light his eyes looked frightened. She had never seen him like this, and she couldn't move. He seemed about to speak, but suddenly his body brushed past her. She still didn't move, her heart hammering in her chest. She heard the door open and click shut, the storm louder for that instant. Heard his car start. Heard him turn in the driveway. Listened until there was only rain lashing the windows.

She walked into the kitchen and opened the fridge door. She lifted out the plate with the thinly sliced translucent snapper carefully arranged in a circle on the ivory ceramic with tomatoes, peppers, and olives in the center. She forced herself not to remember what she'd been thinking about him as she prepared the fish. She carried it into the dining room and set it gently on the table as if she were serving him. About to return for a fork and a clean plate, she saw his jacket still hanging over one of the chair backs. She sat down next to it and almost reached for it. Instead, her left hand moved to her face; her thumb and forefinger gripped the bridge of her nose as her eyelids squeezed tight to the point of pain.

THIRTEEN

Telecommunication stocks had been down before Jay Chevalier's announcement of free phone service, but in the months after, they began to plummet, and many companies were going bankrupt. There was even speculation that e-mail and the post office would be severely affected. It was conceivable that in the near future all verbal personal and business communication would take place over LiveCell phones. Most people simply preferred it. Jay Chevalier refused another buyout offer. Those who had tendered this—as they thought of it—*final* offer, were stunned and angered that he wouldn't sell the company at any price, that he would not listen to reason.

Two weeks after their unfortunate evening, Jay had asked Mary again if she would attempt the phone infusion. She'd turned him down, telling him he was wrong about her, she wasn't capable of something like that. Hoping more time would heal the rift, he'd waited and tried once more to convince her. She'd flatly refused. Jay continued working as if none of it mattered, but he wasn't the same person he'd been two months ago.

"Mary?"

"Hey Deirdre, what's up? Still at the factory?"

"I guess you're working late too. How's it going over there?"

"You mean besides this FDA thing?"

"What *fucks* they are. I couldn't believe it when I heard. *Headaches?*

Nightmares? Come on. That is *so* lame. I mean, we've been using these phones constantly for way over a year now. Do we have headaches? No. Like *hello*! I mean—*buzzer*!"

"It's ridiculous, but we still have to deal with it. I just wish the media hadn't turned so against us. That makes it worse."

"I can't believe these people coming up with the complaints, and the FDA buying it, or pretending to buy it. First it was cell phones, now they're fine and it's us. Like, check the bank accounts of those complaining."

"Duncan has."

"Really?"

"Almost every one of them he was able to check . . ."

"Can't we use that?"

"Legal says it's only circumstantial proof; all were cash deposits."

"How is Duncan anyway?" said Deirdre.

"He's still depressed he sold his stock. He gets more and more upset about it, calculating how much he's lost—not made is more like it—he says *lost*. Almost every day he says he's going to buy in again, but he doesn't. He should have bought back in after he first sold. Now the stock is so high I'd be worried about buying it, especially with this FDA thing hanging over our heads. That's already affected our stock price a little, and the press is probably just revving up. I'm sure it'll only get worse. The media thrives on nailing us. Somebody out there hates LiveCell, and they must have a lot of power." She paused. "Anything from Wendy Smith?"

"Nothing since she disappeared. But you know, I think someone tipped her off. I mean, we were *that* close to a deal, and then she's just gone, no trace. It didn't make any sense. You know, after I revealed her real name at the meeting, you'd think Duncan would've found something out about her like he can, but nothing."

"When phone calls were still traceable, Duncan told me he'd found that Wendy'd made two calls to Alden Stone Associates. Then a few days after Wendy disappeared and I asked him about it, he denied it."

"*Too* weird. You think Wendell Alden is after us?"

"I think it's the father and his connections. I'm not sure how much Wendell has to do with it, but the father has connections everywhere. He's in the Republican inner circle, and the corporate inner circle. They *all* have every reason to hate us."

"Did you tell Jay?" said Deirdre. Mary didn't need to answer. "And you got the usual? Figures. He can really make you so mad sometimes." A pause. "There's something about Duncan that's been bugging me. He's changed and something about him isn't right. You know what Jimmy Hakken calls him? . . . The donut."

They both giggled for a moment.

"I feel the same way," said Mary.

"You do? Really?"

"Something about him *isn't* right, but Jay insists he's okay, so what can we do? Does he try to get information out of you?" A short pause. "He's obsessed with figuring out how the phones work."

"You know, don't you?"

"Did Jay tell you I knew?"

"I think we're the only ones who know. Don't you love talking on these phones? You can say whatever you want." She hesitated. "I can't be in there when he infuses. I've tried it a bunch of times, but it like really freaks me out. I feel so weird. He tells me it's because I fight against it, but I can't help it I guess. Did he tell you about the first time?"

Mary didn't answer. *So*, he's been trying it with Deirdre. This upset her though she realized she wasn't being fair. It wasn't as if they were having sex.

"His heart stopped," said Deirdre. "I had to like give him CPR."

"*His* heart stopped?"

"It was awful. I thought he'd died. Like forever."

They were silent for a moment. She wondered why *he* hadn't told her any of this.

"Do you know Luke Delamar?" said Deirdre.

"I don't think so."

"He's one of Jimmy's original gang members, like was his lieutenant or something, you know how they have all those Army positions. Jimmy insisted I take him for security. I just can't get a read on him, so I thought you might have an idea about it. He never talks, I mean like, *not at all*, and he stares at me so strange I get shivers."

"What's he look like?"

"Big. Really big, with long black hair and beard. Rides an old Harley."

"Oh, yeah, I've seen him. He *is* scary."

"I just don't know what to do about him."

"Have you asked Jay?"

"You know how Jay is about that kind of stuff, the weirder they are the more he seems to like them, and I can't bother him with things that are my responsibility."

"You can't tell Jay this either, but there's something I need to tell you," said Mary.

"What?"

"I don't know if I should tell you. I don't want you to be frightened."

"*Please*, tell me."

"My place has been gone through, all my stuff. I know someone has been in my house."

"*No way.* Are you sure?"

"As sure as I can be. At first I thought it might be Trisha, my cleaning lady, but when I asked her I could tell it wasn't her."

"That is *so* creepy. Who do you think it was? What do you think they were looking for?"

"So it hasn't happened to you?"

"I'm pretty sure not. I'll be way more alert."

"Now every time I go home at night I wonder if someone's waiting for me."

"How about new locks, or a security system?"

"I did the locks already, and I guess I'll put in a security system. Though by the time the cops . . . I wanted privacy, living out there, but now I wish I had some close neighbors."

"You want to stay with me for a while? I got plenty of room with Wendy gone."

"I'll be okay."

"You sure? It would be fun."

A pause.

"Hey, you eaten?" said Deirdre.

"Not yet."

"Dos Reales in half an hour?"

"Give me forty-five, I have a few things to finish up."

"Cool," and they ended the call.

Deirdre was relieved Jay had insisted her factory go back to one shift. After two months of doubles everyone was exhausted; she didn't know how Jimmy Hakken's crew had managed the triple shifts; those gang guys really were tough. Neither factory was meeting demand anyway, even at a combined output of fifty-thousand phones a day. Jay couldn't keep infusing phones at the rate he was—even he had limitations.

She locked both the inner and outer doors and walked across the empty parking lot to her station wagon. No sky tonight, just a cold swirling November fog, the two parking-lot lights wreathed in hazy incandescence.

When she arrived at Dos Reales she had to circle a few minutes to find a place to park in the overfull lot. Then she waited outside by the entrance, listening for the Porsche. She'd already called Ricky, so she wasn't concerned about getting a table. Soon there was a flash of silver and Mary pulled in, one smooth line to the only empty spot—just vacated, right in front. *Such style.* It made her feel awkward and gawky. Silver must be Mary's color, again realizing her lack of one. They hugged each other—Deirdre held it a little longer than necessary—and they entered the restaurant.

"It's strange being here without Jay," said Deirdre, once they'd been seated in a corner booth.

"I've never seen it so crowded." Mary looked around. "This place is getting very popular."

"Yeah, almost *too* popular, but Ricky still takes really good care of us. He treats Jay like a big celebrity now, and Jay is so uncomfortable about it, it's like *way* funny."

"Jay uncomfortable?"

"Absolutely. He can't stand being fussed over. He was in and out of the factory quick tonight; he seemed preoccupied. There's like, a lot of pressure on him." She leaned closer and lowered her voice. "The really weird thing to me is that Jay can't sell the company anyway, because without him to infuse the phones . . . There must be all these tech geeks trying like crazy to figure out how the phones work."

"He thinks I can do it."

"What?"

For a moment, Mary glanced away. "He thinks I can learn to infuse the phones."

"No way!" She said it louder than she expected and told herself to calm down. Being alone with Mary excited her more than she liked to admit.

"I know I can't do it. I told him I don't even want to try."

Like, why not? she thought. Like what would be cooler than that?

"He wants to run this experiment," said Mary, "and he wants you to be there."

"What kind of experiment?"

"I'm supposed to be at the factory, and Jay would infuse from his office through two LiveCell phones—his and mine. He says he wants you there in case something goes wrong. After what you told me about these severe reactions, I finally understand why he's concerned."

"Are you going to do it?"

"I don't think so. Don't tell him this, but I actually used to *love* being there when he infused. But I can't handle it anymore."

Deirdre studied her face. "Mary, can I ask you a personal question?"

The waiter stopped them, placing fresh-made tortilla chips and salsa on the table, apologized for keeping them waiting and asked if they wanted a cocktail. Deirdre ordered a vodka rocks and Mary a beer. They decided to share appetizers.

As the waiter left, Mary said, "You want to ask about me and Jay, but I can't talk about it." She looked away.

Deirdre reached over and touched her hand. "I'm sorry; I shouldn't have asked. I just know something has changed between you two—like way icy."

Mary continued to look out at the restaurant; then the stunning gray eyes found Deirdre's again.

"Seriously, it's like Antarctica," said Deirdre, trying to lighten things. "He told me something a few weeks ago. He said that when we really love someone, it's difficult for us to understand if our love isn't returned with the same intensity that we give. We believe all we have to do is love that person more, like more intensely, and eventually they'll love us the same way too."

"He told you that?"

"I kind of think he told me so I'd tell you."

"I wonder if he's ever been in love. He's such a loner. I keep wondering if he's ever truly loved anyone. Maybe he extracted too much of his damn *pineal* gland."

Now Deirdre knew there was something really wrong. Worse than she'd thought. "You know, I asked him that, about the loving somebody thing. He wouldn't answer."

Mary didn't respond.

"I guess you know me though, Miss Persistent."

Mary still said nothing.

"Okay, okay. He said—'For lack of a better word, God.'"

"*God?*"

"But when I asked him if he was like religious, he said not at all. He went into this whole weird thing about nature being God, and about this continuum of energy, about accessing this energy and understanding that there are things like more important than your personal desires and everything."

The drinks and appetizers arrived and they ordered the rest of their meal. They worked at their beverages, cactus salad and flautas. Deirdre reached over and took Mary's hand again, turned it so she could see her watch; it was just an excuse to touch her. She was so damn horny with Wendy gone.

"Those colored dots are amazing, so beautiful like colored stars. The things he thinks of. I can't wait to get one."

"He said Swatch snagged on something, but they should be in production pretty soon. You should tell him you want one, maybe he can get you an early sample." Mary pulled her hand away.

"I can wait. Besides, he gave it to you, that means a lot."

They paused, and Deirdre felt awkward. "Did you hear about Jimmy and the whole Native American thing?"

Mary shook her head. "I think the Jimmy Hakken gossip must stay over at the factories. Most everyone in our office is still nervous about him."

"Besides Duncan?"

"Cliff Thompson seems sort of all right about him, but everyone else? Yeah—but tell me the story."

"Jimmy's talking with Jay at the factory and like *all* serious tells him he thinks he might have some Native American blood on his mom's side. And Jay's all, *So?* You know, like he would, and Jimmy gets quiet. So Jay, of course, senses Jimmy's all upset, so he asks him what the Hakken is and Jimmy tells him. Then Jay says according to his mom his father was half-Finnish, so now Jimmy's forgotten all about the Native American thing. Now he's all Nordic, which fits. The guy might as well be a Viking."

"Jimmy Hakken might actually have another side."

"Yeah, you don't see it at first, not right off, but he does. Like me, he's trying to educate himself more."

"Hakken has worked out. I *never* would've believed it. I remember Jay telling me he was going to run the old factory after you went to the new one. I thought he'd really lost it, that maybe his arm had poisoned his brain." A pause. "Deirdre . . . I'm sorry I doubted you about the Wendy Smith thing."

"That's okay, I think everyone did."

"Not Jay."

"No?"

"I think he may have been a little concerned, but I remember him saying that he trusted you and that was the end of it."

"That whole Wendy thing was kinda weird, but the sex was *really* great, her body was just incredible. Probably not as lovely as yours though."

They were both quiet.

"You're blushing," said Deirdre.

"Sorry."

"Have you ever had sex with a woman?"

"No."

"Really?"

"I haven't had much sex," she said, kind of blurting it out.

"*You?* No way. I can't believe it. You're so incredibly attractive. You're actually beautiful, *really* beautiful. Aw-oh, I'm making you blush again."

"Maybe we should talk about something else?"

"I didn't mean to upset you."

"It just never worked out for me. I never met the right person. When you grow up on a farm, particularly a dairy farm, you have to be home a lot to do chores, so in high school I rarely dated, and then in college I was still living at—"

"*Mary*, I think it's sweet, really. You don't need to apologize. I think it's really cool and appealing. It just surprised me because you're *so* beautiful and *so* smart you could have like anyone you wanted."

"Not anyone."

Deirdre broke the silence again. "I wouldn't give up." She placed her hand on Mary's once more. "I'm *really* sorry I upset you. There I am again, Miss Say-the-wrong-thing." She searched Mary's face. "If you ever need someone to talk to or anything, anything at all . . . okay?"

Deirdre wasn't sure what made her return to the factory that night. It wasn't like she didn't sometimes come back to check, but she was almost positive she'd locked both sets of doors and knew everything else was okay. Maybe it was just restlessness after her dinner with Mary and an excuse not to go home to an empty bed. She kept thinking about Mary. In so many ways Mary was more beautiful than Wendy, not in the same flashy way, but in a quiet one that Deirdre found more and more appealing. It was her coloring rather than her features: that glowing skin and gray eyes, all that rich brown hair, and lately, she could sense Mary's emotion and sensuality beneath her polished manner. After talking with her at the restaurant, she was positive Mary wasn't having an affair with Jay. Though Deirdre knew she didn't have a chance with her, she couldn't help dreaming about it. For the past hour she'd been driving around aimlessly, and since she needed something to do besides obsess, she ended up at the factory.

The wind had abated and fog was draped like a damp hush over the world, only electric lights and neon transcending the monochrome gloom. Two mercury-vapor lights were casting ineffectual violet halos in the factory lot. As she parked the wagon she almost changed her mind and headed for a nightcap before the bars closed. But she was already here, she might as well check.

She shuffled across the gravel; finding the front doors was like reading Braille. She tested the knob and it turned. "Huh," she said out loud, still sure she'd locked it. She pulled open the door and—

A hand grabbed her arm, wrenched her inside. She screamed. Her arm was forced up toward the center of her back. She couldn't see who'd attacked her, the alcove illuminated by only a flashlight. She stopped screaming as the pain intensified. Couldn't believe this was happening— again.

"That's a lot better," said a male voice. "Not that anyone can hear you out here."

"What do you want?" She couldn't move. "Who are you?"

He paused, then chuckled to himself—a hollow nervous chuckle. "I can't fucking believe it. It's you."

"What do you want?" she said again.

"You could start by opening this *fucking* door." She didn't answer. "Did you hear me? Open—the fucking—door!"

"I can't."

He drove her arm farther up toward her shoulders, forcing her onto the toes of her sneakers.

"I can't, *really*, I don't know how."

"The fuck you don't, you goofy bitch. I've been listening to your stupid voice for an hour. For some fucking reason my recording won't activate the voice code. Now, *Open it*."

"Please, you're hurting me."

"If you don't open this door . . ."

"You're breaking my arm."

"Open it."

"Let me go. *Now!*"

He hesitated, lightening his grip for an instant; she was able to drop back on the soles of her shoes and get her balance. She sensed uncertainty, so she kicked back as hard as she could. The heel of her sneaker collided squarely with his shin. He cried out, hopping clumsily on one foot as he attempted to maintain his hold. It was this cry that alerted Luke Delamar.

"Fucking goofy bitch," the guy yelled. As they struggled, he lost his grip on her arm. He barely managed to contain her flailing arms with his, trying to subdue her attack by hugging her from behind. But his efforts were futile anyway; a black fury was approaching by the second.

Luke burst through the open door. "Fuck me!" the guy screamed. He released Deirdre, backing madly. Luke charged, bear-hugged and tackled, his entire weight crushing the guy into the floor. There was the tremendous crash of bodies against planks, and then a long silence, neither moving.

"You okay?" Luke asked her quietly over his shoulder.

"I'm all right."

The guy began fighting for breath, an awful strangled gargle emanating from his gaping mouth, eyes bulging like a dead cod. Luke disengaged himself, patted down the intruder for weapons, and stood.

"What're you doing here?" she said to Luke.

He kept his eyes on the intruder. "I check the building twice a night." He leaned down, a look of concern on his face. "Just try to relax, buddy. Relax and the breath will come." He turned to her. "Who is this guy?"

"I have no idea."

"I guess I whomped him kinda hard."

"He wanted me to open the voice lock. He seems to know who I am."

"Did he try to hurt you?"

"He tried . . . no, not really. He just talked big." A pause. "Luke?" His wary expression. "Thanks, thank you," she said.

Just for an instant he grinned, then kneeled back down. "Buddy, you got to relax, okay?"

Finally a gasp, his ashen face wet with sweat, his lips blue. After a fourth or fifth attempt, he managed a few breaths and lifted his head. Saw Luke. "Don't kill me"—a labored breath—*please*—just don't kill me." He started coughing, nearly vomited.

"Who are you?" said Luke.

"*Fuck*—what a day. I knew—I shouldn'ta—taken—this goddamn job. I even got lost—stumbling around—the goddamn fog—trying to find—

this place." A wheezing pause. "Fuck *me*. Then it takes an eternity—to disarm the security system. I told her—I don't want—this goddamn job. But she—'*We need the money*,'" he imitated a shrill female voice. "We always need—the money—because she spends—*all* the money. *Fuck!*" he yelled out to no one in particular. "Now I'll be back in—and she'll be fucking—everybody in town—again. I *knew*—I just knew—I shouldn'ta taken—this job."

Deirdre noticed a backpack and small tape recorder resting near the flashlight. She turned on the alcove overhead, everything blinking into bright focus, and opened the pack. "Luke."

He walked over and examined the contents of the pack. "C-four, plastic explosive." Luke went back to the intruder, glaring at him.

"*What?*" said the guy, looking up at Luke.

"Why?"

"Why what, for fuck's sake?"

"Why blow up our factory?"

"What are you talking about?"

Luke continued to stare at him. "Why?" He said it very quietly.

The guy raised his eyebrows. "*Money?*"

"Someone hired you?"

The guy nodded.

"Who hired you?"

"You think they tell me? *Hi, my name is Fuck-head and I want you to blow up this building, so just in case you get caught you can tell everyone.*"

"Who?" said Luke again.

"Don't look at me like that. You already broke my back, my ribs—and my head is killing me. I think I got fucking whiplash."

"Who?"

"I don't know *who*, okay?"

"Who?"

"What're you? A fucking owl from hell?"

Luke reached down and slapped him across the face. The force of the blow snapped his head around like a chiropractor adjusting someone's neck.

"You need to learn better manners," said Luke. "And you swear too much. There's a lady present."

It took the guy some minutes to recover from the slap, and he wasn't quiet about it. A red welt was blossoming, and his eye was beginning to swell shut. "Look, I'm sorry," he finally said, trying to sit up but only managing to drag himself slightly against the wall. "It's just been a bad fuc—a bad day, *okay?*"

"Who paid you?"

"Listen, *honest*, I just get an envelope. At a drop-off point. Inside is the address, half-payment, and any particulars. In this case it was the recorder that was supposed to open the fucking—sorry—the voice lock and some info on the security system. That's the truth."

"Wendy Smith, she must have recorded my voice," said Deirdre. "*Goddamnit!* How could I have been so stupid?"

"We changed the outer locks," said Luke.

"It wasn't enough."

"It was." He grinned. "Should we kill him?" He winked at Deirdre so the guy couldn't see.

"Sure, why not? Let's kill him, but I want to like torture him some first."

"Wait a minute, what the fuck're you two talking about? It was just a job. I own two LiveCell phones for fuck's sake. They're great phones. Really great phones. *Fantastic* fucking phones. That's why I didn't want to take this job. Listen, let's talk this over. You can have all the money. Or all the money I got—half the money for the job. That's ten thousand, five thousand each." He watched them intently.

"I think I'd rather torture him," she said.

"What the fuck's wrong with you? Did I hurt you? *No.* I was just trying to do a job."

"You called me a *goofy* bitch. Twice."

"Listen, you're not goofy at all. Not in the least, and I mean that. It was that door. I mean, a fuc—sorry—an hour I couldn't get it open." He was near tears, his pain probably increasing as the shock wore off.

"You come in here to blow up our livelihood. You won't tell us who paid you, and you don't expect us to kill you?" said Luke.

"Just listen—" He cowered, attempting to inch farther away along the wall. "Listen to me. I told you: I just get a phone call with a pickup point. That's *all*. Fuck, stop looking at me like that. Listen, I can get more money."

"How should we torture him?" said Luke over his shoulder.

"Let's burn him. Like real slowly."

"What the fuck's wrong with you? I don't know *anything*, you gotta believe me. What a day," he muttered. "What a jewel of a day. She's probably already out fucking somebody because I'm late."

Luke was beside Deirdre. "Should we call Mr. Chevalier?" he whispered.

"I hate to bother him. I'm sure he's asleep. Jay would probably let him go."

"Police?"

"They didn't do much last time. Do we want the publicity? You know how the press has been like savaging us lately? They'll probably say he tried to blow up the factory because of headaches he got from his Live-Cell."

"I think he told us all he knows."

"Hey," begged the guy from the corner. "Just listen, *please*! You gotta believe me. I told you the truth. Besides, I'll probably never walk again, isn't that enough?"

"You want me to call an ambulance?" said Luke.

"And bring the fucking cops? I was thinking you might wanna accept my offer."

"Not if you keep swearing."

"Sorry, really, I am. Lady, I'm sorry." He paused, brightening. "So we've a deal?"

"Hey," Luke said, "*fuck you*." Deirdre started giggling. Luke moved in the guy's direction. "If you take their money and don't blow up the building what happens?"

"They're gonna come after me."

"Who will?"

"The contact person. Whoever's the go-between. Somebody."

"And?"

"Fuck if— Never happened to me before. They'll want their money. Who wouldn't? Are you gonna let me go? Listen, you want me to ask around. They'll figure me for a snitch, but fuck it, I could try."

"Where's the money?"

"In my jacket."

"Let me have it."

The guy reached slowly into his pocket, groaning, and pulled out an envelope. Luke reached down and took it, handed it to Deirdre.

"If you find out who set this up, you can have this back."

"You serious? You're gonna let me go?"

"You think we want you here?"

"I know this sounds really stupid, but I don't think I can get up by myself."

"Try," said Luke, "before I change my mind." He turned back to Deirdre and whispered, "This okay with you?"

She nodded.

The guy rolled slowly onto his side and attempted to get his feet under him, yet with each movement he yelped louder and the sweat poured. He gave them an embarrassed smile.

Luke lifted him onto his feet, the guy biting his lip to stifle the scream.

"Listen," he said once he was more or less standing, leaning heavily against Luke. "You two've been real decent to me. I'm really sorry about . . . you know. Nothing personal. *Okay?*"

"Shut up," said Luke. Then to Deirdre, "Can we take him in your car? I always park a couple blocks away not to alert anyone. Besides, a ride on mine might kill him. We better drop him at SF General, though it's more than he deserves."

Luke emptied the guy's pockets, stuffed everything into the backpack, and tossed it into the wagon. The guy screamed at every step down, but Luke finally got him into the backseat. She drove, the fog still so thick she pulled on the wipers. At the hospital, they propped him up against a wall near an emergency room door. With all the noise he was making, they knew it wouldn't be long.

As they rolled again, Luke said, "Can I buy you a drink?"

"Aren't the bars closed?"

"I know a place—and we can certainly afford it."

She grinned at him, and Luke winked.

FOURTEEN

"Come on, man—*one* more. Come on, baby, juss one more time." Sammy guided the bar as it slowly moved downward, his massive cupped hands as if in offering under the knurled metal. The bar rested across Jay's chest for less than an instant, and then Jay drove the weight upward, his arms quivering slightly as the bar hesitated in mid-stroke, Sammy's two index fingers assisting fractionally. "That's it, come on, baby, you got it, you got it," he said again. With a last reserve of strength, Jay forced the bar to the full extension of his arms. Sammy immediately gripped it and settled it with a loud clank onto the steel bench rack, the six big cast-iron plates rattling against each other.

"Man, I think you stronger now than before. *Damn*, that's seven reps. What you weighing these days?"

"I'm back around one-eighty," said Jay as he lay prone and panting on the weight bench.

"Man, I don't want to hear about it. You lifting almost as much as me, and I got close to sixty pounds on you."

"When I boxed I didn't lift that much—Pete wouldn't let me—but it feels good now."

Jay popped up off the bench and stretched his arms out behind him, enjoying the burn in his muscles. His wounded arm was finally normal again. Looking around he was relieved the Cyclone gym hadn't decorated for Christmas. It was the time of year when he felt he didn't fit anywhere, a time for families, not orphans. It brought back bittersweet memories of the Northeast and his mother, or at least some vague early memory of Christmas there. He wasn't sure how much of it was really his and how much of it he'd invented as a child. His grandfather had said that Christmas wasn't his people's holiday—wouldn't have a thing to do with it. And now, with him gone, there would never be anyone to ask. It also dredged up those leaden holidays at the orphanage, or his Christmases as a young man when he waited the time out alone in diners or cheap rooms. It was not his favorite couple weeks.

"You ready?" he said to Sammy.

"Naw, man, enough is enough."

"You sure?"

"I gettin' soft in my old age. You must have real strong ligaments." Sammy shook his head. "You too strong for your own good."

"Shall we hit the heavy bag for a while?"

"Let's shower and head down to Felix's for some of that crazy hop water they got down there. You know, that stuff that foam up, come in those little glasses? bubbles all running around inside? all you got to do is ask for it? We'll play some soul music on the juke. Man, I got to hear that Bobby Womack—I love that shit. I got a CD in the Benz now, but it sound best at Felix's on a Saturday afternoon. We get Felix to turn it up for us. I wanna show you his place. An icon 'round this neighborhood." He paused. "Where you park?"

"On Edes around Ninety-sixth Street."

"Then you walk right by. Blue neon say *Lounge?*"

"I've noticed it before. A beautiful old sign."

"Wait till you see the inside. Oh man, I *love* this time a year—and I got me the day and the night off, too."

"Where's Jolene?"

"Didn't I tell you? Jolene and the kids on the plane to Acapulco yesterday. I couldn't stay down there no full two weeks; Nick need my ass at the room, and I get all bored lyin' on a beach anyhow, so I go down later and join 'em for Christmas. Can you believe that shit? Acapulco for Christmas. But she want it so bad, I say, honey, you want an *A*-capulco Christmas, you got your sweet self an *A*-capulco Christmas. Man, I got to haul all the gifts down there on an air-o-plane. And I'm talking these two monster motherfucking suitcases. That why I not working out too much today—got to save my strength for them suitcases. But today, today baby, daddy gonna drink some beer and rye whiskey."

"Nice to see you in such a good mood."

"Christmastime, man. I got that holiday spirit pumpin' my veins. And thanks to you I don't got to struggle my ass no more. Thanks to you, this the best year of my life, and my family's life. Man, I set up college funds for all my kids a month ago. I didn't tell you . . . I done sold all my stock."

He watched Jay for his reaction. "Not 'cause I don't believe in your ass, you know I do. I done it 'cause I don't need no more money, I make enough, and I didn't wanna worry no more about it." He put his arm around Jay. "Man, I knew you was good luck the minute I laid eyes on your ass. I never told you, but I borrow that first twenty large I put in LiveCell, Jolene screaming at me when she find out. '*How we ever gonna pay this back?*' she said. '*Are you out of your damn mind?*' And now—I her fucking hero, and it all 'cause a you."

Jay looked embarrassed.

"Man, you juss shrivel all up anybody say they love you. You quiet again today. Few months ago, you start to defrost, now you all on quiet again. Jay, you can't let those motherfuckers bug you. I been readin' the papers, and I dig they after your ass again, but I telling you man, those fucks will never rest till they own it all. They coded to do juss that. They got to make sure we *all* juss as fucking miserable as they are. They can't rest till they make everybody on earth miserable."

Sammy studied him again. "Maybe you juss sell it to them? They ain't gonna rest otherwise, you and I both know that. And you got to ask yourself why? I mean, you give the world this beautiful thing, and now everybody talk all over for free, but they got to fuck with it." He examined his friend. "Come on, man. We don' worry about it none today. We go talk with my man Felix. We let those beer angels soothe your weary mind. And Felix got a holiday special you got to try. Let's shower up."

They walked out of the free weight room into the boxing part of the gym. As they headed for the locker room everyone greeted Sammy and gave Jay the nod.

"You change a lot of people's lives around here. They too shy to tell you, but they tell me." He paused. "Man, there you go again, looking all funny. We got to find you a good woman, get on with the *de*frost."

"Sammy, I'm fine," he said.

"Yeah, you fine, I know you fine, I juss wanna see a smile on my main man." They stripped down for their showers. "You gonna take some steam today?"

"You?"

"If you want. Man, I all ready right now for my holiday afternoon."

"Let's just shower and head to the bar then. My treat."

Sammy glared at him. "No way. This my afternoon, my place, my treat. Right?"

Jay nodded, and finally smiled at his friend. Sammy winked, grabbed a clean towel and headed for the showers.

" . . . across a hundred and tenth street . . ." Sammy sang quietly along with Bobby Womack. Then at the *uhh-wu-wu-wu* part he allowed his voice to rise above the volume of the jukebox. Nobody minded in the least.

Entering Felix's Lounge for the first time was like entering a still photograph from a book, *Lost Barrooms from the Late 1930s*. Of course in the thirties the windows wouldn't have had iron grates, and the door, now protected by steel mesh, would have opened with a push—no wait until being recognized and buzzed into the place. The bar itself had remained the same though, with its horseshoe shape at the entrance-end and its thick curved mahogany lip, the top a sanded and alcohol-stained teak. The same huge mirror corralled by polished wood, a graceful arch with vertical amber lights resembling Grecian pillars, sentinels of the liquor-bottle forest. Mahogany booths and tables lined the right wall beyond the horseshoe section. The cornice of a rusty and tarnished tin ceiling was hung with paper streamers and oversized Christmas decorations. In the center of the bar was a massive punch bowl surrounded by mugs as new-borns surround a mother, next to this a red plastic ladle, and on the red glass bowl and mugs, white silk-screened script that read *Tom and Jerry*.

Sammy'd started with one, a Christmas tradition, Tyrone adding rum and boiling water to the egg mixture ladled from the punch bowl, top-ping it with a *pfft* of whipped cream and a shake of nutmeg. Since Tyrone had inherited the lounge twenty-four years ago, most of his patrons called him Felix though no one remembered the original Felix. When Sammy introduced him to Jay, he shook Jay's hand with great seriousness and told him his money was no good in his place; whatever he wanted was on the house. Sammy told Felix he'd have to wait in line.

Sammy emptied his Tom and Jerry, got up and walked to the front door, signaled Felix to buzz it open. Holding the door with his foot to keep it from springing shut, he leaned forward and looked down Edes Street in the same direction Jay had parked the Cutlass. Then he came back and sat down again.

"They gone," he said to no one in particular.

"What's at?" said Felix from down the bar.

"Man, you running craps in the back, you peddling crack, you serving minors?"

"Sammy, *what* you talking about?"

"You know anything 'bout a chocolate sedan with two ugly white boys inside? Look like an unmarked."

"Never seen it before."

"Man, juss look wrong to me, but they gone now. Look like some stray vice boys or some shit like that." Felix went back to stacking glasses.

"You want another Jerry?" said Sammy. Jay told him one was enough. "You right," he said quietly so Felix wouldn't hear. "They lovely, but they awful sweet, and I like sweet." Then, calling down to the old bartender, "Felix, my man, set us up a couple of frosties."

"Blue Ribbon?"

"What else."

"Shorts?"

"Now you talking, brother."

"Calvert?"

Sammy just grinned. He turned to Jay. "So what's going on? I know there something. Company stuff, the bad press? There something else? You got woman troubles? I hate to see you with the blues at Christmastime."

"I'm fine," he said as Sammy searched him. "Truly, I'm okay." Jay watched Felix pouring the drafts, then back at Sammy. "This is a wonderful place. Thanks for bringing me here."

Sammy placed a hand on his shoulder. "You need something, all you got to do is ask, but you know that."

As they talked and drank, customers began to drift in, the door buzzer heralding each fresh group or single—that vague nudge of cool air moving down the bar—almost everyone already gussied up for the holidays though Christmas was still a week and a couple of days away. The bar began to fill; another bartender arrived to help Felix pour drinks, and a waitress began working the tables. Only a few patrons seemed surprised to see Jay on a stool beside Sammy. Many came over to say Hey to Sammy, ask about Jolene, the children, and meet Jay. There was a lot of laughter, and after a couple hours Sammy leaned over to his friend and said, "Baby, you finally on *de*frost."

"I'm better, thanks to you."

"You really can't tell Sammy what's bugging you?"

The bar was busy now, which offered its own kind of privacy. Jay felt he should tell Sammy something; he knew Sammy would be hurt if he didn't.

"I'm worried about my people."

"LiveCell?"

"Someone tried to blow up one of our factories."

"*Motherfucker.*"

"It was a paid job. Untraceable. Two of my people interrupted the man in the middle of the night. It was a fluke they happened to be there."

"Damn, man. Now they trying to burn your ass out." He shook his head in sadness. "You use David Artega?"

"Unofficially, but the thing was confused. My people dropped the arsonist off outside San Francisco General. A man was admitted that night with broken ribs and internal injuries, but he disappeared sometime before morning. The ER doctor assured Artega the guy must've had help leaving. We have the wallet, but the information was a dead end, an alias. He even used a different alias at the hospital. Artega thinks he was out of the country by that afternoon. My people also took ten thousand off him, which he told them was half the job, but Artega thought fifty-thousand was probably the figure."

"Why didn't your people turn him over to Artega?"

"I don't think either of them have much faith in the police, and though Deirdre saw Artega once, it's not as if she knows him. And you'd have to meet Luke to understand. It takes some people a long time to believe in a good cop."

"I hear you. David didn't clue me in."

"I asked him to tell no one." Jay drained his beer. "Let me buy you and Felix a drink. Let's get back in the spirit."

"Man, glad you told me. I understand better. I told you man, you making some waves; you changing things for them big money boys. I love you for it brother, and I respect your ass all the more. But, baby, you can't let this shit get you down—it bound to happen. They bound to try and set you back, but I know you, you keep coming. Man, I wish I coulda seen you in the ring, I bet you never quit coming."

Jay didn't tell him about the death threats. There'd been a second one since he'd mentioned the first to Mary. The second was identical: DESIST OR DIE across plain white paper. He hadn't told Detective Artega either. Jay didn't take the threats seriously—how could he? It seemed too stupid, too amateurish. The people after him were not amateurs. They had every possible resource available and no one watching them. They could do what they liked as long as they kept the truth out of the media, and therefore from the public. He understood that the rules were inequitable.

Felix was pleased that Jay wanted to buy him a drink. He opened one of the latched doors and reached far into the cooler, pulled out a big brown bottle, brought it over with a glass to their section of the bar.

"This the Xingu beer, the *black* beer, come all the way from the Brazil jungle. Make a man strong where it counts." He poured it out—it looked like oil—and raised the glass. "Thank you, Jay. Merry Christmas."

They all raised their beverages and toasted each other, Felix draining off half his glass and humming his approval loudly.

"Felix, I don't know how you can drink that skanky shit," said Sammy.

"You juss don't know what's good."

Sammy pretended to strangle himself with one hand, his tongue sticking out. He started chuckling. "Man, you juss like that shit 'cause it got snakes and crocodiles on the label. Remind you a your two ex-wives." Sammy slapped his thigh now, winked at Jay.

Felix said, "Even at Christmastime he got to fun an old man."

"You ain't that old."

"Jay, how old you think I am?"

Jay examined him. "Mid-fifties?"

"I be sixty-seven in June," he said with pride.

"You serious?" said Sammy, no longer laughing. "Man, I had no idea you that old. Maybe I should start drinking that shit."

"You juss keep drinkin' what you drinkin'," Felix said, grinned at Jay, and went off to serve a customer.

"That Felix too much. I remember him from when I's a kid, coming in here after school when it empty, juss the regulars nursing hangovers, and he give us pop—but I never figure how old he must be. He never change. Only his wives." He looked around. "Man, I got to go play that juke again." Sammy sauntered over to the throbbing jukebox and began feeding it dollars.

Jay did feel a little better. The joy and faith in Sammy relaxed him, and he decided his premonitions might be wrong. After all, it was Christmastime, a time of goodwill and fellowship, not a time of fear. Everyone in the bar exuded positive feelings. Why couldn't he? These past months he'd fought an underlying uneasiness that wouldn't rest, and he worried he was putting his people at risk. Was he pushing too hard, too quickly? Had he calculated everything carefully enough? Had he underestimated the viciousness of the opposition?

After the bomb attempt he'd called a special department heads meeting and cautioned everyone that working at LiveCell might be a lot riskier than he'd foreseen. He'd asked each of them how they felt and what they wanted to do.

Jimmy Hakken spoke first. He said, "My crew are ready for any-thing—*period*. We're on constant alert. Got sentries posted around the clock. No one is blowing up my factory—*period*."

Jay knew that in Jimmy Hakken he'd fostered something that was getting out of hand, yet he also sensed how content Hakken was, as if he'd lived his whole life to fill this role, and if anyone knew the importance of that, it was Jay. However, though Jay would never admit it to anyone, Hakken's devout loyalty made him very uncomfortable.

Deirdre, though she'd absorbed the brunt of the physical attacks against the company, said, "Like I'm going to worry now? Like I'd ever let you down after what you've done for me?"

Her words moved Jay so much that he'd gotten out of his chair and looked out the window at the small rectangle of bay, a silver-gray on that morning. He noticed Mary examining his eyes as he sat down. She was always observing—so astute.

Mary addressed the group. She said, "LiveCell is doing something important, something worthwhile, and that's worth the risk for me."

Jay knew he'd hurt Mary deeply, but she seemed to manage to hide her pain in public. How could he make amends? He couldn't tell her the truth, that was for certain. But now she was unwilling to attempt infusing the phones—he wasn't sure why—and he felt daily that he was running out of time. Time was always the problem.

Chet Simmons was next. Since the day Jay hadn't blamed him for the black-box fiasco and had reassured him that he would never be fired for doing his best, he viewed Jay with quiet but intense fondness. It was as if he'd never had an adult male friend and thought of Jay as his best friend.

At the meeting, "I'm in," was all he said. After he spoke, his eyes flickered downward in embarrassment, and then he glanced shyly at Jimmy Hakken. Hakken gave him a closed-fist salute.

Both Cliff Thompson and Randy Dyer said they would do whatever it took. They were outraged and stunned by the surreptitious undermining and violence. They'd been in the corporate world all their working lives and had never imagined anything like this. It brought the fight out in both of them.

Cliff Thompson said, "I'm agonized by the drop in stock price, but I'm certain it'll rebound once the press and the Food and Drug Administration back off. In some of the smaller newspapers, a counter-attack has surfaced, which is great. People's loyalties to the phones have strengthened, if anything; sales are up, and worldwide sales are just beginning. We've lost a few battles, but we're certain to win the war."

Duncan had been drawing further and further into himself over the last months. He must have sensed that Mary and Deirdre were privy to things he wasn't; of course, his suspicions were grounded. Then there was his sexual obsession with Mary, which had only intensified.

As they waited for his decision at the meeting, he said, "LiveCell is garnering some very powerful enemies. It doesn't seem worth the risk to hold on to it. Jay, as you said, it's getting dangerous for everyone. Why don't you just sell it? I'm sure the new owners would allow everyone to remain, the sale would ease tensions, and we could still achieve the same goals. I don't see any reason not to sell."

Jay asked the others how they felt. They were unanimously against him selling. "There's one reason," said Jay. After more discussion, Duncan finally agreed to stay.

Sammy walked back from the juke, dancing to The Spinners doing "I'll Be Around," his big body imitating a steam locomotive pulling out of a station, his arms churning like the engine's drivers. He took his stool beside Jay again, singing the refrain: "*Ba*by, whenever you call me, I'll be there; whenever you want me, I'll be there; whenever you need me, I'll be there—I'll be around." He gripped Jay's shoulder. "Man, this one *sweet* afternoon."

"The best," said Jay. "I feel renewed." But he didn't; there was still a nasty pressure in his chest.

"That those beer angels doin' their strut. They make a new man outa ya. *For they are the beer angels, and they comfort and make new the weary.* Psalm One-Fifty-One." Sammy chuckled. "Man, I love this place."

Jay nodded.

"Juss seein' you smile, pay me back. You *need* take some time off like this. Man can't work all the time. We should do this every Saturday."

"Next time is my treat."

"Now you talking."

Sammy signaled Felix by swinging his hand as if he had a lasso. After the round arrived, he said, "Where you wanna go eat? Or you want something right here? The cook be in anytime now, and she fry a mean steak. Or we take the Benz, go anywhere you say. My treat, wherever you wanna go."

Jay looked up at the clock over the bar again, though he knew the time. "I have to take off after this beer. I still have a few things to do at both factories."

"Ah, man, no way, we juss gettin' started."

Jay saw the disappointment. "Let me have about an hour and a half and I'll meet you back here. Save my stool. Actually, I would love to eat right here."

"Now you talking, baby. We have some steaks, bake potatoes, biscuits and beans." He slapped Jay on the shoulder again. "I walk you to your car. You still driving that jalopy?"

"It's time for a new one. Just haven't gotten around to it."

When they left Felix's Lounge, the twilight had reached that exact interval between day and night. A time when we believe everything appears more beautiful and magical. The blue neon of *Lounge* against its metal signboard appeared almost transposed from the vibrant hue of the sky. The *Felix's* had been long burnt out. Below the sign, the street was fairly busy on that Saturday night; maybe neighbors were less afraid to be outside because of the holiday season. Some teenagers on skateboards and high-tech scooters clattered and banged along the sidewalks as they practiced stunts, a few leaners and stragglers in big down parkas watched their kids or argued and chatted with each other, drinking from screwed-up paper bags.

Sammy inhaled the cool evening air and let out a sigh. "Man, I must be crazy, but I always think Oakland have a special smell. Smell like home to me. Tonight it smell like happiness." They turned left out of the door, walked slowly down Edes. This time Sammy didn't notice the dark-brown sedan as it jerked out of a parking spot and drove at them. If he had noticed, he probably wouldn't have recognized it—the headlights on bright blinded his view. He didn't pay enough attention either when the sedan skidded to a stop just in front of them, about ten yards away. At that moment, Jay was looking across the street at two young kids playing tag and giggling, so it was only Sammy who vaguely saw the sedan's door swing open. A white man leapt out, double-gripped an automatic, pointed it at Jay. Then Sammy reacted. With a sudden violent spasm he sprinted at the gun. He was already running hard, his head down, hunched over, when the man fired twice in rapid succession; a silencer muffled the explosions. The first bullet struck him in the chest but did not slow him. The second shot hit him high in the stomach. The gunman, seeing this huge black man charging him, jumped back into the sedan and screamed, "*Go, go!*" The tires squealed and smoked. The sedan lurched forward, careening away, the car door slamming shut from the acceleration. A third and fourth shot were fired out of the passenger window at Jay Chevalier. Only one of those bullets was ever found.

Sammy stopped running. He swayed as Jay caught up to him. Jay grabbed him as he collapsed, attempting to cushion his fall as best as he could. People on the street started yelling, running toward them. Jay begged someone to call an ambulance. For this one thing his LiveCell wouldn't work without the black box.

He looked at his friend lying on the sidewalk, at Sammy's face gray in the twilight, at his usually animated eyes dull and half-closed, at a small bubble of blood forming on his lips. He didn't want to look any lower. He pulled off his sports coat and gently covered part of Sammy's body with it. He wiped blood from Sammy's lips and chin, wiped the sweat off Sammy's forehead with his fingers.

"You're going to be okay," he said. "You're going to be okay. Just hold on."

Sammy seemed to hear him and his eyes focused a little.

"You're going to be okay," he said again.

He heard a siren. He sensed people gathered around him but didn't listen to what they were saying. Most just stood and stared, a few of them spoke:

"Damn, that Sammy—Sammy Holmes."

"Samuel Holmes, yeah, I remember him, he use to be a boxer."

"Why somebody shoot him? What the fuck?"

Jay saw Sammy's lips move. He bent down close, placing his ear next to his friend's lips.

"Jolene," he heard him say.

Jay waiting.

"Jay? You there?"

He told him he was there, "*I'm here. You're going to be okay.*" Sammy tried to say something more but his eyes went dull again, and they closed. A minute passed. Jay didn't notice Felix's hand on his shoulder, or all the people murmuring. Another minute. The wavering cry of a siren growing louder. Sammy not moving. Jay not moving, his eyes locked on his friend's face, his hands trembling.

It was then, during that eerie period of empty waiting, when everyone standing there was startled by a horrible sound. Jay Chevalier looked toward the heavens and he bellowed like a wounded animal.

FIFTEEN

Detective Artega was off duty, leaving San Francisco by the Bay Bridge on his way home, when he heard the call on his radio. He was considering dropping by Felix's for a holiday drink anyway, so he responded to the call, joining the scene shortly after the arrival of two other cruisers and an ambulance. Artega pushed through the dark huddle of spectators, approached the victim being loaded onto a stretcher, saw the face in the electric glare. He looked around in disbelief. Then he recognized Jay Chevalier against the darkness, being questioned by an officer. He walked over to them. Though Artega lived nearby, he didn't have jurisdiction in Oakland. However, by pushing the issue, he managed to free Jay from further questioning. He told Jay he'd meet him at Highland Hospital when the police had finished. By then the EMTs had loaded Sammy into the ambulance, and the siren pierced the subdued street. Artega watched Chevalier hurry to his car.

Jay followed the same route as the ambulance in his Cutlass, assailed by blurred images of tubes and IVs being stuck into his friend, wires being attached to his bloody chest. By the time he'd stashed the Cutlass and entered the hospital, Sammy was already in the operating room. Fighting to stay calm, Jay inquired at the front desk, then cornered the triage nurse. He told her he'd pay for everything, to *please* spare no cost, just save his friend. Twice he consulted the head ER doctor who reassured him that the surgeon was extremely capable and that someone would alert him immediately when the operation was finished. Finally he found a seat. Marooned in the crowded waiting room, he looked like a week-old piece of lost luggage that no one would ever claim.

Jay was suffering from a pain just beneath his ribcage that made it difficult for him to breathe. He knew he needed to livecell Jolene. He wondered if Artega was aware that she was in Mexico. The image of Jolene and the children at the beach—the kids giggling, jumping together, turning their naked backs to the waves, chasing each other along the smooth sand—was randomly spiked by the memory of Pete's heart attack in the boxing gym. He tried to concentrate on the phone call he had to make. But what was he supposed to say? "Your husband has been shot in front of a bar so he won't be going anywhere for Christmas. He saved my life and would be fine now if it wasn't for me."

After managing to remain in the waiting room for about half an hour, he walked outside into the night air. Below him he could see Christmas lights shaken onto the dark hills like a rain of colored stars. The sight sickened him. He took out his phone.

"Mary," he said when she answered.

"Hey, it's you. Deirdre just livecelled and asked why you weren't answering calls. She expected you at the factory a while ago." And then anxiously, "Is something wrong?"

"There's been an accident."

"Are you okay?"

"It's Sammy. He's been shot."

"*Shot?*"

"A man jumped out of a car near the gym and tried to kill me. Sammy—" His voice broke. "Sammy saved my life."

"Oh my God. Is Sammy all right?"

"He's in surgery. I'm at Highland Hospital. He ran at the gun and he was shot, twice."

"Oh *no*."

A pause and he sensed her question.

"They assured me that everything possible is being done."

"Is Jolene there?"

"She's in Acapulco with the children. Sammy was going to meet them there for Christmas." Again, he couldn't speak. "I need to call her. I need to tell her."

"I'll call her."

Another silence. He shivered in his T-shirt, his blood-soaked sports coat gone.

"Jay, you don't sound good."

He didn't answer.

"I'm going to close up here. I'll be there in forty minutes."

"Mary?"

They listened to each other.

"Sammy can't die," he said. "You should have seen him today, he . . ."

"I'll livecell Jolene and I'll be there as soon as I can."

Detective Artega arrived at the hospital alone. He spotted Chevalier standing outside and headed over. They talked about Sammy. Then he suggested they go inside—it was damn cold as far as he was concerned—and they walked back in. The waiting room was over-crowded, so he asked a nurse if there was a vacant area to use, and she reluctantly pointed out a small cubicle down the hall. He perched uncomfortably on the examining bed and Jay took a plastic chair.

"I made some calls. Oakland's allowing me to assist. I figured you'd rather talk to me than a stranger."

Jay didn't respond.

"Did anyone know you and Sammy were going to be at the Lounge?"

Jay shook his head. "I didn't even know until he suggested it."

"And you walked directly there from the Cyclone?"

Jay nodded.

"What time?"

"We left the gym around two."

"So you were at the Lounge about two and a half hours. You ever go to Felix's after workouts?"

"Never."

Artega paused for a few seconds, thinking. "I know you gave the other officer your description of the shooting. If you don't mind, give it to me again."

Artega listened: how Jay's attention was drawn from the kids across the street by Sammy's sudden movement; the dark sedan; the man dressed in black, maybe dark-brown or blue, dark gloves on his hands, white face, black hair, medium build, no one Jay recognized; the two shots. Sammy had blocked much of his view of the gunman, and Jay hadn't seen the driver or noticed the car leaving; his attention was on Sammy. Artega wrote it all down.

"Why?" said Jay.

"Why what?"

"Why did he run at the gun? He could have saved himself."

"You think they wanted you?"

Jay nodded.

"You didn't mention this before."

"I've had two death threats."

"When?"

"First one was four months ago, the other a few weeks ago."

"How were they delivered?"

"What do you mean?"

"Phone call, message machine, e-mail, letter?"

"Letter, regular mail, sent to me at LiveCell, Harcourt Building address."

"Do you have them?"

"I threw them out."

Artega looked away, tempted to shake his head. Why had Chevalier kept them to himself? "What did they say?"

"Desist or die."

Artega saw in the sick pallor and eyes what Chevalier was putting himself through, how badly he was beating himself up. "Jay, listen to me. Sammy's street smart, and he knew the gunman could kill both of you no matter what either of you did. His best chance was what he took—for both of you. Maybe the shooter would abort the hit, or panic and miss. Sammy might have gotten to him before he fired. From what you tell me, he almost did." He looked away from Jay's face. He didn't like what he saw.

Sensing a call, he pulled out his LiveCell phone. "Artega," he said. He listened, keeping his eyes off Chevalier. "The trunk? . . . Couple rounds missing? . . . *Four*? . . . Prints? . . . Potential DNA? . . . Anything else in the vehicle? . . . Let me know." He slid the phone back into his pocket. "They found the car and the gun. They're still searching for evidence, but I don't think there'll be much. Gun had four rounds missing. There were two other shots fired?"

"After Sammy went down. As they drove away."

"Listen to me. You don't *know* they wanted you. No one knew you were in the bar, so it might be much more random than you think."

"He was shot because of me." Chevalier glared, jerked out of the chair, and banged out of the room.

Artega found him outside. He was standing with his arms across his chest, staring out at the city. Artega lit a Camel and stood some yards away, idly chewing his thumbnail on the hand that held the cigarette, flicking a stray fleck of tobacco from his lip. He didn't know what more to say to the guy. He'd already tried a few explanations, attempting to give the guy an out, though he figured Chevalier would never take the false way out of anything.

One thing was likely—if Sammy hadn't reacted the way he did, the gunman would have killed Chevalier. But how did the killers know they'd be in Felix's Lounge? That bugged him. Who tipped them off? It also bothered him that Oakland had been chosen for the hit, though the intelligence of it was obvious: if Sammy and Jay had both died, the killing would have appeared to be two more inextricable drug-related deaths, and even with Jay Chevalier's celebrity, any media attention would have died down quickly. He was not going to let that—

"Mr. Chevalier?" a nurse called from the brightly lit entrance of the hospital. Chevalier spun and headed toward the building. Artega cringed when he caught his expression. He hated to see a tough man unravel. "Is he okay?" he heard Chevalier say. "The doctor will speak with you now," was all she said. People working in hospitals all used the same clichés, he thought. He guessed they needed them. What the hell, he used them too. He extinguished his smoke in the outdoor canister, exhaled before the doors, and followed.

He joined the surgeon and Chevalier, who'd just been introduced. As Artega shook hands, he couldn't help but notice how doctors' hands were always the same—cool, baby smooth, and dry. Unlike a cop's.

"Mr. Chevalier," the surgeon said, employing that classic solemn manner, "I've just gotten off the telephone with Mrs. Holmes in Mexico, and she tells me you're a friend of the family." Jay nodded. "Detective, she asked if you were here. Mr. Holmes is in serious though reasonably stable condition, for now. We abated the internal bleeding though reoccurrence is always a concern. We are re-inflating his lung. One lung was severely damaged. We removed the bullet that entered the lung, but the second is too close to the spinal column to remove. He's lost a great deal of blood, which is being replaced. Both bullets entered at a fortuitously angled trajectory. If either had been angled differently he would have died instantly. He's a strong man." He paused. "We'll keep him ventilated overnight. I wish I had better news."

"So he's going to be okay?" said Jay.

"It's too early to tell. As I said, he is a very strong man."

"May I see him?"

"Let him rest for some hours. If his signs are good, you can visit him for a few minutes, though it's unlikely he'll be conscious. He's being kept heavily sedated while on the ventilator." He started to turn away, then rotated back. "By the way, your phones are an incredible product. We use them in the hospital; they save time and therefore lives."

When Mary arrived it took her a while to find Jay. He was in a small sitting room on the second floor down the hall from where they'd wheeled Sammy, the trauma ICU, a wing for patients requiring constant monitoring. When she found him, they embraced.

"How is he?" she said.

He told her.

She didn't ask him how *he* was doing. That was obvious, and it scared her. Now she wished she hadn't been so cold to him after he rejected her.

"I spoke with Jolene," she said, trying to sound normal. "I booked them a flight. They'll get in tomorrow. The last flight today from Acapulco to Oakland left at three. They arrive at eight tomorrow night. I offered to rent something and pick them up at the airport, but Jolene's sister's going to do it. I gave Jolene all the information I had. Did she call here?"

Jay nodded.

"I also let Deirdre and Jimmy Hakken know what happened. And I told Nick Brignolia at the poolroom."

Jay just stared at her.

"Do you know that man?" she whispered, noticing Artega watching her, the only other person in the sitting room.

"Detective Artega. A friend of Sammy's."

Artega got up and was introduced.

"I can't believe this happened," she said to him.

"We don't know anything yet. Though some people noticed the car, no one except Jay admitted to seeing the actual shooting or the face of the gunman. I told Jay there's no proof they were after Sammy or him. It might've been a mistake."

"Sammy noticed the car," Jay said, almost to himself.

"What?" Artega said.

"Sammy," Jay said louder, "as we entered the bar, he noticed the car. I remember he went back outside to see if it was still there. He said it looked wrong to him. He thought they were vice cops. He asked Felix if he knew anything about it."

"Was your Cutlass parked beyond the Lounge?"

Artega saw it now. The hit was supposed to take place as Chevalier left the gym alone. The gunman had waited between the gym and Jay's car to intercept him as he walked back. Simple. Going into Felix's and the presence of Sammy had been unexpected. At first the killers had aborted the hit, then changed their minds. They'd circled back and waited until Jay exited the bar. Shit, *everyone* must have seen them. White people were always noted in that neighborhood.

"Who knows you work out on Saturdays at the Cyclone?" he said.

Chevalier turned away and slumped into one of the chairs. Artega watched Jay's hands wash back and forth across the pallid brow, the fingers pressing at the eye sockets. Artega sensed what he was thinking: that it had stared him in the face. Chevalier would realize he could have saved them both, that he should've known what the car meant when Sammy spotted it. The death threats should have alerted him. That was probably their intention, to alert Chevalier. Professionals don't alert victims. *Shit*, the poor bastard. Many times it was that way; once you knew something and all the pieces fit, it seemed so damn obvious—afterwards.

The woman answered his question about the Cyclone: "Many people at the office know. They think it's odd that Jay goes to Oakland to work out. Most of them wouldn't have much to do with that neighborhood."

"I suppose we don't have the best reputation."

They sized each other up.

She said, "Jay thinks someone was trying to kill him. Do you think that's true?"

"Seems likely. Sammy was in the wrong place at the wrong time." There was no longer any point in giving the guy an out.

The woman sat down. Sat next to Chevalier and placed her arm around him. Artega stood awkwardly not knowing what to do. He thought of calling to see if anything new had turned up, but he'd just be killing time. He wanted to find the shooter, though not as much as he wanted whoever ordered the hit. But he recognized the futility of any emotion. The only chance was if someone had made a mistake, and professionals rarely made mistakes.

He glanced back at Chevalier, watched him straighten, scrub his forehead with his fist, turn to the woman.

"We will suspend all operations at LiveCell until further notice," he said. "We'll close it down."

She removed her arm. "*What?* My God, Jay, what are you talking about?"

"This can't go on. I can't put anyone else in jeopardy."

She looked as if she were trying to accept what he'd said, but wasn't doing a very good job.

"I think you need to give this a little more time."

He didn't answer.

"You're upset right now. We all are. I really think it would be a mistake to decide this now."

"I've decided. I want you to let everyone know," he said. "I want it in all the media."

"When?" she said, sounding frustrated. "Can't you at least wait until tomorrow?"

"No. As soon as possible. There's no time left."

"Shouldn't we at least have a department heads meeting first?"

"No. I won't take the risk. If LiveCell shuts down, there will be no reason for them to keep trying to destroy us. They win."

It took the press about four hours after the fact to discover that a seemingly random shooting in Oakland of a retired second-rate boxer and bartender, Samuel W. Holmes, was a huge story. LIVECELL TO CLOSE was the first headline to saturate the streets. Detective Artega kept the press away from the sitting room by stationing an officer in the hallway. Jay refused to leave the hospital and wouldn't eat. He left the room only once to go downstairs and donate blood, shoving silently past a few pushy, diehard reporters and television people. Some of Sammy's close friends and relatives arrived—Artega monitoring who should be allowed in—and they settled around the room, no one saying much, a few of the women in tears.

When the doctor checked his patient again, he decided there could be no visitors in Sammy's room that night. Artega exited to eat supper, and then at about ten-thirty he went home, leaving the stationed officer. Most everyone else had left as well. Mary retired at quarter past eleven. She told Jay she'd be back early in the morning before she officially shut down LiveCell as he requested.

Just after Mary left, Nick Brignolia entered the sitting room. He'd closed the poolroom early. He shook hands with Jay and took a chair across the room. The old man didn't look much better than Jay did. After half an hour, he withdrew as well.

Sometime after midnight the hospital finally drifted into a hush, and the ICU nurse appeared preoccupied. Jay sneaked down the hall and into the dimly lit room of his wounded friend. He stood silently beside the bed, gently cupping Sammy's shoulder. The ventilator tube in his mouth, Sammy didn't respond to his presence, each machine-controlled breath and the inertness of the big body so painful for Jay.

Jay Chevalier had reached a moment in his life when his intentions and actions, no matter how carefully considered, generated currents that he couldn't foresee or control. He'd already known this intellectually, but now he felt slammed by the reality, and it broke his confidence. He still believed in what he'd been doing, yet for the first time, the cost had changed, and the price was too high.

He'd always known that the end never justified the means. His phones were the means, and though he had visualized his prayer for what they might offer, about what the phones might help accomplish for humanity, an increased closeness to the continuum, he accepted that the end would always, and should always, be out of his control. Otherwise he would be like them, like the Wendell Aldens of the world—dictating, controlling, deciding the fate of others. Even at DuPont, he'd immediately sensed that his discovery would generate conflict and violence. He just hadn't realized it could be directed at anyone but himself. If only Sammy hadn't offered to walk him to his car. He saw Sammy running at the gun, saw the recoil from the automatic, the bullets striking the body, felt himself embracing his falling friend, felt the overwhelming weight of him in his arms, the acrid smell of the gunpowder—

And then Jay had an intuition.

He walked quickly over to the closet in the corner of the room, and though the closet was dark, he found what he was looking for. He grabbed the plastic bag with Sammy's belongings, and reaching inside, his hand rummaging, located the bloody pants. From one of the pockets, he pulled out the object he needed. He moved to the bed and placed it next to Sammy's head. Jay retrieved his own LiveCell.

"Sammy," he said, though his mouth didn't move and there was no sound. "Sammy, it's Jay, can you hear me?"

He waited. Nothing. He repeated it. Still nothing.

Then, "You?" he heard in his mind.

"It's me . . . Jay."

He waited.

"Jolene?"

"She's on her way. Be here tomorrow, with the kids. They're flying up tomorrow."

A pause.

"Fucked up, bad."

"Sammy, you're going to be okay, you just have to hang in there. You've been—"

"Jolene . . . love her . . . my babies . . . love 'em so much."

Jay felt the tears on his cheeks. "I'll tell her. Don't worry about anything, everything will be taken care of. Sammy, I'm . . . what you did for me. I'm so sorry, I wish it had been—

"Naw, don't you be—"

"*What* are you doing in here?"

Jay turned. The night nurse. Steel-haired, stout, the bosom of her white uniform like a spinnaker in a gale.

"I see you on the monitor, hiding in the shadows. You can't be in here," she said, looking around the room. She snapped on the lights and walked over to Jay. "What you doing with his stuff on the floor? . . . You crying," she said matter-of-factly. "What's this by his head?" She reached over and picked up Sammy's LiveCell. "This his?" Jay nodded. "Come on now, you got to leave him alone so the man can res' hisself." She guided Jay to the door with her large hand. "You that phone man, ain't you?" He nodded again. "Son, don' you worry yourself so much. He in the Lord's hands. He gonna be all right."

He searched her face. She wasn't going to let him stay no matter what, so he returned to the sitting room.

After ten minutes she brought him a styrofoam cup of coffee. "You drink this. It good and hot with plenty sugar an' cream. I can tell you ain't gonna sleep."

"Can I see him again?" he said.

"You let him res'. That his best chance." She looked down at him. "Son, you got to let the poor man res'," and she went back to her duties.

As the elderly nurse had predicted, he didn't sleep. His mind toiled all night with the relentless momentum of a dam run-off. When Mary arrived a little after six, she carried a white paper bag with some warm bakery rolls, butter, cheddar cheese, and a plastic bottle of fresh carrot juice.

"You have to eat something," she said.

He sipped tentatively at the juice.

"Jay, you really look bad. I'm being serious."

"I'm fine," he said.

"You *have* to eat something or you're going to collapse."

She handed him a buttered roll with cheese in it. "Please!" He ate it.

There was no news on Sammy.

At around noon, when Mary returned from closing down LiveCell and the two factories, she found Jay in the same place—emotionally and physically. She'd no sooner greeted the people she knew in the sitting room than everyone's attention was drawn to a commotion in the hallway. After twenty minutes they saw a doctor walking slowly toward them.

Jay stood. The doctor told them what had happened. Jay staggered over to a wall. He punched it so hard that his fist went clear through the Sheetrock.

On the following Tuesday afternoon, Jay huddled at his desk and stared out the window. All three of LiveCell's floors in the Harcourt Building were vacant and dark. It was like an old school after hours, so dead and lifeless it almost provoked the need to shout. He sat in his orange office, drinking Lord Calvert out of a coffee mug with his left hand, his right hand swollen and bruised. His phone had been paging him constantly. He ignored it. All he did was focus on the gloomy rectangle of bay as rain washed down the thermopane. The wake and funeral were tomorrow. Both would be held at the Oakland Baptist Church. Jolene had asked him to say a few words in Sammy's memory. Would he have refused her anything?

There was a knock on his closed door. He ignored it, but after a moment the door opened.

"Hey," a voice said. "Chevalier."

He glanced over; there stood Jimmy Hakken—wet, dressed in black. A grim sight.

"Man, I know you ain't seeing nobody. Believe me, MacKensie made that *really* fucking clear. I'm here anyway."

He lumbered in, set a paper bag on the floor, ripped it open, separated two sixteen ounce cans of beer from their plastic carrying caddie, snapped in the pull tabs, and placed one on the desk in front of Jay. He tilted back the other for a lengthy drink and settled in the chair in his awkward, sprawled way. He didn't say a word for five or six minutes, until he'd downed the beer. Then he reached for the bag and exchanged cans, opened a second one.

"You know I ain't no good at talking." He took a sip. "I'm gonna anyway."

Jay had barely moved since Hakken had walked in, but now he reached for the can of beer.

Hakken reacted by holding out his can in a particularly solemn way, and he drank when Jay did.

Jimmy Hakken was never in a hurry to talk. Today he needed words to serve him and he was probably worried; they'd rarely served him in the past. He tried anyway: "I asked MacKensie about what happened. She don't give information easy—I'll give her that. But then I said, look, we are on the same fucking side here."

Jay sipped at his cold can.

Hakken leaned forward in his chair, set down his beer, and stared in his intense way.

"Listen," he said, "Chevalier—I'm just gonna tell you straight what's in my heart. That's all I can do, okay?

"This thing you started, it's bigger than you now. I dig you made it, like it's yours, but it's *ours*, too. I understan' Holmes is dead. I know how bad that hurts, because I lost my mom when I was young, and I lost a best friend, got his skull on my desk. It still hurts me, *all* the fucking time. But by quitting, you hurt all of us. And not just your crew. Bunch of people count on us; they need our phones. Lives're changing 'cause of us. Listen, the stock got fucking hammered yesterday—*hammered*. Everyone suddenly all paranoid that LiveCell is closed down for good. Fuck that— we can't close down. What matters is that we get more phones out there. You always said that, right?" He paused. "You can't quit on us. *Please*."— the last word a croak.

It was probably the longest speech Jimmy Hakken had ever made, and might have been one of the few times in his life that he'd said please.

Jay stared out at the rain again. Maybe three or four minutes passed, neither of them moving. Jay turned back to Hakken.

"Sammy is dead because of me. He has five children. Any one of you might be next."

"When you stand up for what you believe in, when you change things, there's risk. It shows we got 'em scared, Chevalier. Think about that! Yeah there's lots of fucking risk. They make sure of that. But quitting's worse."

Now Jay stared at the beer can.

"Listen, would you have taken a bullet for Holmes?"

Jay nodded.

"Would you take one for me?"

Jay nodded again.

"So let's fucking get back to work."

Nick Brignolia did not open the poolroom on Sunday. Sunday afternoon, when Mary called him from the hospital with the news, he'd gone back to bed. Monday he'd only left his bedroom to eat a little reheated spaghetti. Tuesday around noon, he showered, shaved, dressed, then huddled in his recliner, trying to listen to Puccini's *La Boheme*, but before one side had played, he turned it off.

He couldn't believe Sammy'd been shot down too. Was everyone he cared about going to be taken from him? Gunned down?

After three hours of sitting in the growing darkness, he got up and looked for the LiveCell phone his brother had sent him from Boston with a note that said: *You ever need to call me use this phone. Nick, call me, I miss you. We are getting old.*

Nick had never used the phone; it seemed too strange to him, but he knew all he had to do was pick it up, say his brother's name, and then "okay." As he held it, the phone began to luminesce in the darkness. He pronounced his brother's name very loudly at the phone and placed it against his ear, not expecting it to work. But soon he heard a "Yeah."

"Anthony, that you?"

"Nicky. Jesus! You called me."

"Yeah."

"How are you?"

Nick couldn't answer.

"Hey, you okay? You sick? You don't sound so good."

"Anthony, I need to ask you for a favor."

"Go ahead, Nicky, *anything*," his brother said.

SIXTEEN

The day after Sammy's funeral, Mary was exhausted. She couldn't dim the image of Jolene and her five solemn children huddled together near the grave as the coffin was lowered slowly into cold darkness. A damp morning fog had changed to a chill drizzle, the group of mourners shivering as the first shovel of dirt struck the mahogany. It wasn't going to be much of a Christmas for any of them. Weeks before, Mary had planned to return to Vermont for the holidays, but now she didn't have the heart for the trip. Her mother had begged her to come home anyway; it had been too long between visits. However, Mary had still reluctantly told her she simply couldn't this year. Christmas at home was emotional enough under normal circumstances.

The second day after the funeral, Mary showed up for work at the usual hour. Jay had livecelled her the evening before and said, "Do you want to go back to work tomorrow?" She was very relieved by his decision; a farm girl believed in working through sadness and depression. She wondered what had made Jay change his mind, but she didn't ask. For most of the morning she fielded phone calls from inside the company and attended to writing a press release about LiveCell resuming production. In the afternoon she brought it to Jay to be reviewed. A silence caved in on them—they could barely look at each other—but at least it was a start. Mercifully, Jay decided they should quit around three.

As she headed home from the Harcourt Building she drove too fast, was frustrated by slower cars, used the shrill cry of her horn twice and got the finger once. She realized she deserved it and slowed down. No sense in someone else dying. Tears edged into her eyes. She turned into her long driveway and pulled up in front of her place but didn't get out right away. Ever since her house had been searched, she was alert on coming home, always slightly nervous. But today she merely stared dully at the rain-stained windshield, too done in to move.

When she unlocked the door and entered the hall, she immediately knew something was wrong. It was the smell. No sooner the thought than a man walked out from her kitchen. She didn't scream, she froze, terrified.

"Miss MacKensie?" he said.

He wore a pale gray suit with the jacket open, a coral tie and matching shirt. He was straightening the jacket as if he'd just put it on. She'd never seen a man of his modest height with a thicker chest. Was he the one who'd shot Sammy?

"Are you going to kill me?" she said, her mind churning, but strangely calm now that it was actually happening. Could she make the door before he caught her, or pulled his gun? She saw the dark edge of what must be a holster. Would it hurt terribly? Could she reach her car before he shot her? She doubted it. He looked extremely capable, and her body felt like lead, her legs immobile. "Are you?"

"What're you talking about?" He smiled. With the smile she couldn't help but notice that he had a surprisingly handsome boyish face, probably wasn't much older than she was. His black hair was freshly combed straight back, not a strand out of place, his accent probably Massachusetts Italian. She didn't know if it would matter to notice these details; her mind recorded them involuntarily.

"Come in here, I want you to taste something," he said.

What was he talking about?

"Come in the kitchen. I want ya to try somethin'. Tell me what you think."

She continued to stare at him.

"Miss MacKensie, please. Just a taste. I been cooking all afternoon."

"Who are you?"

"*Me?* Frankie Demanno. Who do ya think?"

"Do I know you?"

"We never met." He glanced away for an instant. "Nick didn't tell ya?"

"Tell me what?"

Now he looked embarrassed, and this reassured her just a little.

"Miss MacKensie, *hey*, I'm sorry. I'm Frankie Demanno, from Boston. I work for Nick's brother, Anthony Brignolia. I'm here to keep an eye on you. Now, please, come in here. You gotta try this," and he turned and walked into her kitchen.

She stood rigidly, her legs still weak at the knees, but then she did, not even sure why—she followed him into the kitchen. He waited there holding something out. A brand-new wooden spoon—not one of hers—his other huge hand cradled underneath to catch any drips. He guided the spoon slowly to her lips, and she, not knowing what else to do, tasted his sauce.

Her eyes lit up. "My God, that *is* good."

"You like it?"

"It's fantastic."

He reddened a little, reached for an almost empty bottle of wine. He poured a glass, offered it to her. Then he quickly cut some bread from a crusty loaf and held out the board with the slices on it. "Here, dip the bread in the sauce if you want. I'll have dinner ready in a couple minutes. I'm gonna fry some sole to go with the linguini. That be okay?"

She took a piece of bread and dipped, washed it down with the wine, which was dry and delicious.

"Where did you get all this stuff?"

"Nick and I did some shopping before he dropped me off. We know a grocery out here. I'm sorry I surprised you. Nick was supposed to call you and explain things."

"This sauce is unbelievable. Really."

"My own recipe."

"You shave the garlic with a razor?"

He looked at her and smiled. He really had quite a smile. "I just chop it fine, cook it very light in lots of olive oil, a good olive oil, first press. That razor stuff is for the movies. But my secret is Parmesan rind. You cook it right in the sauce, remove it at the end. And I use canned tomatoes, they taste better than fresh to me, and to cut the acidity I cook some carrots in the sauce. Nothing fancy. Simple is better."

"I need to sit down," she said.

"Sure, sure, whatever you want."

Mary moved to one of the dining room chairs and slumped down. The adrenaline that had pumped through her system while she was waiting to be shot had left her weak. Not to mention everything else. Frankie brought in his wine and sat beside her.

"I'm sorry about the death of your friend," he said, his earnest face showing concern. He had lovely eyes too, amber-brown, long lashes.

"Mr. Dematto, let me get this—"

"De*manno*, but please call me Frankie."

"What are you doing here? How did you get into my house?"

"Mary—can I call you Mary?" She nodded. "I'm sorry I scared ya. Like I said, Nick was supposed to call and tell you. I'm here to see nothing bad happens to you. It's that simple. Nick figured you might not go for no protection, so I thought if you met me first, you might see it's not such a bad idea. I hoped maybe you taste my cooking, you might like to keep me around a while. I love to cook."

"You're going to cook for me?"

"If you'll have me, yeah, 'course."

"You came all the way from Boston not knowing if this would work out?"

"Sure. Why not?"

"So Nick asked his brother for this?"

"Yeah."

"I still don't get it."

"Nick can't lose nobody else. He thinks very highly of you. Tells me you're some kinda pool wizard." He grinned then, as if he sensed he was winning her over.

"Maybe I should call Nick?"

"Sure, you want. Maybe you wanna eat first? You look a little peaked. Here, lemme get ya another wine."

He brought back a fresh bottle, filled their glasses with the deep-red liquid. They sat and drank, both looking out the window at the last hesitating light over the ocean. For Mary, the situation was extremely awkward, but though she didn't like to admit it, she felt a great sense of relief. And it didn't hurt that he was so good looking. She was too exhausted to figure it all out; she trusted Nick, and for the time being that was enough. Besides, if Frankie's sauce was any indication . . .

That evening Frankie Demanno moved into one of Mary's guest rooms. He cooked and did the dishes. She didn't know a man could be so neat. Nevertheless, if the house hadn't had two bathrooms, she wouldn't have accepted his staying with her. He rode with her to work the next day, complementing the Porsche, asking questions about California, San Francisco, the car, borrowing it the second day to shop for groceries and sightsee while she remained at LiveCell. He nicknamed her Virgin Mary, probably wanting to make it clear to others what their relationship was so as not to embarrass her. The nickname upset her, though he couldn't know why. When her cleaning lady came on Friday, Frankie said he'd take care of the house cleaning. Mary insisted Trisha continue, and he looked relieved. It was Frankie who suggested they should invite everyone to a big Christmas dinner. "We all need some cheering up; something good to eat never hurts," he said. "I'll take care of everything." And he did.

First he asked her about her traditions: how did she celebrate Christmas with her family? She explained about how her grandfather cut a balsam fir tree on the farm a few days before the Eve, soon to be decorated with dozens of live candles; about listening to Dylan Thomas reading *A Child's Christmas In Wales* on the old phonograph in the parlor as the candles burned and the scent of balsam was released from the heat of the flames; about her mother baking all kinds of special cookies and fruit breads. Frankie asked her, with a worried look that made her laugh, if live candles weren't dangerous on a Christmas tree. She told him only if the tree wasn't freshly cut. He quizzed her about the bakeries and wanted some of the recipes. When she livecelled home, her mom said she would e-mail the recipes and asked Mary, again, to come home: "Why would you bake those things there when I've already made them here?" Mary reassured her that she would visit in the spring. She couldn't seem to mention her new roommate.

To the Christmas dinner they invited Deirdre and Jimmy Hakken; Duncan, sounding disconcerted by the invitation, decided to stay home with his mother; David Artega, very busy now with the Samuel Holmes case, had family as well; Mary thought of Jolene and the kids, but knew they'd be with her parents and sister; Nick Brignolia simply asked what time and what to bring; and Jay, hesitating at first, accepted. Mary, disliking herself for the thought, knowing it wasn't the time for it, still hoped that Jay might get a little jealous of Frankie Demanno. "But he just doesn't think about me that way," she admitted, and didn't have a clue how to change it. "I don't want to be *virgin* Mary much longer."

Mary and Frankie spent the next two days shopping and preparing for their party. They found gifts for everyone, and her spirits continued to improve. It was during one of these shopping trips that an incident occurred. It altered her perception of Frankie Demanno.

They'd been walking back together across an unlit gravel lot to where they'd parked, Frankie carrying a bag of smoked salmon, fresh clams and mussels. As they approached her Porsche he slowed, set the bag quietly on the ground. He motioned for her to stay put, his face set in an alertness she'd never seen. He unbuttoned his jacket and walked toward her car. Then Mary saw the two men.

"What're you doin'?" said Frankie, his voice cold. It was still calm, yet without any trace of humor or softness. The inflection was new to her.

"What's it to you, chief?" one of the men said.

Frankie moved in close to the guy who'd spoken, standing only a few feet away.

"You got a problem, chief?" the man said.

"Yeah. You."

The man's hand snapped toward his pocket. Before it got there, Frankie reacted. Mary had never seen a person of his bulk move so fast. His right shoe stamped on the guy's foot, the hard edge of the sole scraping down the length of shin. At the same time his open hand chopped the guy in the Adam's apple. In seconds, the guy was on the gravel choking, grabbing his shin. Later, Mary would remember it as rather comical.

Frankie turned to the other one. "You too?"

That guy grabbed his partner and dragged him across the lot.

Frankie returned to Mary, picking up the bag of seafood. "Sorry you had to see that," he said, looking embarrassed.

He definitely had two sides. "What *were* they doing?" she said.

"I think they liked your car, maybe too much."

She could tell he was protecting her from the truth. She knew then that the Aldens, or whoever, were still after LiveCell. Anger flooded her. It wasn't that she hadn't expected it, but something about Christmas had made her less wary. Had they sent these two men so she'd tell Jay? So that she'd be scared? Were they testing Frankie Demanno? She questioned him again about the incident, but all he said was, "You don't need to worry, Mary, that's why I'm here."

Frankie liked to read different newspaper articles to Mary as they breakfasted. She was reminded of an angelic, aging choirboy as he sat there in his reading glasses and perfectly ironed sports shirts. He was actually in his early thirties, his birthday four years and a few days from hers, but sometimes he could look so young. The coverage of LiveCell in the smaller alternative papers fascinated him. "The only papers not owned by the corporate political dynasty," she told him.

A grass roots movement supporting LiveCell had emerged in ever-widening circles since the FDA had attempted to undermine the company with the allegations that the phones caused headaches and disturbed sleep. Many people had responded in defense of LiveCell, yet the mainstream media had ignored their rebuttals, which only intensified their certainty that something was wrong. As people used LiveCell phones, many developed an intuitive awareness and became progressively more difficult to dupe. They felt that with the nation's economy ruined, with the leaders of big business having looted half of America's corporate wealth, with civil rights being removed in the false name of Homeland Security, that LiveCell phones were one of the only good things they had left. The shooting of Samuel Holmes had further fueled the movement and intensified people's anger. Many were demanding that his killer be found, and conspiracy theories were voiced. Many sensed that Jay was the actual target of the Holmes hit, and they wanted to know who'd ordered his death.

Frankie read to her: "One columnist writes in here, 'A senator and his family were murdered to gain control of the house, why not Jay Chevalier?'" The primary media ignored all the real stories, yet the discrepancy in reporting was becoming embarrassingly noticeable. "This Jay Chevalier guy," Frankie said, "is becoming a people's hero, same as that Cuban guy, Che Guevara."

On Christmas morning Mary was as excited as a child. She'd bought something special for Jay. It was quite a find, and she believed Jay would be thrilled, though how could anyone ever tell with him? Mary got up early and took a leisurely bath. She dressed with care, the smell of coffee and bacon from the kitchen mingling with her bath oil and lotions. Having Frankie Demanno around was like having a gentleman's gentleman. And it was all free, courtesy of Mr. Anthony Brignolia. But is anything ever really free? she wondered. Anthony Brignolia must want something. As she combed out the tangles in her wet hair, she glanced at one of the Christmas cards leaning against the bureau's mirror: a Santa Claus on a reindeer roping a steer. It seemed ages ago that she'd ridden in Garland's pickup truck, and she wondered if he was maintaining his indomitable spirit. There was also a recent letter from Kelly Harris; she reread a few sentences.

With all these LiveCell phones not many people are writing letters anymore. Strange to think of myself as old-fashioned. I have to admit something about those phones: I find them almost too intimate, too intense. I look forward to seeing you for Christmas—

She thought about Kelly for a minute and was startled that her perception of him had changed. She still loved him dearly and missed him, yet he was no longer quite the hero, or mentor, that he'd once been. It was because he had never accomplished anything, she realized, he hadn't used his abilities—he had hidden from them. But she was sure he'd done the best he could. And he'd always had plenty of heart; that was why she loved him.

Had she changed that much in a year and a half? Something passed through her, an energy that shot up her spine, and it forced her to sit on the bed. Then, in a moment of pure calm, she could feel the entire planet surrounding her with all its complexity and all its contrast, all its desire and all its need, all its anger and all its love. As if she could almost touch everyone she cared about, and she felt Sammy somehow with her as well. Was this what Jay meant by the continuum?

After a while she breathed deeply, stood, checked herself in the mirror one more time, and went to wish Frankie Demanno a Merry Christmas.

A few minutes after they finished breakfast, a courier knocked on the door with a long cylindrical burlap-wrapped package addressed to Mary MacKensie. Frankie carried it inside for her. "Fresh cut," he said. It was a balsam fir tree. From his bedroom he hauled a bright-green metal tree stand, Christmas tree candles, and shiny tin holders that clipped onto the branches and pivoted to allow the candles to point vertically.

"I can't believe this," she said. They set up the tree in the corner of the living room facing the ocean. He brought out multicolored lights and an overly generous assortment of ornaments.

"I made a few phone calls," he said. "They shipped everything. I hid the boxes under my bed. I thought that tree guy was never gonna get here. 'Course he'd be dead if he didn't." He winked at her, but she wasn't absolutely certain he was kidding.

Around noon, Frankie, wearing an apron with an embroidered elf over his big chest, started preparing crostini in olive oil to be served with fresh ricotta, anchovy slivers, and a cannellini puree with herbs. When the guests arrived, these would be flanked by a slab of Parmesan and shaved Pecorino, crisply fried whole baby artichokes, clams casino, and grilled marinated plump Mediterranean sardines. A chestnut and mushroom stuffed goose to honor Mary's New England roots was ready for the oven. Yesterday he'd prepared a spicy tomato sauce for the spaghetti; today he'd add chopped lobster claws.

Soon it was early afternoon, the kitchen exhaling a variety of wonderful vapors. They opened a bottle of champagne, toasting the day, sitting out on the deck in the Adirondack chairs facing the sun. Frankie, though he enjoyed his red wine while cooking, wasn't really much of a drinker. Their first night had been an exception, and with a tiny smile she realized even he might get nervous on occasion. There is something in life to frighten everyone.

Nick Brignolia was the first to arrive, dressed in a black suit, starched white shirt, and cardinal-red tie with a modest diamond tiepin. He carried an enormous bouquet of roses. While Mary went into the kitchen to arrange them in a vase, Frankie offered Nick a glass of wine. The old man shook his head: "Later, later I will have one. I talk to Anthony this morning. My brother wish everyone a Merry Christmas."—calling this to Mary as she walked out of the kitchen. "Frankie, he thinks he make a crazy mistake to send his best guy out here. He miss your cooking."

"He may miss it a long time. I like it out here." He glanced at Mary, or where she'd been a moment ago setting the flowers on the table. She was fiddling with something on the tree. His eyes followed her, as if he were hoping for a reaction.

"He might be coming to visit," Nick said to him.

"When?"—a flicker of concern.

"In a few weeks."

"Why?"

"I don't know, maybe for your cooking."

"Maybe to see you?"

"Maybe."

Deirdre and Jimmy Hakken arrived together in her station wagon. Hakken was his usual black-clad tattooed self with the addition of a pendulous candy-cane-striped stocking hat and a cloth bag full of presents. He made a very ominous Santa. Deirdre wore a new pants suit and a fresh stylish hairdo. After Mary hugged her, she looked her up and down still holding her hands.

"Deirdre," she said, "you look fantastic. What a beautiful suit."

"I just bought it," she said, blushing.

"What a great color on you."

"I hoped you might like it; I mean, the suit. They called the color like antique plum or something. Silly name."

"Fantastic color though."

Mary introduced everyone, and Frankie greeted the new guests with a wide smile. Deirdre shrieked on seeing the table of food, and he explained his appetizers to her. Jimmy Hakken was mute as usual, first setting his big bag near the tree, then observing Frankie carefully, probably having heard something about him, maybe noting how relaxed and easygoing he seemed. Regardless, Hakken remained withdrawn and serious. Mary offered champagne, which everyone but Hakken accepted. He had a beer. Always the outsider, she thought.

"That tree is so beautiful," said Deirdre. "And all the red candles look really nice. Oh, my, God, they're real."

"We're going to light them," said Mary.

"No way!"

"Frankie had the tree cut in the wild. That way it has the right spaces between the branches for candles. With pruned Christmas trees the branches are too close together, and you never know when they've been cut."

"That is *way* cool. I didn't know anyone still did it. I mean, have real burning candles." A pause. "Is Jay coming?"

"He said he was. He's a bit late, isn't he? I'll livecell him." She set down her glass. "Jay? . . . okay, good. We were just making sure." She turned to Deirdre. "He's on his way. I don't think he's so big on Christmas." She glanced at the three men talking around the dining room table: Frankie telling a funny story, Nick carefully sipping his champagne, Hakken listening with rapt attention, the strange stocking hat such a contrast to his demeanor.

Deirdre leaned closer to Mary, lowered her voice. "We're always going to worry about Jay now, aren't we?"

"At least he decided to go back to work. I was terrified he wouldn't reopen LiveCell. The idea of being beaten by those bastards irked me to no end, but I knew Jay had to work through it in his own way. Remember Detective Artega?"

"Sure. Tall, lanky, dark. From the shooting at the factory. The only cop that seemed to believe Jay."

"In the last few days he's made some headway on Sammy's death. Michael Pegonis has—"

"Who?"

"From that night, the ex-security guy who shot Jay in the arm."

"That big asshole."

"He worked for Alden Stone Associates. He's contacted Artega and says he has information on the shooting. He wants immunity and protection from Artega, and two million from Jay. Jay doesn't trust the whole thing. Artega wants him to go along, see where it leads."

"Are you and Jay doing better?"

"Because he's telling me these things?"

"Not just that."

Mary examined her. Deirdre wanted to know if she was going to attempt the phone infusion. Had Jay been talking to her about it? Asked her to say something? She couldn't open herself to him like that again, it was too destructive. Or what if she fought against the infusion as Deirdre had? What if Jay's heart stopped?

"I don't think I can," she said.

"It's like, *real* important that you try."

Mary only nodded, then glanced over at the men.

"Frankie's awful cute, isn't he?" said Deirdre.

Mary suddenly felt that maybe Deirdre was getting too damn intuitive.

"Aw-oh, I'm making you blush again," she said.

"It's not that way with Frankie and me."

"Hey," said Frankie from across the room, his ears burning. "What's the huddle about? Come on and join us."

"He's right," said Mary. "It's Christmas." Besides, she wanted off the subject.

Jay finally arrived, Cutlass sounding terminal. It had developed an ominous rapping, a noise that secretly pleased Mary. She'd heard him coming—who couldn't?—and stood now in the open doorway as he parked. Everyone had kept the space free in front of her two-car garage as she'd requested, and Jay followed suit. He jumped out and walked toward her, dressed the same as on the first day she saw him.

"Merry Christmas," he called. "Sorry I'm late. Car isn't running so well."

They embraced. His body just seemed to fit hers. He was warm too, even in only the T-shirt. Why hadn't he dressed up? Was it from being preoccupied, or from being a bit of a Scrooge? But being an orphan, what kind of good feelings could he have about Christmas? Of course, he never dressed up except in Deirdre's jacket anyway, which, come to think of it, she hadn't seen in weeks.

When they entered the house, everyone got up to greet Jay, even Nick. Deirdre threw her arms around him, and Mary again felt jealous; they seemed so close, their relationship uncomplicated. Frankie and Jay had met briefly at the office, but they shook hands now with no readable expression. Mary wondered how they felt about each other. Frankie treated Jay as if he were a celebrity. Maybe he was? Would she ever stop feeling this way around him? She tried to put him out of her mind and concentrated on her hostess duties, taking beverage orders, pouring champagne, passing out plates and napkins. Jay decided to join Jimmy Hakken and drink beer. He *would*.

After about an hour Mary couldn't contain her excitement, couldn't wait any longer. She also wanted to do it while there was still plenty of light outside. She double winked Frankie—their signal. He excused himself, and she kept Jay occupied. She'd made sure the CD player was loaded and that the volume was up enough. She gave Frankie five or six minutes and glanced outside. She told Jay she needed to show him something in the dooryard. He followed her.

Resting in front of her garage was an arctic blue 1965 Chevrolet station wagon with an enormous red ribbon and bow around it. "Merry Christmas, Jay," she said.

He walked up to the car, caressed a fender for a few moments, turned back to her, put his arms around her, kissed her cheek. "It is beautiful," he said, releasing her.

"I know the paint isn't perfect," she said, ignoring the placement of his kiss. "Especially on the roof. And it has the one dent, but it *is* all original, even the paint. You can see cracks in the lacquer. I thought you would prefer it that way. It runs like a top."

"It's perfect," he said. "The best."

By then the others had come out of the house and gathered around. "Oh my God, it's an Impala," said Deirdre. "And not a lowrider. Like how did that happen?"

They told Jay to get in, to try it on, see how it fit. Behind the wheel he actually looked like a tough celebrity as he smiled out the rolled down window at them. The car really did fit him.

"Let's all go for a ride," said Mary, and they climbed onto the blue Naugahyde bench seats. Jay fired up the rumbling engine and backed up the wagon, Mary beside him, Frankie riding shotgun, the other three behind. His old Cutlass wasn't a small car, but he acted as though he were backing up an ocean liner.

They drove slowly, coasted through the Christmas day, the road all but empty, hazy afternoon sun in the yellow grass as they paralleled the shoreline. Nick told them how his first car in Boston had been just like this one: "A sixty-nine Buick sedan, maroon color with the black seats." Frankie looked over his shoulder and said, "Same car exactly, Nick," and everyone laughed. For the first time since Sammy'd been shot, Mary felt some life come back into Jay.

As the sun began to color the sky over the Pacific, Frankie said he hated to end the family outing, but he had to get the goose out of the oven. Jay carefully turned the big boat and, with the water on their right now, motored back.

It was still light when they returned but it was whispering. After mooring the Impala, Jay walked over and popped the trunk of the Cutlass, removed five packages. Jimmy Hakken, still in his incongruous hat, helped him carry them into the house. Frankie had shot into the kitchen and was a whirl of activity. He explained he didn't need help, just quiet to concentrate. Everyone else settled in the dining and living room as a hot appetizer of fragrant steamed mussels strayed from the stove accompanied by loaves of crusty Italian bread. Though another bottle of champagne was opened, Jay and Hakken stayed stubbornly with beer. Nick sipped his one glass of red wine, commenting twice about how good it was. Mary had vodka for Deirdre, but after one on ice, she joined the champagne drinkers. Mary played Perry Como and Frank Sinatra for Nick, and Nat King Cole sang "Chestnuts Roasting on an Open Fire." As dusk gently dimmed the room, they turned on the tree lights.

Mary and Jay set the table, and soon everyone except Frankie was seated—Jimmy Hakken finally removed his hat, exposing his freshly shaved head—and a procession of food began to arrive from the kitchen. First there was a chilled seafood salad with fresh squid, sea scallops, and shrimp, the pale creatures glistening in herbed olive oil, capers and hot peppers, each glass bowl containing a tentacled squid head like a small violet crown. This was followed by his spaghetti with signature red sauce laden with lobster bits. Accompanying the goose, steamed broccoli rabe, and mashed potatoes latticed by fried sage leaves. A salad of radicchio, arugula, and frisee, a turbulent coil of reds and greens finished the main course.

"Everyone get enough to eat?" he said.

"Frankie, best meal I have since I leave Boston," said Nick, setting his napkin firmly beside his plate.

Mary raised her glass. "I'd like to propose a toast. To Frankie, who not only supplied us with one of the finest meals I have ever eaten, *and* provided the beautiful tree, but also, with his humor and his calm, helped at a very difficult time."

He looked down as they drank to him, then his eyes came up, searching hers.

"That was like, unbelievable. Everything was *so* good. I don't think I've ever eaten so much. I mean, my God, who has?"

"Is everyone ready for coffee and dessert?" said Mary. "Frankie baked some cookies from my mother's recipes."

"Nick, I picked up a pannetone for you. Traditional recipe. And I got a bottle of anisette, of course."

"I think I call Anthony, tell him you staying here now with us."

Jay said, "Mary, and Frankie. It was a lovely idea to have this meal, and to invite all of us to share it. This is the nicest Christmas I've ever had. You've all been very considerate not talking about Sammy's death. If I may, I would ask that we drink to our friend's memory and to his family. I talked with Jolene earlier today, and she asked us to drink to Sammy's memory tonight." He looked above their faces. He held out his glass, and they waited. "Sammy . . ." If he had more to add, he couldn't manage it. They all drank.

Jimmy Hakken, standing on a chair, lit the top half of the tree candles. Frankie, after giving Mary another gift, a CD with *A Child's Christmas in Wales* on it, lit the rest. They sat on chairs and sofas, each person with a full beverage, all other lights turned off. " . . . *and out of all sound except the distant speaking of voices I sometimes hear a moment before sleep, . . . All the Christmases roll down toward the two-tongued sea, like a cold and headlong moon bundling down the sky . . .*" Each of the three-dozen candles with a starred halo, the tinsel icicles wavering restlessly in the rising heat of the flames, the ornaments reflecting, the warmed balsam sap beginning to scent the air. " . . . *I said some words to the close and holy darkness, and then I slept.*"

"I've never seen anything so totally beautiful," said Deirdre, after they'd blown out the candles and put the room lights back on. "I mean, it was just *so* amazing."

It was time to open the rest of the presents. Mary gave Frankie a pair of handmade Italian loafers in oxblood-colored leather, Deirdre a visit to a fancy spa, Nick season tickets to the opera. Mary and Deirdre gave Jimmy Hakken an exact plaster copy of a winged gargoyle cast from Notre Dame cathedral for his office.

"I wondered what that blanket-wrapped thing was in the wagon," he said.

Nick gave everyone a very delicate hand-blown glass ornament imported from Italy. Deirdre gave Mary hand-embroidered silk pajamas with a matching robe, and Jay a new sports jacket.

"What happened to your other one?" said Mary.

"It got lost," he said.

Jimmy Hakken presented each of them with a wrapped box, each box a different size and in a different wrapping paper. But inside, each person found the identical chunky silver pendant, cast from the same obviously hand-carved mold, attached to a leather lanyard. Everyone was a bit dumbfounded. At the silence, Hakken said, "Luke Delamar's buddy, he does metal, he made 'em up for me. I told him to go all out, no skimping, real actual silver." He looked around at their faces. "It's the eye inside the hand . . . I got one too. We all got one." Still no one spoke, they just kept staring at their pendants.

Finally Frankie said, "Keeps off the evil eye?"

"Right," said Hakken, brightening. "*Right*, they're real good luck."

Jay gave each of them a framed drawing by a Maine artist. All five drawings were of falling lit matches, the burning matches and flames realistic against backgrounds more sketchy, dark and brooding as if with an ominous hint of storm, the paper itself scratched. Mary said the drawings reminded her of the painting in Jay's office. Jimmy Hakken kept examining his drawing, nodding his head as if the image made special sense to him.

Nick excused himself around ten, kissing Mary carefully on each cheek before he left. It was the first time he'd shown such affection. When it was near midnight, the others decided it was time. Mary saw them off as Frankie began to clean up. Soon Deirdre's station wagon roared down the road, Hakken at the wheel. "I only had beer," he'd said as if beer didn't count as drinking. Jay abandoned the Cutlass, told Mary he'd have it towed tomorrow, and the Impala's round taillights slowly disappeared down her road. She stood looking into the darkness long after he was gone. Then she turned abruptly and went back into the house.

After Frankie finished cleaning the kitchen—he insisted she didn't help—they sat together and drank a last glass of champagne.

"I think it went really well," she said, feeling a tiredness beginning to tug after the long day. "First time I've seen Jay come out of his shell since the shooting. I was glad he brought up Sammy. Maybe he's beginning to heal. Maybe we all are."

"He's a very tough guy. You see that right away."

"You haven't seen him at his best."

"Don't need to. I can tell. I also see the loyalty he generates."

She looked at the tree, the stubs of the burnt-down candles, the multicolored lights still on. "Your food was beyond belief, and the tree, and everything," she said.

"Mary?"

She heard something in his voice.

"I have here one last little present for you." He took something out of his pocket. "I know we haven't known each other very long, but I wanted to get this for you." He slid it toward her. "Merry Christmas."

A flat box wrapped in blue paper with a white ribbon.

"Please," he said.

She slowly unwrapped it. Found a felt-covered box of the same shade of blue. Inside were two large pearl earrings. She didn't speak right away.

"Frankie, these are very beautiful, but I don't know if I can accept them."

"I don't have no family. I got no one to spend money on. It would mean a lot to me if you'd accept them as a token of my friendship."

She stared at him, and he glanced away.

"Don't decide right now, okay? Just give it a few days. What's it gonna hurt—a few days. *Please?*"

She continued to look at him, and finally, unable to make up her mind, she said she would give it a few days.

SEVENTEEN

Two and a half weeks after the holidays, Jay Chevalier sat at his desk, working. Though he'd been showing up at LiveCell every day since Christmas, it was only in the last few days that his former motivation had returned. He reached for his phone: David Artega.

They greeted each other, and the detective said, "Normally I'd come see you in person to tell you this, but I'm gradually getting used to the fact that these phones are secure."

Jay waited. Something had gone wrong. Lately, Artega had been having trouble with the Samuel Holmes case. Jay knew it was partially his fault because he'd refused to negotiate with Michael Pegonis.

Artega said, "They've removed me from the case without explanation. Even the Chief couldn't believe it. He told me off the record that he had no choice, the pressure came from high up."

"Did they replace you?"

"If you want to call it that."

They were both silent.

Then Artega, "It gets to me, putting up with this kind of political bullshit year after year. I know it's part of the job, but it shouldn't be."

"It can change," said Jay with more emotion than usual.

"What do you mean? No one can change that shit. Those assholes know they can get away with it; they always have. At least the public around here seems to be on LiveCell's side. Just when you think America is asleep, it wakes up."

Another pause.

"Michael Pegonis," said Artega.

"Yeah?"

"Gone, disappeared. Untraceable."

Jay's expression darkened further. He waited for Artega to speak.

"Listen, you need me for anything, livecell, okay?"

"Done."

"And listen, I haven't given up."

They ended the call. Almost immediately Jay had another, but he ignored it for the moment. He waited until he no longer felt like punching something.

"Hey, Jay, how's it going?" It was Frankie Demanno.

"Good. You?"

"Perfect, perfect. So we still on for three-thirty?"

Jay was silent.

"Perfect. I'm picking him up at the airport and bringing him directly to you." Jay didn't respond to this either; they'd already discussed these details. "Okay, see you then."

"Frankie?"

"Yeah."

"Are you nervous about something?"

"'Course not."

They said good-bye.

Jay got back to work, yet after only ten or twelve minutes, Mary appeared in his doorway. He motioned her in.

"You look upset," she said.

"Artega called. He's been taken off the case."

"It's been too quiet lately. Almost three weeks now and nothing interesting happening—no one shooting at us, no demolition attempts, no false press, no new spies, even the FDA backing down a bit, or at least no fresh attacks."—she hadn't told him about the two men waiting for her and Frankie by the car—"I'm glad I have a bodyguard. I don't know why you refuse one."

"He just called."

"Was he out in his new car?"

"I think so."

"He's like a kid with that car. Frankie always drove Cadillacs. He'd never been in a Porsche until mine. You never know what will get to someone."

"How's he been lately?" said Jay.

She hesitated. "A little preoccupied, now that you mention it. Why?"

"Has he ever asked about how the phones work?"

"Never. What's going on?"

"You know who is meeting with me today?"

She shook her head and waited.

"Anthony Brignolia."

"Wow."

"I had Duncan check him out this morning. He found almost nothing. Surprised even Duncan. Brignolia doesn't seem to exist in the form of digital information. Duncan's been at it for hours."

"Is he coming to visit Nick?"

"Nick hasn't been mentioned. He's coming here directly from the airport. You'd think after all those years, something like twenty, he might want to see his brother first."

"I wonder why Frankie didn't tell me?"

"He was instructed not to. Frankie asked me to keep it quiet as well, and asked that our meeting remain secret. Brignolia doesn't want anyone to know we're meeting."

"Do you know what kind of business he's in?"

"Frankie wouldn't tell me."

"Sammy revealed a few things one afternoon at the poolroom . . ." and she told him about the shooting of Nick's wife and son and how it was connected with his brother's business. As she told the story, Jay got very still. Every shooting would bring back Sammy's death for him.

"Will you greet him when he arrives?" he said. "I want your impression."

At precisely three-thirty, the front desk rang. Jay livecelled Mary to meet the guests. Within perhaps five or six minutes, the three of them entered his orange office. Jay came around from behind his desk and extended his arm.

"Mr. Brignolia," he said, "Welcome to LiveCell. I see you've met Mary MacKensie." He said hello to Frankie Demanno.

Anthony Brignolia was younger than his brother and of a more delicate stature. His hair was black and expensively cut, and Jay wondered if he dyed it since Nick's was almost white. He also lacked Nick's humped nose—maybe his had been fixed. His midnight-blue hand-tailored

English suit hung perfectly, a pale-ivory Egyptian cotton shirt and deep-maroon silk tie matched the understated taste of his faux-tortoiseshell wire-rimmed glasses. A glance at Jay's blue T-shirt and worn jeans brought a ripple of surprise across his brow. It was instantly suppressed.

"Doctor Chevalier," he said, "this is a great honor for me." Jay's hand surrounded the gentle clasp of Brignolia's fingers.

Frankie waited by the door, his posture more rigid than normal, a box under one arm. Brignolia made a slight movement of his head and Frankie set the box on the desk. "That'll be all, Demanno," he said, and Frankie turned to leave.

"Mr. Brignolia," said Jay, "would you care for a coffee, something else?" Brignolia shook his head curtly. "Thanks Mary, thanks for showing them up. So long, Frankie."

Frankie nodded, Mary winked so only Jay saw it, and they both withdrew.

Brignolia glanced back at the open door.

"I always leave it open," said Jay. "Would you feel more comfortable if it were closed?"

"If it isn't a problem."

Jay was forced to circle around the motionless Brignolia to close the door. "Please, sit down." He gestured toward his collection of mismatched armchairs.

Brignolia ignored his offer and stepped over to the framed Ryder reproduction, studying it for an unhurried moment; then he chose a chair.

Jay settled in behind his desk again. He wasn't going to give Brignolia any advantages; it fascinated him too much to watch the man work.

"Ryder's *Toilers on a Sea*, isn't it?" Brignolia said.

"Yes," said Jay, though the title was *The Toilers of the Sea*. Still, the man must know something about art, and wanted him to realize it.

"I thank you for seeing me. I've brought you a small gift."

Jay glanced at the plain cardboard box, rectilinear and about as long as his arm.

"Please," said Brignolia, gesturing slightly toward it.

Jay stood up and slid the carton to his side of the desk with one hand. Using a penknife, he cut through the packing tape, opened one end, and pulled out a second box. This had a tight fitting lid that needed to be slowly lifted to break the suction of air. Inside, protected by gray foam, was something long and plastic-wrapped. He knew what the gift was and carefully loosened the almost twelve-pound object from its foam cradle, unwrapped the plastic, and set the model train engine on his desk. It was a masterpiece in brass, handmade in Korea, each part faithfully reproduced and painted just like the original engine. It could run, sound, and smoke just like a real one.

"A Union Pacific Big Boy," said Jay. "Many consider it the most powerful steam locomotive ever produced." He actually preferred smaller engines like Berkshires and Hudsons.

"I asked the man for the finest one they had. Did he do all right?"

Jay nodded. "How do you know I run O gauge trains?"

"I know a great deal about you, Doctor Chevalier."

Jay looked up from studying the model. "Then you should call me Jay. Thank you for the gift, it's very thoughtful."

"If it brings you pleasure, I'm pleased." The minimal smile was something the two brothers had in common, though Anthony's was even less demonstrative than Nick's. Where Nick's grimace had some warmth, with Anthony, there was none.

Neither said anything; both waited for the other to speak. Jay didn't want his silence to become rude. "So why are you here?" he said.

Anthony Brignolia searched Chevalier's face and spoke immediately. "LiveCell is changing the world. This change has only begun." He paused. "The world runs on information. Up until your telephones most information could be accessed, traced. All conventional methods leave footprints and can be bugged—until LiveCell. Your telephones are secure *and* leave no trail—it changes everything."

"I thought the world ran on commodities?"

Brignolia almost smiled. "You're right," he said. "First salt, then oil, now drugs and silicon chips, maybe water or LiveCell phones soon—but with information you control those who control the commodities."

"Is that what you do?" Jay said.

Brignolia stared at Jay as if he were attempting to look into him. "I am going to be honest with you. I understand you're an honest man. A rare thing at your level. And I know why you're honest. You care more about honesty than money or power."

Jay was silent.

"What I do is leverage situations for clients. I do this with information."

Still nothing from Jay. His silence irritated Brignolia.

"You might be surprised at some of the things we've handled. For instance, a recent Supreme Court decision over an election. I don't tell you this to impress you, only so you know at what level we operate. Most people have things to hide, and usually these things can destroy them if made public. Of course, much of the media can be controlled, either for or against someone. Many times people have something they want very much and can be manipulated that way. But then there is you. Seems you have nothing to hide and no price."

"Do you know who killed Samuel Holmes?"

"Holmes, the black man. He had courage—a waste. I know he was your friend and I'm sorry for your loss. I know the bullet was intended for you. You've been very lucky, and now I watch as the small newspapers take up your cause. It's given you a little more time."

"Did you have anything to do with it?"

Brignolia was startled. "Of course not. Such methods are barbaric and stupid; they're from thirty years ago. There's rarely a need for killing. It should always be avoided. It's messy. Jay, I fear you misunderstand me. I do not like or respect these people."

"Yet you work for them."

"It's my business."

"Don't they have their own organizations?"

"They fight amongst themselves for power, they're not secure, they have no loyalty. Look at the mess the FDA made. Headaches? What fools. They spent a fortune and it hardly affected LiveCell at all."

"What do you want from me?"

Brignolia stopped talking and looked down at his pants. He needlessly readjusted the crease at each knee.

"I fear I've given you the wrong impression, though it's refreshing to talk with someone so direct." Brignolia waited and received only silence again. "If you want the killer of this Samuel Holmes, I will get him for you."

"Mr. Brignolia, what is it that you want?"

"I want to save your life."

"And you think it needs saving?"

"Yes."

"Why do you think my life is in danger?"

"You don't know?" Brignolia sensed he'd gained something, finally, and paused. "You're a dangerous man. To those in control, you are upsetting their world, the very way that it functions, the fundamental laws under which it operates. You don't think they realize that people using

LiveCell phones are changing? And now the public is believing in you more and more."

"That's ridiculous. I only invented a new kind of telephone."

His mouth flashed the cold half-smile. "You're teasing me now. Do you know that DuPont Chemical Company has a team of lawyers that have been desperate to sue you? But you're too smart, and do not patent your telephone, so what can they do? And still no one can figure out how it works. You're an amazing man, Chevalier."

They were silent again. Brignolia wondered if his outburst had been advisable. How can you read a man like this? How can you figure out a man when you don't know what he wants, or what gets to him? At least he knew that everyone wants to stay alive, no one wants to die.

"So?" said Jay.

Chevalier was going to be killed and this was how he responded? Brignolia decided he hadn't made himself clear enough. "I can keep you alive. It will be difficult, but I believe I can do this. Without me you'll be killed. This I have no doubt about; this I know."

"I thought killing was out of style?"

"You joke with me again, but they're desperate, and they'll kill you. It's their only solution now."

"So what do you want from me?" Jay said it once more.

Brignolia paused, wondering if it was the right moment. He'd waited a long time for this, and he wanted it more than anything he'd ever desired. He kept the excitement out of his voice.

"You need me. I offer the network to protect you and all your people. I can leverage the press in your favor, which will bring the masses behind you, which will further protect you. I know you say you don't care about money, yet this I bring also. I'll assist you in managing the business so that every person on earth has a LiveCell telephone. China alone is worth billions. With this income, and the changes it will bring to the power structure, we can take control. Then we do whatever you want. We destroy corruption, dishonesty, we build all the orphan houses you want."

"You know about that?"

"Most altruism, everyone does it for reward, for publicity. They even pretend they don't want publicity and then quietly allow their altruism to be discovered. Not you."

"And what do you want in return?"

"Half of your stock holdings in LiveCell, which I believe is thirty percent of the company, and my people will make up half your board of directors."

"Does Frankie know?" he said.

Brignolia was shocked. He makes his final offer and Chevalier asks him about one of his employees? "Know what?"

"Why he was sent out here," said Jay.

"He was sent out here because my brother called me and asked for a favor to protect the girl. There is no one better at that than Demanno. Besides, it had to be someone the girl would accept."

"And that was the only reason?"

"I sent Demanno for both reasons. That is the truth."

Jay paused. "I think LiveCell is fine as it is."

Brignolia looked down; he did not want Chevalier to read his expression. He faced Jay again. "I don't think you realize the truth of what I am telling you. You do not know these people like I do."

"But you work for them?"

"Without their approval, very little is possible. They destroy what gets in their way, and they'll destroy you. You need me."

Brignolia sensed he was losing him. He didn't understand this man who seemed unafraid to die. Was he bluffing? He knew Chevalier was too intelligent not to see some truth in what he was saying, yet he wasn't interested in his offer. And he was offering the man his life, for God's sake. He knew Chevalier had turned down every financial offer. Where was this man's weakness? Everyone had something. *Everyone.* Chevalier didn't appear to be involved with anyone and seemed impervious to coercion. A very difficult person.

When Chevalier remained silent, Brignolia said again, "I work for them, but I don't like it. They treat me always as if I'm beneath them, with their careful condescension, and talk to me as if we're in a stupid gangster movie, only because I was born Sicilian. They hide behind their manners, yet their arrogance is sickening. And they're not that smart, this I know, but they're ruthless when it comes to protecting their world. They consider it an untouchable right, something they've been granted by being born into it. They know nothing about working people, people like you and me. These are men who would allow their own buildings to be bombed and children to die, just to remain in power. Chevalier, we can bring them down. Together, we can beat them." It was as close to a plea as Anthony Brignolia had ever made.

Jay got up from his desk and walked to the window. The blue-green in the bay was fading to a blue-gray. He could see a few white caps, the red stern of a boat and its wake as it disappeared behind a building. It was probably going to start raining again. For a moment his mind went to northern Maine. He imagined the snow there now, that crystalline blue curve of a snow field on a clear late January afternoon, maybe a sliver of moon just showing in the eastern sky. He thought of the snow covering his mother's grave; he thought of his grandfather and wondered if the cabin was still standing. He turned back to Anthony Brignolia.

"Mr. Brignolia, I appreciate your offer and your belief in LiveCell. I know you came a long way to talk to me. Allow me a few days, perhaps a week, to consider your proposal. It would not be just my decision, many people make up this company. Would that be okay?"

Brignolia stood. He extended his hand. They shook.

"Yes, that would be fine," he said. "Any details you would like from me, please call."

Jay examined him, and just as Brignolia was about to turn away he said, "Is Alden Stone Associates one of your clients?"

There was a minute jolt in Brignolia's eyes; he didn't need an answer. "I'll walk you down," he said.

It was almost dark outside. San Francisco pulsed with electric light as most offices and stores were still open for business. She'd brought them each a mug of coffee from the lounge.

"So what did you think of him?" said Jay.

"He looks a lot like Nick except for the hair and the nose, but that's where the resemblance ends. He has none of the vulnerability or tenderness. Not that Nick doesn't try to hide his, but if Anthony is hiding his, he's doing one incredible job. What did he want?"

"Half of my LiveCell stock and half the board."

"*Jesus!* Why does he think you would sell to him if you turned down all other offers?"

"I'm not sure. He wants it badly. I know that."

"Don't they all."

"If he has other holdings, which he probably has, he would take control of the company."

She looked at him—at his calm eyes, a bit tired since Sammy's death; at the strong jaw, the carved angles of his pale, battered face; at the close-cropped hair with its increase of gray. Her senses almost too aware when she was with him, still so affected by his presence that it annoyed her. Then she noticed the locomotive on his desk.

"Was that in the box? How did he know you liked trains?"

"He seems to have researched me rather thoroughly."

"He doesn't know about the Siuslaw Road house does he?"

"Can't imagine how. I bought the trains here in San Francisco, so that was easy to trace. He possesses a great deal of information though. He calls you *the girl.*"

"The girl—that's kind of funny. My mom and grandmother always call themselves girls, so I'm not so hung up about that as some women are. It's kind of a New England thing, I guess, older women calling themselves girls, but of course he's Italian, isn't he? So, tell me, are you going to consider his offer?"

He glanced over at the train. "Probably not."

She felt instantly relieved. "Jay, let me take you out tonight," she said, even though she knew how it would end.

"Okay," he said. "Where to? Your choice."

"How 'bout Italian?"

He laughed. "Brignolia said to me, '*Now you are joking with me,*' I don't think he was used to that, anyone kidding him."

"Did you really tease him?" she said.

"Sure, why not?"

And then, in this moment of happiness, she said, "Don't you want to have children?" And though she didn't add, "with me," it was obvious.

It stopped him. He went to the window again, gripped the frame above his head, stared out at the lit windows of other buildings. Rain was just visible in puddles on some of the lower roofs and in the reflected surface of the pavement below. In some of the adjacent offices, a few people were standing much as he was, gazing out at other buildings, or at the rain, or at a moment in their own lives. Everyone has these complicated lives, he thought, all of us battling with our desires and our needs, and all of us connected in a way that so few realize.

"I'm sorry," she said. "I wish I hadn't said that."

He turned back to her.

"I'm glad you said it. I'm just not sure how to answer you. It's not a simple answer."

"Let's forget I said it. *Please.*"

"I know you've been upset with me for a while."

"Let's talk about something else, okay? Where shall we go eat?" He relented for the moment. "Your choice, but my car."

She brightened. "How's it running?"

"It purrs, and as you knew, the color is perfect and even the dent gives me pleasure. The fact that the paint is so old, I can imagine the person who sprayed it at Chevrolet in the sixties. It's like an antique that's never been refinished with all its stories intact in the finish." He walked back from the window. "Even with all the fancy cars in California, people wave at me. Seeing the car seems to cheer them up, allows them to remember something, maybe a more carefree time in America when people still believed in the promise."

And then he said, "Mary, I want to answer what you said before. It's important."

Noticing her face, he continued anyway.

"As you can imagine, because I was an orphan, parenthood would be a very serious thing for me. I'd have to be sure that I could be there for a child. As things are, I have to concentrate on LiveCell for now. I can't think about anything else."

He sat beside her and placed his hand gently over hers.

"I know I upset you when I ran from you. It had nothing to do with you, or your attractiveness, or what I feel for you." He paused. "You have given so much of yourself to LiveCell, and I hate to ask for anything more, but Mary, I still need you to learn how to infuse the phones. We are running out of time."

It was Mary who looked out at the rain now.

EIGHTEEN

She stood in the humid gloom, her LiveCell held tightly to her ear. Jay was talking to her from his office, explaining a few last details, telling her not to be nervous. How could she not be nervous? Deirdre appeared to be just as uneasy. Mary gazed out into the shadowy stillness at the rows and rows of inert vesseled telephones, each waiting to come to life.

The evening after Anthony Brignolia's visit, Jay had taken her out for dinner. He didn't bring up the infusion experiment again, but she sensed it was on his mind the entire time. She could tell how worried he was, and when she got home she decided she was being selfish and called him. Jay was right: personal needs were not a priority, LiveCell was what mattered.

The next day after work she drove over to the factory. The crew was gone, the parking lot empty except for Deirdre's wagon, and something about that solitary car surrounded by all that vacant gravel made her realize that Deirdre must be lonely too. In her own way, all she had was Live-Cell and Jay. He'd taken them both over. As she parked and got out, her stomach fluttered. Deirdre met her at the door and led her into the clean room.

"I sure hope your heart isn't going to do anything weird," Deirdre said. "Of course, I wouldn't mind so much giving you CPR, you know?" Mary looked at her. "Sorry, I'm only fooling. I guess I'm a bit jumpy."

Mary stood where Jay usually stood. "Why does he always have the lights off?"

"I'm not sure," said Deirdre, "he just always asks for it that way, so I figured you'd want it the same. Maybe it's so he can tell, like when the phones are infused, you know, when they start glowing and all."

Mary livecelled Jay.

"Open yourself," she heard him say. "Don't *try* to do anything, except remain empty of fear, and if you feel strange don't react against it, allow yourself simply to embrace it."

My God. Does he do it on purpose?

"I don't believe this could hurt you or I wouldn't experiment with it. If you have random thoughts, don't suppress them. It's a kind of concentration, yet you don't concentrate on anything specific. Allow the continuum to do all the work. Remember you and I are only a medium."

"Can I stand? I notice you kneel."

"Yes, kneel, definitely kneel. Sorry I should have remembered that. For one thing your mind won't waste effort balancing your body, and in case you get dizzy, you won't have so far to fall."

Great. "Why do you always keep all the lights off?" she said.

"It reduces your visual-stimulus input. I recommend you close your eyes as well. Are you ready?" he said.

"I think so."

"You sure?"

She told him she was. Kneeled on the cool vinyl tile. Glanced at Deirdre and winked. She didn't want her to know how nervous she was. Deirdre gave a tentative half-smile. Mary gripped her LiveCell and closed her eyes.

Immediately thoughts and remembered sensations tumbled through her brain: The first time he stared at her in the boardroom. The time he told her she was fired and then their embrace. The way he looked on Christmas sitting in the Impala. Her hand rubbing his jeans the evening he ran from her.

At first she had only these random images and feelings, along with an unusually vivid sense of him. But then why wouldn't she? She could imagine him behind his desk with the phone to his ear. Or maybe he was kneeling? Gradually an energy began to flutter inside her, fill her, a kind of tingling pulse, starting at her brain and reaching out toward her extremities through her arms and legs. *Oh no*, this was what she had been afraid of: what if *that* happens? And in front of Deirdre. She remembered

Jay telling her not to resist, and she tried to calm herself. It wasn't easy, but she knew how important this was. It wasn't the moment for personal reticence; it was all just in the line of duty when you worked for LiveCell. At least it was dark in there.

She allowed it, and the tingling grew in intensity, and then the sensation was so overwhelming that she was beyond concern or fear, or even, in a strange way, sexual feelings. It was a connectedness with Jay, or maybe something way beyond him, something she hadn't known existed. And then came the realization that she was vibrating; not that her body was moving, but that her mind was vibrating at a perfect frequency. It was almost a second orgasm but at the same time it was like the one perfect moment after, prolonged and with a purity of emotionlessness that transcended everything. After an indefinite interval—she had no concept of time—she opened her eyes. She realized she was crying. She got clumsily to her feet and saw the field of phones glowing and pulsing gently in front of her. It was like a field of soft light caressed by a tender breeze.

Deirdre let out a cry. "Oh, my, God! You did it! Mary, you did it. I can't believe it. This is *so* totally amazing."

"Mary?" she heard Jay whisper inside her brain. He seemed far away and very close in the same instant. She couldn't respond. She wondered if this was like giving birth with the pain inverted to pleasure. "Mary? Are you okay? I feel like we did it," he said. His voice still came from a tremendous distance. She realized she'd been holding the LiveCell next to her hip. She brought it closer, but still couldn't say anything.

"Are the phones infused?" he said.

Why did she have to answer? He must know. My God, why is he doing this to me? Doesn't he realize how this makes me feel? It was exactly what she had been frightened of.

She turned to Deirdre, her tears probably visible in the gentle yellow radiance of the LiveCells.

"Mary, are you okay?"

They looked at each other, and Mary's arms opened, and with only an instant of hesitation Deirdre embraced her. Mary felt the strong arms tighten around her and buried her head into Deirdre's neck and shoulder. They held each other for some minutes. Finally they separated.

"I have to go home," said Mary. "This is all too much for me."

Deirdre nodded.

It was then that Mary realized Jay was still on the phone. "Everything's okay," she said to him. "The phones are infused." She ended the call before he could speak.

"Are you, like, sure you're all right?" said Deirdre.

"I need some time alone. I can't even begin to tell you what that was like."

"You want me to drive you?"

Mary shook her head.

"This might sound, like really corny, but I'm *so* glad I know you. And no matter what happens, I wouldn't trade any of this for the world."

Mary thought a moment. "I guess you're right. I wouldn't either."

She left Deirdre in the clean room, went down the hall, stood at the doorway of the factory, trying to get some equilibrium back. The early darkness submerged her in blueness as she crunched unsteadily across the gravel to her car. She slumped onto the familiar leather seat, but didn't reach for her keys. For a second she considered just going to the office to see him, but she couldn't face his presence right then. Where she really wanted to go was home, back to Vermont. To see the farm again, and her parents. To run her hands through Pilgrim's fur and throw the old dog some sticks. She wondered if Pilgrim could even run anymore, with that strange three-legged gait. She wanted to waste away a lazy afternoon of nine-ball with Kelly on that cranky old pool table. She wished Jay would just forget everything and fly to Vermont with her—just for a week. Of course Vermont would be snowed in, but no one would care. The fireplace at the farm would be roaring with maple and oak and birch, her mom would bake a ham or roast a turkey; they'd all sit around the big dining room table and sip hot mulled cider and talk. At night the full moon would illuminate silver-white ferns of frost on the upstairs bedroom windows, those patterns that were like overdrawn constellations with meteor tails, the lacy mappings of a frozen winter sky. They could go cross-country skiing or snowshoeing or even sledding. She imagined Jay on a sled in his blue T-shirt screaming down an icy hillside, grinning madly. The whole idea excited her unduly. "My God, what's wrong with me?" she said out loud. She knew nothing would have changed for him. And then somewhere deep in herself she realized that what Jay wanted would never be what she wanted.

And she sensed he was trying to livecell her. She didn't answer. Let him suffer too!

She wished she could at least head for Jake's poolroom and practice some nine-ball. Her hands itched to hold her cue again. Anything to take

her mind off this feeling. Since Sammy died, she hadn't been back to
Jake's. She still didn't have the heart to walk in and not find him behind
the bar in one of his crazy bowling shirts, setting a draft in front of her,
saying, 'Hey, girl, how's things?' and sliding her the salt shaker, then turning, his big shoulders moving under the shirt, to fix her a crab roll. Would
Nick keep the poolroom open? But what would he do if he closed it?

Her mind was untethered, ricocheting from thought to desire. Had
the infusion affected it somehow? Maybe the continuum was too much
for her? No, she felt connected to everything in a way she never had, as
if she could almost see all the infinite particles that formed existence.

Finally she fired up the car, headed toward the highway as it started
to rain. Snarled in traffic approaching the Golden Gate Bridge, she
waited as all that was visible through the windshield was reduced to
streaming red and gray. She didn't even play a CD while the Porsche
crawled forward in line. Instead she thought about her life, and realized
it would always be a complicated layering of things to deal with and sort
through. It was her nature to become involved, not to retreat from emotion or what scared or confused her. She also newly understood that
something incredible held all of them in its embrace, whether people
were aware of it or not. Knowing this was miraculous, even if it didn't
change anything else. No wonder Jay missed those days with his grandfather. We must all have a core memory that we love.

Then Frankie livecelled. "Are you on your way?" he said.

She touched the wiper control, and the world beyond the windshield
popped into focus. "Just clearing the bridge."

"Dinner'll be ready by the time you get home."

"I'm afraid I'm not that hungry."

"Don't worry, I'll hold it back—no problem. We'll have a couple
wines—build the appetite. Or you want champagne? I got something real
important to discuss with you. Okay?"

Oh, great. Is everyone always in love with the wrong person?

Frankie hadn't been with her on the drives back and forth to Live-
Cell for almost a week; she'd insisted on going alone. Since Christmas,
he'd become progressively preoccupied and distant, almost sulky, yet this
change in him was subtle because he hid his emotions. Regardless, she
could tell something was up. Was it the pearl earrings? She'd tried to give
them back a few days after the holidays, but on witnessing his brave smile
and the pain in his eyes—a new expression and one she never wanted to
see again—she'd told him she'd keep them. But maybe the damage was

already done? Some situations just don't have good solutions. The earrings had remained untouched on top of her bureau, deserted in their blue box.

When she arrived home, she was greeted by the familiar smells of Italian cooking. Frankie came out of the kitchen in another apron, this one with a big bunch of sprouting carrots on it, and handed her a glass of wine.

"How was your day?" he said.

"Fine, the usual," she said. She'd only infused twenty-four-thousand living phones by being a human medium as a continuum of energy passed through her body and mind, giving her the strangest orgasm she'd ever experienced, and now she was even more in love with this guy whose pineal gland was missing and who insisted on saving the world instead of fucking her.

"You work too much," he said.

"You think so?"

He snapped around and went back into the kitchen. Had her tone been nasty? She hadn't meant it to be. She followed him.

"And your day?" she said, trying to sound friendly.

He looked at her. He sure had romantic eyes. Maybe she'd been missing something that was right in front of her?

"I've been called back to Boston." He was watching for her response.

"Why?" she said. "I don't need protecting any longer?"

"Mr. Brignolia doesn't give explanations."

"And?"

"I like it out here."

"So, stay."

"You don't understand."

"What's there not to understand? If you don't want to go back to Boston, stay here. Are you worried you couldn't find another job? I'm sure Jay would hire you. I know he likes you. I don't know how much Brignolia pays you, but I'm sure Jay would match it."

"Mary, that's not the problem."

"What is?"

He glanced around the kitchen as if seeing if anyone was listening. "You don't say no to Anthony Brignolia."

"Jay did." She regretted it instantly.

"I know," he said.

"Anthony told you?"

"Mr. Brignolia never says anything he don't have to. I got a friend in the organization. There're always leaks, always ways of finding stuff out." He paused. "Let's sit down, okay?"

Frankie adjusted a few things on the stove, and they brought their wines into the dining room.

"If it got out that I told you this, it'd be real bad for me," he said.

She said nothing.

"Mary, I'm gonna be dead honest with you, because it's important and there isn't much time. You know I have feelings for you. I know you don't have the same feelings for me. I accept this." He held up his hand. "Please, let me finish. I really can't do this twice. I know who you have feelings for, and I see he's an incredible man, more than I could ever hope to be." Again he quieted her with his hand. "What I'm about to tell you, you must pass on to him. I do this because of how much I care for you. I do it only for you."

She waited.

"Jay's in danger. Mr. Brignolia was dead serious about that." He saw her expression. "Didn't Jay tell you any of this?" She shook her head. "I guess he wouldn't. He wouldn't wan' you to worry. Besides, the guy's a loner, a true loner." He glanced out the window. "They know Jay needs to attend the phones every day. Without this, the phones won't work. This true?"

Mary wasn't sure how to answer. She was frightened he knew that, and even more frightened that others outside the company knew it as well. Had they found out about the infusion process or were they guessing? But how could they find out? Deirdre would never tell, and of course Jay wouldn't. Who else had found out? Jimmy Hakken? No way—he'd sooner die. And then she felt even more afraid. Was Frankie Demanno really on their side, or was he setting up something for Brignolia? Had he been sent out here by Brignolia to spy on her? No, Nick called Brignolia. But what if—

"You don't have to tell me," he said.

Her intuition said to trust him, but she was still worried. "He doesn't need to be with the phones every day," she said. At least not after today. Jay always seemed to do things in the nick of time.

"Good. That's critical. Then you got to prove this by having Jay disappear. No one should know where he is. No one. This will give them pause, and give LiveCell more time. Right now, they think all they have to do is off Jay, and LiveCell's finished."

How the hell had they found that out? She attempted to keep her emotion out of her voice. "Brignolia's going to kill him?"

"Mr. Brignolia does what serves Mr. Brignolia. For now, saving Live-Cell fits his interests. I think he's waiting for Jay to change his mind and accept the offer. The people after Jay are the same fucking inner circle that call all the shots in this country. Brignolia works for them, not the other way around."

"But you work for him."

It stopped him. "I'm questioning that."

"Were you told to spy on me?"

"Yeah, but also to protect you. Once I met you, I never spied." He searched her face. "Mary, you gotta believe me. I'm on your side."

"Why not quit Brignolia and work for Jay then?"

"You mean that? I mean, you personally? You want me to stay?"

His intensity scared her. "Will Brignolia have you killed if you quit?"

"Mary, I grew up real hard. I been with Mr. Brignolia since I was a teenager. He kinda took me in, took care of me. But everything has a price. You're right, I don't think I can work for him no more. Being out here with you has forced me to look at a lotta stuff. I never considered other ways to live. His way was what I knew, and I didn't question it. Not until I came out here and—"

She knew where he was headed again. "I'll talk to Jay."

"Yeah, warn him. He needs to disappear—soon."

"How soon?"

"He probably has a couple weeks. Hard to tell."

"I'll call him tonight. I'll also talk to him about hiring you."

"Wait a bit. Give it a few weeks. I've gotta go back to Boston. There's no way around that, but I'm gonna try and talk to Mr. Brignolia, not that—"

There was a piercing wail. They saw smoke coiling in from the kitchen.

"Oh, shit," he said, jumping out of his chair and plowing into the fumes.

She sat, stunned by the entire day. She could hear Frankie banging around, a window being opened, a dishtowel slapped at the alarm, which finally chirped silent, Frankie muttering under his breath. She went to the door and peered in.

He stood near a couple smoldering pans. "Dinner, I gotta say, is nowhere near my usual standard. I turned the damn oven heat in the wrong direction."

"Can I take you out for dinner?" she said.

"You want to?"

She looked at him, this stocky Italian in his silly carrot apron, holding a dishtowel. "I'd love to."

"Really?"

"Yes, really."

"Your Porsche or mine?"—a big smile now.

"Yours." She headed for the door.

As he was putting on his sports jacket, he noticed the apron. He untied it and tossed it into the kitchen.

NINETEEN

Frankie Demanno orchestrated the disappearance. Jay grumbled about the procedures being excessive, and Frankie said, "Hey, please, this is what I do, allow me to take care of it." He wasn't worried about outside surveillance but saw no reason not to be thorough: "Hey, what's the point otherwise?" He insisted that only Jay know his destination and that his departure be kept secret except among the three of them; Mary could fill everyone in after Jay was hidden. His disappearance had to be sudden and unexpected.

The day of Jay's departure, Frankie again checked the Impala for tracking devices. If there had been any kind of transponder signal he would have picked it up; it was clean. Renting or buying another vehicle would be more obtrusive than using the Chevy. The car could be ditched later, but changing cars before the departure left tracks unless the second car was stolen. He couldn't imagine Jay agreeing to steal cars.

That night, he had Jay drop off the Impala in a quiet parking lot where he was waiting. He watched Mary pull in and collect Jay. Frankie planned to rendezvous with them later at a rest stop on the 101. From there Chevalier would be on his own.

Frankie waited about fifteen minutes before walking across the dark lot in his new charcoal-brown trench coat, pleased it was raining. He didn't look around, but went directly to the Impala, unlocked the door with a spare set of keys, hopped in, fired the engine, and eased the wagon into the street. Just the right amount of traffic, he thought, checking the rearview mirror. With his hand on the spindly wheel, he felt as if he were maneuvering a barge. He understood the car had been a gift, but still didn't get why Chevalier didn't drive something else; the man could afford anything he desired. These people really do need looking after, he muttered. It would be so easy for him to slip a tracking device into the car now. Chevalier was a strange guy, trusting, but at the same time he seemed to know exactly what he was doing, and maybe even what other people planned to do. As if he were able to see into a person and—

A strangled cry from right behind him. Frankie jolted. What the fuck was that? Without turning, he noiselessly released his nine-millimeter Beretta from its holster, his ears searching madly. Approaching a red light on Market, he hit the brake and rotated, the barrel instantly locating the culprit. A very ugly cat with a missing ear, yellow paws gripping the back of the rear bench, was staring at him. The animal opened its mouth and squallered again. Two more cats slunk from hiding. Jesus, these must be Chevalier's goddamn cats. He's bringing them! But then, why the fuck not? He holstered the gun and looked around for more surprises. He noticed the floor of the backseat was jammed with paper grocery bags, and he reached over and opened one. It was full of frozen chicken pot pies, starting to thaw, soaking the bottom of the bags. Another held cat food. Christ, what a character this Chevalier was.

Someone blipped a horn. Frankie straightened and the light was green. As he drove again, the ugly yellow cat leapt forward and started to purr on the seat beside him. Frankie scratched along the animal's backbone. The tom arched, bounded into Frankie's lap, nuzzling an elbow with his teeth. Damn thing was gonna get yellow hair all over his new coat, maybe even fleas. Nonetheless, he allowed the cat to remain in his lap. So, Chevalier was going to hole up somewhere. And the poor guy would be forced to eat those horrible pies—*sacrilege*. For a moment he considered accompanying Jay to make sure he had something to eat, but it was an idle thought. Mr. Brignolia had let him know again that he was expected immediately. He had to face whatever it was, try to reason with the man. But why did it have to be right then? What a mess they were all in.

On the outskirts of San Francisco he checked to see if he was followed. This was second nature; he merely backtracked a few times, pulling over occasionally and watching. Assured, he entered the designated rest stop, berthed the barge in the darkest corner, doused the lights, the rain collecting on the windshield, muddling the view of the on-ramp lights and the highway. The other two cats wandered forward, probably relieved the car was stationary. Out of curiosity, he opened the last shopping bag—those same damp awful pies and a six pack of canned beer. It was too cruel to contemplate.

Within ten minutes a silver Porsche pulled up behind him, switched off its lights. He met Jay halfway between the two cars.

"You leave first," Frankie said. "We'll check your back for a few miles, then you're on your own." Jay nodded. The guy really does look right into you, even in the dark. They stood in the rain for some moments. Since Jay said nothing, he said, "I figure to be in Boston maybe a week, hopefully no longer. I'll try ta get back as soon as I can." A pause. "Jay, I really appreciate your offer. Oh, and hey, remember, cash only, no cards." Jay nodded again. "Keys are in it." He motioned to the Impala. "I didn't lose any cats. That yellow guy with the ear is real friendly."

"Had him since Delaware." Jay gave Frankie's wet shoulder a firm grip. "Thanks for everything. Take care of Mary. She needs you."

Frankie walked to the idling Porsche and slid in beside her. She was staring straight ahead. The Impala's four brake lights flared red for an instant, then slowly diminished like a closing aperture.

"He's gonna be fine," he said. "There is no way anyone can track him now. Okay, let's follow."

Mary engaged first gear and accelerated up through two gears hard enough to wiggle the rear-end on the wet tarmac.

"Easy," said Frankie. "Are you okay?"

"I don't have a good feeling about this. I'm not sure why."

"Hey, nothing can go wrong. He disappears for a while, no one can get to him because no one knows where he is. LiveCell runs fine without him, it takes some pressure off, we figure our next move. It's our best option, until we got a better one. Besides, you'll be talking to him every day on a phone that can't be traced. Where's the problem? Anything looks suspicious, he calls."

Soon they identified the unique iconography of the Impala's taillights in the distance. Frankie said to hang back and maintain distance. He'd checked all the cars they passed, but at this point he wasn't concerned; being thorough was habit. "Okay," he said at the next exit sign. Mary livecelled Jay and told him they were headed back, she'd call him tomorrow. Frankie studied her again, knew she was upset, but didn't know what he could do about it.

The next day she put Frankie on a flight to Logan. He'd stored his car in her garage, staying up until eleven the night before to wax it. She hadn't waxed hers once. "It's leased for heaven's sake," she said, watching him polish, laughing at him.

"Who cares if it's leased. It's a fine machine and deserves to be pampered. I want it to be puffed when I get back." He draped it meticulously with a new high-tech car cover.

"And I thought I had it bad."

Mary ran LiveCell while Jay was absent. Heading the company was overwhelming, not to mention needing to infuse new phones every day. No wonder Jay had so little time for anything else. Of course, *he* didn't have a near orgasm every other time he infused.

Four days after Frankie left for Boston, she heard from Detective Artega.

"Something is wrong," he said over his LiveCell.

"How? What?"

"You're under surveillance, and it's not our people."

"Are you sure?"

"Believe me, cops know how to recognize other cops. But these guys—I have no idea. Maybe Feds, but not your usual Feds. Both factories are being monitored, and your offices at the Harcourt. These guys are extremely professional."

"What do you think it means?"

"Must have to do with Jay disappearing. Maybe they want to validate he's actually gone."

"They must be looking for him then," she said.

"Likely."

"One lucky thing is that the public doesn't know what he looks like. With virtually no photos in the media except the high school and Harvard shots, he'd be difficult to spot."

"These guys probably have surveillance shots, but at least his face isn't part of the public consciousness like most celebrities' . . . Mary, do you know where he is?"

"Why?"

"He won't answer his phone."

"I spoke with him today. He's fine."

"Thanks for telling me. Know you're being watched every minute."

"We really appreciate all your efforts."

"Sorry if I scared you."

"It's creepy, isn't it?"

"A lot of stuff has been surprising even me lately. I thought I'd seen it all."

After finishing with Artega she immediately livecelled Jimmy Hakken. He muttered that he'd thought the same thing but didn't want to alarm her until he was absolutely sure. His crew had spotted them. It had started three days ago.

"What bugs me is how quick they knew Chevalier'd gone to ground. MacKensie—we might have a leak. You want my boys to take care of this? Feds don't scare us none."

"It would only make things worse."

"We're on full alert. Just give the word."

Jesus, did he think he could fight anyone? But he probably didn't care. He was probably ready, maybe even eager, to die for his cause. He really was like a medieval knight. Jimmy Hakken also wanted to know if Jay was okay. Jay must not be taking calls from anyone except her, but why?

She called Frankie about the surveillance. She could tell he was trying not to worry her; she wasn't fooled. He said he'd check around and see if he could get a read.

The next morning Mary felt so restless she figured she must be getting sick, but she didn't have any other symptoms. Too busy to listen to her uneasiness, she decided it was probably stress. But by the middle of the afternoon she knew it was something worse. Kelly Harris called her from the farm.

"Mary," he said.

That one word turned her uneasiness to dread.

"Where's Jay?" he said.

"He's in hiding."

"Have you spoken with him?"

"Not today. Yesterday, last night late."

"Can you call him?"

She only nodded but she knew he heard her.

"Call him. I can't get him."

"What's wrong, Kelly?" She knew Jay hadn't been answering other people's calls. This was different.

"Something's not right."

"I'll call you as soon as I can," she said, her heart pounding.

She livecelled Jay.

He didn't answer. She tried to stay calm. It doesn't mean anything yet, he could just be away from his phone. But Kelly's fear tortured her. He could be wrong this time. He has to be wrong! She forced herself to wait five minutes by her watch and tried again. Fuck! She waited and tried one more time. She didn't call Kelly back; she couldn't handle it.

At about fifteen minutes before four, Frankie livecelled from the North End.

"Mary?"

"What's wrong?" she said, her heart already lurching in her chest.

"I found this out minutes ago. You got a rat. I don't know who it is, but someone way on the inside sold you out."

"Fuck," she said.

"Mary, hold tight, it might not be too bad. I'm gettin' the next flight out in the morning—I already missed the last one today. D'you have any idea who it might be?"

"Yes."

"I'll be in at ten-twenty-two, United one-sixty-three. Can you meet me?"

"Yeah."

"You should call Jay right now. We're gonna need him to figure this out. Something is real fucked 'cause I never seen Mr. Brignolia this pissed. Something or someone has screwed him big time. Is there a way the rat could guess where Jay is?"

"You can never tell with him, if it's who I think it is."

"When I get there, I'll get it out of the bastard, *believe me*. After you speak with Jay, you call me. And Mary, please don't worry, we'll straighten this out when I get in."

She tried Jay again. She wondered if Duncan had left for the day. She livecelled him. He answered.

"Duncan, can I see you in my office for a minute?"

"I'm almost out the door."

"It's important." As she spoke she started walking toward his office—quickly.

"I really can't because I have an appointment."

"Duncan. *Now*, please." *Stay calm*, she told herself again. She needed to get information out of him.

"Oh, all right," he said. "I resent that tone though. Frankly, I'm sick of that tone. I'll be there in five or ten minutes. I have something I forgot to do first."

She caught him as he was leaving his office. He had his coat on and his briefcase in hand.

"What do you want that is so goddamn important?" he said, backing away, retreating into his office again.

Just by the look in his eyes, she knew. She kicked the door closed. "Duncan, what have you done?"

"What are you talking about? . . . Why are you looking at me like that?"

"Duncan, what have you done?"

"I'm going home. I have better things to do. This is ridiculous." He started to walk around her. She didn't move.

"Duncan," she said as his hand touched the doorknob. "Would you rather talk with Jimmy Hakken?"

He stopped. A sick smile came over his face. "You think I'm worried about that scarecrow any more? He's being watched as we speak. All I have to do is say the word."

"You sold us out." She didn't even raise her voice; she was stating a fact. It was all so clear. She realized she'd sensed it all along.

"LiveCell was going down anyway," he said. "You didn't have a chance. It didn't matter what I did."

"How could you?"

"Do any of you have any idea how the real world works? Do you even have a clue? You're such a bunch of idealist misfits you're blind to reality. Don't you realize what a mess it would be if the Third World had free, secure communication? Or the Chinese? Or the Muslims? But do any of you geniuses ever think of that? And look at all the trouble you've already caused in this country. His phones are stirring people up, changing people, don't you see that? We could have a revolution in this country and then where would we be? You think this can just go on?" He shook his head. "Well, it's not going to happen."

"You hate him, don't you?"

"What are you talking about?"

"A truly decent and kind man and you hate him." She tried to keep the anger out of her voice, but Duncan reacted anyway, his voice louder.

"Hate him? Who do you think tried to warn him? Who sent him two warnings? Who pleaded with him to sell the company? Who tried to make all of you see reality? And all I got in return was his holier-than-thou attitude. Who does he think he is always running around in that T-shirt showing off his muscular arms, always pretending to be so calm, *so* together like nothing could ever get to him. He treated me like a servant: '*Duncan* find this out, *Duncan* find that out,' but where it mattered he wouldn't listen to me. And you. I loved you. You have no idea how much I loved you." His voice broke with emotion. "I would have done anything for you if you had given me a chance, but instead you wanted *him*. What was it about me that you couldn't give me one single chance? And to think I would have made you rich and treated you like a queen."

"Did they pay you yet?"

That stopped him. "Not all of it, but they will."

"Who? Alden Stone Associates?"

"When the dyke told us about Wendy Smith and the possible information deal, I paid attention."—*so that's who had tipped Wendy off*, thought Mary—"You all figured I was so devastated about selling my stock, but I saw a way to make even more money. I could see with Chevalier's stubbornness and inability to compromise that eventually LiveCell had to go down. It was only a matter of time. So I contacted Wendell's father."—*he must have contacted him through Wendy*—"Mr. Alden and his connections are the people who are actually running this country. They control things you could never even imagine. They listen to me and treat me with respect, not like you and Chevalier and that dyke and totem pole."

"You've been working for Alden." She knew it was true but could barely believe that anyone could be such a traitor.

"If Chevalier had been allowed to continue, look who he would've sold out to. You think I was going to let that happen? You think I'd work for Brignolia? Wouldn't that have been great—to give *those* people the most important technology on earth."

"How do you know about that?"

"I bugged his office."

"You bugged Jay's office?"

"You and Chevalier are so naive."

"And I suppose you know how the phones work? Is that what you sold to Alden?"

He smirked and stood straighter. "I know he has some kind of device that implants intelligence into the brain-like cell aggregate. I know he used it every day and now you probably are. If that scarecrow didn't have the factories crawling with thugs, I'd know more. With my help, their lab techs can almost produce the supposedly magic cell mutation by now.

Once we get whatever device imparts the intelligence, we'll have it. We'll get it soon, believe me. And we'll patent it!"

As Duncan talked, Mary quietly tried to reach Jay again. She knew she had to keep Duncan talking. Anything he revealed might be helpful.

"If the phones are supposed to be a menace," she said, "why does Alden want them so badly?"

"For themselves. Not for everyone else. Chevalier could have been selling those phones for a fortune—to the right people. But did he listen to me? Think of the military and corporate applications. Think if our generals and leaders had increased intuitiveness over everyone else? We would control the world. Instead he lets the masses have them, cheap, ridiculously cheap, and the sales are spreading outside the country. We'll see if his beloved masses can save him now. Or that scarecrow and his goons. You're all being watched. You can't go anywhere without being tracked. So try to go to the media, or the cops, or the supposed Mafia. See how far any of you get. You can't move an inch without being followed and stopped."

"They'll never find Jay."

A laugh escaped him. "Shows how much you know. I suppose you think your fancy hit man is infallible? Well he isn't. There are three tracking devices already implanted that will lead our people right to Chevalier."

"We checked. There are none." She was feeling ill.

"You didn't check the cats, did you?" He laughed again. "A simple little dime-sized transponder was cyanoacrylated in a small slit in the epidermis under the fur of each cat. Virtually undetectable. It couldn't have been easier getting someone into that dumpy room of his at the Y. I knew Mr. Love-every-fucked-up-misfit would take those mutant cats with him no matter where he went. They've probably found him by now, no matter where he is. And he thought he was smarter than me." He was chuckling with satisfaction.

Mary put her phone to her lips, the bitterness in her heart almost choking her. Her call was answered within seconds.

"Duncan has sold us out," she said. "Because of him, they may have gotten to Jay already. I think Duncan has caused enough trouble, but be careful, he seems to think his new friends can protect him."—she watched Duncan's arrogant face change to concern, veins appearing on his forehead—"He's right here, in his office at the Harcourt Building."

Jimmy Hakken merely grunted, and she could imagine him already running to his car. She was glad he wasn't after her. She couldn't think of anything worse.

"Who was that?"—his voice shrill. It was now Duncan who looked sick.

"Hakken," she said.

"You, fucking, bitch!" he screamed and ran at her with his arms out as if to strangle. She waited, not moving. At the last instant she drop-kicked him in the groin. He fell to the floor, writhing in pain, grabbing himself, moaning. Though it disgusted her to get close to him, she reached down and slipped his LiveCell phone out of his suit coat pocket and left the office. She tried to get him out of her mind; she had too many other things to do.

TWENTY

Mary headed toward her car out of habit. As she walked she livecelled Deirdre, putting her in charge of the company, explaining most of what had happened as quickly as possible. She also talked with Chet Simmons and Cliff Thompson, telling them Deirdre would now be the acting CEO, but not mentioning anything about Jay. On reaching the parking-garage door she hesitated, her mind racing.

Maybe Duncan had lied about the cats? Maybe they wanted her to run to Jay so they could follow? She tried him again and told her Live-Cell to ring him every ten minutes. Now she had to assume the worst. Kelly wouldn't have called otherwise. She forced herself to remain logical and suppressed her worst fears.

She had to get to Jay, yet travel undetected. With everyone in the company being watched, she could rely on no one. Any member of Live-Cell could be picked up and held on some pretext. But if they'd found Jay, she'd need help. Frankie would arrive in the morning, but hours could make the difference. She couldn't wait. She needed a gun and someone to help her, someone they weren't watching, someone outside the company, someone willing and tough. Artega flashed into her mind, but who knew what his orders were? Nick was too old. If only Sammy weren't—

Garland McKeen!

She livecelled.

"Yeah-boy."

"Garland?"

"Naw—nobody here by that name."

"There isn't?" LiveCells never misdialed.

"No, ma'am."

She could hear a faint metallic noise of maybe a horse shaking a bridle, rain drumming against what might be a tarp, and just then the bellow of a steer. Sounds that made her instantly homesick.

"I'm trying to find Garland McKeen . . . Hank. Do you know—"

"Hell, why didn't you say so? Thought you were a bill collector. Who's this?"

"Mary, Mary MacKensie."

"Oh, boy."

"I met Hank about—"

"Believe me, I know. Know *all* about it."

"Who am I speaking with please?"

"Hank's pa, who d'ya think?"

"Mr. McKeen, I really need to reach Hank."

"Hell, he's out by Taylor Creek. Suppose I could get him. He know your number?"

"Does he still have a LiveCell phone?"

"Yup."

"Then if he just thinks of me, it should work."

"All he does is think of you," he muttered. "These new-fangled phones do that?"

"That's why I don't understand getting you instead of Hank."

"Hank juss give me his phone for today 'cause I done left mine at the house. It musta confused the little critter. You know these dang phones amaze me. Sure makes things a heck of a lot easier around here. Hank kept trying to convince me, and I gotta admit—"

"Mr. McKeen, it's urgent I speak with Hank right away."

"Gotcha. Light's draining fast anyway. Hank'll be headed back any time now, but I'll try to get him for ya."

"Thanks."

"You bet."

Mary didn't enter the parking garage. It might be under surveillance, or her car bugged. But she had to get out of the building undetected, before Jimmy Hakken arrived. He might be tailed, and who knew what would happen when he found Duncan. She didn't want to know. Quickly, she walked back to the elevator and rode down to the main floor.

"Manuel," she said, approaching the front desk.

He looked up from a magazine. "Oh, hey there."

"Is there a way of sneaking out of this building?"—her tone light-hearted.

"Someone you don't want to see out front?" He grinned, and she winked back. "Of course, dear, I know a way. All you do is take the elevator down to the basement . . ." and he explained it to her. Didn't ask any questions, just told her what she needed to know. Some people just understood. She thanked him, and he returned to his magazine.

She followed Manuel's directions, and in six or seven minutes, after lots of duct work, conduits, throbbing machinery, hard-to-find light switches, one wrong turn, she shoved open a rusty door and stepped into an alley. A light rain. She cursed—her coat was still in her office. At least she had her purse; she'd just buy another coat. Why hadn't Garland called? Hadn't her urgency been clear to his father? Should she livecell Frankie? It had been almost half an hour; he was probably getting anxious. But she needed to talk with Garland first. She still couldn't bear to talk with Kelly again. She shivered—the drizzle was worsening—and headed down the alley away from the front of the Harcourt Building. Without a glance, her head down, she entered the sidewalk at Ellis and blended into the crowd of pedestrians. Frankie had told her, "Someone looking around nervously is easy to spot. Why wave a flag?" Every morning he'd shared tidbits like this at breakfast. The memory made her long to be back at her dining room table, listening to Frankie over a cup of his coffee. It's true: we rarely appreciate what we have until it's gone.

In a clothing store, she found a grayish green raincoat, wondering if she was thinking camouflage. Her shoes were okay, they had decent soles. She was relieved that she hadn't chosen heels or a skirt that morning. As the sales girl handed back her card, she asked to use the washroom.

Mary locked the door, took out her phone, thought "Garland," picturing him vividly.

"Yeah-boy."

"Garland?"

"Mary! That really you?"

"It's me."

He let out a hoot; he hadn't changed.

"So how you been? *Dang*, is it ever good to hear from you."

"Didn't your father let you know I called?"

"He told me you might ring, not that these ring. Give me my phone back in case."

"He didn't tell you to call immediately?"

"Pa's not real good at messages. You sound a little bit upset. You okay?"

"I'm afraid I need some help."

"Anything. You know that."

"I hate to ask you this, but I need to get to the Oregon coast—tonight. Some people are watching me. I can't use my car, and I don't dare rent one."

His voice changed. "Who's after you?"

"This could be very dangerous."

"Bet this has to do with your phones. Been reading every newspaper with any coverage. I can guess what's going on. Listen, gonna tell Pa, chores is most done anyway. I'll get the truck and bet I can be in the city in something like four five hours. That be okay?"

"Yes."

"Goddang, I'm on my way then."

"Garland, I think we might need a gun."

"Rifle, shotgun, or handgun?"

"I'm not sure."

".357 long barrel. Matched pair, used to be Grandpa's. They'll be loaded and ready—Remington Golden Sabers. I'll throw a rifle on the rack too."

She wasn't sure exactly what he was talking about, but at least they'd have guns. "I hate to put you in this mess," she said.

"There's some things I just know about, shooting's one of 'em."

"Garland?"

"Yeah?"

"This could be dangerous. *Very* dangerous. I have no idea what we're headed into. It might be nothing, but I doubt it. We might get shot at."

"So?"

"I just want you to be really sure you want to do this."

"Yep, sure do."

"You're really something, you know that?"

He hooted again and they ended the call.

Though she tried to hold them back, tears filled her eyes. She saw him galloping a horse through the rain, grabbing and loading the guns, jumping in the truck, roaring along a dirt road to the highway, sliding onto the pavement and accelerating toward her.

She pulled herself together. Called Frankie and filled him in. When she got to the Garland part he went cold.

"Who is this guy?" he said.

"Hank McKeen. He's a cowboy." She didn't use *Garland*. Maybe that's why he preferred *Hank*.

"A cowboy?"

"From up north."

"What kinda *cow*boy?"

"His family runs cattle."

"But how do you know this guy?"

"Frankie, we don't have time for this."

A pause. "But you can trust this guy?"

"I believe I can."

"Okay, sorry. Damn, if only I was on that last flight out. This is driving me nuts. And I still think you gotta wait for me. *Please*. I'm trained for this. You and the cowboy aren't."

"It might be too late. Who knows what they might be doing to Jay. You know I have to try."

He fell silent.

"Maybe I could get a flight into Portland?" he said. "Closer to Chevalier. Only trouble might be getting a gun. I'm not sure who we got up in Oregon, not one of our big areas. This new airport security sucks. Anyway, either airport, I get in, I rent a car—use my alias—head to Siuslaw, or however you say it. You still trying to reach Jay?"

"Every ten minutes."

"He told ya where he was gonna hole up?"

"I just knew."

"Shoulda been a perfect location." A lull. "The *cats*! Those people are sick. Mary . . . I'm so fuckin' sorry."

"You're not to blame."

"I'm supposed to be a professional. I shoulda debugged the car one more time."

"Frankie, don't beat yourself up. No one would've suspected the cats."

They stopped talking.

He broke the silence: "Please wait for me. I don't know nothing about this *cow*boy."

They'd already been over it, and he knew she had to go.

"Okay, okay. On the map, there are only two direct ways to get there—one-o-one, or interstate five. You and the cowboy are gonna get stopped."

"But they don't know his truck."

"Don't matter. They only gotta watch two roads, and real soon they gonna know you're missing if they don't already. They'd be fools not to stake out the two roads, especially at night with light traffic. Even if the cowboy's truck crossed a few checkpoints, that right there, it's over. They only need six men. Let me think on it and call you back. And Mary, I'll check in every hour, okay?"

"Thanks."

"You're doing fine, lose the purse and keep moving. They gonna have a hard time finding you in the city, but they'll be looking, *hard*. Be a disaster for them if the two major players in LiveCell vanish at once. Even they couldn't keep that out of the media. The public would demand an explanation. Try not to worry too much about Jay, we don't know nothing yet. He could be all right and just not answering. At the worst, they just want information outta him. He's too popular right now for—"

A knock on the bathroom door. "Miss, are you okay in there?"

"Yes," she called. "Be right out."

"What was that?" said Frankie.

"Store clerk. Got to go."

"Okay, later."

Exiting the washroom she assured the clerk that she was all right, just an upset stomach. "You do look a little pale," said the girl.

Back on the street, she tossed her purse into a trash bin, stuffing only those things where a transponder couldn't be concealed into her raincoat pockets. Duncan's phone she threw into the bin as if it burned her hand, but it upset her to lose the purse—she remembered the day she bought it, so pleased to find that rare shade of silvered leather—but what else could she do? Maybe someone would find it and be delighted. Frankie had told her he wasn't worried about her shoes or clothes. "You got way too many to bug 'em all," he'd muttered. "Take a thousand transponders." She was relieved to hear him joking, knowing he was going through hell. But weren't they all.

Mary tried to keep out of the rain, stay in peopled areas, and avoid doing anything unusual that might draw attention, which wasn't easy since she constantly imagined a hand grabbing her: "Miss MacKensie, come with us, we have some questions to ask you," or whatever that kind of agent said. She'd never dealt with the FBI, the CIA, or whoever had been directed to watch LiveCell. She'd never even had a speeding ticket, which was a miracle considering how she drove. What lies had the surveillance teams been fed about Jay and LiveCell? She knew cops did what they were told and kept their questions to themselves. And to think that America had been founded on the right to question authority.

Even with her LiveCell trying Jay every ten minutes, she called every five, knowing it was pointless. She had to accept it. He was in trouble. She finally livecelled Kelly; they could barely speak. She couldn't afford to break down again and ended the call. It was the same with Deirdre. Frankie called but hadn't solved the problem of getting Garland's truck to Oregon undetected.

And then Garland checked in: "Mary. Got her running at over eighty. Hit ninety on the hills. Be there even sooner." She could hear the thing hammering down the highway.

"Don't get a ticket."

"Don't plan on it. Not many cops on these roads anyhow. Never knew this rig could run this fast. Just passed Red Bluff. Dang, can't wait to see ya."

God, was everything a delight to him?

They decided to meet in the parking lot of a Safeway off Market—full of cars pulling in and out, a busy Friday evening. Mary wheeled around an empty cart, not really sure why, it probably looked silly, maybe even suspicious, but she needed to do something other than stand. Garland would be there any minute. As she glanced at some of the other shoppers, she yearned to be worrying about what flavor of ice cream to buy, the price of lemons, or even calming an upset child. Again, she forced herself to remain fixed on what she had to do.

She heard it though she didn't realize it was his truck. She just wondered who was driving around without a muffler. It was a sound you heard in Vermont, where road salt ate exhaust systems, not San Francisco. As the deafening rumble pulled into the lot she saw who it was. Nothing like a clandestine operation.

He parked in a space close to her, shut off the truck, and hopped down. He was still wearing his yellow rain slicker and pants from ranching, the same battered Resistol set back on his head. Well, at least he didn't have the guns out, firing them into the air.

"Sorry 'bout the racket," he said, a sheepish grin on his face. "Frigging manifold pipe come loose at the muffler. Musta been jarred a bit on our road, and then the backpressure at ninety blew her apart. She was holding up pretty good till she sheared plum off."

"Let's talk in the truck." She shoved the shopping cart near the front bumper and got in. He jumped up behind the wheel, and she scanned the parking lot, nervously. No one seemed the least bit interested in them.

"You made great time," she said, and he grinned. He really did look a bit like James Dean—James Dean with a smashed up nose. "Don't worry about the muffler. Frankie doesn't think it's safe to take your truck anyway."

"Who's *Frankie?*"

"A friend of mine."

"He goin' with us?"

"He's in Boston."

"Then how would he know?"

"Believe me, he would."

Something touched his features. But only for an instant.

"Garland, I think Jay's in trouble."

"Chevalier?"

She explained the situation to him. "We have to get to Jay. Obviously your truck's out—too late to get it fixed. Maybe *you* could rent a car at the airport? No one would be monitoring your credit cards. *Shit.*"

"What?"

"I bought this coat with one of my cards. They probably already know about the transaction."

He squirmed in his seat, reached inside his rain pants for his back pocket. "Mary . . ." He hesitated.

"What is it? Tell me."

"Don't have my wallet." He hammered the dash. "Dang. See I never take it when I'm working, and I was racing to—"

"We'll just have to think of something else."

"Forgot the rifle, too." He rubbed one of his huge hands across his forehead, stomped his boot into the floor pan of the truck. "God dammit!"

"Garland, come on. It's just great you're here."

She reached for her phone and thought Frankie. He answered instantly. She explained the current complications. He said, "Any rental at the airport be checked no matter whose card you used. No muffler? And you're sure about this cowboy?"

Did men ever stop being roosters? And then she thought of Jay and had to stem her emotion once again.

"God*dang*, I know what we can do." It was Garland.

"Hold on one second, Frankie."

"Freights! We can hop a freight out. They run right up near the coast in Oregon."

"You mean get on a train?"

"Sure."

"We can just get on one?"

"Sure. Hop on and ride. Be easy."

"Where do we get on?"

"Just find a freight yard. Follow the tracks."

"You've done this?" Something in his voice concerned her.

He hesitated. "Not exactly, but kinda."

"Garland, do you know how or not?"

"Well, a guy working at the ranch talked about it. He hopped freights when picking apples and got to liking it. I know we can do it. We just check and see if one is heading north. They move good too, once they get rolling."

She relayed this to Frankie. He was reluctant at first but came around to the idea. "They'd never look for you there. You're safe and it gets you north of any checkpoints. We stay in constant touch. I book into Portland and pick you up in my rental." Frankie checked MapQuest and found a big yard in Oakland. She vaguely remembered seeing it and thought she could get close based on his directions.

"Let's get moving," she said to Garland. He ignited the truck—it sounded like an ailing Nascar—and they rumbled out of the Safeway lot and pointed the Chevy for the freight yards.

Frankie continued, "The cowboy have a gun?"

She told him.

"What's he got?"

She asked Garland and relayed it.

"Dinosaurs—but a good weapon and a great bullet. Okay, you get close if you can, but not too close. Wherever the train stops, livecell me from there. I pick ya up around noon, we head to the house, the cowboy and me got guns. If those fuckers have Jay, I want them."

Maybe the overt noise of the muffler worked as a cover? Who on surveillance would take notice of anyone drawing so much attention to themselves? Besides, would one of the principles of the multi-million-dollar LiveCell be driving around with a grinning cowboy in a battered ranch truck with all the windows rolled down to prevent carbon-monoxide poisoning? Mary still hid behind the hood of her raincoat and hunkered down on the bench seat. She wasn't taking any chances. It also protected her from the cold drizzle blowing through the window.

They found the freight yard in Oakland without too much trouble—and without a ticket for noise violation. Locating one of the roads that led down to the yard took a few extra minutes. It was almost nine-thirty by the time they parked. Garland put the guns in a dirty canvas tote from which he'd removed some fencing tools. He'd left the top chamber on each gun empty. "Pa calls that the dead man's chamber. Ten shots should be enough anyhow." He suggested she stash anything loose in the bag as well. "If we have to run for a train you don't want things jumping out. Your pockets don't even have flaps." She handed him her wallet and phone. He wrapped everything carefully in a small wool horse blanket, secured the brittle leather straps, checked the buckles. He tossed it over his shoulder, and they walked out over the thistle and weed-studded ground toward the rows and rows of dark freight cars.

"Guy told me you just ask any brakeman and they'll tell you what's headed where. Though we got to stay clear of the bull; that's a railroad cop. They drive around in unmarked cars. If you see somebody let me know."

"Garland, are you sure we can do this?"

Shrouded in cold fog, the vast freight yard brooded, the distant noises of the city vague from across the expanse. Though she could hear a diesel switcher revving and the bang of an occasional coupler, it was oddly quiet, even the traffic on the freeway above her more muted. As they walked, a gentle rain became visible in the puddles. Large mercury-vapor lights on long masts strained to illuminate central sections of the yard, managing only a dead silver against darkness and the dull orange sky. A heavy smell of diesel oil, creosote, and tar mixed with the earthiness of ground and the freshness of rain. As they approached the freight cars, she felt vulnerable surrounded by so much ominous steel.

"Guy said never walk between cars. You never know when they're gonna move. Always climb up the rungs and over the couplers." As if on cue, a string of five coal hoppers whispered out of the fog, rolling ominously toward them. They jumped aside, their backs against the graffiti and rust-covered flank of a car on the adjacent track.

"There isn't much room," she said. There wasn't. She couldn't stretch out her arms without touching freight cars. "I'm really not sure about this."

"You'll be okay once we get on board."

"Why were those cars moving around like that without an engine?"

"Hump yard. They run 'em over a big hump back there and a computer sets the switches so they end up on the right track. That's how they form trains. That's why you never step between switch points, 'cause you can't know when they're gonna close. Take your foot right off."

Great. "How do you know all this stuff?"

"Same guy. We worked together over a year. All he talked about, every day. Obsessed with it. I been wanting to do this ever since."

They came to the end of a long string of auto carriers and crossed over more tracks. She'd never realized there could be so many tracks, must be well over two dozen. She glanced down for snapping switch points that could bite a foot clean off, checked for more stealth freight cars creeping out of the mist. Then at Garland—headed into the unknown, rain dripping off his hat and slicker, the bag of guns over his shoulder, that incurable grin on his face. She was stunned that her life had arrived at this place, that this was her only moment of reality, that such a moment existed at all, accompanying this cowboy through a freight yard on a rainy February night hoping to save—

"Hey, look." He pointed.

Leaning between two freight cars, a guy was checking something with a flashlight. He straightened, spoke into what looked like a LiveCell phone, and waved the light beam above his head toward the front of the train.

They walked up to him.

"Hey there, bub," said Garland.

He didn't turn, continued talking into the phone.

"A brakeman," Garland whispered to her. There was the long blast of a diesel horn, a wheel creaked and they heard a distant metallic groan. The sound increased, reached them with a tremendous *k-chang*, and the train jerked forward a few inches. The brakeman faced them.

"Say what?"

"We're looking for a train north," said Garland.

"North?" His gristled face peered at them, his cap pulled down against the rain. The train was beginning to rattle and moan as it slowly gained momentum. "Where you people want to go to?"

"Oregon," said Garland.

"Well," he said slowly, pointing his flashlight. "That's the OAPO headed for Davis. She'll be dropping some there, and then heading on up past Redding to Klamath Falls."

"So it's going to Oregon?"

He thought a minute. "Sure thing. Where else would it go?"

Garland turned to her. "Quick, unbutton your coat so you can run. That's our train."

"Hey," the brakeman called after them, "I wouldn't be trying to get on that; she's already goin' way too fast."

Garland jogged beside her in the loose gravel ballast as a variety of freight cars slowly passed. "There's an open boxcar," he said. "Can you make it? We got to be quick."

For all Garland's railroad explanations, he hadn't mentioned how to jump a moving train. It was too late to ask now. She ran beside the boxcar and placed her hands on the wet wood of the floor. A lot higher than she would have liked, almost at her shoulders. She hesitated, felt a flush of sweat, but knew she had to try; the train was moving faster and faster by the second. *Now!* She threw up a leg, her heel catching in the iron door guide, her ass hanging in the air. Her hands started slipping, a splinter bit her palm, her body began to fall backwards. She screamed.

Suddenly strong hands found her and pitched her into the car. She quickly got to her knees. Garland was still running. He'd lost a little ground against the increasing speed of the train. "Come on," she cried. He gained on the car again, reached out for the floor, but just when his palms were on the boards, the canvas tote swung from his shoulder. He caught it as it fell in front of him. The save threw his body out of balance and he careened toward the car, his shoulder whacking the side, spinning him askew. "No!" she yelled. Somehow he righted himself and managed to keep running.

"Come on, Garland. You can make it. Come on!" Again he was abreast of the car, his feet flying, the bag held tightly in his hands. "Here," he said, and tossed it at her. She reached out frantically. A leather strap scraped her fingers as she grabbed for it. But the bag fell between them onto the gravel and disappeared in an instant. "Dang," he muttered. With a last crazy lunge, he caught the edge of the metal door with his left hand and hung there for a moment, his legs dangling over the blurred ground, his other arm flailing like a rodeo rider on a bull. She leapt toward him to pull him into the car. Somehow he maintained his grip on the door edge, brought his other arm into steadiness, and grabbed the rusty door runner. From there it was a matter of seconds and he was lying on the boxcar floor, his small chest heaving, his left hand bleeding.

"My God," she said. "Are you okay?"

"I lost—the guns."

"My fault. I should've been ready. God, I can't believe you made it."
She looked down at him—being small and very strong had its advantages.
No one else could have possibly managed that. "Maybe when we come
back we can find your guns. Or let's call someone to pick them up." *Oh
shit!* "Do you have your phone?"

"With the guns."

"We don't have either phone." It was a statement of dread. It had
been so long since she'd been without a LiveCell; she felt utter panic, cut
off from everything. But she didn't want Garland to realize how upset she
was. No guns, no phones, no money. It was a complete disaster.

He got slowly to his feet and looked at his hand.

"Is it okay?"

"Just a gash. Had worse."

Blood cleaned most of the rust from the wound. She tore some strips
from the lining of her coat and bound his hand, his missing finger looking so sad.

The freight continued to pick up speed, the boxcar vibrated and rat-
tled, the wheels pounding on the rails. They gripped the edge of the door
opening to keep their balance, their feet spread wide. It would've been
difficult to talk above the racket. The sound of clanging crossing gates
approached and receded, the flashing disks visible for a few seconds, an
explosion of red across their faces. Streetlights and waiting auto headlights swirled around the interior of the boxcar like search beacons, then
left them in darkness again. After perhaps fifteen minutes, the rough track
improved and they tried to talk.

"What we gonna do without guns?" he said.

She gestured at her ear.

He said it again louder, almost shouting.

She shrugged. "Maybe Frankie can get a gun."

"You think there's a bunch of 'em got Chevalier?"

"I don't know anything. There's no way of knowing."

"Suppose not. You cold? You're shivering."

"I'm okay."

He took off his yellow slicker and pulled his sweater over his head
and handed it to her. "Sorry it's not too clean."

She accepted the sweater.

"You all right?" he said.

"I guess. This has been a long day."

She took off her wet raincoat and got the sweater on, smelling cattle in the wool as she pulled it over her head. They were the same size, she couldn't help noticing. She put her raincoat back on, thanked him, and he grinned. Within ten minutes she stopped shivering so badly and felt somewhat better. They'd left the lights of the city behind, loping now through long fields of soaked fruit or nut trees. Every so often the diesel horn cried out at the far front of their train.

"Are you going to be warm enough?" she said. He looked miserable in the rain slicker with his arms wrapped across his chest.

The roadbed had smoothed still more, and they didn't need to shout any longer.

"I'm sorry about your grandfather's guns."

"First the muffler, then no wallet, forgot the rifle, dropped the guns. Sorry I made such a frigging mess of this."

"You didn't. God, I thought you were going to fall. I'll never understand how you did that." She glanced out at the blurred darkness. "I'm just not sure what to do now."

"We go up there. Maybe there ain't too many of 'em. They got guns, just got ta take one."

Garland really was an eternal optimist. His courage was as natural to him as his joy in being alive. She was still terrified. Now she couldn't contact Frankie, and the only place to meet was at Siuslaw. If only she had a LiveCell, maybe Jay would finally answer and this would all end.

They rode through the wet night, the rain occasionally intensifying, blowing in through the open door. Garland used a scrap piece of two by four and closed it some. He then jammed the lumber in the door guide. "Guy told me these doors can slam shut. Sometimes riders get locked in. Ain't good."

At Davis the freight stopped and either picked up or set out some cars, just as the brakeman had predicted. Garland hung in the doorway and tried to see through the drizzle, the shimmer of electricity that was Sacramento behind him. "She's a long one. Bet they got half-dozen engines up there." He hopped down onto the gravel ballast, looked up at her. "Not that you'll need it, but you ever wanna jump a freight again, this is how you do it." He positioned his hands palms down on the floor, and in one quick motion rotated his body onto his ass and rolled into the car. "Shoulda shown you that before. Practiced it at the ranch." He came and sat beside her. She looked at her watch, the familiar glide of the colored light. The blue dot was past ten, the red after six. Garland noticed the watch and she told him about it. She silently prayed once more that Jay was all right. The train creaked, humped, and began rolling again.

They thundered through the darkness. As the miles clicked past, Garland got quieter, almost sullen. She'd never seem him like this. Nearly an hour had gone by and he'd said almost nothing. Something was wrong. Maybe he was having second thoughts?

"You okay?"

"Yep."

"Is it the guns?"

"Naw."

"You sure?"

"Yep."

She continued to examine him.

"Just hungry. Shoulda et something. Nothing since lunch."

"You know, I didn't eat either. That was a mistake. I'm hungry too. Very hungry."

After a few more minutes, he said, "I ain't so good if I don't eat."

"What do you mean?"

"Don't run too good."

"Blood sugar?"

"Yep."

"Oh no. Are you diabetic?"

"Naw. Ain't that bad. Just hypoglycemer. Be okay."

"We should have brought something to eat."

"I'd justa dropped it."

"We're quite the pair aren't we?"

This brought a bit of a grin, and they both started giggling.

They crossed a long girder bridge at Lake Shasta, and for an instant it was as if the boxcar had rolled into black nothingness; then they wound along Sacramento River Canyon. Though the rain had stopped, the air felt like snow. It had been a couple years since she'd seen snow. Above them, in the higher elevations, vast reaches of vague whiteness were spiked with pine. The freight slowed somewhere north of the lake and eventually lurched to a stop. The silence was more pronounced after the racket of the moving train. They sat on the wet doorsill, their raincoats protecting them, waiting for the train to begin moving again. Garland was shivering badly, and she kept rubbing her arms with her hands, her feet frozen.

"See that yellow sign?"

He glanced toward where she was pointing.

"Maybe it's a bar or a gas station. Too late for a store to be open. We need to get something to eat and we need to warm up." And maybe someone there had a LiveCell phone. That would be a godsend.

"Can't," he said.

"What do you mean?"

"Might be left here. She won't stop long."

"It's more important we get food."

She let herself down, held out her hand to him. "Come on."

He shook his head vigorously, the brim of his Resistol shuddering. "Be okay, really. Got to get to Chevalier. Maybe there's only two or three of 'em."

"Garland, come on." She had to say it a few more times. Reached up and took his hand. Pleaded with him in a way that got him moving.

They walked along the gravel beside the dark freight, passing articulated auto carriers and chemical tank cars, a few fruit reefers. He said they'd been real fortunate to find an empty boxcar. Soon a cracked plastic illuminated sign, Trackside Bar, and a *Rainier* neon clarified out of the icy darkness. Like two coal miners who had been trapped in a tunnel, they trudged toward this one spot of brightness.

TWENTY-ONE

On entering the Trackside Bar, they were swamped by a warm fetid haze with a stench that almost drove Mary back outside; she had to remind herself why they were there. Garland had guessed the train would pause for around fifteen or twenty minutes before heading north again. That might be enough time unless it left sooner, but the diesel horn would likely signal twice—then they had to run, immediately. At least the tracks were directly across the street.

She peered through the rank smoke. A pool table. All four patrons and barman turned as they approached; only the jukebox ignored them, strumming out a bleary country ballad. Not one of them looked even remotely like a LiveCell user. She planned on asking anyway. The bartender, his eyes mere slits, exhaled and stuffed out his cigarette in an overloaded ashtray.

"Hep you?"

"Kitchen still open?"

"Nope."

"Is there anything to eat, anything you could make us? We're pretty hungry."

The bartender shook his head curtly. "We're 'bout closed."

Someone sitting at the end of the bar mumbled, "Honey, I got something . . . eat," and two or three of the others started snickering. She ignored the comment, hoping Garland hadn't heard it.

"Just some chips, pretzels maybe?" She glanced at a snack rack behind him.

There was no reaction.

"Please. We're really hungry."

The bartender swiveled and grabbed two small bags of chips and tossed them on the bar. "Dollar."—sounded like a grunt.

"Any coffee?" She got the *Nope* again. They needed something to drink, something to bring up their blood sugar. "Two drafts then, Rainier not Bud, and two bags of those pretzels, and some Slim Jims." As he started pulling the beers, Mary walked down the bar, his pig-like eyes following her. Garland was watching her as well, it probably dawning on him that they didn't have a dime. She singled out the one who must have made the nasty comment—mullet haircut, bulky steroided muscles, low forehead, and an open short-sleeved shirt cheerfully printed in pineapples. "So, any of you play pool?" she said to him.

"And I suppose you do?" said Mullet.

She nodded.

"How much you wanna play for? Or maybe a sweet innocent thing like you wants to play for something asides money?" He gave her a confident leer. *Jesus*, this guy was too much. A skinny woman next to him whacked his arm. She sniffed a few times and her rabbit eyes darted nervously.

"How about if we play for fun?" said Mary. She looked right at him, though it disgusted her.

"I won enough fun. Don't your little cowboy there play pool?"

She shook her head.

"You think you can handle me?"

"I haven't been playing much lately, but I still think I can beat you." *God*, this was awful.

"Why not put your money where your mouth is then?" He stood, made a show of expanding his hairy chest, and took some quarters from his change pile. "Allow me."

She glanced at Garland eating chips ravenously. The bartender set down the drafts, and Garland drained his. He asked for another, the bartender said something, and Garland pointed at Mary. His blood sugar must be climbing, his body warming; the grin returned. He was like Popeye with his can of spinach.

Mullet fed the pool table quarters, slammed home the chrome lever, and fifteen balls dropped onto the shelf with a *ker-blunk*. Mary examined some cues. She didn't eyeball the shaft for straightness or roll the cue on the pool table to see if it was warped. All that mattered in a cue was the condition of the tip, and she selected the best one. Garland brought her a draft and the bags of snacks. She couldn't believe how good they tasted, stale pretzels and cheap beer.

Mullet racked the balls, ordering the solids and stripes obsessively. She winced, the clock ticking in her mind. It took him forever to rack the balls, sliding the triangle back and forth along the felt. He was probably showing off those puffy muscles. They didn't have time for this. Her ears kept listening for the call of the diesel horn; if they missed the train, what would they do? Steal a car? Did Garland know how? She just wanted to get out of this place.

Mullet looked up from his completed rack. "So what you wanna play for?"

"Two dollars?" she said.

"How about a fin?"

She nodded. At least some of it was easy.

"You can break," he said.

She intentionally held the cue wrong, forming a clumsy bridge with her thumb sticking up and gripping the stick at the very end of the butt. On her break, she purposely miscued. "Oh, damn." She wanted him to break the balls.

"Go again," he said with a wave of his arm.

"No, not when playing for money. It's your shot."

He turned and retrieved his drink, took a long sip, grabbed his smokes and lit a cigarette, inhaling deeply. Only then did he approach the pool table. This was all driving her crazy, but she knew she had to remain calm. He broke with a big flourish, sank two balls, both stripes. He looked to his audience for approval. Sitting beside the skinny woman were two men, both in camouflage pants. To Mary they all appeared to have been hatched from the same egg. They matched the place—fake wood paneling, filthy plywood floor, rotating plastic beer light featuring the Budweiser Clydesdales, the pool table lit by a miniature Nascar.

Mullet hammered in two more balls and missed a cut shot by three inches. He still seemed very pleased with his performance. "Okay, honey, your turn. Let's see what you can do."

She missed. "Nice try," he said. But by missing she locked a solid in one of the pocket jaws, leaving it just at the edge of the hole. "Didn't leave me much, did ya?" he said.

Garland brought her more food and beer, and a glass of orange juice. It had been a long time since she'd eaten a Slim Jim. Did they even have any nutritional value? The juice was a good idea, she should have thought of that, but the situation unhinged her.

Mullet tried a bank shot and missed. Why did they always shoot so hard? She holed two solids, exclaiming as each ball fell. Don't overdo it, she told herself, trying to settle her nerves. She locked another solid in a pocket. He sank a couple more, squinting through the smoke of his cigarette. He was left with one stripe and the eight now. Since Mary had two of the pockets bottled up, his only choice was another bank shot. He missed. She allowed herself to sink only two more, but left him nothing, snookering the cue ball. He stared at the table. Did he suspect something? He missed his ball entirely.

"Isn't that a scratch?" she said, knowing it was.

"No fucking way. Only on the eight. You scratch the eight, you lose."

Time-wise, she had to end this, and did. She drove the cue ball off three rails getting position for an easy shot down the rail on the eight so it looked like luck.

He scowled and threw a five at the table. "Let's play for twenty, see how good you really are." He was irritated now, hopefully not too irritated. There was something behind his sexual bluster that was disturbing.

She approached the bartender, placed the five on the bar. "How much?"

"Fourteen-fifty," he said. More than she figured. For an instant she thought she heard the train call out.

"You gonna play or not?" said Mullet, loud, right in her ear, his breath like rotten meat.

She jerked away from him. "Rack 'em."

"For twenty?"

"Twenty. Let's go." She glanced back at the bartender. He was still staring at her through those slits, but she couldn't read his expression.

She waited again while Mullet went through his inane racking procedure. He kept looking up at her, and it went right into her stomach. She wanted to get out of there immediately—something was beyond wrong. She glanced at Garland; he winked at her. Nothing ever seemed to bother him.

This time she broke using her normal stance. One solid fell and she quickly ran through the rest of her balls; Mullet, seeing she wasn't missing, tried every obnoxious trick—screeching the chalk, saying, "Don't miss," just as she stroked, moving around in her line of sight. As she got ready for her easy eight-ball shot, the bartender called out, "Hey, you."

She straightened and turned.

"You gonna pay me or not?" His arms across his chest, those eyes.

"Just a second." She leaned back over to play her last shot.

A striped ball blocked it.

"What are you doing?" she said to Mullet.

"What're you talking about?"

"You moved one of your balls."

"Fuck you, what're you talking about?"

"You moved that fourteen ball. My shot was clear before, now it isn't."

"You sayin' I cheated?"

One of the louts got up off his bar stool and headed toward the exit. The skinny woman licked her broken-out upper lip and sniffed. Garland moved quietly beside Mary.

"You moved the ball," he said to Mullet. "Bub, that's no frigging way to play pool. Put it back."

"Dickhead—stay out of it before you get hurt."

Mary addressed the bystanders. "Did any of you see him move the ball?"

"Nope," said one. The others shook their heads.

"It's your shot, *dearie*," said the skinny woman, her eyes gleaming. "Either make it or pay up."

The bartender: "You don't hit that eight, you lose. Them's house rules."

They all watched her. She saw what she'd only sensed before—real trouble. This was no longer about an uneasy feeling, bad smells, or a pool game. They all knew something she didn't. Her heart raced. She stared at the table, not sure what to do, her mind numb.

Then Garland whispered, "The curvy thing."

Inverting the cue stick to a forty-five degree angle, she masséd the cue ball around the fourteen and into the eight, sinking it perfectly. A silence. A very ominous silence. It was broken by the mournful blast of a diesel horn.

"Just pay the bartender the twenty," she said to Mullet. "We have to go."

His face made her flinch.

"Maybe you need a *real* fucking lesson on the pool table—with your legs spread. Dickhead the toy cowboy can watch."

The skinny woman, spit spraying from her mouth, said, "Now you'll get yours, you uppity bitch."

The one at the door snapped the deadbolt.

It was then that Garland reacted. He picked up the heavy bar-table cue ball, and with a throw that had made him a local legend when he played shortstop as a teenager, he threw hard to first. He got the man out at the door; the cue ball ricocheted off his jaw, whacked into the wall, and down he went with a screaming thud.

"Run!" Garland yelled as he grabbed her pool stick. "Don't think, just run. I'll be okay."

She did. Found the door, stepping over the body lying near the threshold, the man holding his mouth, bellowing. The bartender yelled something she didn't understand, peripherally someone was darting toward her. She could almost feel him grabbing her when she heard a sharp crack. She fumbled with the bolt, her hands shaking. Got it turned, threw open the door, and plunged into the darkness.

She ran, cold fresh air surrounding her like a blessing. For an instant she slowed and glanced back. Through one of the windows was Garland, a pool stick gripped in both hands. He swung, struck Mullet squarely on the side of the head, the mouth opening in a contorted scream. Garland must have been one hell of a batter, too. Then she saw a body darken the doorway and she ran again.

Life sometimes works out for just a moment. Sometimes that moment is when we need it most. As she ran across the street to the moving freight train, there in the dull light of the bar sign was a vacant boxcar gliding toward her. She ran beside it, and remembering what Garland had shown her, managed to get in without too much trouble; thank God for his quick lesson. Her heart pounded as she kneeled on the wet boards, looking for him to appear. "Garland," she yelled. She repeated his name over and over, searched the retreating door of the bar, saw only what looked like the bartender standing in the road. He saved me, Garland saved me, he saved me, the train wheels chanted. Some part of her was still back there with him—

The freight cried out again as it surged toward the north, toward Jay Chevalier.

The temperature began to drop as the train struggled up a long grade. Snowflakes flew in out of the darkness until a barely discernible band of dim white formed on the boxcar floor. She jumped up and down, her feet frozen, teeth chattering, body shuddering, her coat pulled tightly around her like waning hope. Without this wool sweater . . .

Garland's courage overwhelmed her again; she could see his face and body, the pure force of it in that small frame. That incredible power and agility had always been just beneath the grin. And then she remembered about borrowing a phone. But she was almost certain no one would've had a LiveCell in that repulsive place.

The train had passed Klamath Falls about an hour ago, her watch the only light—a prayer for Jay. The freight crested a summit and began a long downhill run picking up speed with every mile, brakes and flanges squealing, the acrid-smelling smoke of overheating metal biting her sinuses. The train charged into the icy blackness like a runaway nightmare, and all her thoughts were eclipsed by the cold. She'd never known the fear of freezing to death. She did now, and forced herself to keep moving, tired as she was, the short meal and beers having long deserted her. "When this train stops and I can see any kind of civilization, I have to get off or I'm going to die."

Outside Eugene, Oregon, the freight finally came to rest. She'd noticed highway signs for the city when the tracks paralleled a road. The radiant colored dots read a few minutes before six. She let herself down out of the boxcar and immediately fell onto the gravel, her joints that cold. She picked herself up and walked stiffly up the yard, one hand bruised, her shoulder aching. Garland had been right, it was a very long freight. Though the temperature was milder, she still shivered and knew it would take her a long time to get warm. At least she was shivering; at her coldest during the night, she'd stopped. That had scared her the most.

Out of the chrome pre-dawn there appeared a concrete structure with a half-dozen work trucks and pickups angled next to it. Not seeing anything besides more tracks and freight cars, she approached the building, the metal door with YARD OFFICE above it. She stood, uncertain. After last night, she was leery entering any place where strange men would be. But she had to take the chance, and opened the door.

Two men were sitting over some papers at one of the cafeteria-style tables. They looked up, their faces unfriendly. Regardless, she forced herself to walk a few feet into the room, the heavy door drawing shut behind her with a *clunk*. The older one got to his feet.

"What do you want?"

She couldn't seem to say anything. He approached her tentatively, warily.

"You're not allowed in here."

He looked her up and down; she instantly got a queasy feeling.

"Did you just come in on the OAPO out of Klamath?"

She nodded. He came closer.

"You look awful cold."

"I am." Her teeth started chattering again from the heat of the room. She felt her legs go weak and knew she was about to fall again. There was a bench near the door and she just made it.

"Bill," he said over his shoulder. "Get the little lady a cup of coffee, lots of cream and sugar." He addressed her again: "You must be froze. It was goddamn cold even in the cab up there tonight."

"You drove the train?"

"Yeah, what else? We just switched out crews. I logged my twelve, or a few minutes less, and another crew will take her into Portland. You trying to get to Portland?"

She shook her head. He moved towards her, sat down beside her. For a long second she was terrified he was going to reach over and touch her. She sensed that he wanted to. Not again! And without Garland to protect her.

"All my years with the railroad, I've never seen a lady riding alone. Rarely see wimin ridin', alone or not. If I'd known you was back there, I would've let you ride with me in the unit. We could've kept each other warm." He showed his yellow teeth, his eyes moving down to her chest and staying there. The other man approached with the coffee. She took the styrofoam cup, and he returned to his paperwork without a word. She sipped the coffee hungrily, feeling the hot liquid running into her stomach. She needed to get her strength back.

"Are you staying here in town?" the engineer said.

"I'm trying to get to the coast." She could tell he couldn't figure her out. That was in her favor.

"Where about?"

Should she tell him? She was too exhausted to care. "Near the Old Siuslaw Road."

"At the edge of the National Forest. You got family there?"

She nodded. Then added, "My husband."

"He lets you ride freights?"

"It's a long story," she said, unable to think of anything else.

"What's his name?"

For a frantic moment she couldn't remember the name on the mailbox, then realized it probably didn't matter. "Madsen," she said as it came to her. "John Madsen."

"Don't think I know him."

He seemed to reach some kind of decision about her. "I live over in that direction. Tell you what, let me finish up a few things here, and I'll take you part way."

Should she do this? Would it be safe? But what other options did she have without any money? Was the five dollars in her pocket? She was too exhausted to think clearly, so she agreed, finished the last of her coffee. "Is there a washroom?"

"Right through that door down the hall on your left."

She stood. "Thanks, that coffee really helped. I can't tell you how much." Be polite with him, but not friendly.

"You want another?"

"Yes, please, in just a minute."

He smiled and she got that queasy feeling in her stomach again. She set her empty cup on the bench and headed to the washroom.

What Mary saw in the mirror was a shock. She barely recognized herself. Only ten hours and she looked like a vagabond. Her skin was grimy and smudged, her eyes laced with red, her hair a tangled mess halfway to dreads, and with the filthy wet coat and Garland's sweater . . . She made only a few minor repairs, realizing she shouldn't make herself more attractive.

He still looked her over strangely when she returned from the washroom. She accepted a second cup of coffee, followed him outside to his pickup. As they got rolling he slid on the heat, turned up the fan. She no longer shivered and chattered, but the cold from the train was still in her bones and the heat was welcome; she held her wet shoes near the hot-air vent. Rain came down again, the wipers beat back and forth. The engineer tried to make conversation at first, but she told him she was too tired to talk, if he didn't mind. The less familiar, the better.

She looked out at the illuminated triangle of highway through the rain, a gauntlet of dark pine on each side. As she got closer to Jay, the reality hit her. If only she had a gun. That jolted her mind to Garland.

She might have gotten him killed by asking him to help her. But Garland had to be okay. Somehow she couldn't imagine that he wasn't. He'd have gotten out of that bar; she'd never seen anyone who could move so fast. She thought of Frankie flying across the country, probably somewhere over the Midwest by now. He would drive directly to her when he got off the plane, but he probably wouldn't arrive until noon. He'd be frantic. If only she had her phone—

"You know," said the engineer, "I keep thinkin' I've seen you some place before. You look kinda familiar to me. Could I of seen your picture somewheres?" He was studying her again with quick glances as he drove. Men and their fucking glances.

She kept her eyes on the road ahead. "No, I couldn't imagine where." He'd probably seen her in one of her TV news interviews, or maybe in one of the magazine articles. Should she ask him to help her? Maybe he had a LiveCell phone, or even a gun. But could she trust him? Would his sympathies be with LiveCell? Was it worth the risk? After what had happened in the bar, her faith in strangers was gone. He might do just the opposite of what she asked. She wasn't sure what to do, so she did nothing.

He stopped at the junction of the 101 and Old Siuslaw Road. As she reached for the door handle, he grabbed her arm.

"Why not come to my place for breakfast? It's ridiculous lettin' such a pretty young thing as you out in the rain like this. You could dry off yer clothes. I got an electric drier. You could take a shower an' clean up. I bet you clean up nice."

"My husband's waiting."

"Funny kinda husband, lettin' you run around like this."

She pulled away from his grip, jumped down, shut the door, and prepared to run—but he simply drove off. The queasy feeling in her stomach receded as his truck headed into the gray light of morning. She waited a few minutes in case he came back, ready to run into the woods. Blessed silence. Fixing her hood against the rain, she began walking along the pavement, and before too long, she reached the graveled section of the road. She forced herself not to run; she needed what little energy she had left.

Eventually the mailbox with Raymond Madsen came into focus out of the fog. She angled past it, left the Siuslaw Road and headed along the drive rutted with scrub-pine roots. The rain had abated somewhat; it was fully morning and she smelled the sea. The wet pine and brackish fog

revived the memory of when she'd been there before, stopping her new
Porsche to check her face and hair in the vanity mirror. Though only a
bit over a year ago, it was an eternity away.

Mary examined the ground for tracks, not sure what she was looking
for. In the thick pine-needle bed she couldn't tell much. At least one car
had driven along it, maybe two. "I don't know what to expect. I don't
know how to do this." If only she had Frankie telling her how to
approach the house, or Garland beside her—Garland *and* two guns. That
had been the plan, not this. She couldn't slow the beating of her heart.

The distant thundering of breakers, muted as it attempted to breach
the fog, made her think of the painting in his office. The image plagued
her; she couldn't shake it in her exhaustion, and she started to envision
Jay as the boat careening above the turmoiled waves, the chaos of the
world. And she was merely a passenger in the boat, the violent sea supporting them both, allowing them to thrust toward the sky, toward their
dreams, yet also just as willing to destroy. And then she remembered the
moon, saw Jay as the moon, and started to run.

There was his blue wagon with a black sedan parked tight behind it,
blocking it in. The sight of the strange car stopped her. A sudden pain
between her eyes almost knocked her down. She knelt for a moment on
the wet pine needles, fought back the nausea, attempted to calm her
breathing. She listened. Nothing, only her heart pumping madly. The
house was dark. The smell of burnt wood. She noticed a faint drift of
smoke at the chimney. What appeared to be a body was lying on the
porch near the door.

Slowly, with careful steps, she approached from along the edge of the
drive, her hurt shoulder brushing wet pine, her mind screaming, *Don't let
it be him*. If someone glanced outside, they could shoot her, and she did-
n't care. The front door was open. She saw that though her eyes were
fixed on the prone body. A *suit*! It was wearing a suit! A gun lay beside
it. She picked it up, the pistol heavy and alien in her hand—evil. The
body lay face down against the rotten porch boards, a dark stain under it.
She couldn't bring herself to examine the corpse from any closer, and she
didn't check if the gun was loaded—what would it matter?

She tried to think logically. If one of them was dead, maybe the others were dead too. If not, would they have left the body? Wouldn't they
have dragged it inside? Taken the gun? Or was it a trap? She wanted to
call out for Jay. She studied the darkness beyond the doorway. Just some
derailed toy train cars on their sides, some disheveled track. She crept

along the porch as quietly as she could, praying she wouldn't break through one of the bad planks and make a noise. She peered over a windowsill. There, barely visible in the firelight, propped up against an armchair, was Jay. He held a gun loosely in his hand. Another body was on the floor. She ran.

"Jay," she called. "It's me—Mary." She listened at the doorway. Silence—the ocean—silence. Entering the front hall she called out again, the gun ready in her hand, stepping over ruined trains and track. She heard a faint something. When she got to Jay his cheeks were wet. She crouched down next to him, the gun falling from her hand.

"You're okay," he said. She could barely hear him, his voice a whisper, his lips almost blue, his face like wax. "They told me they had you, that you'd be tortured—"

"—You've been shot. You need an ambulance."

He shook his head very gently, his eyelids wavering with the pain it caused him.

"Where's your LiveCell?" she said.

"Destroyed."

She looked around the room quickly; were there only two men?

"Mary . . . you're okay. Everyone all right?" His eyes searched her face.

She told him yes, though she had no idea. "Were there only two?" He nodded with his eyes. She noticed his hands. "My God, what did they do to you?" His hands and especially his wrists were burned, blistered. She reached down and carefully removed the gun from his right hand. The fingers seemed to be numb, the knuckles chafed and covered in dried blood.

"Taped," he said. "Hands. Dragged myself to the fire." She cringed at the horror of it.

"Jay, we need to get you to a hospital. Did they have phones?"

"Won't work." And she realized the frustrating truth of it. Though Jay had created the phones, they would still only work with permission from each owner.

"I'll drive you. Can you move?"

He shook his head again, winced. "May I . . . a glass water?"

She stood up and ran to the kitchen, found a clean glass, turned the tap, heard a pump and generator somewhere below rumble on, let the water run cold a second, filled it, ran back. Though the burns to his hands were not on his fingers, she held the glass to his lips; she didn't think he had any feeling in his hands.

"Thanks," he said after he drank, his voice a little louder. She fought back the tears again.

"What can I do? You need help. I can't carry you by myself."

"Don't be upset."

She tried to quiet herself. "Is there anything I can do?"

"Thought they . . . more time." His eyes half-closed, the lids flickering.

"How bad is the pain?"

He opened his eyes, gazed at her for a long time with such overwhelming love that she began to tremble. "For once, I'm not so fine," he said, and attempted a smile.

Her tears fell then, running down her face, completely beyond her control.

"Mary, please . . . it's okay. What matters . . . you're safe, you're here. I knew you would come." His eyes flared for an instant and then shut tight. A spasm ran through his body as if it were her own.

"Jay? . . . Jay? . . . No—" she cried. "You can't die, please, don't die. God, please don't die. I can't live without you." She placed her arms around him and pulled him to her, his head resting against her chest, against her soaked raincoat. "I love you," she whispered. "I love you so much."

She was never sure how long she held him. She remembered eventually setting his head gently on the floor, carefully straightening his body. She remembered stroking his face, bringing her lips to his, their second kiss, her tears landing on his forehead, running along his broken nose, down his pocked temples. She remembered finding Jimmy Hakken's gift of the ugly silver pendant around his neck, and starting to laugh hysterically, uncontrollably. She remembered taking off her raincoat and covering him with it. She remembered walking into the kitchen and staring out the window, her tears like the rain on the glass, moving down her face in the same hapless way. She remembered thinking about what they'd done to him. The anger, the strangling rage poisoning her until she screamed; she must have kicked something repeatedly, her foot was still sore. She remembered drinking a beer with his blood on her hand. She remembered managing a few bites of cold leftover chicken pot pie, telling herself she had to eat or she'd faint. The cats finally came out of hiding and rubbed against her legs. She fed them and realized that she had to get out of the house, that soon others would know something was wrong and come looking.

Her mind began working logically again, and she reconstructed what might have happened. The two men must have surprised and bound Jay the previous morning—if only she'd tried to call him then, if only she'd listened to her premonitions, if only Kelly had known a few hours sooner. The two men worked on him all day, threatening him with her torture and who knew what else, not realizing the rage they were generating; he would have remained calm, waiting, unyielding. They must have attempted some kind of injection because there was a hypodermic on a table. Maybe Jay was immune from drinking so much of his Grandfather's distillate? Her mind drifted to the evening when they sat on her porch as the storm swept in from the Pacific, Jay sipping champagne, telling her about his grandfather, about the phones, about how they could stop him; and then Jay walking away, leaving her, and she started sobbing again—

She controlled her thoughts. Anthony Brignolia must have known about Duncan and the plan to interrogate and possibly kill Jay. That's why he was so angry; he must've attempted to dissuade Alden and his connections and failed. He probably hoped Jay would still come around to his offer in time. Frankie learned part of this through his contact, and he called just before four, warning her about Duncan. It was obvious Jay gave up nothing important over the last twenty-four hours or the men would have been gone when she arrived.

As she'd ridden the freight through the mountains, the two men must have left Jay alone for a moment, or dozed off. Jay freed himself by inching to the fireplace and burning through his bound hands, ripping through his leg bonds—she found burnt and torn tape. He attacked one of the men, killing him and taking his gun. The second man had fired, the bullet striking Jay in the stomach, and Jay had shot him, the man struggling to flee until he collapsed on the porch.

Then she thought: Jay didn't ask her who sold him out, or how his attackers found him, or even why she'd arrived alone and soaking wet. All he'd said was, "I knew you'd come." And for a frightening instant, she wondered how much Jay had known all along. Had he known he was going to be killed? Had he believed that only by dying he could save Live-Cell?—and save her?

He must have foreseen a lot of it. He'd probably known all along that Duncan would betray him, that she would find him here, and that Live-Cell would be saved because of his death. Maybe that's why he couldn't allow himself to love her? Why he ran from her? He knew how soon he was going to die. She wished they'd shared those moments together anyway. How could someone who knew so much, have known so little about some things?

But Jay Chevalier had his dream, his vision. Whatever had happened to him in the northern Maine wilderness as his eyes locked on the heavens had changed him and guided him. He'd been willing to do anything to realize that dream, this vision he had for humanity, his belief in the continuum, even up to extracting cells from his own brain and accepting that he would have to be killed in order for his prophecy to continue. For her, that held something far beyond any unfulfilled yearning or unrequited feelings.

Mary walked outside, limping slightly from her sore foot, her whole body aching. The Impala. She considered using it to escape. But it was boxed in, and there was no way she was going near those two corpses for the sedan's keys, and besides, she'd be more exposed in a car. Frankie would be there soon enough anyway. He'd have landed in Portland by mid-morning and should arrive within an hour. He'd be able to find the Old Siuslaw Road and the mailbox.

And once she got his phone, she'd livecell Deirdre and Artega, engage enough media and police so that no one, not even the Aldens, would be able to cover up Jay's murder. What they'd managed with Sammy's killing would not happen again. And once the world knew what the Aldens and their associates had done, they would be forced to leave LiveCell alone. Frankie could handle things until the press and police arrived. She needed desperately to find out how Garland was, but wasn't so sure she wanted to know what had happened between Jimmy Hakken and Duncan. She tried to lock her mind on the future.

As she headed down the drive toward the mailbox—ready to jump into the pines if she heard a vehicle—she saw the rain had stopped and that it was going to clear, the sun already working through the fog. She heard a tremendous *whoosh* and glanced up.

Above her, in the open lane between the low trees, the sky was filled with birds, hundreds of them, maybe thousands, all flying silently until they turned together in great synchronous arcs of dark pearlescent color. A part of her was drawn up toward the myriad beating wings, and somewhere inside her mind she felt a voice. She didn't hear it, it didn't speak in words, it spoke in feelings. And then she knew why Jay had needed her to be next to him when he died, and he was there, inside her, and she almost laughed at the pure wonder of it. She listened and she knew exactly what she had to do.

EPILOGUE

Frankie Demanno and Mary MacKensie gazed out her dining room window at the Pacific Ocean. Each held a flute, the chill of the white wine dulling the sides of the glasses. Two cases had been delivered by a special courier, sent from Anthony Brignolia's native village in Sicily. The attached note read: *The world has suffered a great loss, but for you Mary it has been the greatest. Wise people in my village say that this wine can bring the soul back to life. Please drink it in the memory of a great man.* Brignolia also made Frankie a rare gift; he released him from whatever unwritten contract had bound him.

Over the past three weeks, Frankie had been very gentle with her, saying little, respecting her grief, but finally she had to ask him to stop cooking so many special dishes for her. Every time she stepped in the door, he was bringing her something else. If only she'd been the least bit hungry.

From the moment she'd spotted his rental car on the Siuslaw Road, he'd assisted her in every way. He'd summoned the local police and the press to the murder scene and protected her from too much questioning. He'd driven her home, prepared hot chicken broth and fresh vegetable juice with ginger, brought it to her in bed. He'd stayed up most of that first night, sitting at the dining room table, sipping coffee with anisette, glancing in at her every so often during her fitful attempt at sleep.

It was Chet Simmons, LiveCell's meek purchasing head, who asked Mary if he might be allowed to organize Jay Chevalier's funeral. The event was national news, all the major media in friendly attendance—they had switched sides just as Jay had foreseen. Thousands of people came, some from as far as Iceland and Australia. Kelly Harris and Mary's parents flew in from Vermont, staying the week with her. Kelly looked so bad she worried he was back on heroin. "I'd look a lot better if I was," he said. "Believe me." Frankie moved to a motel during her parents' stay, but still came by to cook, her mother eyeing him strangely at first—after all, he was from Massachusetts—but relenting slightly after she tasted a few of his specialties.

At the funeral, the Brignolia brothers were standing side by side. Detective Artega—he'd been put in charge of the Samuel Holmes case again—and what appeared to be at least half the San Francisco police department were there. Almost everyone from the Cyclone gym and most of the staff from the Mexican restaurant Dos Reales. Everyone from Live-Cell and all their families. Manuel, who cried the entire time. But no one had anticipated the intensity and breadth of emotion surrounding Jay Chevalier's death. It seemed as if the entire nation was in mourning. Frankie suggested Mary give a eulogy. He said she was head of LiveCell now; Jay had left her his sixty percent of the company, and she needed to show the world that she was unafraid and ready to continue his legacy. He felt it was important. And when Mary finished speaking, she was about the only one without damp eyes. What she felt for Jay was beyond tears.

The procession of thousands was led by Luke and Jimmy Hakken along with the entire crew, many on choppers, all dressed in black, armbands across their tattooed biceps. The gang had voted to make Chevalier a Druid posthumously, the first and probably last time such an honor was given. Mary had offered Hakken the blue Impala, and he'd accepted, along with adopting the three cats—no one else wanted the mangy creatures. "It wasn't their fucking fault," he said. And then he stared at her for a long Hakken moment. "MacKensie, you know I ain't gonna let this end here." She wasn't sure what he meant, but it chilled her nonetheless.

"So they dropped the charges?" Frankie took a sip of wine, looking out over the ocean.

"Garland's so famous since the story got picked up, they'd be idiots to sue for assault."

"He put three of 'em in the hospital? They were kinda vague in the paper."

"The one he hit with the cue ball has a broken jaw and missing teeth. The one who tried to grab me has a smashed knee. The woman tried to attack him and scratched him, doing more damage than the men. He told me he couldn't hit a woman, but he managed to throw her off, and she disappeared when she heard the siren; the bartender had called the cops. He was the only lucky one. When the cops got there, Garland was having a beer, the bartender in awe. He told the cops what really happened. I guess he'd been scared of that one guy for years and was relieved to be rid of him."

"That the guy who wanted to rape you?"

She nodded.

"What happened to him?"

"Garland said to me, '*I don't usually lose my temper, but the way that guy was talking to you made me frigging mad.*' I guess that guy is still in the hospital. They're not sure when he'll be out. And Garland did all that with a bandaged hand."

"You were right—he's some cowboy."

"I offered him a job at LiveCell, at any pay. You know what he said? '*Naw, I just know ranching. Wouldn't be no good at nothing else.*'"

"You got his accent down."

"That was a good suggestion about buying him the exact same guns. Thanks again for that. I just wish I could do something more for him."

They paused, sipped their wine.

"Frankie . . . I want you to work with me at LiveCell."

"As a bodyguard? I used to think I was the best, now I'm not so sure."

"I want you to be in charge of public relations, but I also want you to be my right hand."

"Public *relations?*"

"You'd be very good."

"Really?"

She nodded. He hid behind another sip of wine.

"So how did Jimmy Hakken do it?" She changed the subject. "You know about that stuff."

"Duncan?"

"Yeah. They couldn't find a mark on his body. Nothing. It took the cops weeks even to figure out he'd been in the room."

He shook his head. "I really don't know. Something I never learned. That Hakken is one strange bird."

"Duncan still hasn't spoken or moved. They have to feed him."

"Do they think he'll ever come out of it?"

"I talked to the neurologist at the hospital a few days ago, and he said a massive trauma like this could take years."

"Hakken's a scary guy. Probably good he disappeared."

"Even for you? I didn't think you were scared of anything."

"Everybody is scared of something. The only person I met not scared of nothing was Jay Chevalier."

They both went silent. She excused herself and left the room. He worried he'd said the wrong thing. When she returned a few minutes later, her hair was pulled back.

"The earrings," he said.

"They look okay?"

"You kiddin' me?" He couldn't take his eyes off her. "Mary, you know—"

"Not yet. *Please.* Give me a little more time."

He nodded. After some awkward moments she checked her watch. "I need to go over to the factories. Deirdre will call any minute if I don't get going. She's become a wicked worrywart. Not that I blame her."

"You go over there every day now."

"You want to come with me?"

He shrugged.

"So, you accept my job offer?"

"You kiddin' me? You know how I feel."

"Then I want to show you something."

"At the factory?"

"Yeah."

"What?"

"If I told you, you wouldn't believe me."

THE END

Eric Green *lives on the Maine Coast with his wife. He was born in northern New Hampshire, rode freights across the country as a teenager, made his living as a visual artist for thirty years, and writes the syndicated award-winning column "The Penobscot Falcon."*

CPSIA information can be obtained at www.ICGtesting.com
Printed in the USA
BVOW070732220213

313915BV00002B/2/P